Outstanding Reviews for *The Warriors of God:*

"Christie tells an intriguing story in straightforward fashion . . . All too credible in its details, and the climactic battle for the White House is a genuine page-turner."
—*Publishers Weekly*

"A fascinating account of terrorist preparation and attack."
—*Ormond Beach,* FL *Observer*

"Mr. Christie keeps this story moving along, and it will hold the attention."
—*The New York Times*

"Christie does more than provide a riveting read. His startling story alerts readers in memorable fashion to the threat of terrorism and the difficulties of defending against it."
—J.E. Greenwood, Col. USMC (Ret.)
Editor, *Marine Corps Gazette*

"Christie is clever with his writing. I found the plot so believable, I wanted to call the White House and tell them to read this book. This would make a fingernail-to-elbow chewing movie."
—*Tulsa World*

THE

WARRIORS

OF

GOD

WILLIAM CHRISTIE

Smp

ST. MARTIN'S PAPERBACKS

This is a work of fiction. Although existing U.S. government agencies and military units are depicted, everything occurring within the framework of these institutions is the product of the author's imagination. Some locations have been altered, some have not, to suit the purposes of the narrative. All characters and events are entirely fictitious, and any resemblances to actual persons, living or dead, is accidental.

Published by arrangement with Presidio Press

THE WARRIORS OF GOD

Copyright © 1992 by William Christie.

Library of Congress Catalog Card Number: 92-14292

ISBN: 0-312-95393-3

Printed in the United States of America

Lyford Books hardcover edition published 1992
St. Martin's Paperbacks edition / April 1995

St. Martin's Paperbacks are published by St. Martin's Press, 175 Fifth Avenue, New York, N.Y. 10010.

10 9 8 7 6 5 4 3 2 1

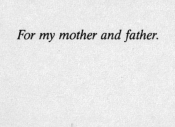

For my mother and father.

ACKNOWLEDGMENTS

I would like to express my thanks to:

Kevin Frankovich, for generously allowing both me and Richard Welsh the use of his apartment.

JoEllen Sumner, for her time in researching material that, unfortunately, did not make it into the final draft.

Jim and Beth King, for everything.

All my friends, particularly those in the Marine Corps, for their constant support and encouragement.

Bob Tate, my editor at Presidio Press. Our relationship began, as I'm sure many have in the book trade, with the editor asking himself, "What kind of loon did I get stuck with this time?" Throughout the production of this novel, Bob had to deal with my strange sense of humor, several episodes of authorial hysteria, and the occasional threat of physical violence (though never directed at him). He handled it all with utter calm, exceptional presence of mind, and complete professionalism.

Finally, my agent, Larry Gershel, of Wieser & Wieser. When things were exceptionally bleak, Larry believed. What more can I say?

PART ONE

Therefore I say: Know your enemy and know yourself; in a hundred battles you will never be in peril.

When you are ignorant of the enemy but know yourself, your chances of winning and losing are equal.

If ignorant both of your enemy and of yourself, you are certain in every battle to be in peril.

SUN TSU, *The Art of War*

CHAPTER 1

THERE WOULD BE no moon that night in the Persian Gulf. As the sun set, a single dhow slipped out of its berth in the port of Dubai and headed out to sea. The port, actually a wide inlet called The Creek, served as both harbor and sewer for the largest city in the seven states of the United Arab Emirates. Dubai had been a hub of regional trade even before the oil boom, and the port was usually so crowded that the dhows moored two or three abreast in the section of the long quay reserved for them. These large, distinctive wooden ships, with sharply pointed bows and high, square sterns, have been used for fishing, trading, and smuggling throughout the Middle East for over a thousand years. Sailing by their own schedules and manned with crews from all over the region, the dhow fleets were rarely equipped with radios, lights, or more than basic navigational aids. This made them a constant irritant to commercial shipping, and their movements very hard to keep track of.

Nearing the outer harbor, the dhow came upon the Cypriot-registered freighter *Antonia*. She was anchored, presumably waiting for dawn to move into a berth. A painting platform hung from the *Antonia*'s side, and two crewmen were relaxing on it, enjoying the evening. They had obviously made little progress, as the hull was brown from accumulated rust. Four large plastic paint containers sat beside them.

The dhow made a sharp turn to pass close by the freighter. As it slowly approached, both crewmen slipped off the platform and into the water. The paint pails were tied to their waists and floated along behind. The men swam with silent breaststrokes into the path of the dhow. As it passed, the swimmers grabbed ropes trailing in the water and pulled themselves into the boat. Once they were aboard, the dhow crew reeled in the pails.

From the bridge of the helicopter carrier USS *Makin Island* (LPH-13), the halo of light from Dubai was the only visible illumination. The *Makin Island* was one of five ships of the Persian Gulf Amphibious Ready Group, embarking a twenty-two-hundred-man Marine Corps expeditionary unit: a reinforced infantry battalion, helicopter squadron, and support unit specially trained for short-duration amphibious and helicopterborne raids and to support U.S. special operations.

The United States normally deployed marine expeditionary units, called MEUs, only with the Seventh Fleet in the Pacific and the Sixth Fleet in the Mediterranean. But in the aftermath of the 1991 war with Iraq, another MEU was regularly assigned to the Middle East Task Force. The political realities of the region made it impossible for American troops to be permanently stationed on land there, but the war with Iraq had shown the United States the need to maintain some kind of presence in the region, to prevent further instability. And the moderate Arab states of the Gulf still had reason to feel insecure. The Arab world had split into several opposing camps, and the hard-liners and moderates in Iran were engaged in a battle for power whose outcome was completely unpredictable.

So, delicate compromises were made. A U.S. Navy task force patrolled the Persian Gulf, and an aircraft carrier battle group remained in the Indian Ocean. Air force squadrons flew into Saudi Arabia on periodic exercises. Army tanks and heavy equipment were left behind in Saudi warehouses. And the marines served as an off-shore quick-reaction unit.

The Iranians, once again a major power in the region, were infuriated by this. Always deeply suspicious of U.S. motives, they believed a permanent American military force in the region to be a far greater danger to their interests than Iraqi aggression. The Iranians repeatedly issued communiqués warning that all foreign attempts to gain a foothold in the area would be violently resisted.

The night before the amphibious squadron was scheduled to leave port, the command ship—the dock landing platform (LPD) USS *Franklin*—tied up at the Dubai Naval Base to entertain the base commander and local VIPs. The heavy shipping traffic meant berthing space was at a premium; the *Makin Island* was anchored outside the harbor. Due to the same space limitations, the other ships of the squadron—a dock landing ship (LSD) and two tank landing ships (LSTs)—were visiting about eighty miles away at Abu Dhabi, the capital of the emirates, along with the commander of the Middle East Task Force.

With severe restrictions on the available airspace in the Gulf, the marines were having trouble getting flying time. Anchored near the friendly port of Dubai, the marine helicopter squadron embarked aboard the *Makin Island* took advantage of the opportunity to get in some night flying hours. Except for dimmed landing lights on the flight deck, the ship was blacked out. This was standard procedure. A line of helicopters circled overhead, practicing night formation flying.

As part of the general security precautions while at anchor, several two-man guard teams, made up of one marine and one sailor, were stationed at various points on the ship. During special alerts the Seafox patrol boats operating from the LSD circled the task force, and divers from the attached platoon of Navy Sea-Air-Land commandos, or SEALs, checked the hulls and surrounding waters. But it was not possible to keep divers in the water all night nor to operate the two Seafoxes continuously. So they were used only when intelligence reports indicated a specific threat. In this case, the LSD was in another port.

On the dhow, the two swimmers waited on deck until the captain emerged from the wheelhouse. One swimmer began to walk toward him but was stopped by a loud hiss. Almost hidden beside a pile of fishing nets, a young Arab motioned the swimmer back with a wave of the muzzle of his Belgian FAL automatic rifle.

The captain, a short, burly man with stained work clothes and a three-day beard, came closer and looked the swimmers over. The younger of the two was visibly angry at being held at gunpoint, most likely offended that heroes such as they would be treated so badly. The older one was wary but patient, seemingly relaxed but balanced for quick movement. A dangerous man, the captain thought. In Farsi, the dominant language of Iran, the captain quoted from the Koran: "Believers, make war on the infidels who dwell around you. Deal firmly with them."

The older swimmer replied, also in Farsi: "In retaliation you have a safeguard for your lives; perchance you will guard yourselves against evil."

The captain smiled and motioned to the rifleman, who engaged the safety catch and slid the FAL under the nets. "Welcome," he said, as he strode forward to clutch the two swimmers in an embrace. "May God protect you, and grant you success."

The older swimmer, obviously the leader, satisfied the demands of courtesy. *"Inshallah*—If God wills. You have our thanks; the pickup was perfect."

"It was a good plan," said the captain. "Far better than crossing borders. Fewer things can go wrong." He paused. "The Americans are still anchored in the same place. Are there any changes to the plan?"

"If they are where they should be," said the swimmer, "then there are no changes."

"No changes!" the captain roared incredulously. "This is unprecedented. God willing, we may succeed after all."

"How long before we are in position?" asked the swimmer, immune to the captain's good spirits—and his sarcasm.

"Fifteen minutes," said the captain. "Or as long as you require. We will simply slow down. It will be even more convincing."

"We will need at least thirty minutes, perhaps more, to prepare."

"You shall have it," replied the captain. "And whatever else you require."

"Only the time, and a place to assemble our equipment."

Under a frame draped with fishing nets, the swimmers opened the paint pails by lantern light. The first two pails held swim fins, diving masks, weight belts, sheath knives, an instrument board, and two oxygen rebreathers. The remaining two contained limpet mines and time fuzes. The leader anxiously asked, "Kharosh, are the fuzes and the lime intact?"

"Perfect," replied twenty-two-year-old Jr. Lt. Kharosh Rajabi. "No water entered the pails or the wrapping. What shall I do?"

"You prepare the mines, and I will attend to the rebreathers," said Lt. Comdr. Bashir Sa'idi. He was in his early thirties, a veteran of the war with Iraq. Rajabi was not. Both were members of Number 6 Combat Swimmer Detachment—one of the units known in the Iranian military as special troops.

Sa'idi removed the rebreathers, the small oxygen tanks, and cans of lime from the protective plastic wrapping. The rebreathers were brand-new and the best available, purchased from an English firm that supplied commercial divers. Different from the more common scuba system, the rebreathers looked like inflatable rubber life vests. They were fed by tanks of oxygen; but, instead of being expelled into the water, exhaled air was returned into a rubber bladder, "scrubbed" through a soda-lime absorption unit to remove carbon dioxide and carbon monoxide, and breathed again. A rebreather could be used underwater longer than scuba gear, and did not leave a telltale stream of bubbles. Sa'idi disassembled and checked all the components with the dogged thoroughness of a man who did not lightly trust his life to a piece of machinery.

Rajabi unpacked the six limpet mines from the other pails. The mines were designed to be attached to the side of a ship by a diver and held in place by magnets. The limpets were a new Soviet model, purchased by Iran from North Korea. The bodies of the mines were made of plastic, and each weighed less than ten pounds. The filling was plastic explosive, and the undersides were indented to direct the full force of the blast into the hull of a ship. Instead of using large, heavy conventional magnets to hold them to the target ship, these limpets had small battery-powered electromagnets. When the mine was in place, the magnet was activated by the turn of a key. The small size of the magnets left more space for explosives, with the added benefit that if discovered, the mines could not be removed without the keys to shut off the current. Rajabi carried the limpets to the anchor of the dhow and tested the magnets. They all worked perfectly.

The mines had several chambers for fuzes. Rajabi carefully removed the fountain pen-sized time-delay fuzes from the padded carrying boxes. The fuzes were the standard Soviet lead-increment type. Removing the safety allowed a strip of soft lead to be stretched between two springs. When the lead broke, a firing pin was released to explode a blasting cap. Different lead increments took specific periods of time to break, from minutes to days, at various temperatures. Rajabi prepared two different fuzes for each mine, so there would be a backup if one failed. Making sure the safeties were in place and the blasting caps firmly attached, he screwed the fuzes into the mines. The limpets were now fully armed.

By the time the two Iranians finished, the dhow had reached the outer harbor. Sa'idi and Rajabi stripped down to black cotton shorts and long-sleeved T-shirts. Each wore a combination depth gauge/compass on one wrist, and a waterproof watch on the other. The sheath knives were strapped to their ankles. They donned weight belts and swim fins, then the rebreathers.

As part of a deception plan in the event they were captured or killed, none of their equipment or clothing could be identified as Iranian issue. Both men wore captured Iraqi military identification tags.

The captain of the dhow saw the landing lights of a helicopter before he saw the *Makin Island.* Then, clearly, he picked up the red glow of a cigarette high up in the island, near the bridge. The dhow was eight hundred yards away from the carrier, and the captain did not dare go nearer. He cut the engine and ordered the crew to drop anchor.

As the dhow stopped, Sa'idi took a compass bearing to the *Makin Island.* Quickly, before they attracted any attention, the Iranians fastened to their waists the nylon bags holding the limpets. The two men straddled the side of the dhow farthest from the American ship. They filled the rebreather bladders with oxygen, carefully expelled the air from their lungs, and took the first breath. They gave each other the thumbs-up to signal that the rebreathers were working. Then they set the units for maximum oxygen flow to compensate for the heavy load and exertion of the first leg of the swim. Sa'idi reached over and clipped his three-meter nylon buddy line to Rajabi's waist, so they could maintain contact in the darkness. They adjusted their masks, leaned out over the railing, and fell backward into the water.

• • •

The fantail lookout on the *Makin Island* had been following the movement of the dhow by watching its lanterns in the darkness. When the sailor saw the lights stop, he pressed the button on his sound-powered phone and called the bridge.

The captain was sitting in his padded leather chair, facing the flight deck. He was always there during flight quarters, and—like most ship captains, who fervently believe disaster will strike when they are sleeping—he was exhausted. When informed of the message from the fantail watch, he snapped, "Well, what's it doing?" This prompted another exchange over the phone, and the crewman on the signal bridge began to scan through the huge observation binoculars.

"Sir, it's sitting there dead in the water," reported the seaman at the phone.

"How far away?"

"About nine hundred meters."

The captain reached for the phone at his side and pushed the button for Primary Flight Control. "This is the captain, let me speak to the air boss." There was a slight pause. "Boss, we've got a small boat nine hundred meters off the stern. Have you got a bird available to take a look? . . . All right, I'll be listening on HDC." The captain turned to the signalman, a third-class petty officer. "Punch up HDC-1."

"Aye, aye, Sir." The petty officer turned to pipe the primary Helicopter Direction Control frequency into the speakers on the bridge.

In response to the summons, a Marine Corps AH-1W Cobra gunship broke off from its escort position on the flank of the helicopter formation circling the ship. The Cobra pilot headed for the dhow. The copilot/weapons operator focused his night-vision goggles on the boat. The nose-mounted 20mm cannon, slaved to a sight on his helmet, followed his every move. There was little natural light for the goggles to magnify, and the Cobra gunner knew that turning on the white spotlight would make the helicopter a perfect target. Fortunately, the dhow's lantern threw off enough light to give a decent green-tinted image of the deck. He looked for a moment and pressed the microphone button on his stick.

"Just a regular dhow, fishing nets and all. Looks like their engine quit. The engine hatches are open, and they seem to be working on it. *Makin,* you read that?"

"That's affirmative," replied the air boss. "Do they look like they need any help?"

"Negative," said the Cobra copilot. "They're waving at us, signaling everything is okay, and pointing to the sail."

"Roger," said the air boss. He spoke into his phone. "Captain, did you read that?"

"I got it, Boss," said the captain. "It's the same old story. We'll give him time to get out of there, but if he stays too long or gets closer, I'll move him." He put down the phone and turned to the officer of the deck. "I want to know immediately if that dhow drifts toward us," the captain ordered. "You make sure there's a god-damned pair of eyeballs on that thing every second, you understand me?"

"Aye, aye, Sir," said the officer of the deck.

The two Iranians swam at a depth of twenty feet, deep enough to avoid agitating the phosphorescent organisms near the surface, and leaving a visible trail. In his hands Sa'idi carried an instrument board—this was a small plastic tablet with a compass and depth gauge mounted in the center and a luminous line down the middle to indicate direction. Holding the board in front of him, he could continually follow the preset compass bearing without interfering with his swimming motion. Nothing else was visible in the solid darkness. The temperature of the water was over eighty-five degrees, and the small amount that seeped into his mouthpiece tasted of oil.

Rajabi swam directly above, holding onto the back

harness of Sa'idi's rebreather so there would be no stop-and-go jerking on the safety line or the dragging that would occur if the swimmers were not in physical contact. Sa'idi was pleased that the hull sounds he was hearing were on the same path as the compass bearing and that there were no sounds of underwater explosions. A sure protection against divers is to periodically drop explosives into the water around a ship. But the Americans had never been known to do this. With a tap Sa'idi signaled to Rajabi that he was moving nearer the surface, and Rajabi tapped back. They rose gradually, so they would not mistakenly pass under the ship in the darkness.

Then the compass needle began to oscillate. It meant they were close; the metal hull of the ship was interfering with the compass. Sa'idi signaled Rajabi, and they swam carefully toward the now-loud noises that emanated from the ship.

A few more meters and the water seemed to become even darker. The instrument board touched the steel hull. Sa'idi had not seen the hull, though he sensed it. Rajabi began to move down the hull, and Sa'idi pulled angrily on the buddy cord. They had to proceed carefully, since they had no idea of their exact location on the ship. It was easy to become disoriented in the pitch blackness, especially when the compass did not work.

Feeling their way, the Iranians slowly swam down the length of the *Makin Island*. The mass of the ship projecting over their heads created the illusion of being enclosed by the steel hull. They fought the claustrophobia by concentrating on swimming and staying in contact with the ship. Their movements made little swirls of phosphorescence in the water, but they were so close to the hull that it could be seen only from the side catwalks. And the catwalks were closed during flight operations.

Reaching the bow seemed to take a long time. Then they went back the way they had come, this time measuring the distance. As they reached midship Rajabi, intent on remembering his count, did not notice the increased turbulence of the water. One more kick of his fins and he was caught. Realizing what was happening, he kicked and clawed at the water, to no avail. Bouncing about in the swirl, Rajabi was slammed into one of the underwater openings that sucked seawater into the ship. The snap of the buddy line jerked Sa'idi away from the hull. In one cool movement he swept his knife out of its sheath, cut the line, and kicked backward.

Judging he was clear, Sa'idi floated motionless, listening quietly in the dark for the hull sounds. Hearing nothing except machinery, he moved back to regain contact. Touching the cold steel once again, he slowly slid down the hull to find Rajabi. He felt the turbulence, but it was lessened—Rajabi's arms and upper body were pinned against one of the gratings and were held in place by the strong suction. Feeling a leg, Sa'idi moved his hands up Rajabi's body. He was alive but unable to free himself. The bag of mines dangled free. Sa'idi cut the bag loose and tied it to his belt. He paused to think. The intakes probably became obstructed often. Discovering the blockage, would the Americans turn off the flow and free Kharosh? He decided not. Several different intakes must flow to the same system. Sa'idi moved in front of Rajabi until their face masks were touching. Rajabi's eyes were wide behind the mask. Sa'idi squeezed his friend's shoulder, then reached down and turned off the oxygen flow. Rajabi closed his eyes. Sa'idi cut the air hose, then moved away so he would not have to watch. There would be no prisoner to interrogate and no blood in the water to attract sharks. No one on the surface saw the boil of air bubbles, which quickly subsided.

Trying to recall the measurements, Sa'idi believed he had just passed midship. He faced the hull, wishing Rajabi was with him to guard against any interruption. Though the American SEALs did not usually patrol around hulls, he knew he would be helpless against an attack while placing the mines.

He removed a limpet from the nylon bag. Pressing the mine against the hull with one hand, he turned the key that activated the magnet with the other. He pulled at the mine, but it was firmly attached. Sa'idi removed the key and let it fall to the seafloor below. If he was discovered, the Americans could not remove the mine before it exploded. He pulled the secondary safety from the first fuze. The pin came out easily. If the fuze had been defective and the firing pin had fallen, it would have pressed against the safety, preventing it from being removed. Reassured, Sa'idi pulled the primary safety. Then he activated the fuzes of two other mines while they were still in his bag, so the three would explode simultaneously.

Sa'idi moved down the hull to attach the second mine ten meters from the first, on the same level. As he reached to turn the magnet key, the ship moved and the mine slipped from his grasp. Windmilling with his hands, Sa'idi brought up his feet, and the mine landed on top of his swim fins. Holding his breath, Sa'idi carefully lifted his feet. Using one hand to keep himself level, he grabbed the mine with the other. The plastic mine was slippery; but juggling it, he managed to get a grip on the underside indentation. Sa'idi was furious with himself. After all his training, to ruin such a vital mission with a careless mistake. He concentrated on slowing his breathing to reduce oxygen consumption, then attached the mine without further difficulty. He placed the third limpet above the other two, forming a triangle.

Moving methodically toward the stern, Sa'idi placed one mine on the propeller shaft and one on the rudder. He attached the last at the base of the hull, near the propeller shaft, to open a hole if the limpet on the shaft did not succeed. Free of the weight of the mines, he adjusted his oxygen-flow control to a lower setting. Sa'idi cleared the hull, took another compass bearing, and began swimming steadily.

• • •

On the bridge of the *Makin Island,* the officer of the deck hung up the phone and turned to the captain. "Sir, the dhow is still in the same location."

"Very well," said the captain. "Signal the command ship and request they inform the U.A.E. Coast Guard."

"Aye, aye, Sir." As the OOD walked by the phone, it buzzed again. He picked it up and listened a moment. "Sir, the dhow got its engines working and is clearing the area at this time."

"Good," said the captain. "Belay that signal."

Sa'idi checked his watch to see how long he had been swimming. He should be near the dhow. The compass bearing would get him in the general vicinity, but either he or the dhow could have moved with the current. He would go a little farther before he risked surfacing for a look.

A hundred meters more and he heard metallic tapping—a wrench striking metal plate. He drifted a moment to be sure of the direction, then swam toward the sound. The tapping became more distinct, and he could discern the faint outline of the dhow's hull. He moved to the side opposite the tapping and broke the surface beneath a lookout, who was so startled he almost fell into the water. Regaining his composure, the lookout pushed a rope ladder over the side. Sa'idi, weary from the exertion and the tension, slipped twice before he managed to get aboard. As the swimmer lay on the deck, the captain of the dhow walked over and asked, "And your companion?"

"Get moving, now!" the swimmer snapped.

The captain nodded. He unleashed a quick stream of Arabic, the anchor was lifted, and the engine started.

As the dhow moved out into the Persian Gulf, Sa'idi forced himself to rise from the hard comfort of the deck. He emptied the oxygen tank of the rebreather and punctured the hose and bladder. He packed all his diving gear, except the knife, into one of the plastic paint pails.

Sa'idi resealed the top of the pail and, with the knife, punched holes in the sides and bottom. He kicked the pail overboard. It bobbed twice in the wake of the dhow, then filled with water and sank. The weight belt carried it to the bottom.

Well out to sea, the captain of the dhow studied his charts. When the dhow was outside the emirates' territorial waters, he ordered the anchor dropped once again. He took a plastic suitcase from under the bunk in his cabin and brought it on deck. Inside, nestled in foam rubber, was a radio that would transmit a narrow-beam UHF beacon. Using the set's own compass, he extended the directional antenna, confirmed the frequency setting, and turned it on. The set began transmitting a continuous signal. The captain turned to one of the crew. "Put up the recognition light."

The crewman took a large battery-powered lantern from a wooden locker near the bow. The white globe was covered with translucent green plastic. The young Arab turned on the lantern and hung it at the bow.

Twenty-five minutes later they heard the whine of a gas turbine engine, which changed to a scream. Though the Iranian Navy British Hovercraft BH-7 cut its engine back five hundred yards away, the dhow crew's ears still rang. The Hovercraft came alongside the dhow and two crewmen threw lines, which brought the vessels side by side. The front hatch of the Hovercraft opened, and the dhow crew could see several men; two were carrying machine guns, and one held the unmistakable silhouette of a Soviet RPG-7 antitank rocket launcher. A voice called from the Hovercraft, in Farsi, again quoting the Koran: "God has cursed the unbelievers, and prepared for them a blaze."

Sa'idi stepped out on deck. "Neither their riches nor their children will in the least save them from God's wrath. They shall become the fuel of the fire."

"Come aboard, brother," said the voice from the Hovercraft. Sa'idi stepped over the rail and pulled himself up the rope. Hands from the Hovercraft reached for him and helped him aboard.

"Is the mission accomplished?" inquired the voice.

"Completely," Sa'idi said.

"Where is the other?" the voice asked harshly.

"In Paradise."

"Will there be any evidence?" demanded the voice.

"None," replied Sa'idi.

"Then finish it," the voice said to his men on the Hovercraft.

The two lines holding the dhow were suddenly cut, a spotlight snapped on, and the machine gunners opened fire. The West German MG3 machine guns, firing at a cyclic rate of twelve hundred rounds per minute, sounded like tearing cloth. The gunners squeezed off ten-round bursts to keep the barrels from burning out. There was terrible screaming from the dhow—cries that it was a mistake, cries for mercy. Anyone approaching the rails was cut down. While the gunners methodically swept their fire back and forth, two satchel charges—canvas bags loaded with twenty pounds of plastic explosive—were thrown onto the deck. When the two craft had separated, the RPG gunner fired rockets into the deckhouse, blowing the wooden structure apart. But no one saw a dark shape slip over one side.

The gunmen scrambled back into the Hovercraft, and the Gnome gas turbine screamed to life. The Hovercraft moved five hundred meters away and waited. The satchel charges exploded with the signature white flash of plastic explosive, showering the water with debris. What was left of the hull sank quickly. The spotlight swept carefully over the floating wreckage, and then clicked off.

The Hovercraft went to full throttle and headed for Iran, skipping over the calm sea at fifty knots. It reached the Revolutionary Guard naval base at Bandar Abbas before daylight.

CHAPTER 2

It was 0420 on the USS *Makin Island,* and the midwatch was entering that particularly boring period of the morning when staying alert was almost impossible. Flight quarters had been secured, and the aircraft integrity watch ensured that all the helicopters were properly chained to the flight deck. The logbook reported a slight problem when one of the saltwater intakes became blocked. Another intake had been opened, and the system was running normally. The captain retired to his sea cabin for some rest before the ship weighed anchor.

In the marines' berthing area near the engine room, LCpl. Brian Hawkins tossed and turned in the narrow confines of his bunk, appropriately known in the naval service as a rack. One deck above, a sadistic sailor dragged a set of tie-down chains across the aircraft hangar. The members of the crew condemned to the night existence of the midwatch saw no reason to modify their behavior for those lucky ones who were allowed to sleep in the relative quiet and cool of the evening. After all, those who now tried to sleep would show no consideration as the midwatch tried to rest in the noise and heat of the day. So this particular sailor took his revenge every night, dropping equipment and dragging chains with vengeful glee, tormenting Hawkins as Marley's ghost tormented Scrooge. Hawkins lived in the uppermost of four vertically stacked bunk beds, six feet above the berthing deck and sandwiched in a sea of other bunks. For a six-month deployment, an infantry company—over 150 marines—lived in a space smaller than one floor of a typical family house.

The top bunk did have its advantages, though. No one stepped on your face or groin while climbing into the rack, or swept a broom or mop onto it during field day. And if living on top meant there were pipes and electrical cables in your face and that the vibrations from the upper deck reverberated through your body, it also meant that you didn't have some lardass sagging so deeply into the mattress springs above that you were pinned to your rack, unable to move or turn over. And you got a clear shot at the air-conditioning, if it was working. The air came pure and cool from the vents above, yet to filter down through four layers of bodies seasoning in the tropical heat.

On the bridge, the officer of the deck yawned over a cup of coffee and fought off the terrible temptation to sit in the captain's chair.

At 0423 the three mines near the engine room exploded almost simultaneously. They blew a hole in the hull over twenty-five feet in diameter. A wall of water under incredible pressure rushed into the lower levels of the ship. On the bridge, the impact knocked over crew, coffee pots, binoculars, and other loose gear. After the initial shock, the officer of the deck pulled himself to his feet and tripped the general quarters alarm. The yeoman screamed into the 1MC, the shipwide public-address system: "General quarters, general quarters! This is not a drill, this is *not* a drill!"

Under normal conditions, an LPH maintains material condition yoke, which means there is free access between compartments and decks. During general quarters, the condition changes to zebra, and all hatches are sealed to prevent the spread of water and fire. In an LPH, unlike smaller warships, only the decks below the hangar deck can be sealed off from each other. The hangar deck and vehicle stowage are huge open spaces covering almost the entire length of the ship. And the decks above are linked by large stairwells, fore and aft. During a general quarters drill setting condition zebra can take over ten minutes, since personnel need time to move throughout the ship to their stations. Needless to say, it takes longer at night and in the confusion and stress of a real emergency.

Just before the explosion, Hawkins lay listening to the cacophony of snores and creaking springs. The compartment was barely visible in the dim red night-lights. Then an enormous hammering bang vibrated through the hull, and the ship lurched violently to one side. Hawkins was nearly thrown out of his rack—only the aluminum guardrails held him in. There was a roaring sound of water under pressure. Ten marines whose bunks lay against the bulkhead died instantly when the steel wall shattered and the sea came pouring in. The night-lights flickered, went out, and came back on. At the far end of the compartment several marines forced open the wooden door to the port-side ladderwell and charged up the stairs. But the weight of the rushing water soon forced the inward-opening door shut, and it could not be moved. Darkness and confusion made the situation worse as the berthing area became jammed with panicked, shouting marines, thrashing in the now–chest-deep water and trying to climb over each other to get out.

The engine room flooded before it could be sealed off, the water spreading to the decks below. Electrical power was lost, but battery-powered emergency lights came on automatically. Alert crewmen in several compartments had quickly secured hatches but were trapped as these isolated pockets were surrounded by water. The ladderwells were clogged with marines and sailors who had escaped the berthing areas and were trying to make their way to the flight deck.

The captain, still wearing his skivvies, ran onto the bridge as the crew tried to sort out the damage-control reports. "Was it a missile?" he yelled to no one in particular.

"Underwater explosion," shouted the officer of the deck, juggling two phones. "No contact with the engine room, the whole deck is flooding fast."

"Jesus," groaned the captain. "Have we gotten a message off yet?"

"Yes, Sir," said the OOD. "The command ship says they can get fireboats here in an hour. Tugs will take longer. We've got nothing but emergency power right now."

The stern rose violently from the water as the remaining limpets on the propeller shaft, rudder, and hull exploded. The screw was cut almost completely through, and the rudder hung limply. The hull at the base of the stern buckled, and water began to pour down the propeller shaft and into the ship.

The weight of the water in its hull caused the *Makin Island* to roll gently to starboard. The port anchor chain groaned as it accepted more of the ship's weight. The roll stopped, and the ship listed more than fifteen degrees. A CH-46 transport helicopter broke its chains and slid off the flight deck into the water. The captain watched it in dismay. "We're not going to be able to get the birds off," he said. The bridge crew failed to hear him in the din of panic. The ship settled lower into the water.

On the fight deck many marines, not waiting for direction from the navy, had activated some of the large life rafts that hung along the catwalk in canisters that looked like oil drums. The rafts were in the water and had begun to inflate, still secured to the ship by a line. As the

Makin Island settled deeper in the water, men on the high side jumped into the darkness as chief petty officers screamed for them to remain on the ship.

Hawkins looked down into the bunk below. Private First Class Garvey was staring, shocked, at the screaming men and the rising water. Hawkins leaned over, grabbed Garvey by the T-shirt, and shouted, "Hang onto me and don't let go for nothing. Just do what I do."

Anyone but a recent graduate of boot camp would have doomed them by not moving until he knew what was going on and all his questions had been answered. But Garvey, simply relieved that someone had taken charge, followed him without a word.

As the water rose to the bottom of his mattress, Hawkins grabbed a cluster of cables that ran overhead toward the starboard ladderwell. He slipped into the water. Garvey followed. Hawkins pulled himself hand over hand along the cables, moving toward the entrance to the ladderwell, which was now underwater. Then the battery lamps were submerged, the water only a foot below the overhead. The plunging darkness and rising water made claustrophobia inevitable. Hawkins tried to control his panic by concentrating on the cables. Through many hours of idle observation while lying in his rack, he knew they ended near the entrance to the stairwell.

Hawkins looked back. Garvey was dealing with his fear by keeping his eyes screwed shut and chanting, "Oh fuck, oh fuck, oh fuck" in a continuous litany. Hawkins had intended to dive down, find the ladderwell, and come back up for Garvey. But the water was only six inches below the overhead—and there was no time for two trips. Hawkins felt the end of the cables. He couldn't see anything. The screams were so loud he thought his eardrums would burst. They were running out of air space. Hawkins turned, put his face to Garvey's ear, and interrupted his chanting by shouting, "Grab onto my waist and kick as hard as you can. We'll go on the count of three."

"Okay," Garvey gasped.

"Ready . . . one, two, three!"

They plunged below the water, and Hawkins opened his eyes. He couldn't see anything in the darkness. Disoriented, he lost his sense of direction, and the twisting of his body in the turbulence sent him off course. Propelled forward by Garvey's panicked kicking, his head slammed into something soft and yielding. Feeling with his hands, he realized it was a body. He almost expelled his breath. Still moving forward, he hit something solid. Feeling again, more tentatively this time, he realized that it was the line of bunks that ran parallel to the ladderwell. Grabbing the aluminum tubing of the bunk frame, he pulled himself along. Reaching the end, he felt frantically around the corner for some sign of the ladderwell. Garvey's arms squeezed his waist so tightly that they were forcing out what little air he had left in his lungs. Pushed forward by the kicking, Hawkins felt what had to be the tubing of the handrail. He grabbed it with his left hand and pulled. He felt the steps below with his right hand. The pressure in his lungs was unbearable. Hawkins pulled himself up the handrail with the strength of desperation. He fought the desire to take a breath. Garvey had stopped kicking, but was still hanging onto his waist. It couldn't be much farther, the ladderwell wasn't that long. Again, his head struck something hard. Sweet Jesus, the hatch that was usually pinned up out of the way was now shut tight. In the middle of the hatch was a smaller access hatch, the size of a man's shoulders, that opened by turning a wheel. Hawkins's thrashing hands found the wheel, but it wouldn't turn. The rising water was putting pressure against the locking catches, and they wouldn't budge. Hawkins wedged his feet against the side of the ladderwell and used the force of his entire body against the wheel. The quick movement caused Garvey to slip off, but Hawkins didn't notice. The wheel moved an inch. Feeling himself blacking out, Hawkins coiled his body for a last desperate push. The wheel gave in his hands, and he turned it wildly. Finally the force of the water popped the hatch, and Hawkins bobbed up through the fountain of water erupting through the opening.

Halfway through the hatch, Hawkins inhaled air in great, wheezing gasps. Hands grabbed his arms and pulled him through. It took him a moment to realize that Garvey wasn't there. Unable to speak, Hawkins pointed at the opening until an enormous khaki-clad chief petty officer realized what he meant. The chief plunged headfirst through the hatch until only his legs were visible. His legs swung about as he rooted through the water. Then he emerged—first his torso, then his head, and finally his arm, which was wrapped around Garvey's head. True to his rank, he bellowed to the nearest sailors: "Well, give me a fucking hand!"

Two sailors pulled Garvey through the hatch. "Any more?" shouted the chief. Hawkins shook his head. The chief levered the hatch back down and secured it while the sailors began CPR on Garvey. After five breaths, Garvey spewed out a lungful of saltwater into a sailor's face and began to breathe on his own.

The chief leaned wearily against the bulkhead. He pointed to Hawkins and one of the sailors. "Rest until you get your wind, and then put him on a stretcher and get him topside." He paused to take a long breath. "If you see any officers, tell them we need more people to get the fire in the galley under control."

Hawkins was just starting to breathe normally. He felt a little put upon. After all, he had just gotten Garvey out of serious shit, a real act of fucking heroism, and now they wanted him to drag the boot up three flights of stairs. Couldn't they find a spare squid around here? As he opened his mouth to bitch, the chief said, gently this time, "We can't spare anybody else." Hawkins nodded.

The sailor pulled a metal-framed stretcher from its

mounting on the bulkhead, and they strapped Garvey into it. The ship was tilted to one side, making it difficult to get up the ladderwell. As they crouched to get the stretcher through the hatch leading to the main stairway, Hawkins kept up a running conversation with Garvey, who was beginning to come around.

"You might want to consider dying, Garvey, because if you don't, you *will* pay for this, I shit you not. Personally, if I was you I'd tell the Doc I strained my back and get a medical discharge, because if you come back to the company you're going to be my house mouse for the rest of your time in the corps, you bastard. It's not good enough I save your ass—I have to break mine carrying you out of this scow. First I'm blown up, then drowned, then I get a fucking hernia. You better plan on supporting me for the rest of your fucking life."

The sailor on the other end of the stretcher listened in amazement, then began laughing so hard it weakened him, and he nearly dropped the stretcher. Goddamn marines! The world falls to shit, the ship is sinking, and he's making me laugh. What kind of rocks do they find these animals under?

Garvey began to perk up. He didn't think Hawk would be giving him all that shit if he was going to die.

There was chaos at the top of the stairwell, the level just below the flight deck. The corridors were filled with smoke and people rushing back and forth shouting orders and passing messages. Hawkins attributed the confusion to the fact that they were near officers' country. A crowd was trying to push its way through the open door leading to the flight deck. Hawkins looked first at the mob of men, then at the sailor carrying the other end of the stretcher.

"I've had about enough of this bullshit, my arms are falling off. Just keep pushing on this thing, and we'll get through."

"Right behind you," yelled the sailor.

"Take it easy, Garve," said Hawkins, looking down

into the stretcher. "Don't strain yourself or nothing." Garvey, strapped down tightly, just grinned uneasily. Hawkins would surely drop him if he said anything wise.

Hawkins turned to the crowd at the hatch. "Gangway, gangway, serious casualty here. Make way, make way," he yelled, butting at the bodies in front of him. "Make way, we got a man hurt bad here." His voice rose several decibels as the men in front grudgingly made room. "Goddammit, you people get the fuck out of the way before this guy dies!"

They emerged from the hatch to a dark morning sky just showing traces of red. A short stairway led them to the tilted flight deck. It was crowded with shouting sailors and marines; some were jumping into the water. On each aircraft elevator were rows of casualties waiting to be winched into one of the helicopters buzzing around the ship. Circling in dangerous proximity to one another were American Seahawks from the nearby destroyers, two British Lynxes, and some French Gazelles that must have come from the shore.

Patrolboats, customs boats, fireboats, tugs, and dhows poured from the port, all attracted to the *Makin Island.* Four tugs attempted to nudge the ship into shallower water, but could not. Localized fires burned throughout the interior of the ship, but the fireboats could do little except supply hoses and pumps. Fortunately, the explosion had barely missed the access elevator into the ammunition magazine. Also spared were the tanks containing high-octane JP fuel for the helicopters. A slight error in measurement had saved the *Makin Island.*

Hawkins and the sailor pushed through the crowd and set the stretcher down on the aft elevator, near one of the medical teams.

"I'm going to shove off now," said the sailor. "You guys take it easy."

"Thanks a lot for everything, mate," said Hawkins, shaking his hand.

"Now listen, Garve," said Hawkins, bending over the

stretcher. "I've got to see about getting off this thing. Now for Christ's sake, if they ask you, tell them you're dying. If they find out you've just got some water in your ear, they'll never let you off."

"Thanks, Hawk," said Garvey as Hawkins stood up and got his bearings.

"You'll pay, Garvey," yelled Hawkins, as he disappeared into the crowd. "You will definitely pay for this."

As the first light of dawn illuminated the scene, the captain's gaze was fixed on the flight deck. "All personnel except damage control lay to the flight deck," he ordered. "But do not, repeat, do not abandon ship." In this confusion, he thought, we'll lose more people than we'll save. The command ship came up on the radio, and the captain turned away to make his report to the task force commander.

At 0535, with only the upper deck and flight deck above water, the captain of the USS *Makin Island* abandoned his ship. He was the last man off.

CHAPTER 3

"OVER THREE HUNDRED dead," breathed the president of the United States, as he stared disbelievingly at the paper in his hands.

"Most are missing," said the secretary of defense. "They still haven't been able to get a firm count."

The president put down the message and accepted a cup of coffee from the White House chief of staff. "And the survivor from the fishing boat, the one our frigate picked up. He definitely said that it was an Iranian mission?"

"He said the two divers they dropped off to attack the *Makin Island* were active-duty Iranian naval officers," the secretary of defense replied. "He was the mate and quite well informed. It seems that the fishing boat had been doing odd jobs for Iranian intelligence for the last few years. One of the divers was lost in the attack, and the other was transferred to an Iranian Navy Hovercraft. The Hovercraft destroyed the fishing boat, evidently to silence the witnesses."

"But missed the mate, our smoking gun," said the president. "What's the latest word on the *Makin Island?*"

The chairman of the Joint Chiefs of Staff, Adm. John Armstrong, broke in. "Sir, we don't think we'll lose her, but it will take some time to get the clear picture."

"It'll probably be a write-off," the secretary of defense said bluntly. "An old LPH like *Makin Island* may not even be worth the cost of salvaging." The secretary had made his reputation in Washington as a conservative military reformer and was feared and disliked both for his clout with the president and for his willingness to take on sacred cows. A highly decorated company commander in the 101st Airborne in Vietnam, the secretary's bitter memories of the military leadership at that time tended to color his relations with the generals and admirals in the Pentagon.

Admiral Armstrong was a big, bluff, heavyset man. Although inclining to fat, he was still an intimidating figure at the apex of his career. After one of his legendary ass chewings, strong officers had been known to leave his presence with knotted stomachs, quivering lower lips, and knocking knees. Now the admiral was both angry and tired. Several of the cabinet members, considered tough men in the political arena, flinched involuntarily whenever the admiral punctuated his speech by slapping his meaty hands on the arms of his chair. He regarded the secretary of defense and his clique of reformers as military dilettantes, men who wanted to change things without having paid the price of long service that he had.

During their frequent disagreements the secretary would often make a point of staring fixedly at the rows of ribbons on the admiral's chest, where combat decorations were conspicuously absent.

The secretary of state looked up from the messages he was reading. "It appears we were mistaken," he said, "in thinking their economic situation would force the Iranians to be more pragmatic about better relations with us —or even to begin to act rationally. But that, of course, is a separate issue." This secretary had made his reputation in academia and rarely used the first person singular except when taking credit.

The secretary of defense noticeably rolled his eyes to the heavens.

The president's habit was to sit back and allow his advisers to fight it out before he made a decision. He also liked to take his time and gauge the possible public reaction to any move. Now, he didn't think waiting would be possible, and his anxiety was apparent. "It *is* a separate issue," he said. "The pertinent question is what our response should be."

"As much as I hate to admit it," said the secretary of defense. "Iran's strategy is brilliant. They've left us with only three choices: to capitulate and leave the Gulf, to remain and face more attacks, or to retaliate and take the chance of starting another major war."

"They're betting that after Iraq we won't have the will to crank everything up again and confront them," said the national security adviser. "But we really have only two choices; there's no way we can withdraw and leave the Iranians in control of the Gulf."

"I agree," said the secretary of defense. "So we must respond."

"Another war?" the secretary of state asked. "Is that what you have in mind?"

"It's been an undeclared war," the secretary of defense replied, "ever since they took over our embassy."

"What are you suggesting?" said the president.

"We have to reply to this attack, without becoming drawn into a larger conflict with Iran," said the secretary of defense. "So any strike has to be undertaken with that in mind." The secretary looked up from his papers and met the president's gaze. "We should eliminate the oil terminals and storage facilities on Kharg Island in the Gulf. It would cripple Iran's war-making ability in one decisive strike."

"There are other good reasons to take it out," said the national security adviser, throwing in with Defense. "The Iraqis tried to destroy Kharg for years, and they didn't have the equipment, expertise, or guts to do it. It would be a tremendous psychological blow if we did it in one strike. It's an island, so we can better achieve air superiority and recover any downed pilots. And the number of civilians killed would be relatively small."

The national security adviser was a former air force general, a technocrat whose invaluable performance on the White House and National Security Council staffs launched him to the policy level upon retirement.

"Has it occurred to anyone what kind of impact this will have on world oil supply?" asked the secretary of state, shaking his head for effect. It was his favorite gesture.

"The Iranians are obviously counting on the fact that we can't afford to cut off their oil," said the admiral.

"I think they've miscalculated," said the director of the Central Intelligence Agency. "There's still a lot of unused production capacity out there."

"If the OPEC countries are willing to use it," countered the secretary of state, slightly more desperate as another voice weighed in against him.

"They will," said the national security adviser. "Money talks. Saudi Arabia and Kuwait will probably make up the difference by themselves. They've come through before, and I'm sure they will again. After all, for them we're the only game in town right now."

"What of Iran's response to all this?" asked the secretary of state. "Even as we speak we're starting to get indications from third countries that the Iranians want to begin new talks."

"Of course they do," the national security adviser said scornfully. "It's the old game played to perfection. They hit and then ask for negotiations, to make it politically difficult for us to strike back. We've talked and talked, but there's just no way Iran is going to permit us to reestablish relations—not for a price we're willing to pay."

"There are a hundred different power blocs in Iran," said the secretary of state. "They have a lot of influence, and they often act independently of the government. This is what we could be dealing with."

"That's the same old crap from the hostage crisis," the secretary of defense said. "It's a beautiful way for the

Iranian government to avoid responsibility. They just made it clear what they think about moderation. We have to hit them. Quickly, and hard."

"At the very least," said the secretary of state, directly to the president, "they'll step up terrorism around the globe. Will we be prepared for the consequences of that?"

"The Iranians obviously weighed the consequences before they acted," the secretary of defense said quickly, before the president could speak. "Every time they've moved against us, they accepted our carefully weighed response, found the cost to be low, and came back for more. Now they're waiting to see what we do—or don't do. And if we don't respond it means more attacks, both in the Gulf and around the world."

The president said nothing.

"And what of their response?" said the secretary of state, feeling the full weight of opinion against him. "We could put ourselves in an untenable position. The Iranians just may not act the way we wish them to."

"I'll tell you what happens if we do nothing," the secretary of defense said angrily. "The Iranians will smell weakness and step up the pressure to get us out of the Gulf. We either act or go home—there's no other way."

"Turn that around," said the secretary of state. "The hard-liners in Teheran are egging us on. If we hit Iran, we smash all the bridges we were trying to build. And it could isolate us even more in the Arab world."

"I don't agree," said the national security adviser. "The Arabs don't care what we do to the Persians. Iran is the big threat now—the Arabs would love to see her cut back down."

"We've discussed this time and time again," said the president. "And each time there's been agreement that an attack on Kharg is the preferable response to a major attack on American interests. It may only shut their oil off temporarily, but they'll know that we can hit again whenever we choose." He took off his glasses and set them on the desk. Without glasses, the president looked very tired. He rubbed his eyes. "And frankly, hitting Kharg is our only choice, especially with definite proof of Iranian involvement. It's clear we must do something." He turned to the CIA director. "But before we move, I want a complete evaluation of the possible impact on world oil supply and prices—and I want it quickly."

"Yes, Mr. President," the director replied.

"Now, to change the subject," the president said. "Let's discuss our military options."

"It'll have to be carrier air," said the secretary of defense. "Nobody in the region is going to let us launch air force planes from their bases, not for this."

The president frowned. "I'm uncomfortable with the prospect of shot-down American fliers. Even the slightest chance of it happening is unacceptable."

"We don't necessarily have to use air power to take out the facilities on the island," Admiral Armstrong said. He was not a naval aviator and had few debts to that constituency within the navy.

"What do you propose?" the president asked.

"Cruise missiles, Sir."

They all nodded. The missiles had been stars in the war with Iraq.

"Can we do it all with Tomahawks?" the national security adviser asked the admiral. "Or will we have to follow up with air strikes?"

"Just missiles," said the admiral. "The targets on Kharg are ideal for them."

"Then I don't understand why we need to pay for planes at all," the secretary of state said abruptly.

"Tomahawks are ideal for specialized strikes against heavily defended targets, when it would be suicide to send planes. But the missiles cost over a million apiece," the national security adviser told him. "And that's just for a thousand-pound warhead. A plane can carry many thousands of pounds and, if it doesn't get shot down, it can fly a lot of missions."

"And one other reason," the secretary of defense added dryly. "Smart missiles don't determine the force structure, but pilots do. And if you screw with pilots' planes, you find them and their lobby dancing on your desk."

"All right," said the president, putting an end to it. "I've got some questions for the admiral."

"Yes, Sir," said the admiral.

"What do we have in the Gulf right now to deliver the missiles?"

The admiral consulted one of his briefing books. "Sir, we have an Aegis cruiser stationed with the battle group there. We can use her for the strike, but she'll need more missiles than are normally carried. We can fly them and the technical people to the island of Diego Garcia in the Indian Ocean and transfer them to the ship there."

"Mr. President, there's something else we should take into consideration," said the CIA director.

"And what's that?" asked the president.

"The Iranians own some of the tankers they use to shuttle the oil out of Kharg, and they lease some. The ones they lease are owned by Greek-, Panamanian- and Liberian-registered companies, and the crews are a mix of several nationalities. Some of these leased tankers will be sunk, and crews may be killed." He stopped abruptly, feeling he had made his point.

"They've been operating in a war zone and making a fortune out of it," the secretary of defense said dismissively. "They know the risks. Besides, they probably went through Iraqi attacks during the war."

"There's just one small problem with that argument," the secretary of state said, with every bit of condescension he could muster. "The Greeks are going to see a slight difference when the United States of America sinks their ships and kills their citizens. The respective governments are going to have to be warned, if not of the attacks, then of the danger to their people."

"Jesus Christ!" exclaimed the secretary of defense. "Tell the Greeks and it'll be in Teheran before the day is out."

"That may be so," the president said. "But we can't just sally forth and kill the citizens of our allies." He thought for a moment. "We'll make a general statement to all countries that the United States will not be responsible for the safety of anyone working or residing in Iran."

"I believe that will be sufficient, Mr. President," said the secretary of state.

"I agree," said the secretary of defense, magnanimous in victory. "If we make that statement right now and some time elapses until our response, the Iranians will take it as an empty threat."

"Good," said the president. "Admiral Armstrong, I want you to plan an operation with the objective of destroying everything of value on Kharg Island. I want the operation kept under the tightest possible security, and I want to be briefed as soon as possible. If you need to move more ships into the area, let me know and we'll do it right away. But I don't want anything done without my approval."

"Aye, aye, Sir," said the admiral.

"Other than that," said the president, "I want a briefing prepared for the press. But we'll wait until all the information is in. Let's get it right, but let's hurry.

"That's it. Does anyone have anything else? All right, thank you, gentlemen."

CHAPTER 4

THE CAPTAIN OF the Aegis cruiser USS *Buna* (CG-78) shifted anxiously in his padded chair in the ship's combat information center, studying the blue screens that displayed information generated by the Aegis system's SPY-1 radars. While sailing in the Persian Gulf within range of Iran, the screens were watched with more than usual concentration. It was nearing dawn, but inside the superstructure of the ship one could tell only from the set of clocks on the bulkhead.

The previous night the captain had been awakened by a flash message ordering him to execute Operation Black Knife at 0225 zulu, or Greenwich mean time, the designation used in all military communication to eliminate confusion with local time zones. Adjusted for the local time, it meant he would launch the attack on Kharg Island at 0525. For security the code name was meaningless, having been selected from a computer-generated list. If the mission succeeded it would be renamed something suitably patriotic before the initial press release.

The time was 0500, and the captain couldn't seem to get comfortable. In this type of engagement, it wasn't the normal fear for self-preservation that set him on edge. The Iranians had little chance of interfering with the mission. It was the other small, cumulative fears that haunted him as they have haunted the captains of all ships. The captain has ultimate, total, and complete responsibility for hundreds of men and hundreds of millions of dollars worth of irreplaceable ship. He is responsible for everything that happens or fails to happen on his ship but has no way to personally ensure that the thousands of minor daily tasks essential to the survival of that ship are actually carried out. Ah, but the reward. A ship's captain is the only truly absolute monarch left in the modern world, with total authority over his realm. Absolute authority and absolute responsibility, a sobering mixture.

On this mission all eyes in the United States would be scrutinizing his actions, applauding his success, or analyzing his failure. So the fear of a mistake, of a technical malfunction, of disgrace and the end of a career were not only very real but of far more immediate concern to him than the faint possibility of physical danger.

On Kharg Island the night brought no respite from work. Loading a supertanker with oil takes fifteen hours, and the job went on around the clock.

Kharg sits thirty miles off the coast of Iran, in the western Persian Gulf. It is two miles wide and six miles long, a barren lump of white sand and boulders. Until 1958, when it was realized that the then-new supertankers, drawing sixty or seventy feet of water, could not put in at any of the ports along the coast of Iran, Kharg served as the shah's own Devil's Island. It accommodated "communists"—that is, any opponents of the regime.

Oil reached Kharg in six huge underwater pipes from the pumping station at Ganaveh, on the mainland. The tank farm was positioned on a 220-foot hill so the oil could flow down to the waiting ships by gravity, if need be. There were forty-five storage tanks, including nine with a million-barrel capacity. Tankers took on oil at two huge terminals: on the east side, the T-shaped Kharg Terminal, which could handle ships of up to 250,000 tons; on the west side, the Sea Island Terminal, where the largest tankers moored to piles driven into the sea bottom and drew oil through underwater pipes. Prior to the revolution, Kharg could load six million barrels of oil a day. At the present time, slightly over three million barrels a day passed through the terminals. The facilities on Kharg included a small airport and a village for its workers and defenders. Fresh water was produced in a desalinization plant fueled by natural gas tapped off from eight oil wells right on the island.

U.S. intelligence judged the air defenses on Kharg to be extremely formidable. They included a battery of American Improved HAWK surface-to-air missiles, with nine separate launchers carrying twenty-seven ready-to-fire missiles. President Reagan's arms-for-hostages deal had provided the Iranians with a complete store of the vital spare parts required by the complex system. There were also three British Rapier missile launchers, originally purchased by the shah. In response to U.S. complaints when spare parts and replacement missiles were provided in 1984, the Thatcher government replied that the items were simply nonlethal equipment not covered by any embargo. The Kharg defenses were bolstered by the compact and formidable Swedish RBS-70 laser-guided missile, supplied for hard cash through the good offices of the Bofors Company, by way of Singapore. Over five thousand missiles were shipped before the officially neutral and antimilitarist Swedish government stopped the sales in the glare of unfavorable publicity. The island was also liberally sown with Soviet 23mm and 57mm antiaircraft guns, the latter radar-controlled. Farther out in the Gulf, offshore oil platforms fitted with portable radars provided limited early warning.

As dawn approached and reveille sounded throughout the island, air-defense troops and oil workers sat in groups and ate their breakfasts of unleavened bread, cheese, and yogurt.

The attack began at 0520, when EA-6B Prowler electronic countermeasures aircraft operating from the aircraft carrier USS *Theodore Roosevelt* fired AGM-88 high-speed anti-radiation missiles (HARMs) at the radars on the offshore oil platforms. The missiles homed in on the emissions of the radar sets and obliterated them. The Prowlers then isolated the platforms' radio frequencies and began jamming, preventing the Iranians from sounding an alarm.

At 0525, the USS *Buna* turned out of the wind so the exhaust of the missiles, when they were fired, would not obscure the view of the video cameras recording the launch. Between the ship's superstructure and the forward five-inch gun were sixty-one rectangular hatches. Each covered a built-in missile-launch canister. The absence of a conventional launcher meant that missiles could be fired faster, in greater numbers, and in any combination of types. Near the stern were sixty-one more missile cells. The Aegis cruiser normally carried a mixture of Tomahawk and Standard antiaircraft missiles in the cells. In this case the Standards were displaced by thirty extra Tomahawks.

In the CIC the captain gave the command to fire, and the first twelve missiles left their launch cells one after the other, trailing white smoke. The booster rockets fell away after lifting the missiles out of the canisters and clear of the ship. Wings sprang out from the missile bodies and turbofan engines ignited. At this stage the missiles were still traveling almost vertically. At the end of their apex, the twenty-foot–long missiles plunged down toward the water. Close to the water they pulled up, compasses setting them on preprogrammed courses and altimeters keeping them just above the waves and below radar cover. One missile, whose engine failed to start, punched neatly into the water at the end of its trajectory. There were shouted obscenities from the bridge. The *Buna* fired another group of twelve missiles, paused, and rippled off a final six.

The missiles had a short trip, since the *Buna* had been less than eighty miles away from Kharg Island—a distance far short of the Tomahawks' maximum range. Still several miles from the island, they climbed slightly, and each missile's radar came on. The guidance systems compared the radar pictures to the digital maps stored in their electronic memories and made adjustments to the courses. The missiles split up, heading for different targets. They ignored the radar reflectors the Iranians had installed on buoys to attract Iraqi Exocet missiles. An Iranian technician manning a HAWK-battery low-altitude search radar spotted the missiles emerging from the clutter caused by radar beams bouncing off the ocean waves. He screamed a warning to his officer.

The Tomahawks came out of the rising sun at over five hundred miles an hour. From a distance the missiles seemed to float over the waves, but they closed on the island with deceptive quickness. The first three, designated to suppress the antiaircraft defenses, screamed overhead. Plates in the undersides of the missiles fell clear, and small cylindrical objects fluttered to the ground, stabilized by white streamers. Three Rapier missile launchers arrayed on the high ground near the tank farm disappeared in the small, sharp explosions of the BLU/97B bomblets. The exploding Rapiers added to the show, corkscrewing through the air. One missile dumped the last of its 166 bomblets on two Soviet Flat Face and Flap Wheel radars and plunged into a battery of 57mm guns, its unburned jet fuel adding to the conflagration. The remaining two missiles banked across the island, compared the terrain to that of their programmed routes, and dropped bomblets on the three HAWK missile radars and three target-illumination trailers before crashing into the control vans. Without radars the HAWK missiles were useless. Some gun crews desperately tried to bring their weapons to bear. But as will happen, many simply stood and stared, dumbfounded.

The next group of three Tomahawks, with thousand-pound high-explosive warheads, emerged from the smoke of the first explosions. The three missiles flew

across the island and smashed into the Sea Island Terminal, the explosions shattering the pilings and cracking
open the two oil pipelines running from the island. The
shock waves from the blasts broke windows all over
Kharg.

The last five missiles of the first wave followed. Four
slammed into the Kharg Terminal, the thousand-pound
warheads cutting the connection between the mile-long
T-shaped terminal and the island and exploding where
the two sections of the terminal came together. One
exploded in midair from either a malfunction or a lucky
hit by the antiaircraft guns.

The next wave, twelve missiles, came in seconds later.
An RBS-70 missile streaked out from the island but lost
its target in the smoke and the glare of the sun. Several
23mm guns finally started hammering away, but the
twenty-one-inch diameter of the missiles did not present
much of a target. The speeding Tomahawks broke from
their group to pursue different objectives. Six headed for
the pipelines bringing oil from the mainland. Five made
it; the computer on one malfunctioned and it passed
over the island out to sea, flying until it ran out of fuel.
Two flew parallel over the airfield, scattering bomblets
over the runway before crashing into the control tower
and hangar. The remaining four flew into the Kharg
Terminal and destroyed supertanker berths. The explosions cut and ignited the oil lines on the terminal; the
fires spread to the loading supertankers.

The last six missiles created the most spectacular
damage. Following the long axis of the island in echelon,
the Tomahawks dispensed their bomblets over the fuel
farm. Emptied of their cargo, two crashed into the
desalinization plant. The exploding rocket fuel ignited
the stores of natural gas to create an enormous fireball.
The only source of fresh water was gone. The remaining
missiles plunged onto four of the island's eight oil wells.

The million-barrel fuel tanks caught fire and began to
melt from the top down, like giant slabs of milk choco-

late. Burning oil from the pumping station and tanks flowed down the hill from the fuel farm like lava, and crews abandoned their antiaircraft guns before they were engulfed by the flames. The intense heat cracked the surfaces of roads, melted any pipelines that had been spared, and created a strong wind as the fires drew in oxygen to feed themselves. A choking cloud of oily black smoke covered the whole island, and the surrounding waters became dark from spilled oil.

The attack was finished one minute after the first missile exploded. Helicopters with rescue crews flew in hours later from the mainland, and one crashed in the unusual drafts created by the fire. Smaller ships were able to enter the tiny harbor used by resupply vessels, but efforts were hampered by the flow of casualties and the thousands of shouting workers demanding to be taken off. An accurate count was impossible, but it was estimated that over several hundred had died. Fires were still burning a week later. International companies specializing in fighting oil fires refused to enter the war zone.

Predictably, massive demonstrations erupted throughout Iran demanding revenge. The United States issued a quick statement threatening even more massive retaliation for any further acts of terrorism. The governments of the Gulf states sighed in collective relief, but of course said little publicly.

In the United States, public opinion was heavily in favor of the attack. There was muted criticism of its scale and devastation, but the widely held view was that it was high time something was done about the Iranians. The American media, as usual terrified of being on the wrong side of an issue, scaled down coverage after the first few hysterical days. Television reports from the scene were drastically curtailed when a jittery Iranian gun crew shot down a chartered helicopter as those inside tried to obtain dramatic pictures of the destruction.

Countries that depended on Iranian oil exports expressed outrage at the American attack, and the international community experienced a few weeks of anxiety over higher energy prices. Oil companies made killings from the volatility of the crude oil spot markets. But, predictably, the oil-producing countries, already strapped for foreign exchange, soon seized the opportunity for extra revenue by cheating on their OPEC production quotas and thus made up the shortfall.

In the Philippines, Greece, and India, the native countries of most of the supertanker crews—and none favorably disposed toward the United States—there were demands for compensation and angry demonstrations outside American embassies.

Despite the usual condemnations from the Left, the reaction in Europe was temperate. After the attack on the *Makin Island,* the action against Kharg was seen as justifiable.

Two uneventful months passed, and the alerts were relaxed. Iranian protests to the World Court and the United Nations were dismissed as face-saving gestures, the anti-imperialist rhetoric as the usual hyperbole.

PART TWO

Such men as had the fear of God before them and as made some conscience of what they did . . . the plain russet-coated captain that knows what he fights for and loves what he knows.

Letters and Speeches of Oliver Cromwell,
by THOMAS CARLYLE

CHAPTER 5

THE MAIN PARKING lot of the Pentagon was always crowded long before 9:00 in the morning. An unwritten military commandment states that you must arrive at work before your commanding officer and leave after him—if you want your career to progress. Those stationed at the Pentagon followed the commandment religiously. With so much to do, and so many staff officers to do it, the ability to find an ax and vigorously grind it was greatly admired.

Richard Welsh did not have a much-coveted reserved space and therefore had to park far out in the lot. Normally he felt pity for those early arrivers and didn't mind the walk. But today it was raining, and as he splashed his way to work he cursed them all as apple polishers.

Welsh was soaked by the time he made it to his entrance. He passed through the security check, and as usual the irony of his presence as a civilian in this building was not lost on him. His career path could not be called logical.

After high school, Welsh had managed to obtain a naval Reserve Officers' Training Course (ROTC) scholarship, necessary to pay for college. During the required summer cruises he developed a burning hatred for ships and the navy, enduring both until he could enter the Marine Corps. He found his calling there as an infantry officer. A year and a half later he was in Beirut, part of the unit flown in to reinforce the marine battalion landing team (BLT) devastated by a terrorist truck bomb.

Welsh was in Lebanon less than a month before the BLT was relieved. He left disillusioned and disgusted. If he had stayed longer perhaps he would have thought differently, much the way people who put an enormous investment into a worthless enterprise can never quite bring themselves to admit it was wrong. He resigned after fulfilling his service commitment, two years later.

Having become fond of Washington during officer training at Quantico, Welsh managed to get a job as an aide to a Midwestern congressman. It was not a success. The man treated his staff worse than Welsh would ever have dreamed of treating any of his enlisted men. He soon grew tired of picking up the congressman's laundry and running errands for the congressman's wife. Then a friend who worked for a member of the Armed Services Committee mentioned a Pentagon post he thought Welsh might find interesting. So at age thirty-one he found himself in a new job. At least it would pay the bills until he could get his law school applications together.

As he made his way to the offices of the assistant secretary of defense for special operations/low-intensity conflict, Welsh was forced to admit that if one only looked at the working conditions, then whoever said the third time was the charm had to be a jerk. Pentagon offices were once-decent-sized rooms that had been ruthlessly partitioned into a staggering number of smaller cubicles. Each individual space was just large enough to do a deep knee bend in without cracking into the desk. And the noise level was only slightly less than that of a 747 revving for takeoff.

Yet even such less-than-lavish surroundings were the result of bloody and savage bureaucratic battles fought between the military, the office of the secretary of defense, and the Congress. Working for Congress had exposed Welsh to the Byzantine processes of high-level policy-making, but that was nothing compared to the story behind the creation of his department. It was like attempting an explanation of the daily workings of the U.S. military—no outsider would ever believe it.

The greatest handicap the office labored under was the regular military's traditional lack of interest in special operations. Two contradictory views prevailed: one held that special operations skimmed off the cream of personnel and resources better used by regular units; the other held that special ops personnel were uncontrollable thugs. Special operations units had always been starved or disbanded in peacetime, then frantically slapped together during war or some emergency, usually with dubious results.

Welsh often thought this bias had a root in the culture. Military operations using economy of force were very attractive to a country with limited resources, such as Great Britain. But the American mentality was somewhat different. Instead of asking why they should use two divisions for a mission they could accomplish with twenty men, Americans asked why they should use twenty men when they could use two divisions.

After the disasters of the hostage rescue mission in Iran and the Grenada invasion, the Congress, in a rare bipartisan effort, placed all special operations forces under a unified command with separate budget authority. This was called United States Special Operations Command, or SOCOM.

The core units were Special Forces Operational Detachment Delta, better known as the Delta Force; SEAL Team 6, the navy's Delta equivalent, responsible for waterborne counterterrorist missions; the army's 160th Special Operations Aviation Regiment; and air force special ops transports, helicopters, and combat control teams. Also part of the command were the army Ranger regiment and Special Forces groups, special warfare support units, and all navy SEAL teams.

But what followed next, Welsh often thought ruefully, could not be described as willing and cheerful obedience to orders. The services simply declined to give up con-

trol of their units. It wasn't overt disobedience, of
course, just that nobody quite understood the plan. Congress had to threaten to withhold the money appropri-
ated for the new command. Two secretaries of defense
issued written orders. And the services slowly, grudgingly gave in. But Welsh had to give the brass credit: they
didn't give up.

To give SOCOM an advocate at the civilian command
level, and to break the military's habit of diverting special operations funds to other uses, Congress created the
office of assistant secretary of defense for special opera-
tions/low-intensity conflict. The military leadership tried
to place the staff in an office building in Rosslyn, Virginia, claiming there just wasn't any available space in
the Pentagon. Welsh thought it was a nice touch that the
lease on the building had only eighteen months left to
run. Congress screamed, and room in the Pentagon
somehow became available.

Welsh's friends liked to tell him that only a dumb ex-
jarhead would jump aboard such a sinking ship. But
Welsh really did enjoy his job. A regular marine grunt
was nowhere near Special Forces caliber, but a solid
background in infantry tactics enabled him to judge
what was really going on. He also discovered a talent for
analysis. The frustration level was usually just as high as
in the military, but sometimes he actually felt that he
could make a difference.

Welsh had barely hung up his suit jacket when a muscular navy lieutenant in summer whites sauntered into
the cubicle. Above his ribbons sat the SEAL badge,
which they called the Budweiser—a large gold emblem
with rampant eagle perched above trident, anchor, and
flintlock pistol. Accordingly, the length of the officer's
blond hair skirted even liberal navy regulations, as did
his moustache. To Welsh it all was a sure sign of the
corruption of an Annapolis graduate—a conditioned
anal retentive set free among a group of nonconformist

military wild men. Coffee cup in hand, the lieutenant crashed into an unoccupied chair.

Welsh shook his head in mock disgust. "Jesus, I can't even sit down before some squid comes in here to shoot the shit. Don't they give you people any work to do?"

Lieutenant Roger Miles sipped his coffee and planted both feet on the desktop, knowing full well that Welsh reserved that location for his own hoofs. "Bullshit. If you'd get your ass in here earlier you wouldn't have these problems."

Welsh smiled and casually picked up the K-Bar combat knife he used as a letter opener. The feet came off the desk quickly. One day Miles had been a little slow and lost his shoelaces. "Good morning to you too, Rog," Welsh said cheerfully. Miles was a good man. The other services didn't always send their best to liaison duty, but the navy didn't consider SEALs housebroken, and that made them unfit for most staff jobs.

"Good morning, Rich," Miles replied. "How was the date last night?"

Welsh groaned. "Let me get some coffee first."

Returning from the coffee mess, Welsh was nearly trampled in the narrow aisle by a scowling air force lieutenant colonel. "Morning, Colonel," Welsh offered. The man sped by with a grunt.

Miles was still in the cubicle when Welsh returned. "I almost got run over by Colonel Livingston," Welsh announced. "Who pissed in his Cheerios this morning?"

Miles laughed appreciatively. "The full colonels' promotion list came out today, and guess who wasn't on it?"

"What a shame," said Welsh, with patent insincerity.

"You never liked him anyway."

"Not since the day he tried to convince me that a light colonel outranked my GS rating, and that I should call him Sir."

"And you told him to stick it up his ass."

Welsh shrugged. "I don't have those Pavlovian reactions to rank anymore. I've been out too long, and working here at Fort Fumble doesn't foster much respect for authority. Besides, the only reason that prick is here is to tell the air force brass everything we do. Just like you."

"Not me," Miles protested. "I just do the heavy lifting. My superiors take care of navy politics. Now, what about the date?"

"Another epic saga of weirdness, disappointment, and personal humiliation."

"Oh?" asked Miles, with an anticipatory grin.

"I couldn't believe it," said Welsh. "Halfway through dinner she wonders out loud why she can't sustain a relationship."

"What did you say? I'm kind of interested—that type of woman won't have anything to do with a warmonger like me."

"I didn't say a thing; I just kept stuffing food in my stupid mouth. I was so rattled I can't even remember what I had to eat. I mean, you can call me a tight-ass, but I usually try not to strip myself emotionally naked on the first date. And this was after she'd spent the previous half hour filling me in on why men are pigs."

"Well, you *are* pigs," Carol Bondurant said casually, as she walked into the cubicle with a message binder in her arms. Carol was one of the secretary's administrative aides.

"Of course we are, Carol," said Welsh. "That's beside the point. I just expect you women to have the good grace not to cut on us to our faces. You can do that among yourselves."

"We haven't given up trying to improve you," Carol said.

"Any time you want to improve me, Carol, you're welcome," Miles said imploringly, expanding his pectorals for her inspection.

Bondurant, peering over her glasses at him, took a moment to form her reply. Welsh shook his head sadly and waited for it. "Thanks," Carol said, "but right now this is the only impossible job I want."

The pectorals deflated, but Miles took the rejection with good humor. "I'm going to write a book," he announced, rising from the chair. *"Women Who Complain About Men, and Why They Don't Get Dates."* He left to continue his rounds.

Carol sat down, taking care to smooth her tailored suit. "You don't find guys with his class every day," she said.

Welsh leaned back in the chair and put his feet up on the desk. Carol was his best friend in the office. She had one of the sharpest brains around and didn't mind letting the boys know she was smarter than they were. Welsh loved it but imagined her lack of tact was why she was working in a department nobody wanted. "What was it you came in here for, Carol?"

She waved the heavy binder menacingly. "Are you going to look at the top-secret message traffic, or not?"

"Anything interesting?"

"The usual. Nothing you won't see on the news tonight." It was their standard joke. Not because secrets were carelessly leaked, which of course they were. But because the mass of top secrets that spewed daily from the top secret printers were, with the exception of a few actual nuggets, either useless garbage or the same information the Cable News Network broke every half hour.

"How many new messages this morning?"

"A ton."

"Carol, you know it arouses me when you're so specific."

She had a wonderful laugh. "It makes no difference, we only get to see what the almighty powers decide we need."

"Don't be cynical," said Welsh. "It's great intelligence, real helpful. An airliner may be hijacked in Europe today—country unknown, airline unknown; possibility of terrorist incident against American targets in the Philippines. . . . Christ, every time we do something the market in rumors goes up."

"So, do you want this?"

"Leave it on the desk," Welsh sighed. "I'll see if I can work up the enthusiasm to slog through it. That is, if you don't want to smuggle it out under your clothing so I can read it tonight." He pretended to examine her body in some detail, as if looking for likely hiding places.

He got a blush, but Carol was quick. "Not for anything less than a movie deal," she retorted. "By the way, the secretary wants to see you at 10:00."

The assistant secretary of defense for special operations was simply called the secretary in the office, since the actual secretary of defense was as remote as the Almighty. "What did I do now?" Welsh asked mournfully.

"He wants to discuss your memo. And I don't think he's happy, so heads up."

"Thanks, this should be interesting. I'm glad I sent out all my law school applications."

"Did you really?"

"Uh-huh. Please keep it quiet, though."

"No problem," Carol said. "I'm thinking of going for my MBA pretty soon."

"Approaching burnout?"

"You know it."

Waiting in the secretary's outer office, Welsh reviewed his options. The secretary either liked his most recent memorandum and had some questions or hated it and was planning to chew his ass. Considering Carol's tip and the memo's content, he guessed it was the latter.

The new secretary had no background in special operations, but Welsh thought they could have done a lot worse. The political realities of the job demanded that the secretary have either expertise and no political pull or connections but no experience.

The secretary had done well in his bid for a government appointment, but he didn't have enough juice to get a meatier job. Welsh always maintained that public servants on that level came in only two types: patricians or dealers. The secretary was a dealer, and even though Welsh liked the man, he just couldn't bring himself to trust him.

The intercom buzzed and Welsh was told to go into the inner office. The secretary was talking on the phone and waved him into a chair. The secretary normally sat on the couch for meetings, but today he remained behind his desk. Welsh sighed and took out his notes. Use the desk to establish the appropriate emotional barrier between you and your employee—Management 101. Welsh tried to remain expressionless; he'd always been told he wore his emotions on his face.

The secretary hung up the phone. "Richard," he said, waving Welsh's memo in the air, "I've read this very carefully. I ask for a readiness evaluation, and I get this. So I'm eager to hear the reasoning behind it." He leaned back and grasped the arms of his chair tightly.

Welsh cleared his throat. "Could you narrow that down a bit, Sir?"

"I can. I want to know why you think we're not ready to perform our counterterrorism mission."

Now the tricky part, thought Welsh. "No, Sir, that's not what I wrote. I said that the major problems we have in command and control, strategy, and intelligence are going to make it very difficult for us to carry out our missions."

"Go on," the secretary said.

Welsh took a deep breath. So it was going to be hard to get. Everybody and his brother knew what the frigging problems were. "Sir, we've spent a great deal of money and effort building up first-class counterterrorist forces, but we've also built up an incredibly bloated command and control system. The units of countries that have done successful hostage rescues all have final say over the planning of their operations and direct command access to the head of state—the person who'll actually order their use. And those heads of state have detailed knowledge of the units involved—they've even participated in training exercises. Here, every decision and plan has to pass through the National Security Council, cabinet members, and the joint chiefs. All of them are capable of changing anything as they see fit. The president just signs off and prays that it works."

"Rich," the secretary said patiently. "That's the way the system's been set up for us to run. We're not independent, we're part of the Department of Defense."

"But that means everything as far as readiness," said Welsh, flipping a page of his notes. "The nature of terrorist incidents forces us to move quickly. But with our command structure it's impossible to make a decision in a timely fashion. All the internal negotiation, review, and revision gives the advantage to the adversary. It makes our lack of strategy even more of a problem."

"Now you're joking," the secretary interrupted. "Every one of our units has its procedures down to a tee."

"That's not what I mean, Sir. I'm talking about strategy, not tactics. The units develop their tactics and procedures, but in a vacuum. Strategy is how we intend to use them, and that comes from the top. We do contingency exercises all the time, and the troops get a good workout. But the real decision makers are never there, just some low-level role players who happen to be available that day. We don't do any real planning—we're just reactive, and we always end up running out of time. Our current setup puts us in roughly the same position that we were in during the Iran rescue."

"C'mon, Rich," the secretary said paternally, "you're overreacting. Look how well we did in Panama and Iraq. We've got a handle on things now."

Welsh paused. Did the secretary really believe that? "Sir, Panama is a country where we've stationed troops for ninety years. And even then we went for the massive conventional attack, which proves the joint chiefs don't trust special ops and don't have the faintest idea how to use us. Ten of the dead and ninety-three of the wounded were from our command alone, and that's an incredibly high casualty rate. On the plus side, Delta did a really fine job getting that guy out of prison. In Iraq we had to fight like bastards to even be used. Then it was just support of conventional operations, long-range strategic reconnaissance, and short-duration raids. The bombing campaign masked our insertions, and we had total air superiority. Even then we took our losses, not to mention the usual intelligence screwups. But the men were fantastic. All our shooters are the very best. But the actual assault is the least of our problems."

"I thought that was the whole point," said the secretary.

"No, Sir," Welsh said. "It isn't. In hostage rescue missions intelligence is the most important thing. We did a lot of good things in Iraq, but we couldn't have rescued our POWs even if we'd wanted to because we couldn't find them all. We may know whenever the Russian president goes to the toilet, but if we couldn't find Noriega in a country we practically owned, then we can't get the detailed intel we need for a rescue in a country that's a much harder intelligence target."

"Again, Rich, that's out of our hands." The secretary shook his head sadly. "You just don't understand these things. If we keep running to Congress, our stock of goodwill is going to dry up." The secretary said it in a flat tone, as if he were giving testimony. Having taken the scent of the air, he was ready to bring the conversation to a close.

Welsh had known all along that the man wasn't about to bother the secretary of defense, or go anywhere near Congress, or generally fuck up his career by trying to change things he didn't even think could be changed. Welsh had written the memo for the sake of his own conscience. Which was an easy thing to keep, he had to admit, if you didn't have a family to support or a career to advance.

"Once you take away the Russians," said Welsh, "there are damn few other countries able or willing to

challenge us in a conventional military manner. The
Iraqis were just dumb; they misread us and thought they
could get away clean. And our military finally got to do
what it always wanted—refight World War II. Sophisticated, deniable, government-sponsored terrorism is going to be the war of the future. A few years ago, when I
was in the marines, the SEALs did a surprise exercise
where they penetrated the harbor at Norfolk Navy Base,
slapped mines on every ship of value, and no one ever
knew they were there. And the admirals are only paying
attention now that it actually happened to them in the
Gulf. Sir, I'm bringing all this up because I think the
Iranians are about to do something big."

"And why do you think that?" the secretary asked
with a sigh of exasperation.

Welsh forced down a sudden impulse to twist the little
bastard's head off. "I'm sure they're going to retaliate
for Kharg Island. When we let the shah into the country
for medical treatment, they took over our embassy. They
sent the truck bomb when we went into Lebanon. *Vin-
cennes* shoots down their airliner and Pan Am 103 gets
blown up. We move into their backyard and they plant a
mine on *Makin Island.* These people don't just talk an
eye for an eye, they live it."

The secretary nodded solemnly, as if granting the
point. "So you think it's going to be an equivalent economic target?"

"Not necessarily. They may think Kharg is a signal
we're taking the gloves off, and they have nothing more
to lose. I believe they'll try to hit us here."

"Nobody else agrees," said the secretary. "They think
it'll be an aircraft bombing or attacks on our interests in
Europe. That's where the terrorist networks are."

"They know we traced Pan Am to them," said Welsh.
"And we're watching the European Shiites and Palestinian splinter groups. *Makin Island* was a sophisticated
operation; it showed the Iranians aren't afraid to try

something that dangerous, even if they have to do it themselves."

The secretary made a few notes on a legal pad. "Rich, you're an intelligent guy and you do good work, but you don't go out of your way to get along with people."

"I'm sorry, Mr. Secretary," said Welsh, but there was no apology in his voice. "You'll find no shortage of people around here who'll tell you what they think you want to hear. The truth is that, after billions of dollars, we still have major deficiencies."

"That doesn't sound like a good Republican conservative talking," the secretary said, trying to make a joke.

Welsh had a mental picture from Beirut of a broken marine body in bloody underwear being pulled from rubble as marines gathered around, trying not to cry. And he remembered everyone responsible doing back flips to cover their asses. "In my experience the people who like to be called conservatives aren't much interested in conserving anything."

"Thank you, Rich," the secretary said. "That will be all."

Fifteen minutes later Carol Bondurant found Welsh sitting quietly in his cubicle, trying to cool down.

"That bad?" she asked.

"That bad," said Welsh. "I have this wonderful talent. I get diarrhea of the mouth and burn all my bridges."

"I don't think you're going to get fired, but don't be surprised if some really crummy jobs start turning up."

"That's what I figured. Why do I keep doing this to myself, Carol?"

Carol gently put her hand on Welsh's arm. "Rich, you're one of the true believers. A guy like you just doesn't understand careerists. You think if you push people hard enough, they'll do the right thing."

"But what if I am right?"

Carol patted his arm. "All it means is that everyone who was wrong ends up hating your guts."

Welsh made it back to his apartment in Arlington

before 6:00. He opened the first of what looked like many beers and flopped down on the couch. The walls were bare; the only other furnishings were an armchair, a TV, and a breakfast table. The bedroom was somewhat better appointed. It held the queensize, the stereo bought in Japan before the dollar crashed, his desk and computer, and overstacked bookcases.

Welsh picked up the remote control and turned on the news. While he still had a job, he probably should get around to buying some furniture.

CHAPTER 6

THE LATE SUMMER heat was intense in Teheran. There would be no rain until late fall, and the air was so dry that at the few remaining sites where construction had not been abandoned, the cement was stored in great uncovered heaps. The wind came down from the high desert and left a layer of fine dust on everything.

What had once been called a village of four million people was now the most expensive city in the world, for the price of war and isolation was food rationing, unemployment, and hyperinflation. After the attack on Kharg Island the Iranian government had ruthlessly crushed any outward expressions of dissent, such as the growing protests against the state of the economy. The government's reach extended into all aspects of everyday life, down to the Komites, the religious police who enforced Islamic dress codes and revolutionary attitude. But although there was widespread discontent, much of the population took fierce pride in their country's rejection of the outside world.

It was sunset, with the usual monotonously brilliant bloody-orange sky courtesy of hydrocarbon pollution. The traffic was still amazingly heavy. Most of the cars were Paykans, a boxy little Fiat clone assembled in Iran before the industry was destroyed by war. Little could be heard over the din of horns as the epically bad Iranian drivers jockeyed for position and ignored the traffic regulations, expressing either Iranian individualism or Shia fatalism, depending upon one's point of view.

Emerging from a clotted mass of traffic, a nondescript Paykan turned onto Takht-e Jamshid Avenue. It was a broad, busy street lined with ten-story buildings and fronted by sidewalks made of ceramic tiles. The vehicle drove up to the south gate of what had once been the Embassy of the United States of America. The wall surrounding the complex had been whitewashed and covered with revolutionary slogans. The sentry box at the gate was occupied by two Pasdaran, or Revolutionary Guards, dressed in tight-fitting light mustard-green fatigues. One guard approached the Paykan with the arrogant swagger of authority, leveling his Kalashnikov AKM assault rifle, the lightweight, modernized version of the famous AK-47. A distinct snap could be heard as he thumbed the safety catch one step down from safe to automatic. The driver carefully handed the guard a pass. After examining the document and the passenger, the guard stiffened to attention and signaled the camera mounted on the wall. The gate opened with a grinding of unlubricated gears, and the Paykan was waved through.

The car came to a stop a short distance from the main gate, next to a long, rectangular, three-story brick building—the former chancery. The lower windows were covered by steel bars and the upper windows were shuttered. Another Pasdaran appeared from a steel door. He saluted and helped the passenger from the car. The guard led the way to the entrance, pressed a buzzer, and held the door open after the electric lock was released. The guest wore the robes of a Shia clergyman and carried a briefcase. The guard bowed respectfully as he passed.

The clergyman acquired another armed escort inside, and he was guided along a corridor and through the steel security door that led to the second floor. The door was heavily battered from the first temporary takeover of the embassy on St. Valentine's Day, 1979, when Ambassador Sullivan frantically phoned the Barzagan government for help on one side of the door, while the radical students hammered on the other side in an equally frantic attempt to reach him.

On the second floor the clergyman was led to an inner conference room guarded by two more armed Pasdaran. He entered the room and was greeted by a small, gray-haired man who grasped his hand and kissed it.

The clergyman, Ayatollah Nashazi, had as a much younger man in the late 1950s become a follower of a group of clergy led by an ayatollah named Ruhollah Khomeini. This group became known as the radicals.

Their movement changed forever on October 26, 1964, when Ayatollah Khomeini made a thundering speech attacking an agreement exempting American military advisers in Iran from Iranian law. He also made clear his bitter hatred for the United States. Nine days afterward he was arrested and exiled to Turkey. A short time later, he moved to Iraq under the protection of its radical government. Nashazi left Iran to join him. For both, the humiliation of exile was underscored by the protection given the Americans who had introduced the hollowness and corruption of Western values and culture into Iran.

Like his mentor, Nashazi believed Iran should be isolated against Western influence and that only the dominance of the clergy would ensure this. He took a hard line in favor of confrontation with the United States, which he and the ayatollah regarded as the principal source of evil in the world.

When Ayatollah Khomeini died in 1989, Nashazi allied himself with the hard-line members of the government who shared the ayatollah's views. They were strongly challenged by those who were shocked by the cost of war and ideological purity, wanted a secular nationalist government, and insisted on the need for Western investment to rebuild and develop the country. As the economy worsened, Nashazi could feel opinion in the government shifting against him. His anger grew.

Even after years of exile, plots, and intrigue, Nashazi

looked like a jolly old man: chubby, round-faced, fond of good food and playing with his grandchildren.

The small gray-haired man, in contrast, had the ascetic look of a biblical prophet. He was forty-nine years old but looked ten years older. He was gaunt, and his face was deeply lined by the stress of being hunted most of his life. His hair was cropped close to the skull, easy to care for but not helping his appearance. Unable to shake the bourgeois Iranian's determination to be properly dressed, he was clad in a worn and indifferently tailored pin-striped suit; his only concession to revolutionary chic was a collarless shirt and no tie. He used the name Amir, which had been his nom de guerre in the Islamic underground.

In the early 1960s, Amir had moved through the country as a recruiter for the underground radical Islamic Nations Party, enlisting religious but uneducated young men from the lower classes of Iranian society. Unlike many of his peers, Amir's fanaticism was offset by a natural wariness and icy calculation. He remained operational while, one by one, his comrades fell into the hands of SAVAK, the shah's secret police, and disappeared to face interrogation and torture, rarely to be heard from again.

After a member of the party assassinated Prime Minister Hassan Ali Mansur in 1965, Amir fled to Iraq and joined the antishah underground there. In late 1968, he was sent to a Palestine Liberation Organization camp in Jordan for advanced intelligence training. The shah's friendliness toward Israel had created an alliance between the Iranian underground and the PLO, particularly since Israel's secret service, the Mossad, had helped the CIA create and train SAVAK in 1957.

The contacts made in the terrorist training camps were the most obvious reason for the Islamic Republic's speed in developing relations with North Korea, Libya, Syria, and the Sandinistas—despite oft-stated revolutionary solidarity.

Amir hurriedly took his leave of Jordan in September 1970, when King Hussein turned the angry Bedouins of his army loose on the camps. While the PLO relocated to Lebanon and nursed its wounds from Black September, Amir returned to the Shia shrine at Najaf in Iraq to join the Ayatollah Khomeini in exile. He followed the ayatollah to France in 1978, when the shah pressured the Iraqi government for his expulsion.

Amir accompanied the ayatollah on his triumphant return to Iran on the first day of February 1979 and began organizing an overseas intelligence service for the new Islamic Republic. Then Iraq invaded Kuwait. With typically Middle Eastern irony, Amir soon found himself dealing with his old enemies, the Israelis, for arms to fight against his former ally, Iraq—now both countries' common enemy.

In acknowledgment of his achievements, Amir was given the use of part of the former American embassy for his headquarters. When the decision to confront the Americans made it too late for the country to turn back, an idea began to take shape. The retaliation he envisioned would be the ultimate coup, but it was so incredibly dangerous Amir doubted he would ever be given permission to put the plan into action.

One thing gave him hope. Although the Iranian president controlled the majority of the *majlis,* the heads of the various ministries and religious power blocs had a great deal of independence. On some issues they even formed a de facto ruling council. Amir knew that the state of the economy was putting great pressure on the hard-liners in the government. He was careful to make it obvious that the success of his plan would catapult the radical clique into power and that failure could be blamed on the moderates and cause their eclipse. Sensing the desperation in the air after the attack on Kharg, he thought his plan had a chance of approval. Then, in accordance with the strict security precautions he had recommended, a courier had arrived and informed him that Ayatollah Nashazi would come to the embassy personally. The ayatollah had even agreed to forgo the comfort of his distinctive Mercedes sedan.

Amir led Nashazi to one of the padded chairs and served tea Near Eastern fashion—heavily sweetened in a glass. An assistant would normally have done this, but Amir had allowed no one else in the room. "May you never be tired," he said, passing the tea and a plate of sweet cookies.

"May you find salvation," replied the cleric. He opened his briefcase and extracted a sheaf of papers. "I presume the room has been checked for listening devices?"

Amir gave no reaction to this stab at his professional vanity. "My people went through fifteen minutes ago. Needless to say, when we first occupied these quarters, we opened the walls and floors. Everything in the room was examined."

"Did you find anything?"

"Some Russian devices, and one that I think was SAVAK."

"And what you had put there, I imagine," Nashazi said.

Amir stirred his tea and said nothing. Their positions brought them into frequent contact, but the two had never managed more than a respectful dislike for each other. Amir's work depended upon the exploitation of human behavior, with all the uncertainties and variations that entailed. The ayatollah's life had been governed by the absolutes of his Faith. They were both products of the same culture and ideology, but if it was true that each man's relationship with the world was shaped by the terms of his own experience, then the two were irreconcilable.

Amir knew Nashazi could not resist theatrics. The tension would have to build before the cleric dropped his bombshell.

True to the prediction, the ayatollah noisily slurped

half his tea before speaking. "Your proposed operation has been approved," he said. He studied Amir's face, but it was unmoved. Amir felt that self-control was not only a mark of professionalism, but the most important aspect of his trade.

"What of the necessary requirements?" Amir asked.

"You mean your conditions, do you not?" said Nashazi. "I told you that you were being too presumptuous. You should be glad you still have your position."

Amir shrugged. "To launch a mission like this and have it end successfully, extraordinary precautions must be taken. The people who undertake it must have the proper support."

"They have given you complete control over this operation," said Nashazi. "You will report to them only through me. As you requested, no one else will know of the existence of the plan. For various reasons they also wish this."

I know, Amir thought, because many in the government would do anything they could to stop it.

The cleric pointed a chubby finger at Amir. "But I warn you of the great responsibility you assume by adopting this arrogant attitude. You realize what the consequences would be if this mission failed, or worse, was exposed."

"I understand," said Amir. "I did not make these conditions out of an inflated sense of my own importance. In my heart I know I cannot succeed otherwise."

"They believed you," said Nashazi. "They also know your feelings about the competence of others in the government and military and about your own importance. But they are convinced your precautions are necessary." He paused to let the impact of his words sink in. "They do have one condition, though."

"And what is that?" asked Amir.

"The other target that was suggested will be dealt with before the main objective."

To Nashazi's satisfaction, Amir was visibly startled.

"Do you realize this is an impossible complication?" he said, leaning forward in his chair. It took him a moment to regain his composure. "The list of targets was presented for their choice, but only one was intended. If things go as planned, there will be complete and total surprise for the first attack, which almost guarantees success. But afterward American security will be on full alert and spare nothing to hunt our people down. It will be impossible for them to remain undetected, let alone mount another operation."

"You have been given your instructions," Nashazi said flatly. "Obey them, or remove yourself from the mission."

"Why must this be?" asked Amir, trying to buy time to develop a counterargument.

"The Americans are the principal enemies of the Faith, the servants of Satan, and justice will be done to them. We punished the American navy for its crimes. The same will be done to the American marines."

"We did that in Beirut," Amir pointed out.

"They will be struck down where they feel most safe," Nashazi continued, as if he had not heard. "It is written in the Twenty-second Sura that God will assist whomever takes a vengeance equal to the injury which has been done to him."

Amir gave no visible reaction. He thought for a moment. "Very well. But I must tell you the chances of the second and most important attack succeeding are not good. Some of our people may be captured alive."

"They are determined," said Nashazi. "And since you mention the chance of capture, why will you not use our Lebanese brothers?"

Amir chose his words carefully, knowing he was on sensitive ground. "Hezbollah are good boys," he said. "And very devout."

"Yes, yes," the cleric interrupted. "Unlike others, extremely devout."

"Devout, yes. And incredibly brave and dedicated."
Amir hesitated. "But . . . unsophisticated."

"What is your point?" Nashazi asked coldly.

"They would stick out like signs in America. They
would have to move through the country without attracting attention. Few have even basic English. They
are hotheads, wild and unused to discipline. This is not a
hijacking, where they could fly into an airport and do the
job quickly, but a very sophisticated mission. By using
Lebanese, we could deny our involvement, but they offer
so little chance of success that it would not be worth-
while to even mount the operation. If you simply want a
spectacular attempt, then use the Lebanese. But if you
want success, you must use our people."

"Very well," said Nashazi. "Your point is taken."

Amir pressed on. "For similar reasons, we must not
take the help of any outside forces. Not Hezbollah, or
the Palestinians, the Syrians, the North Koreans, or any
other."

"Why not?" Nashazi demanded. "Granted, this mission is sensitive. But their help has been invaluable in
the past. They have networks in America."

"It was our only mistake in the attack on the American ship," Amir said. He had not been part of that operation and was very careful of what he said. The extent of
Nashazi's involvement was still unclear to him. "We used
foreigners, and our role in the affair was discovered
when one escaped and talked."

"That was a regrettable error," Nashazi said.

"Errors sometimes happen," Amir replied. "Even in
the best-planned operations." Still trying to change
Nashazi's mind, he added, "It was a shame what came of
it."

The cleric surprised him once again. "Kharg was a
blessing in disguise," he said fiercely. "It will force us to
be independent, to cast off the weaknesses of Western
materialism. Our Afghan brothers have taught us how to
defeat a so-called great power. When we have nothing

they can take away, then our people will not be afraid to fight. They will have their Faith, which is all they need."

"I see," Amir said, deadpan.

"I still do not understand why we should not use the resources of our friends," Nashazi said, returning to the subject at hand.

"The Americans obtain their intelligence two ways," Amir explained patiently. "With machines or dollars. If we use outside help, someone will be tempted to sell our plans for a rich reward. Or the Jews, who have long ears and a great interest in our friends, will inform the Americans. Or a cable or telephone call or radio signal may be intercepted. Someone will use the wrong name, or the wrong passport, and the computers will go mad.

"Also," he added, "in the past, our friends' willingness to help was because their aims were identical to ours. This time, they or the Russians, who keep a close eye on our friends' intelligence services, may not wish to see us succeed."

"I understand," said Nashazi.

"We must use our own people," Amir insisted. "None but the commander will know the objective of the mission until they begin. All communication will be restricted to face-to-face meetings in secure areas or by special couriers. We will ensure success with tight security, secure communications, and our men leaving no traceable evidence. The Americans will of course believe we are responsible. But they will be able to prove nothing, not even to themselves. However, as I have pointed out, there is still the chance the operation could be traced back to us."

"You must prevent that," declared the cleric.

"Our people will have nothing that could give away their nationality," said Amir. "Nothing, that is, except their statement under interrogation."

"Our boys would never talk," Nashazi insisted.

"With the proper stimulation," Amir said dryly, "everyone talks. This I assure you. I will choose the best people, but you must know the risk of two attacks."

"They have made up their minds," said the ayatollah. "And I will not be the one to ask them to change. Now, have you decided who will lead the mission?"

"The man I have in mind has led many difficult operations against our enemies, always successfully. He can plan as well as fight. Also, he speaks fluent English and is familiar with America."

"Oh?" said Nashazi, suspicious of anyone who had come into close contact with the West. "Who is he?"

"He is Maj. Ali Khurbasi."

"That name is familiar."

"He led the attack on the al-Amaya oil terminal," said Amir. "Operation Karbala 3 in late '86."

"Excellent. That began many successes for us. When will he begin?"

"Not immediately," said Amir, with customary vagueness.

The answer only made Nashazi angry. "Why do you delay?"

"I have orders to conduct an operation against the emirates first, as a screen for this one."

"You mean the raid on the pumping station?" Nashazi demanded. "Why use this Khurbasi?"

"He leads our best commando unit." Amir folded his hands in his lap and gave the cleric an emotionless smile. "And I wish to be sure of how good he really is."

"We must move quickly," said Nashazi. "If we wait, we will not have sufficient resources to act. Do you understand this?"

"Yes," said Amir.

"Once again, do you accept the mission?"

"Yes," he said.

"Hundreds are dead on Kharg," said Nashazi, the spy chief fixed in his gaze. For the first time Amir had a close look at the man's eyes, set apart from the old and somewhat kindly face. They were unsettling, with a dangerous luminosity. "The Americans have the knife at our throats, but we will not die quietly. They must pay a great price for our hardship. So you will destroy the president of the United States. In his capital city. In his White House."

Nashazi prepared to leave. Amir took the cleric's hand and kissed it. "May faith be thy daily bread," he said.

"I entrust you to God. May thou be blessed," Nashazi replied formally.

CHAPTER 7

THE TWO IRANIAN Navy Osa-class missile boats moved as close to the shoreline of Umm al-Qaiwain in the United Arab Emirates as their captains dared.

The summer monsoon season was in full force, and several storm fronts skirted the eastern edge of the Persian Gulf. Driving rain and wind made nighttime visibility difficult. The missile boats, not noted for their seakeeping qualities in the best of conditions, wallowed in the chop. The captains were willing to put up with seasickness, since there would be few aircraft flying in such weather. If their plan worked, any chance radar contact would take them for the daily Iranian naval patrol to Abu Musa and Sirri islands, knocked off course by the storm.

Not wanting to risk detection by using their radios, the two boats communicated by blinker light. A Hovercraft would have been the ideal vehicle for this type of work, delivering commandos close enough to the shore to launch their rubber boats. But there were too few to risk more than one at a time, and spare parts were always scarce. If attacked, the captains had strict orders to abandon the commandos and run for the Iranian coast, since their vessels were irreplaceable. The Soviet-built boats, recently purchased from North Korea, were old and of limited capability, but there were few countries willing to provide replacements for Iran's decimated navy.

Of the seven states of the United Arab Emirates,

Umm al-Qaiwain was both the poorest and the least populous, a recent census registering a grand total of seventeen thousand souls. The population was generally confined to the Persian Gulf coast, the few towns little more than small fishing villages. In the emirates only Abu Dhabi, Dubai, and Sharja were oil producers; the other four sheikdoms survived on the largess of their neighbors.

Before siding with Saudi Arabia and the United States during the Gulf War, the emirates had loaded their oil on tankers from the island of Das and the port of el-Zannah, both in the Persian Gulf. But they had watched with great concern the effects of minings, blockades, and attacks on supertankers. There was also the problem of a resurgent and aggressive Iran dominating the entrance to the Gulf. Faced with all this, the sheiks decided to construct an oil pipeline across an overland route to the Gulf of Oman, outside the Straits of Hormuz. If the Persian Gulf was blocked in some future conflict, they did not wish to be dependent on the goodwill of Saudi Arabia or Oman. From the large oil fields of Abu Dhabi in the south, the pipeline followed the coastal highway north to Umm al-Qaiwain, then across the peninsula to the state of Fujaira. Every major consultant informed the sheiks that the project was not economically viable, but they opted to go ahead anyway. Their coffers were bulging from the high oil prices of the Gulf War.

Iran had kept a close eye on the construction, noting the location of a key pumping station and pipeline maintenance facility near a small coastal village north of the capital city, also called Umm al-Qaiwain. This was the commandos' target. During the planning in Iran, an argument had been made for the low-cost option of cutting the pipeline at some secluded place. This had been brusquely rejected as having no impact. Money for repairs meant nothing to the sheiks. But a mission that hit a well-defended target and left destruction and dead men was another thing entirely. Such an act would terrify the sheiks and make it quite clear that the Americans could never protect them.

Except for the blinker lights, the missile boats were blacked out. On each boat three Zodiac rubber boats, already inflated and stowed between the missile launchers, were passed over the side and tied to the hull.

There were fifty-four commandos in all, twenty-seven crammed aboard each missile boat. They slid one by one over the sides of the boats into the Zodiacs. The Zodiacs were slippery from the rain and salt spray, and their light weight caused them to bounce uncontrollably in the waves, springing out to the edge of the mooring lines and then cracking back into the boat. The commandos, straddling the steel decks, had to gauge the swell and launch themselves into the Zodiacs, taking care not to bounce out. The first man into each boat, with no one to help, had it worst. They secured safety lines and grabbed the next commandos as they hit.

One of the Iranians misjudged his jump, slipping off the side into the water between the Zodiac and a missile boat. There was a short but piercing scream as the Zodiac bounced and sandwiched him against the steel hull of the missile boat. After a moment of shock, the commandos resumed loading without a word. The crew of the missile boat got a brief glimpse of the victim as he floated to the surface twenty yards away. They did not turn the boat around to get him.

Soon all the commandos were aboard the Zodiacs. They sat four to a side, with the coxswain in the rear and waterproofed equipment bundles in the center. When the men were settled, each coxswain started his outboard motor, which was specially modified with a cover to dampen the engine noise and an attachment that directed the exhaust underwater. When the captains of the missile boats were sure the outboards were running properly, they gave a blinker signal to each other and then to the rubber boats. The Zodiacs cast off their lines and motored away from the retreating ships. The missile boats came about and sped farther out into the gulf.

The Zodiacs headed for the shore in single file, each signaling the one behind by using a flashlight with a blue lens. There was little interval between the boats, since the Zodiacs did not cut through the waves like rigid-hulled ships. The rubber craft rolled over each swell and plunged into the wave's trough, and it was easy to lose sight of each other. The commandos had to hold on tightly to keep from being thrown out. Soaked by the rain and the spray, they shivered though the air was not cold.

The leader of the Iranian Army commando unit, Maj. Ali Khurbasi, leaned over the bow of the first Zodiac and scanned the area with an American starlight scope wrapped in plastic bags to protect the sensitive electronics from the elements. The drift of the current made a compass bearing useless. Ali was looking for an infrared light signal set up by a reconnaissance team that had swum ashore three nights earlier. The team had been ordered to turn the light on at the arranged launch time and leave it on for six hours in case the main force was delayed.

Ali's stomach was in a knot. So many things could go wrong, and there was no support if they ran into trouble. If the reconnaissance team had been discovered, all surprise would be lost. Worse, if the men had been captured alive and forced to talk, the signal would be the lure for an ambush. But the mission was to attack and be gone before daylight, so the commandos needed an advance reconnaissance of the target and guides to the objective. The recon also reduced the risk of landing in the wrong spot. That would be a disaster. Anything could happen with over fifty men moving around in the darkness, trying to navigate with no point of reference.

The green artificial light of the starlight scope combined with the lurching of the Zodiac to nauseate Ali, but he did not take his eyes from the eyepiece. The overcast and rain reduced the amount of ambient light for the scope to magnify. Ali swore silently. Where was the light? He thought he had seen it through the larger scope in the missile boat—he would not have launched otherwise.

The Zodiac crested a wave, and Ali had to grab onto the boat to keep from falling out. When he brought the scope back to his eyes, he saw the red blob of the infrared light off to the left. He could not believe he had missed it before. Holding the scope in his right hand, he extended his left arm. The coxswain saw the signal and turned the Zodiac to the left. Each of the other boats, following the blue lights ahead, turned with it.

Three hundred meters from the beach, Ali gave another signal. In succession, the other Zodiacs moved up even with the lead boat so all could land together, on line, with all their firepower to the front in case of trouble.

The surf in the Gulf was not strong. But even so, the Zodiacs had to approach the shore at an angle, sliding across the break of the waves. If they landed directly over the break, they risked flipping end over end as the bow dropped over a wave and the stern lifted.

As the bows scraped the sand, the commandos leaped out and threw themselves to the ground, weapons ready. Ali and another commando ran toward the dunes. They were halted by the loud snap of a Kalashnikov safety coming off. "Blue!" came a challenge from ahead.

"Fire!" Ali hissed back. Recognition signals had to be easy to remember but make no sense, so the enemy could not easily guess the countersign.

"Welcome," whispered Lt. Karim Radji, the recon team leader, from behind a clump of sea grass.

Ali turned to the commando beside him. "Go bring them up," he murmured.

Straining under the weight of the Zodiac, outboard, and equipment, the commandos carried their burden up to a depression between two sand dunes. Ali ordered six of the men to take up a hasty defensive position atop the dunes on either side. The other two removed the equipment from the Zodiac and stacked it in the sand. They draped a camouflage net over the boat.

The other crews followed. Ali took Karim off to one side. The lieutenant was a tall, athletic young man of twenty-three, with the build of a soccer player. When not heavily armed and covered with camouflage paint, as he was now, Radji had a boyish face that gave him a look of deceptive innocence. Ali considered Karim the best close-in reconnaissance specialist he had ever known.

Ali took a plastic-laminated map from his pocket. "Tell me what you have," he whispered.

They took out flashlights and spread the map on the sand. Karim pulled a poncho over them so the light would not be seen. The rain pattered down on it as they talked.

"I am glad you are here," Karim said, smiling. "We were becoming tired of living in holes. I have sand in my ears."

Ali grimaced. It was unnatural to make jokes in such a situation, but Karim was always doing it. The boy was wary as a fox, but always seemed utterly casual. Ali envied it. "Any problems?" he asked.

"It was good we had more than a day to do the reconnaissance," Karim said. "We landed in the wrong spot."

"I thought that might happen. There are few landmarks on the shore to navigate by. Was it much trouble?"

"It took some time to figure out where we were," Karim admitted. "We swam ashore six kilometers down the beach. Once we sorted that out, no problems." He pointed to the map. They had to look closely to see the details in the blue light. "I brought Abdul here with me, and the other four are at an observation point near the objective. We checked the route, and found good spots for the mortars and machine guns."

"Do we need to make any changes to the plan?" Ali asked. "Is there anything new or different?"

Karim flipped through his notebook to a sketch diagram of their objective, a complex of squat concrete buildings situated on a low hill. The pump house was in the very center, surrounded by barracks, workshops, a mess and recreation building, and a generator building. The pipeline ran up the low hill directly into the pump house, continuing on its way out the other side. A road led to the village, which was a kilometer away. Another ran out the opposite side, to the coastal highway.

As an acknowledgment of the station's importance, a high chain link fence topped with barbed wire circled the compound. Besides keeping out people and animals, the fence would prematurely detonate any rocket-propelled grenades fired from outside. Inside the fence was a fifteen-meter belt of antipersonnel mines, then a barbed wire apron fence and a four-foot-high earthen bank. A permanent garrison of twenty-five soldiers guarded the complex, mostly Baluchi mercenaries hired in Pakistan. The defenses were more than enough to frighten off the odd saboteur, terrorist gang, or bandit.

Karim traced the diagram with his finger. "We checked the entire perimeter. No problems."

"Good," said Ali. "Did you see ground radar or come across any sensors?" It was his great concern. If those detection devices were present, the force would have to move slowly and with the greatest care.

"No," said Karim. "We saw nothing, and we went very close to the perimeter to check. They are quite lax. The fence and mines make them feel invulnerable."

"Anything else?"

"They allowed the brush outside the fence to grow long. So lazy. We can get very close without being discovered."

"God is generous," Ali said. "But we are wasting time. Be ready to move as soon as I brief everyone."

They clicked off their flashlights and emerged from

under the poncho. Ali was glad to see that his senior
enlisted man, M. Sgt. Musa Sa'ed, had supervised the
unwrapping and distribution of the equipment packs.
The commandos were deployed in a perimeter for security, and his two officers, the sergeant in charge of the
mortar team, and the master sergeant were next to the
boats, awaiting any new orders. Ali quickly briefed them
on the route they would take. He gave them ten minutes
to check their men.

Sitting with his back against the soft hull of a Zodiac,
Ali pulled a tube of camouflage cream from his pocket
and touched up the black camouflage on his face and
hands. He was pleased with two decisions he had already
made. Waiting for the storm had greatly increased their
chances of landing undetected. And landing before midnight gave time to move slowly enough and ensure the
surprise they needed. One man had been lost already,
but better to lose an idiot out to sea than have him
destroy the mission through some carelessness.

Ali forced himself to remain sitting. The temptation
to pace, to do something, was unbearable. But showing
anxiety would make the men nervous. The tension before the attack was the worst part. There were too many
things to think about.

Exactly ten minutes later the commandos soundlessly
came down from the dunes and lined up in single-file
march formation. Ali felt a surge of pride as he walked
down the file and checked his men. They had touched up
their camouflage paint where it had been smeared by the
rain. All their equipment was secured for silent movement. There was no whispering or confusion as they
moved into position. The group was understrength, but
better to have fifty men you could count on than a hundred you were unsure of. The six coxswains would stay
and guard the boats.

He came to little Parviz and squeezed the boy's arm.
Only seventeen, Parviz looked thirteen. He was less than
five and a half feet tall and achingly thin. Unlike the

Revolutionary Guard, the commandos did not usually accept recruits that young. But, at the depot, Parviz, trembling with nervousness and in a high voice, informed Ali that he wanted to be a commando. The other troops had collapsed with laughter, but Ali, unsmiling, told the boy he would be given a chance to prove himself. When accepted into the unit, the lonely boy far from home dogged the heels of his commander in gratitude. Since his gratitude was genuine and not obsequious, Ali tolerated it. Despite his size, Parviz could carry a heavy load without tiring, so Ali made him a radio operator. This would be his first action. "How do you feel?" Ali asked.

"Fine, Sir," the boy whispered, very nervous.

"Have no worry, you will do well," Ali said. "Just stay close to me." Parviz nodded, and Ali moved down the column.

He reached the end of the file and came upon the master sergeant's unmistakable silhouette: short but with the build of a heavyweight wrestler—the same rough shape as a block of granite. They had been friends since before the revolution, and Ali could not imagine soldiering without him. The master sergeant was highly experienced and completely imperturbable. "Make sure none of these blind men gets lost," Ali whispered.

"They will not," Musa assured him in a low voice. He added in a whisper, "Everything is going well."

Ali nudged the master sergeant with his elbow and walked up to take his place at the front of the column, behind Karim and Abdul, the guides. He gave Karim the order to move out.

The column moved quickly but deliberately, so each man could be sure of his footing and step quietly. The rain masked the sounds of their movement.

The commandos wore captured Iraqi Army camouflage battle dress. They were shod in rubber-soled canvas boots, which dried quickly when soaked. Strips of luminous tape were sewn to the backs of their billed caps; the men could stay in formation in total darkness and uneven terrain by following the glowing tapes. They carried nothing that could identify them as Iranian.

Ali believed in light loads, and the men carried a minimum of personal gear: a web belt with four pouches, each holding three thirty-round magazines for the Kalashnikov AKM assault rifles; a bag of grenades; a water bottle; and a knife. All but the two commandos carrying Soviet PKM machine guns were armed with Kalashnikovs. Every man carried a backpack with either demolition gear or ammunition for the mortars, machine guns, or rocket launcher. No man carried more than forty pounds. They had to travel over eight kilometers through rough terrain, and Ali knew all the firepower in the world would be useless if the men were too tired to fight.

From the dunes they passed through a belt of palms, then rocky ground covered with sparse trees and scrub. The available cover was scarce, so the overcast and rain were a blessing. The guides led them around the sides of hills and through draws to keep the column as concealed as possible. Each time they stopped, the master sergeant passed a head count from the rear to the front, letting Ali know everyone was still with him.

Karim halted the column at the base of a hill. "We are at the release point," he whispered to Ali.

Ali's calves ached from the rocky hills, and the insides of his thighs were chafed raw from wet trousers. This was where the various elements of the attack force would break up. "I want to take a look," he replied.

The two men crawled to the top of the hill. Ali had memorized the terrain from maps and photographs. As he saw it through the starlight scope, the plan unfolded in his mind. The hill they were on was almost broadside to the compound; he could see the lights and the pipeline. The road from the complex to the highway was about three hundred meters off to their left. The village was farther out to the right.

It was still raining steadily. "What do you want to do?" Karim whispered.

"Take the support teams and put them in position. We will wait until you come back."

The six-man mortar team collected the backpacks filled with mortar bombs from others in the column and trudged off into the darkness with Karim. The five-man machine-gun team, reduced from six by the accident at sea, picked up their two Soviet PKM general-purpose machine guns and started up the hill. They also carried an RPG-7 rocket-propelled grenade launcher to deal with any armored vehicles. It took two trips to get all the packs filled with rockets and belted machine-gun ammunition to the top. The team members positioned their weapons to cover both the complex and the nearby road. They set out Claymore antipersonnel mines to cover the road, their flanks, and rear. The lieutenant in charge took his West German walkie-talkie out of its protective plastic bag.

Karim dropped off the mortar team in a small piece of flat ground on the side of the hill. They quickly assembled the two Chinese Type 63 lightweight 60mm mortars and prepared a few rounds of ammunition in case of emergency. The sergeant commanding the team crawled to the higher ground to get a compass bearing to the strongpoint and check the distance. Upon his return he gave the crews their firing data and turned on his radio.

It took Ali and the main assault element over an hour to work their way around the compound. The reduced visibility of the rain and overcast made it difficult to navigate, but Karim had an unerring sense of direction. Twice they heard and smelled sheep and had to proceed carefully for fear of running into any herdsmen. Ali was reassured when the huge pipes loomed out of the darkness.

Staying in the shadow of the pipeline, the column of men followed it up to the complex. Fifty meters from the fence they slid into a long drainage ditch. There they linked up with the other four recon men of Karim's team.

The thirty-six commandos had to pack tightly in the small space, praying they had not been seen. They also prayed they would not have to remain long, for the ditch had a strong aroma of sewage, crude oil, and creosote. Ali stationed himself at the top and watched through the starlight scope. Parviz stood guard beside him.

While the commandos waited, the four recon men began their work. They were students of a colonel of the People's Army of Vietnam who had been flown to Iran during the war with Iraq to teach his specialty. The colonel was a member of the Su Doan Dac Cong, the Special Attack Force Command, better known during the Vietnam War as sappers.

Dressed in tight black shorts and T-shirts and covered with black camouflage cream, the Iranian sappers began the job of silently creating a path through the defenses. They worked in pairs, one on either side of the pipeline.

The sappers slithered through the brush up to the fence. After checking for alarm wires, they wrapped thin strips of cloth around the chain link before they cut it, so there would be no metallic snap when the wire parted. They bent back the wire and tied it with string.

Once through the fence they started on the mine belt. The first sapper in each pair crept forward on his stomach. In his left hand he held a long piece of grass, which he gently stroked in front of him. In his right was a blade of stiff plastic, and he used it to probe the ground before moving. Unlike a metal knife, the plastic would not cause any magnetic-influence mines to detonate. When the grass brushed against a trip wire, the sapper gingerly checked it for tension to determine if it was spring-loaded and would activate if cut. If there was no tension, he cut it and moved along. If there was tension and he could not move around the wire, he placed a luminous marker so those following could see it and slip over. When the plastic hit a mine below the sand, the sapper changed his route to move around it. The second man, directly behind, marked the path of the movement using pencil-sized sticks with a swatch of luminous tape on one side. From the perspective of the attackers, the effect was of a two-foot-wide trail bounded by green dots on both sides. Those inside the compound could see nothing.

The sappers' movements were achingly slow. They ignored the rain and the pain in knees and neck and elbows, focusing only on the two feet directly in front of them. After each stop the lead sapper would not continue until his partner laid a flat piece of wood on the ground and pressed an ear to it, listening for movement within the compound.

Ali could clearly see the two luminous paths marking the sapper teams' progress. Unable to do anything but wait for them to penetrate the defenses, he once again felt helpless. A few moments before, he had been occupied and everything was running smoothly. Now his stomach churned, his legs shook so much he had to press them into the sand, and he had to urinate so badly he thought his bladder would burst. The same sensations plagued him before every fight. Ali called it fear and hated himself for his weakness. He thanked God it was dark and no one could see him. The commandos listened carefully, knowing if the sappers were discovered they would have to attack at once.

The sappers were almost inside the perimeter. Finally there was something to do. Ali hunched lower, pulled the walkie-talkie out of his pocket, and told the mortar and machine-gun teams to be ready. They acknowledged. Ali felt the master sergeant move next to him in the darkness. "Tell them to be ready," Ali whispered. Musa disappeared into the ditch.

The sappers cut through the barbed wire apron fence and crawled up the earth berm. They heard the crunch of boots in wet sand approaching. The closest pair flattened themselves out against the mound. The two on the other side of the pipeline unslung their tiny Czech Skorpion machine pistols, giving a quick twist to make sure the sound suppressors were screwed on tightly. The sentry, bundled in a poncho with his helmet mashed over the hood, heard nothing as he strolled around the edge of the berm, grumbling in a low voice about the rain and the army. He heard nothing more after a hand clamped over his mouth and a knife was plunged into his throat and twisted. The sapper's partner caught the rifle before it fell and helped drag the body behind the berm. They listened carefully, but there was just the rain. A flashlight signal was passed to the ditch.

Ali gave the order. There was no hesitation. The commandos had spent a long week in Iran rehearsing every step of the attack on a mockup.

The sappers had strung heavy fishing line from the ditch to the two holes in the fence. Crawling in single file, each commando grasped the line with one hand and silently followed it through the scrub. A team of twelve men made its way to the hole on the left side of the pipeline. Another twelve-man team and twelve more led personally by Ali went through the hole to the right of the pipeline. They moved quickly through the fence and the paths in the mine belt, lining up in their teams behind the earth berm.

Ali kept his walkie-talkie near his mouth the whole time, so he could instantly call for supporting fire from the mortars and machine guns if the three teams were discovered. He was the first through and watched over the berm as the rest came up. Through the starlight scope he could see only a few figures moving in the compound.

Ali had no intention of conducting a conventional attack on the complex, where they would take and clear each building. Two twelve-man assault teams would sweep through the complex to the right and left of the pipeline, eliminating all opposition and causing as much damage as they could. The pipeline was a handy guide,

and the members of each team had been carefully
drilled to fire only on their side of it. Ali would lead his
twelve-man demolition team directly to the pump house.
The entire force would move through the compound as
fast as possible, then break out where the pipeline ran
through the fence on the opposite side. This would put
them on a straight line to the hill to pick up the support
teams, and then back to the boats. They would be gone
before anyone could react.

All the commandos were ready, and Ali gave a whispered order to go. They would keep silent as long as
possible.

The Iranians poured over the top of the berm. Ali's
demolition team spread out behind him as they ran
alongside the pipeline toward the pump house. The familiar feeling of exhilaration had returned; the throbbing in Ali's stomach vanished now that it was time to
act instead of worry.

Two workers came out the side door of the pump
house as the commandos approached. Both froze,
shocked by the sight of so many armed men. Ali cut
them down with two short bursts from his Kalashnikov.
At that the silence was broken, and the Iranian commandos began to scream their battle cry: *"Allahu akbar!"* God is great!

There were explosions and bright flashes on both
sides of the compound as the assault teams worked their
way through. As they raced down the sides of the buildings, the commandos fired at anything moving, stopping
only to toss white phosphorus grenades through windows and doors. The fragments of phosphorus burned at
twelve hundred degrees Celsius, setting fire to anything
they touched until either consumed or deprived of oxygen. The process also threw off thick clouds of white
smoke, which concealed the assault teams as they
moved.

Hardly a shot was fired at them. The few defenders
who had ready weapons and the urge to use them at-

tracted such a massive volume of automatic fire that the
survivors quickly lost their motivation.

Reaching the door to the pump house, Ali found it
locked. From his bag he took a fist-sized ball of plastic
explosive, already primed with a short length of time
fuze dangling free. The rest of the team spread out on
both sides to cover him. Ali pressed the charge into the
bottom of the doorjamb and pulled the friction fuze
igniter before jumping out of the way. A few seconds
later the door and part of the surrounding wall blew in.
Ali pulled the pin from a fragmentation grenade, released the spoon, counted to two, and threw it into the
opening as hard as he could to keep it from being picked
up and thrown back. The grenade exploded, and the two
commandos beside him charged through the door, firing
their AKMs on full automatic. The rest followed quickly,
with Ali bringing up the rear.

Just beyond the doorway was a short hall lined with
offices. The commandos checked each one before moving down the hallway to the pumping machinery.

All the offices were open except the last. Ali stopped,
waiting for a pair of commandos to clear the room before proceeding on. One kicked the door open, and the
other threw in a fragmentation grenade. They crouched
against the wall, waiting to charge in after the detonation.

The grenade exploded, but the flimsy prefabricated
walls did not contain the blast. Ali was leaning against
the wall when it blew down around him. The explosion
was deafening. He felt men running by him. There was a
frantic sound of automatic firing, of magazines emptied
in continuous bursts.

The wood and plaster covering him was knocked
away, and someone pulled him to his feet. He was surprised to see that it was Parviz. Ali checked himself, but
he was only bruised, as were the other two commandos.
The hallway was filled with dust and the acrid explosive
smoke from the grenade.

Ali shouted for the men to go on and begin setting the explosives. Using the wall for balance, he groped his way down the hallway. A dark shape came out of an alcove, hidden by the smoke. Ali thought it was one of his men until he saw the pistol. He grabbed for his Kalashnikov, but it had tangled in his webbing when he fell. Struggling to free the weapon, Ali could not take his eyes from the pistol. The adrenaline made him feel as if he were watching the scene through a telescope. Then a fireball erupted next to his ear. A cluster of slugs hit the man with the pistol in the chest, slamming him to the ground as if pushed by a giant hand, the man's clothing smoldering from the tracers. From the floor Ali looked back and saw Parviz, eyes wide and tongue protruding from the corner of his mouth in concentration, loading a fresh magazine into his assault rifle. The side of Ali's face felt like it was on fire. Touching it, Ali discovered that the muzzle blast from Parviz's AKM had burned off his sideburns. He gave the boy a grateful smile and discovered that his hands were shaking, and the pulse was pounding in his ears. Pushing himself back to his feet with a grunt, Ali motioned for Parviz to follow him down the hall.

The commandos were packing their twenty-pound demolition bags into the pumping machinery. Each bag of plastic explosive was connected to a ring of detonating cord so the charges could all be set off at the same time. Several commandos were sitting down, exhausted. Anger cleared Ali's head. He tried to shout at them, but fear and the smoke had dried out his mouth. It took a large swallow of water to get his voice back. "Clear our way to the other side of the building," he rasped. "Secure the door and hurry, we have to get out of here." The men dashed off.

While they were working, the lights suddenly went out —the assault teams must have hit the generator and power lines. The commandos switched on the flashlights taped to the stocks of their AKMs.

When the explosives were in place, Ali took two

precut lengths of time fuze from his bag. Each had a blasting cap already crimped to one end and a fuze igniter attached to the other. He taped the two blasting caps to the ring of detonating cord. The fuzes would burn for five minutes; if one failed, the other would do the job. He shouted for the team to move out. Parviz still stood guard beside him.

Ali pulled the fuze igniters, and they sprinted through the building. The rest of the team was waiting at the exit on the side opposite from where they had entered. Ali made a quick count to be sure he had everyone, then gave the order to go. Several white phosphorus grenades were thrown back into the compound to screen their movement. The demolition team sprinted down the pipeline, shouting, "Lightning, lightning!" in Farsi as they ran. This was the prearranged running password, so the other commandos lying in wait would know they were friendly.

The assault teams were spread out behind the earth berm on both sides of the pipeline. The sappers had opened another hole in the mine belt and fence for them to exit through. The master sergeant and Karim were waiting as the demolition team dived over the berm.

"Do we have everyone?" Ali shouted. He was still having trouble hearing.

The master sergeant nodded. "Three wounded, nothing serious. They can all walk."

"Lead them out," Ali ordered. "I will be the last."

One by one, the commandos slipped off the berm and through the hole.

Ali signaled the last group, and they charged down the path. Ali was the last man. As he went through the barbed wire apron fence, he stopped to take a last look at the burning complex, tripped, and landed hard on his face.

At that moment a stream of machine-gun fire reached out at them from one of the buildings. One of the commandos was hit. He stumbled, lurching off the path. Ali watched helplessly, then pushed his head into the sand. There was a series of muffled pops and then loud bangs as a string of Italian Valmara 69 bouncing mines burst from the ground and exploded at waist height. The runners disappeared in the explosions.

Ali, unhurt, crawled down the path. "No, no, no," he moaned desperately. The sand was covered with blood. He heard the bullwhip crack of high-velocity slugs passing over his head; the commandos regrouping outside the fence were returning the fire. So were the supporting machine guns. He thought he heard screaming. The mortar team dropped a barrage of high explosive and white phosphorus into the compound. Ali scrambled down the path on his hands and knees. He came across the body of a man and felt for wounds. The familiar lines of the human form abruptly stopped—the right leg was severed, an arm was held only by tendons. Arterial blood pumped furiously. Ali had to look closely to make out the face. It was Parviz. Ali vomited, water and bitter bile. Hands took hold of him and dragged him down the path.

They stopped out of small-arms range to attend to the wounded. Water was splashed in Ali's eyes, and he saw Musa's concerned face in front of him. "I am all right," he said.

Musa spoke from the darkness beside him. "We are ready to move, Commander."

At that moment the pump house exploded in a brilliant flash that lit up the entire area. The commandos were buffeted by the shock wave, and debris began falling all around them. All they could see of the complex was the crude oil from the pipeline burning brightly.

"How many have we lost?" Ali shouted, preparing himself for the answer.

"We carry five dead and eight wounded," the master sergeant told him.

"Did you get Parviz?" Ali demanded.

"We have attended to him and given him morphine," said Musa. "But he has no hope."

"Do we have everyone else?" Ali asked, lowering his voice, reestablishing control. "And all the bodies?"

"Yes," the master sergeant replied.

Ali got to his feet. The commandos were in march formation, waiting for him. "Let us go, then," he said.

The column didn't stop until it arrived at the release point. The mortar and machine-gun teams were waiting, and they all continued on to the boats. All the way back, Ali silently berated himself—if he had only called for the mortars earlier, it would not have happened. The coxswains had the Zodiacs ready, and they wasted no time getting out to sea. The pickup went smoothly; the missile boats had moved very close to the shoreline so as not to miss them.

Parviz was still alive as they left the emirates' territorial waters, though he never regained consciousness. Ali held the boy's hand until he died, just as it was light enough to see clearly.

Ali rose from the deck. Two sailors were watching him with horror in their eyes. Looking down to see what they were staring at, he found that he was completely covered with blood.

CHAPTER 8

"It is good to finally meet you," Amir told Maj. Ali Khurbasi. "I was told you were not wounded in the raid. I trust this is true?"

Ali nodded. They were sitting in Amir's office in the chancery, around the elegant mahogany desk of the previous occupant. There were no mementos in the room, no books other than a large and ornate Koran—none of the things that would give a clue to the personality of the occupant, except perhaps by their absence.

"You did a good job," Amir continued. "We are all very proud, and I have a small reward. Stand to attention." He pressed a buzzer, and an army colonel entered the room.

Surprised, Ali rose to his feet. The colonel read from a piece of paper. "In the name of God, the Compassionate, the Merciful. On this day Maj. Ali Khurbasi is promoted to the rank of lieutenant colonel in the Army of the Islamic Republic of Iran." He finished the usual flowery prose of a promotion document, pinned the new rank to Ali's uniform, shook his hand, and immediately left the room.

"Congratulations," said Amir.

"I have good people," Ali said warily. "They are responsible for any success." With a soldier's natural pessimism, he was convinced this was preparation for something unpleasant. It had to be. He would not have been brought to Teheran to meet with a high-level intelligence chief just for congratulations and a promotion.

"Spoken like a true commander," said Amir. "But you would be held personally responsible for failure, so it is only fair that you receive credit for success." He hesitated. "However, this is not why you have been summoned."

Now it comes, Ali thought.

"I know you deserve a rest," said Amir. "Unfortunately, there is no time. We are preparing a special mission of enormous importance to Iran, and I am authorized to offer you command. You may decline without prejudice."

Of course there will be no prejudice, thought Ali. Everyone will simply forget that I turned down this enormously important mission.

"All I will tell you before you make your decision," said Amir, "is that it will take place outside the country and is far more hazardous than your last operation."

"I have never refused a mission," said Ali.

"I know, but you would be wise to think about this. It is not a mission of martyrdom, but I tell you honestly that your chances of survival are not good."

"I accept," said Ali.

"Do not be hasty," Amir warned. "I will give you a day to consider, if you wish."

"I am a soldier," Ali said simply.

"And a good one," said Amir, embracing him warmly, though Ali barely responded. "You were chosen because I felt you had the best chance of succeeding and returning alive."

"When will I be told of the mission?" asked Ali.

"You will read the order now," said Amir. "And then I will answer any questions."

Ali had to read the authorization twice before he believed it. That he would be given such a mission was incredible. His stomach clenched; he wasn't sure if the reaction was due to the prospect of actually undertaking the task or the fear of failing.

"What do you think?" Amir asked.

Ali chose his words carefully. "I think if I can choose the men, and am allowed enough time to train . . . and if I have the proper support. . . ." He paused. "Yes, God willing, it can be done. In my experience the more improbable an operation seems, the greater the chance of success. The crucial element, of course, is surprise. Can the secret be kept?"

"Only five people will know the entire plan."

"Then the chances are good."

"I am amazed," said Amir. "I expected many more questions from you."

"In that case," Ali said "now that I have passed the point of no return, may I speak frankly?"

"I owe you that, at least," said Amir.

"I must ask why."

"Why what?"

"Why are we doing this?"

"Because we have been attacked, and we must defend ourselves," said Amir, as if talking to a child. "If not, the Americans will continue working to destroy the revolution."

"I know the Americans well," said Ali, "and I hate them more than most because of it. But you know as well as I what will happen if this is traced back to us. We have been given only a taste of the damage they can inflict—at little cost to themselves. The economy is ruined; I can see that by walking through the city. Now the oil is shut off. Dare we take this risk?"

Amir was unaccustomed to disagreement, certainly from army lieutenant colonels. "You speak like a great general," he said angrily. "Would you have us fight their ships and planes with ours, and see us dominated? To lose a ship is nothing to them. If we fight them here in our house, then even if we win our house will be destroyed. This time we will not chop at the giant's fingers while he clubs us with the other hand—we will reach in and pull out his heart. Do you want everything we have done to be for nothing?"

Ali knew he had gone much too far and had no sense of how to get back. So he sat quietly and vowed to accept whatever happened. But not wanting to provoke Amir further, he shook his head, no.

"Oh, so you don't," said Amir, with supreme contempt. "Well, even as we speak there are those who think we should make peace with the Americans; go back to being a servant in our own house. And perhaps like the servant we should thank them for shitting in our face. You disappoint me."

"I am embarrassed," Ali said. "I spoke foolishly. I hope you will not change your mind about giving me the mission. No matter what has been said, I want it very much."

"For a moment I reconsidered. But I want someone who can think, not a puppet. And I must have total commitment. You have another chance to decline the mission, if you wish."

As Amir intended, Ali was humiliated. "I assure you, I am totally committed."

"You are obviously tired," said Amir. "Unfortunately, I can give you little time to rest. You will begin making your plan at once and report to me when it is ready."

"I will accomplish the mission, God willing," said Ali.

"I know you will," said Amir.

A month later they met again in the same office, with intelligence reports and photographs spread over a long table. Amir was unusually brusque; he seemed to Ali to be in a great hurry. It worried Ali, since his great fear was of being forced to carry out someone else's inferior plan.

"I have examined your outline," Amir told him. "I find it very sound."

Ali was relieved. He had provided Amir with only the finished product. Experience had taught him not to give noncombatants a number of choices—they invariably picked the one that sounded most exciting.

"I particularly compliment you on your method of transporting the men to the United States," Amir continued. "Very creative. As a matter of fact the entire plan is quite elegant, particularly the problem of the explosives."

"You honor me," Ali replied. "The transportation of the men and equipment was the most serious problem we faced. The weight of explosives alone was prohibitive. This is why it is so difficult to launch operations against the Americans. We cannot use diplomatic cover, and if we try smuggling we risk a seizure and the loss of surprise. I did not want the force to have to link up with their arms after arrival; enough can go wrong as it is."

"And your solution was brilliantly simple," said Amir.

Ali steeled himself for what he had to say. "As a soldier, I must ask you why we have to attack the marines. It seems so insignificant, compared to killing the president, and gives away all surprise." His hands cut the air. "It is like creeping through the night to a man's house, to murder him, then breaking all the windows and still hoping to catch him asleep."

"Marines, marines," Amir groaned, throwing up his hands. "Why? Because of Lebanon. The old men are obsessed with marines. They think marines are the United States. It is not logical, but they know little of the world."

"Then it can be explained to them."

"They do not wish to have things explained," Amir said flatly. "Their only interest is that their will be carried out. However, if you wish to make the effort I will arrange an appointment."

Ali said nothing.

"I did not think so," said Amir. He shook his head. "I should never have given them a list of targets."

Hearing his own theory confirmed, Ali smiled faintly and gave a resigned shrug. "In any event, your reports on the marine base were invaluable. We can at least strike with minimal risk to our force."

"I thought you might use martyrs," Amir said approvingly.

Ali stared at his papers. "I will require four, which will allow for backups if needed."

"I will provide them," said Amir. "Do not look like that, my friend. These people are not only very useful, but you are giving them what they desire most in the world. And the advantages are obvious, which is why the method is used."

"Yes," Ali said. "And when we set it in motion, our people will be far away from the area and in hiding."

"After all," said Amir. "We do not have jet bombers or cruise missiles. All we possess are people willing to sacrifice for their country and their Faith. Our methods are more destructive, which is fitting. The weapon of the powerless, I have heard it called."

"It is the only solution," said Ali.

"Very good," said Amir. "Now to the White House. How did you come to settle on such a method?"

"I approached it like any other heavily defended objective," Ali said, quick to defend his work. "A detailed reconnaissance to discover the enemy's weaknesses. The plan is as simple as possible, aiming to achieve at least tactical surprise; the execution violent enough to shock the defenders. We strike quickly and get out, before the enemy can counterattack or bring up reinforcements. The only special requirement here is that the attacking force be kept to a minimum, to reduce the chance of being discovered."

"It sounds quite simple," said Amir.

"In combat simple things are very difficult," Ali replied. "And complicated things are impossible. God be praised we do not have to take hostages."

"The psychology would be all wrong," said Amir. "They would negotiate for a common spy, but never the president. And what great thing could we demand that they would actually deliver? No, there is more significance to simply killing the head of state, the most well-known and protected man in America. And destroying him inside his White House is the most important part of it. Nothing else we could possibly do to the Americans would have the same impact. The shock will be felt all over the world."

"You are right, of course," said Ali. He flipped through some pages in his binder. "Agents will have to make a reconnaissance of all possible landing points. Safe houses, vehicles, and supplies must be purchased."

"There is a team available," said Amir. "Their security is airtight, and they are perfectly located for the mission."

Ali nodded. "How much time will we have to train?"

"Not long. Definitely no more than four months."

"That is not long for a mission this complex or important," Ali said pointedly.

"It is a question of security," said Amir. "The more time that goes by, the more likely someone will boast or perhaps quietly gossip—in the strictest of confidence—to make himself seem more important. Then the secret would be revealed geometrically until some curious ear offered it to either the East or the West. The West more likely; Westerners are less mean with their rewards."

"That is a rather harsh judgment."

"I prefer to plan on human weakness rather than be shocked by it."

"Then we must begin selection and training immediately. May I have permission to use my commando company?"

"Unfortunately, only a few selected individuals meet our criteria," said Amir. "As I am sure you understand, each man must be able to speak English. You will be sent volunteers with combat experience, preferably commandos."

"No Pasdaran?" Ali asked, feigning innocence. In the aftermath of the revolution, plans had been made for the ideologically pure and controllable Pasdaran to absorb the pro-Western regular army. But during the war with Iraq, Ayatollah Khomeini realized he would need the army's specialists in armor, artillery, and logistics. So purged officers were recalled to duty, the army's morale and image improved, and army clergymen lost their military authority. The recall was a shrewd calculation: Not only did overall military expertise rise, but the army gave total loyalty to the regime in return for its continued existence. The Pasdaran's first mission had been to execute army troops retreating from the battlefield, giving rise to a long-standing mutual hatred.

"I think it would be too much to expect to combine army and Pasdaran," said Amir, smiling slightly as he imagined the results. "Each Pasdaran unit has its own constituency among the powerful. I want no divided loyalties, no periodic reports leaked to other parties, no battles for control. There will be enough problems without that. The army will do what it is told." And of course, Amir thought to himself, if the mission fails, the army, and therefore the moderates, will be available to receive the blame.

"I understand," Ali said.

Declining Amir's offer of a car, Ali walked back to his quarters at a Teheran army barracks. The streets seemed to be full of young men with missing limbs peddling goods and bunches of flowers, appealing to the public guilt. Ali felt very tired. This new mission was the answer to many prayers, but the desperation it implied only depressed him. So did his once-beloved Teheran. Perhaps this is the end, he thought, and I am to be the one who brings it about. He tried to force the feeling away. None of it was in his hands. *Inshallah.*

Sweating freely from the walk in the shimmering heat, Ali stopped at a small shop to buy a cold drink. There was a prominent picture of a dead son in army uniform, making Ali feel very self-conscious. "There are not many people on the streets for a Friday," he said to the proprietor, trying to make conversation. "It has been several years, but I remember it much more crowded on the Sabbath."

"Many go on picnics," the man said.

"Really?" Ali said, grateful that at least a part of life was as he remembered. "Where do they go?"

The shopkeeper looked at him accusingly. "Behesht e-Zahara."

Ali's face fell. "The cemetery?"

The man slapped Ali's change on the counter. "Everyone has someone there."

Ali took the money and left quickly. As he turned a corner a huge procession of demonstrators emerged from a side street, chanting and carrying banners. It was another Day of Rage, orchestrated to protest the attack on Kharg Island. Ali stepped back against a building. He hated large crowds.

Everyone seemed to be enjoying themselves. A homemade American flag went up in flames—real flags were too expensive to be purchased anymore. Then they burned a Star of David, a Union Jack, and the Soviet hammer and sickle. They all burned, all the flags of the enemies of Islam, the countries conspiring together against Iran, holding her down.

God help us, Ali thought.

CHAPTER 9

AFTER HIS UNSUCCESSFUL meeting with the assistant secretary of defense for special operations, Richard Welsh was given a series of make-work assignments notable only for their drudgery. During this bureaucratic exile, he spent all his spare time working quietly at his desk and signing out masses of intelligence reports.

Carol Bondurant felt so bad for Welsh that not only did she invite him out to dinner, but against her better judgment let him pick the restaurant. Welsh chose a Mexican-American establishment that he claimed was as good as you could find so far north. Carol was a good sport, aside from a small comment about the decor being so loud she needed sunglasses.

They made small talk over margaritas and nachos. Welsh could tell Carol had something on her mind, but he wasn't stupid enough to try and rush a woman into doing something.

It finally came out abruptly after the main courses arrived. Carol looked up from her guacamole salad and announced, "Rich, you've just got to stop pushing this Iran thing. The only thing you're going to accomplish is losing your job."

Welsh's fork was poised before his mouth, and a string of golden cheese trailed languorously down to the plate. "Carol, you know you shouldn't talk shop while eating, it spoils the digestion."

"You'd be lucky to digest that anyway."

"What are you talking about?" Welsh said with mock

outrage, quick to seize any opportunity to change the subject. "These are *chicken* enchiladas."

"And that makes them healthy?" Carol said in exasperation, aware Welsh was trying to sidetrack her.

"You remember all those premeds back in college," Welsh lectured. "They spent all their time in school studying like rats, never having any fun. So of course they spend the rest of their professional careers getting even with the rest of us. That's my theory behind cholesterol and oat bran."

"Thought that up all by yourself, did you?"

"Carol, I only share my philosophy with real pals." Welsh poured her another margarita from the pitcher. "Here, have some more cactus juice. Now are you sure you wouldn't like to order something that actually tastes good?"

"I really prefer French," Carol said with a sigh.

"Hey, I'm a man of the world," said Welsh, deliberately clowning to postpone the inevitable. "I spent a vacation eating my way across France. I have to admit that I prefer beer to wine, but there's just nothing like a beautifully seasoned beef filet, impeccably cooked with a wonderful sauce, and a nice tall Coke with plenty of ice."

"To chew on, right?" Carol said with a giggle.

"Mais certainement."

Carol laughed loudly enough for several nearby heads to turn. Embarrassed, she said, "Rich, let's be serious for a second."

"If you insist," Welsh said in a gallant French accent. But he knew he couldn't put off the discussion anymore. "Carol, there's just no way the Iranians aren't going to strike back at us for Kharg Island. It would be completely out of character for them."

"What about the attack on the emirates?"

"I just don't think it's big enough. And they've never come at us through a third country before, it's always been direct."

"But what can *you* do about it?"

"I'm just playing intelligence analyst," said Welsh. "Maybe I can find something someone missed. God knows I've got enough spare time."

"If you get caught at it, you're gone."

Welsh shrugged. "I'm practically out the door anyway. The thing that worries me is that the Iranians know how we traced Lebanon, Pan Am 103, and *Makin Island* back to them. I'm afraid they've learned from all those mistakes—they're very good at that—and finding clues to the next one will be even tougher."

"Then how do you think you'll be able to find anything?"

"Any big operation aimed at us is going to take quite a few people and a ton of organization. If the Iranians contract it out, which is what they've always done, someone is bound to make a mistake. . . . Shit!" A glop of cheese fell off Welsh's fork and landed in his lap. He vigorously wiped with his napkin and looked up to see Carol smiling at him.

"Rich, even if you come up with something, the secretary won't listen to you," Carol said, as gently as she could.

"That little creep. He couldn't find his asshole with a mirror and a flashlight. . . . Sorry, Carol."

She giggled again. There was obviously no way to talk him out of his obsession. "Rich, now that we're alone, there's something I have to ask you."

"Yes, yes," Welsh said eagerly. "Does it have something to do with acting out a long-repressed sexual fantasy?"

"No," said Carol, in the don't-be-silly tone most women master at an early age. "I want to know how you switch your language on and off like that."

"What do you mean?"

"You can sound like a professor whenever you want to. And then you talk with the guys in the office another way. I'm no shrinking violet, but I've never heard profanity as fluent as you guys use it. And then when you talk to me, you manage to sound almost human." She smiled sweetly.

"Thanks, Carol. No, it's just the Marine Corps. People there don't understand you unless you swear. And marines are true artists of profanity. It's a creative outlet."

"Male societies," she said scornfully. "I suppose you were in a fraternity, too?"

"Nope. In Officer Candidate School I got paid to let people abuse me—and I didn't have to live with them for three years afterward." Welsh paused for a moment. "Carol, if you weren't a good friend, I wouldn't tell you this, but the reason I'm being such a pain about this Iran thing is that I couldn't stand it if something happened that I could have prevented."

"But you've just got to use a little more tact," she pleaded.

"I'm not good at dealing with large institutions, never have been. Maybe a good analyst could tell me why I keep finding myself in them. I've always had to be really sharp, make my work invaluable, because I eventually end up making a pain in the ass of myself. But I just can't keep quiet," he set his glass down hard on the table. "Right now I could just do my work and sit around bitching. That's easy. It's hard to actually do something constructive. I'd never care about bureaucracy or simple incompetence if people's lives weren't always on the line. . . . So," he said, embarrassed that things had gotten so grim, "since you're paying, there's one thing we really should do."

"What's that?" Carol asked with a smile.

"Both have dessert."

"What the hell—why not?"

CHAPTER 10

I<small>T WAS A</small> blustery mid-February day in Merrifield, Virginia. At 11:30 in the morning, a charcoal BMW 325i convertible pulled into the parking lot of the regional post office. Anyone watching would have noticed that the driver did not handle the car with the casual assurance it would seem to demand. Rather, he drove with the cautious hesitation of someone who obviously had regular nightmares about scratches and dented bodywork. This was confirmed when the driver chose a parking space far away from any other car.

The driver was in his midthirties and of medium height, with dark brown hair and pale blue eyes. He was dressed in a well-tailored dark suit that concealed ten extra pounds, a corporate white shirt, and a dark tie. He did not wear a coat. Inside the building he went directly to a wall of post office boxes. The one he opened was a large drawer, chosen for its ability to accommodate parcels. The drawer allowed him to avoid direct contact with any postal workers who might remember his face. He removed a package and left.

Next he drove the BMW to an office building, the steel and glass variety that serves several small companies—one of hundreds of similar buildings that ring the beltway. The man entered, carrying the package, and took the elevator to the third floor. He passed through glass doors that announced the offices of the ITA Chemical Company and waved to the receptionist.

"You weren't gone long, Mr. Brady," she said.

"No, Margaret, just a few errands."

Mr. Brady walked down a hallway. At the end he was greeted by his secretary.

"I thought you went to lunch, Mr. Brady."

"I'm going to work through, Jean. You can go ahead, though. Please leave word not to bother me unless it's urgent." The secretary nodded and began packing various items into her purse. Mr. Brady went through an oak door bearing the legend "Charles M. Brady, President." He locked the door behind him.

The office was done in dark wood paneling, subdued and elegant. It was sparsely but expensively furnished. Mr. Brady turned on the lights and shut the curtains before he set the package on his desk.

Charles M. Brady liked his name. Its origins were sufficiently WASP to be good for business and society. And, depending on the company, he could be Charles, or Charlie, or Chuck. He had been born Hafiz Ghalib.

Hafiz liked to think of himself as following the path of a long line of immigrants who quickly realized that the melting pot was romantic garbage and anglicized their names so the next generation could get along. Except in his case the name change came before the emigration. If anyone remarked about a slight accent, he would describe a childhood spent in Europe as a businessman's son, and the other person would nod knowingly. Americans thought they knew everything.

Ghalib's grandfather had fled Soviet Turkestan with his son in the 1930s, after the rest of the family had been wiped out for resisting Ruslashtirma, or Russification. They slipped over the Afghan border and then into Iran. Hafiz found it ironic that the blue eyes and regular features of his ancestry, which had forced him into so many fights as a youth, should be such an advantage in later years. After graduating with honors in business administration from the Iran Center for Management Studies, the top business program in the country, he had been recruited by Amir not so much for his intelligence but for the absence of a typically prominent Persian nose. His English was superb—indeed, most of the classes at the center had been conducted in English, using Harvard Business School texts. Business opportunities were few in the immediate aftermath of revolution, and Hafiz remembered Amir saying that he would run the type of company he had only dreamed of in Iran.

After two years of intensive training, Hafiz entered the United States in 1983 as a tourist on an Algerian passport. That had promptly been discarded and replaced by the notarized birth certificate of Charles M. Brady. With that document he obtained a driver's license, social security card, passport, and a sheaf of credit cards.

Unlike most young men thinking of going into business for themselves, he had no trouble with capitalization; it was courtesy of the government of Iran. With a letter of credit drawn on the U.S. subsidiary of the National Bank of Greece, he had slowly built up a modest business supplying small institutional chemical users.

The majority of the customers were front companies representing the Islamic Republic of Iran. The business supplied scarce industrial chemicals to Iran, circumventing the embargoes set up in the aftermath of the hostage affair. The chemicals were used to make explosives, rockets, poison gas, and other modern industrial products. The shipments were routed through companies in Brussels, Hamburg, Geneva, Lisbon, Amsterdam, Athens, and on to Iran. The outwardly unsophisticated group of religious revolutionaries in Iran had developed enormous black market networks to fulfill their various commercial needs, and the ITA Chemical Company was just a small part of it. Compared to the network that supplied Iran with aircraft spare parts, electronics, and missiles directly from the stores of the aircraft carrier USS *Kitty Hawk,* ITA was a modest operation, but Hafiz was quite proud.

He had few worries about being caught. He was, after

all, a successful businessman, an American citizen according to his papers, filling legitimate export orders. He loved running the business and the trappings of a successful young professional—the BMW and ranch house bought, at Amir's insistence of course, to maintain his cover.

To keep from attracting unwarranted attention, Hafiz kept the offices of ITA Chemical small and unobtrusive and made sure the staff turned over frequently. The actual chemical products were stored and transferred from a bonded warehouse complex where ITA Chemical leased space. In charge of the warehouse operation was a hardworking and conscientious Iranian immigrant named Mehdi, also an intelligence officer and the second member of his network. The third and fourth members were Mahmoud and Ghulam, who owned a small trucking company that had a contract with ITA Chemical.

Sitting at his desk, Hafiz opened the package he had received in the mail. It was a padded mailer from a bookstore in New Jersey. Inside was a year-old copy of the journal *Foreign Affairs* and a short note on the bookstore letterhead.

"Mr. Brady," the letter began. "Enclosed is the back issue of *Foreign Affairs* you requested, with the article by Dr. Kissinger. We hope you enjoy it. If you require any other back issues of periodicals or any out-of-print books, we would be happy to provide them." The signature was illegible.

Hafiz slit the binding with a penknife and removed the article the letter indicated. From his private bathroom he took a bottle of aftershave and poured some in a glass. He dipped a paintbrush into the solution and applied the wet brush to the paper. The invisible writing between the lines of print slowly became visible. He was surprised to find it in code. Messages of this kind were usually in clear text. He had to stop and get the one-time code pad he kept hidden behind the bookcase, and some graph paper.

The message was interminably long—it ran on for the entire article—and took over an hour to decode. His secretary called on the intercom to say she was back from lunch, and he told her to hold all his calls. When he was done he sat back in his chair, stunned. He nearly forgot to burn the article and the sheet from the one-time pad. With the office door still locked and only his desk light on, he studied the message four times, hoping he was wrong—that somehow he had decoded it improperly. It was no use, nothing was the matter with it.

You knew you wouldn't be here forever, he told himself. They have an objective worth the price of your operation, and so your operation is expendable. One more mission, and back to Iran. He paused for a moment, aware that he had not been thinking of Iran as home.

To get his mind off those thoughts, Hafiz started to do what was familiar—listing the tasks he had to accomplish, deciding how he would accomplish them, and assigning them priorities and completion dates. They had been given very little time. I will have to do the most work, he thought bitterly, because I am the only one who looks American.

After tapping his pen on the desktop for a good minute, Hafiz pressed the intercom. "Jean, please get me Mehdi at the warehouse."

"Yes, sir. Oh, Mr. Brady, you have several messages."

"I'll look at them later. Oh, and after Mehdi get me Hi-Speed Trucking."

"Right away."

Both calls came through, and in the midst of innocuous business conversation Hafiz gave Mehdi and Mahmoud the code word signaling an immediate meeting. Then he took a road atlas down from the bookcase. He had never been to North Carolina. There hadn't been any reason to until now.

* * *

The woman realtor wore a yellow jacket and a Miss America smile. Hafiz noted that she lacked a southern accent but wore a wedding ring, and he guessed she was the wife of a marine. She demanded that he call her Laura and drove him in her station wagon to see the various properties.

Hafiz was not impressed with the town of Jacksonville, North Carolina. The interminable drive through rural flatland over two-lane highways hadn't left him in a receptive mood, and there seemed to be nothing in the town except automobile dealerships and at least one of every type of fast-food restaurant known to man.

They turned onto a dirt road and passed fields that obviously had been uncultivated for some time, overgrown with brown weeds. The sparkle of silver frost saved the scene from a look of complete devastation. There was a modest farmhouse at the end of the road.

"When you mentioned you were looking for a sizable piece of land, I thought of this," Laura told him as they walked from the car. The condensation from her breath hung in the cold air. "It's just a small farm, eight and a half acres. The rest was sold off over the years. The man who owned it passed along, poor soul, and his heirs just put it on the market. The farm hasn't really been worked in years," she said quickly, noting Hafiz's interest in the fields. "It's really too small to be profitable, even with the tobacco subsidy."

"Why is it on the market?" Hafiz asked idly, gazing over at the house.

"Excuse me?"

Hafiz turned to look at her. "I mean, why didn't one of the local developers snap it up before it went to market? It's a bit far from town, but the next housing development is only two miles down the road."

"I see what you mean," she said, stumbling a bit. "Well, to be honest, the water is a problem. The town services haven't got out this far. It would have to be wells, you see."

"Of course," Hafiz said, as they walked around the house. Probably an old underground fuel tank. People ran screaming from that sort of liability nowadays.

Despite that, it had possibilities. He wasn't superstitious of course, but to have the first place look so good was encouraging. It was isolated from the prying eyes of neighbors. The nearby roads weren't very busy. The house was big enough. The barn looked reasonably intact. And the area all around was wide open, for easy observation.

"Is there another way in here?" he asked. "Besides the road we came in on?"

"There's an old plow road that leads through the woods out back," Laura said. "Four-wheelers and dirt bikers used to ride on it, but we closed it off with concrete blocks. The trees are too thick to get around."

"So you would have to cut down some trees to use the road?" Hafiz asked.

"Yes, but nobody would do that."

They walked through the overgrown backyard, past a pitifully rusted swing set. Laura waited outside while Hafiz checked the barn. She explained that she was wearing good shoes. Hafiz didn't blame her; he didn't like rats either.

When he came out, Hafiz took another look around the grounds. Buying it now would save a lot of time. "Let's go back to your office and talk some business," he said to Laura as he guided her to the car.

"Yes, sir."

"Make sure you treat me right, now, Laura. I just closed another property, and I'm ready to deal."

"Yes sir, Mr. Bradford. We surely will."

The next day Hafiz visited agricultural-supply stores. At the first two the clerks totaled up the bill, accepted his money, and loaded the bags into the pickup truck. The third store was different. The gray-haired man behind the counter was the owner, and he was trying to be helpful.

"I don't want to tell you your business, young man," he told Hafiz. "But you really don't need ammonium nitrate fertilizer with this high a percentage of nitrogen for the soil around here."

"To be honest with you," said Hafiz, "I really wouldn't know. You see, my brother-in-law has some land and likes to putter around, you know, experiment." To be completely honest, Hafiz thought, I have no idea why I'm buying nearly a ton of high-nitrogen fertilizer. But I'm certainly glad I'm not buying it all from you. Now shut up and fill the order.

"Then are you sure you want this much?" the man asked.

"That's what he asked for," Hafiz said, shrugging in mock bewilderment.

The proprietor gave up and began filling out the receipt. "I'll never figure folks out," he mumbled. Hafiz responded by flashing him a dazzling smile and pulling out a large roll of bills. "What did you say your name was again?" the man asked, pencil poised over the space on the receipt.

"Beecham," Hafiz said from behind the smile. "Thomas Beecham."

After the ordeal of moving the third load of fifty-pound bags of fertilizer from the pickup to the floor of the barn, Hafiz felt he deserved a rest. All that remained was to pick up mattresses, sheets, towels, that sort of thing. A lot of people would be living in the house, but to avoid attracting attention he would have to buy small quantities from a number of stores. He considered buying food and decided to hold off. He couldn't wait to get back to Virginia.

The Hi-Speed Trucking Company was located in Tysons Corner, Virginia, just north of Merrifield. It was a small office and garage that housed two panel trucks and two flatbeds, all duly certified for handling hazardous cargo. Mahmoud and Ghulam were both the owners and sole employees. Whenever they needed another driver or a helper, they got someone from a temporary firm.

Ghulam was sitting on the floor of the garage, busy packing shipping cartons. Scattered about were reels of electrical wire, boxes of twelve-volt lantern batteries, soldering kits, and other odds and ends. Larger items included four huge industrial-sized glass mixing bowls and stacks of metal garbage cans. Standing near the wall were twelve cylinders of acetylene gas. Adding to the clutter were piles of green one-piece coveralls in various sizes. Boxes of gloves, both rubber and leather, were piled nearby. Ghulam looked at the floor, his packing list, then finally at the still-empty cartons, and sighed in resignation.

The buzzer on the rear door to the garage began ringing. Ghulam stuck a pistol in his belt and quickly walked over to look through the peephole. Ghulam was short and chunky, with a round face that exuded good humor and made him look younger than his twenty-seven years. After a quick glance he opened the door for his partner, Mahmoud, who entered pushing a hand truck piled high with boxes. Mahmoud was Ghulam's opposite: tall; lean; and older, at thirty-two.

"You should have backed the truck in here and then unloaded it," Ghulam said.

Mahmoud waved his hand dismissively. "And where would I put the truck?" he asked, gesturing toward the litter on the floor. "Stop your nagging and help me unload. You sound like an old woman."

"An old woman! You should be shut up in here packing all this junk. You took your time getting the radios."

"The operational fund is almost empty," said Mahmoud, ignoring him. "We will have to get more funds from Hafiz when he returns from North Carolina."

"Are we still leaving next week?"

"Yes, I made all the preparations, just as if we were going on vacation." Mahmoud slapped his forehead."That reminds me," he said, checking his watch. "Mehdi is expecting me to pick up the chemicals." He took a clipboard from the desk and started out the door.

"Fine, just fine," Ghulam shouted after him. "I'll do this all myself."

It was a fifteen-minute drive to the warehouse. Mahmoud parked in one of the docks assigned to ITA Chemical and went up to the offices.

The ITA office door was locked. Mahmoud rattled the doorknob, then resorted to knocking. After a few seconds it opened a crack, and Mehdi peered out. Upon recognizing Mahmoud, he gave a look of relief and opened the door.

"What were you doing?" Mahmoud asked, gesturing toward the flickering computer.

"Just scratching some files," Mehdi replied. He had a pale, bookish face that was set off by an impressive nose. His glasses looked tiny perched upon it. "No sense in leaving anything behind."

"I parked outside dock 12," Mahmoud said. "Is that all right?"

"Fine. The chemicals arrived this morning, and I prepared all the paperwork."

They walked out of the office and downstairs to the warehouse floor. It was deserted.

"I sent all the workers home," said Mehdi. "I told them there were no more orders for the day and since the inventory work had been done they could go. I was a hero."

"I am sure," Mahmoud said politely.

In the special-handling section they came upon ten fifty-five-gallon steel drums with labels warning of corrosive materials.

Mahmoud examined the stenciled identification on the drums, then checked the packet of invoice papers.

"How do you pronounce this?" he asked, pointing to the name of the chemical.

Mehdi told him.

Mahmoud shrugged. "I still haven't figured out why we need this," he said. "What is it used for?"

"Many things. Drugs, polymers, electroplating, developers." Mehdi laughed. "Even spandex fibers."

"Anything else?"

"Yes. Rocket propellant. And explosives."

Mahmoud broke into a smile. "Now I see."

"Keep it to yourself. I should not have told you."

"I will, don't worry."

"Make sure the drums remain sealed, and be very careful. The chemical is toxic if inhaled or swallowed, and it can also be absorbed through the skin. Keep it away from heat. And of course, it is a powerful corrosive."

"Wonderful," said Mahmoud. "And I only have to drive a long distance with it."

Mehdi opened the sliding door of the loading dock and let down a track into the rear of the panel truck. They loaded the drums one at a time, carefully strapping them into the back of the truck.

"Would you like some tea?" Mehdi asked, after the last drum was secured.

"No, thank you," said Mahmoud. "We still have much to do back at the garage."

"Have all your purchases been made?"

"We did the last today. And what of you?"

"I purchased the house in Fredericksburg yesterday."

"Ghulam told me. But why another farm?"

"It isn't really a farm," Mehdi explained. "It's the biggest lot in a development that used to be a farm. It's close to Washington, on Route 95, and the lot gives us some distance from the nearest neighbors. We can use the barn to hide the vehicles. After all, a lot of cars parked around a suburban house every day would attract attention."

"I didn't think of that," Mahmoud said. "What are you doing tonight?"

"I have to pack. I accumulated so many possessions here, it will be much trouble disposing of them."

"I know what you mean," said Mahmoud. "Well, I must go."

"God go with you."

"And you."

Before he pulled out, Mahmoud flipped the diamond-shaped signs mounted on all four sides of the truck to display the black and white placards that warned of a corrosive substance. Leaving the warehouse complex, his shipping papers were checked. The guard remembered him.

"Working late tonight?" the guard asked cheerfully.

"Last run of the day," Mahmoud told him.

"Hell of a thing with those Iranians," the guard stated. "You come from over there, don't you?"

"Those bastards!" Mahmoud spat. "Animals, that's all they are. I could tell you stories you wouldn't believe. We barely got out of there in time, and lucky we did."

"Must have been rough," the guard said sympathetically.

"It was terrible. But we made it over here, and if you work hard you can do all right in this country."

"Wish there was more that felt that way," said the guard.

Mahmoud waved as he pulled out. "Everything turns out for the best," he shouted.

CHAPTER 11

THE OBSERVATION WINDOWS on the bridge of the freighter MV *Treccano Volturno* were wide open, and the bridge crew was enjoying fresh ocean air for the first time in a week. The *Volturno*, owned by Treccano Company of Italy and home ported in Naples, had just cleared the port of Kuala Lumpur, Malaysia, after taking on a cargo of textiles. The harbor pilot's launch could be seen in the distance, heading back to port, and all hands were settling down into the change of routine from port to sea. The midmorning sun had burned off the haze, and the humidity was oppressive.

Gennaro Allessandro, the *Volturno*'s captain, was in good spirits this day, as if glad to be back at sea. In his rough way he joked with the sailors on the bridge, inquiring about the venereal diseases he was convinced they had acquired. The sailors joked back, friendly but not familiar. The captain was amiable but rigidly strict about duty.

The radar operator interrupted the joking. "Captain, there is a small boat approaching at high speed, bearing 240 degrees."

Captain Allessandro quickly turned serious. "Small craft approaching two-four-oh," he boomed to the lookouts. "Can you see it?"

The lookouts trained their binoculars on the heading. "I see something small on bearing two-four-oh," one shouted. "Too far away to tell what it is."

The captain consulted his chart and the radar. "Still in

Malaysian territorial waters," he murmured. "Should not be any trouble this close to shore."

The bridge crew exchanged more glances. Pirates had made their living in the Strait of Malacca and around the Indonesian and Philippine Islands for many hundreds of years. These days they were modern, organized, well armed, and well equipped. Most smaller ships traveling in the area carried weapons. Every year a few disappeared without a trace.

The captain made his decision. "We will not become upset until we know what is going on." He turned to a crewman. "All officers to their stations," he said calmly. The crewman rushed off, considerably more anxious.

The lookout shouted again. "It is a patrol boat," he shouted. "Malaysian Police." The naval contingent of the Malaysian Police served as the country's customs and coast guard.

"Is the boat genuine?" the captain shouted back.

"It has all the markings," the lookout replied. "The lights are flashing, and there are uniformed police on deck."

"Sons of whores," swore the captain. "What could they want? We cleared customs without any problems." He swept his gaze around the bridge. "If anyone on this ship is the cause of this, I will feed him to the fish," he said grimly. For all his joviality, the captain was a Sicilian and could terrify the crew when he wished to. The sailors turned to their duties with more than usual concentration.

The first officer walked onto the bridge. "Do you know what they want, Captain?"

"No, they have not contacted us yet, and I have no intention of calling them first."

The first officer shrugged. "Are there any other ships in the area?" he asked the radar operator.

"No," said the crewman.

The first officer made a gesture of bewilderment. "Then we can only wait."

The radio crackled. *"Treccano Volturno,* this is Royal Malaysian Police. Heave to and drop your ladder, we intend to board. Over." The message was in serviceable but heavily accented Italian, then repeated in excellent public school English, obviously a colonial by-product. The captain, a good Italian Socialist, did not approve of such vestiges of imperialism.

The first officer looked up from a reference book. "British-made Vosper Thornycroft small patrol boat. It checks out."

The captain took up the radio. "Malaysian Police, this is *Treccano Volturno.* What is the meaning of this? Over."

"Routine investigation. Over." the radio crackled.

"But we have already cleared customs," the captain protested into the handset. "You are putting us behind schedule."

"We say again, heave to and drop your ladder. Over."

The captain snorted into the microphone. "Very well, we are complying. Out." He spoke to the helmsman. "Speed one third."

"Speed one third."

The captain turned to the first officer. "Well, drop the ladder. We will find out what they want."

It took some time for the accommodation ladder to be mounted and swung over the starboard side. The metal stairway ended in a platform just above the water, which was draped with old tires to protect the finish of whatever it came in contact with. The police boat pulled alongside, pressing the corner of its bow firmly against the tires, engines churning to maintain contact with the platform.

The first officer stood on the deck at the top of the ladder, waiting for them. Show them what they want, Marco, the captain had said. Call me if necessary or if they want to take someone away. Hurry them along if you can.

One by one, the policemen cautiously jumped from

the bow of their craft onto the platform. There were four in police uniform, and eleven in green battle dress. The first officer noted with some alarm that all were carrying submachine guns.

They tramped up the steps, which bounced frighteningly against the side of the ship. The head policeman stopped at the top of the ladder, tossed a casual salute at the Italian ensign on the stern and another, contemptuous one, at the first officer.

"Permission to come aboard?" he asked in English, as if he did not have fourteen heavily armed men behind him to guarantee permission.

"Permission granted," said the first officer in good English. He saluted nervously. "Welcome aboard." The man didn't look Malay, the first officer thought. But he wasn't sure, there were a hundred different racial groups in the country. He could be Indian.

The policeman gave a signal, and his comrades ran past him and the first officer, spreading out through the ship.

The first officer was flustered. "But . . . but," he sputtered, "this is not necessary. I am prepared to guide you anywhere you wish."

The policeman smiled and pointed a Browning automatic pistol at the space between the first officer's eyes.

"There is no need," he said. "You see, she is ours now."

After several large duffel bags were loaded from the police boat onto the *Treccano Volturno*, the craft swung away and headed back to the coast. The police boat would be guided to some isolated inlet and returned to those who had provided it. The providers may have been moonlighting civil servants, or independent entrepreneurs, or a mixture of both. They simply delivered the boat, accepted a substantial payment, and then disappeared.

Most of the *Volturno*'s crew was locked away in quarters. The officers were held in the wardroom. Those working on the engine and other necessary equipment were under guard. The captain was left on the bridge.

Captain Allessandro did not make any noisy protestations about his ship and his authority or demand to know who his captors were and by what right they had done what they did. He had been a small boy in Sicily during World War II, living there until he went off to sea as a young man. And on that island he had learned that hard-eyed men with machine guns are always the ones in charge and do whatever they please.

The head "policeman," Lieutenant Commander Khabir of the Iranian Naval Infantry, had changed into jeans and a T-shirt, taken from one of the duffel bags. In his belt he still carried the Browning High Power.

Khabir did not introduce himself. "Captain," he said, "we are now in complete control of your ship. We intend no harm toward you or your crew unless you hinder us."

"You are holding us hostage," the captain stated.

"No, as a matter of fact, we are not," Khabir said. "We are merely going to travel with you to your next destination, which is the port of Wilmington, North Carolina, in the United States, is it not?" The captain, surprised, nodded yes.

"Then," said Khabir, "once we reach U.S. waters we will have you divert slightly from your course. It will be no trouble. After that we will slip away one night and leave you in peace. In the meantime my people will supervise your crew and yourself. They will handle the ship's radar and communications and serve as lookouts. Simply do as we command and you will not be harmed. However, any attempt to warn or signal other ships, any failure to follow our orders to the letter, or any attempt to interfere with us will result in one of your crew being shot for each offense. Do you understand this?" The captain nodded sullenly.

"Very good. I warn you that my men are all experienced with ships, so do not attempt any stupid tricks with us. We are serious people."

"No one will interfere with you," the captain said.

"Excellent." Khabir led the captain over to the chart board, where he had tacked down a map with a course already marked. "Then your first task is to bring us to this point."

"Then what?" asked the captain.

"Then I will tell you."

They reached the position in the early afternoon. The captain was instructed to drop anchor, let down the ladder, and prepare a crane to handle cargo. The captain, unused to being anything other than the master of his ship, chain-smoked and relentlessly paced the bridge. The Iranian sailor manning the radar reported one contact at forty kilometers.

The radio broke squelch. A voice called out in English: "Alcazar, this is Blackpool. Come in please. Over."

Khabir took up the handset. "Blackpool, this is Alcazar. We read you loud and clear. Over."

"Roger, Alcazar. May we pass you the videos you wanted?"

"Sorry, no," Khabir answered. "We simply can't fit it into our schedule."

"Very well, hope we see you in Sydney. Blackpool out."

"Alcazar out." The authentications completed, Khabir leaned out the hatch and called to the lookouts on the observation deck in Farsi. "Do you have them in sight?" The Italians gave no indication of recognizing the language.

"I think so," came the answer.

"I want to know when you are sure," Khabir snapped. "And I want to know quickly."

The second lookout saved his friend. "Sir, I have her in sight, bearing 180 degrees, fifteen kilometers."

"That is the way to do it," Khabir said approvingly.

Half an hour later the freighter *Arada* moved to within five hundred meters of the *Volturno* and dropped anchor. The *Arada* had been running cargo between Iran and the Far East for the past six years. The ship had a somewhat seedy reputation and nameless owners who retained their anonymity behind a firm of lawyers and a postal box in Panama. The owners did not care to inquire closely about the type of cargo they carried—only the price. For this reason it would not be going any closer to the United States.

The *Arada* dropped a launch, which motored over and discharged its passengers onto the *Volturno*'s stairs. Khabir was waiting at the gangway to greet the first man up, whom he embraced.

"You are still a magician," said Lt. Col. Ali Khurbasi. "Now let me go and allow my men up the stairs."

Khabir laughed and released him. "It was perfect," he exclaimed. "No problems whatsoever. In fact, it went so smoothly that I worried even more, as if something bad was destined to happen."

"Your reputation is intact," said Ali. "Any problems with the Italians?"

Khabir snorted. "They have more than lived up to their reputation as formidable warriors. So they must indeed be fantastic lovers."

Ali clapped him on the shoulder. "Are you ready for us?"

"Of course, just follow my men. You must be tired."

While the radars of both ships kept watch for any other vessels or aircraft, the launch brought over two boatloads of men, thirty-one in all. Their equipment was winched directly aboard the *Volturno*. When the launch returned, the *Arada* weighed anchor and left the area, its blinker light invoking the blessings of God upon them and their task.

Khabir brought Ali to the bridge as the first stop on a tour of the ship.

"I have brought more friends aboard," Khabir told Captain Allessandro jovially. "Do not worry, they will be no trouble."

The captain just stared at them. "Where will you take my ship now?" he asked.

"Your planned course to your planned destination," said Khabir. "America."

CHAPTER 12

THE *TRECCANO VOLTURNO* sailed into a tropical storm the day after the commandos came on board. Ali waited until the seas were calm to begin his briefings. By then all his men were over their seasickness and able to eat something other than dry crackers and water.

Even after the five months of intense training in the Iranian desert, the endless live-fire rehearsals on a mock-up building, none of the men had any idea of the mission objective. There had been the usual incessant gossip and rumors soldiers love to indulge in. The fact that they all spoke English and had been fitted with American wardrobes made the guesses very accurate, but the secret had been kept.

Ali called a meeting in the sweltering heat of the cargo hold. As he walked forward to address the men, Ali could feel the familiar queasiness in his stomach. For security the moment had been postponed until they were aboard ship, but this only increased his anxiety. What would their reaction be? Though he'd told them how dangerous the mission was, perhaps they thought he was only trying to frighten them. Would they react in anger when they realized how slim the chances really were? The previous night he had lain awake in his bunk, pondering what to do if any refused to go. There was no way you could force men on a mission like this—everyone had to be completely willing if they were to pull it off. Ali prayed that all the emphasis he had put on discipline and teamwork would pay off, and none would even think of letting the others down. But not one to take unnecessary chances, he arranged with Lieutenant Commander Khabir to have some of his men lounging outside the cargo hold—armed, of course.

There were twenty-seven men sitting before him, twenty-seven chosen out of the seventy candidates Amir had provided. Among them were newly promoted Captain Karim Radji and Sergeant Major Musa Sa'ed. The rest were strangers. At the end of training in Iran, Ali had sponsored a celebration, at Musa's suggestion. The sergeant major had been curious when Ali failed to show much enthusiasm. "Why not get to know the men, now the selection is over?" he asked.

"I do not want to know them," Ali said.

"Why not?"

"Because I am tired of getting to know people and watching them die. I have buried too many friends. To me they are a group of good men, strangers, and I wish it to remain that way. Especially for this mission." The sergeant major had only nodded. It was something a soldier could understand.

It was so quiet in the empty hold that the sound of the commandos' breathing echoed off the walls. Ali stood before them and began: "We will land on the East Coast of the United States and be met by a team of our intelligence agents. There we will prepare a truck bomb to attack the nearby U.S. Marine base. After the completion of that phase of the mission, we will assault the White House in Washington and kill the president of the United States."

There was complete silence, broken only by sharp gasps of inhaled breath. The silence continued, and Ali did not move. Then the sergeant major rose from his chair and began to clap his hands. In the span of five seconds, every man was on his feet, applauding wildly and shrieking war cries. Outside the hold Khabir broke into an enormous smile and invited his men down to the galley for a cold drink. The screaming and applause went on for five minutes, as the commandos danced about the cargo deck. Ali heard one of the men shout "God be praised I did not miss this!" His face strained with suppressed emotion, Ali looked over to the sergeant major and could only nod gratefully.

The freighter was not capable of great speed, so the voyage progressed slowly. Ali worried that the commandos would slide into inactivity during the voyage. They held prayers as a unit in the cargo hold, with a compass to point the way to Mecca. They exercised on deck at sunrise and sunset, except when other ships and planes were nearby. During the day the various teams went over their tasks in small groups, studying the maps and photographs Ali had brought aboard. The entire force assembled periodically to go over the details of the mission.

In addition to the commandos, there were four other Iranians who Ali ordered included in all activities. He made it clear that any who did not treat them properly would answer to him.

It had not taken the commandos long to discover that the four had volunteered to be martyrs. Out of earshot, they soon became known as the *Baseej,* after the organization known as *Baseej e-Mustazafin,* or Mobilization of the Deprived. Early in the war with Iraq, the *Baseej* had been formed by mullahs as unarmed volunteers, under age twenty-one and fervently religious, who performed fetch-and-carry tasks behind the front lines for the Pasdaran. Later the *Baseej* picked up weapons and participated in battles, led by their mullahs. Operation Ramadan al-Mubarak in 1982 was the first time they were openly used to clear minefields with their bodies in front of the Pasdaran assault units.

In 1982, on the occasion of the Iranian New Year, the Ayatollah Khomeini announced that, "as a special favor," schoolboys between the ages of twelve and eighteen would be allowed to join the *Baseej* and fight on the battlefields. Their admission papers to the organization were known as Passports to Paradise, and some units were issued cheap plastic keys. These, they were told by the mullahs, would unlock the gates of Heaven unto them.

Among the regular army, with whom they did not normally fight, any suicide volunteer was called a *Baseeji.*

Twice a week Ali inspected the condition of the weapons and equipment and the storage of the ammunition. Every day the sergeant major checked that the men had shaved and bathed, and once a week supervised clothes washing and haircuts. He permitted no facial hair. "By God, do you not want to look to the Americans like harmless clean-cut young gentlemen?" he asked them, to loud laughter. When he was not supervising the commandos, Musa occupied himself with the pile of books he had brought along in his duffel. Karim liked to tease him, saying that intellectual sergeants major gave the army a bad name. Musa ignored him.

During the transit of the Panama Canal, the Italian seamen were locked below deck under heavy guard, their places taken by Khabir's men. The commandos also remained out of sight until the ship was well into the Caribbean. The *Volturno* steered a course through the Windward Passage between Cuba and Haiti, and the men could soon tell they were heading north from the early March chill and rougher seas.

Once they were out into the Atlantic, Ali had the Zodiac boats uncrated and taken on practice runs around the ship. He was relieved to see that the commandos were still sharp, though the men Khabir had provided as boat coxswains were not as skilled as he would have liked. But with only five days before they reached the coast of North Carolina, he decided against any more drills.

Each day now the commandos were grilled unceasingly on the mission plans. Ali insisted that everything be committed to memory. In the privacy of the captain's stateroom, Karim had sifted through the briefing books with an expression of despair. "I believe we have a contingency for everything."

Ali's nerves were taut, and he did not appreciate the humor. "I have a superstition about planning," he said. "If you plan for everything that can possibly go wrong, then in my experience nothing does. But if you neglect anything or are not thorough in your preparation, then for sure something will go wrong."

"I was only making a joke," Karim said quickly.

"I know," Ali said. "But there is a proper time for everything. I am trying to teach you. Remember the saying: Trust in God—but make sure you tie your camel, too."

On the day of the landing, after sunset prayers, Ali assembled the entire force on the cargo deck for a final inspection. The commandos were wearing casual civilian clothing: jeans, sport or polo shirts, sweaters, and light jackets. All of it was American, down to the underwear and socks. Laid out on the deck before each man was his equipment. All but eight commandos would be armed with AKM assault rifles. Extra magazines and grenades were carried in a Chinese webbing harness worn on the chest. These would remain under the jackets.

Musa, Karim, and two other commandos were armed with Israeli Uzi submachine guns whose barrels had been tapped to accept screw-on sound suppressors. Although Uzis were standard Iranian Army issue, dating back to the shah's regime, those weapons were traceable. So the commandos used Uzis that had been supplied by Israel to the old Somoza dictatorship in Nicaragua and sent to Iran in the early 1980s by the Sandinistas.

Four commandos carried the Italian Franchi SPAS-12, a unique twelve-gauge shotgun with both semiautomatic action and a backup pump for emergencies. Ali had decided that opening locked doors with explosives was too slow, and after some experimentation settled on the shotguns. Amir's agents purchased them on the international black market so the serial numbers would be untraceable. In addition to the usual double-aught buckshot and solid slug, the men carried special MPS armor-piercing rounds, also made by Franchi. These would penetrate eight millimeters of steel or four layers of bulletproof glass.

The unit leaders were armed with the Soviet P6 automatic pistol, the standard 9mm Makarov service weapon with a built-in sound suppressor. These were obtained from Syria and the PLO.

Each had a U.S. Resident Alien Identification Card, called a green card, although it is actually taupe. The cards listed countries of origin other than Iran. These documents would account for accented English and were far easier for Amir to provide than twenty-nine untraceable passports. The men had driver's licenses from a number of states, social security cards, and ten thousand dollars cash as emergency escape money. Ali made sure they had memorized the fake names and addresses on the documents.

Each man carried extra clothing in a small shoulder bag. Demolition gear was broken down into small individual loads to be carried in the bags.

All the other equipment—the PKM machine guns, RPG-7s, mortars, grenades, extra magazines, and the various types of ammunition—was packed in waterproof fiberglass containers to be carried in the rubber boats.

As he walked through on his inspection, Ali asked each man questions. He knew they had all the information memorized, but he wanted to show that he was calm and confident—and to communicate that they should be too.

When the inspection was completed and the gear packed away, Ali motioned for them all to gather around him.

"As you all know, in the Battle of Badr, the Prophet and only 319 of the faithful defeated a thousand Meccans. It is written that, 'One was fighting for God; the other was a host of unbelievers. God revealed His will to the angels, saying: I shall be with you. Give courage to the believers. I shall cast terror into the hearts of the infidels. Strike off their heads, strike off the very tips of their fingers!' " Ali's favorite verses from the Koran, learned in childhood, came rushing back. The Eighth Sura, The Spoils. The commandos were nodding their heads in remembrance.

"We few have been chosen to wield the sword of the righteous against the greatest evil in the world, and we dare not fail. 'Believers, do not betray God and the Apostle, nor knowingly violate your trust. Prophet!' " Ali shouted, the sound of his voice echoing through the steel deck. " 'Rouse the faithful to arms. God has now lightened your burden, for He knows that you are weak. If there are a hundred steadfast men among you, they shall vanquish two hundred; and if there are a thousand, they shall, by God's will, defeat two thousand. God is with those that are steadfast.' Remember! He is with us! We are the Warriors of God, and together we will shake the world! *Allah ma'ana!* God is with us!"

"Allah ma'ana!" the commandos screamed back, their faces rapturous. *"Allahu akbar!* . . . *Allahu akbar!* . . . *Allahu akbar!"*

If the wind from the ocean hadn't been so strong, Hafiz Ghalib would have been almost comfortable wrapped in warm clothing and seated on top of the line of sand dunes that stretched down the beach at Topsail Island, North Carolina.

He was not pleased with the landing site—only one road in and out and not many more escape routes beyond that. But the whole rotten coastline was the same. And this stretch of beach was deserted at night this time of year. At least it was close enough to Camp Lejeune that the rubber boats would be passed off as U.S. Marine craft if they were noticed. And it was between the ports of Wilmington and Morehead City, so the ship would blend in with the ocean traffic.

Hafiz took a starlight scope from his carrying bag. It was the current model used by the American military, the AN/PVS-4, purchased by mail order. He couldn't see the ship yet, but it was time. He set up and activated an infrared-filtered strobe light, looking at it through the scope to be sure it was working. There was nothing to do now but wait.

The four black Zodiac inflatable boats were tied to the platform stretching down from the freighter. The boats bounced in the heavy waves, even though the ship had turned against the wind to give them some shelter for the launch.

On the deck above, the commandos were preparing to file down the ladder. They waddled uncomfortably in the loose rubber jumpsuits they wore over their civilian clothes. Their shoulder bags were sheathed in plastic. Khabir stood at the top of the ladder, waiting to see Ali off. They both smiled in the darkness as the sergeant major told the commandos in his deep voice, "As you well know, something is bound not to go according to plan, so be flexible."

A messenger from the bridge ran up to Khabir. "We've spotted the signal," he said, out of breath.

"Very good," said Khabir. "Tell them just enough power to hold the ship steady." The messenger ran off.

Ali looked at his watch; it was 12:50 in the morning. "Begin loading," he called over his shoulder. "I will be last." The commandos filed by.

Ali and Khabir looked at each other for a moment, and then Khabir embraced Ali. "God go with you," Khabir said emotionally, "and grant you success."

Ali returned the embrace. "And may He see you safely home. Thank you for everything." He turned and walked down the stairs to the boats.

The Atlantic was much rougher than the Caspian,

where the coxswains had been trained, and they were having trouble. From the bow of the lead Zodiac, Ali angrily passed orders to signal the other boats to move closer. The outboards were having trouble beating the strong current—the boats had to move almost parallel to the shoreline to stay even with the marker light.

Every time they crossed the peak of a wave, a spray of water would pour over them. Ali cinched the hood of his rubber jumpsuit tighter as icy seawater began to trickle in. His face was already raw from the wind-whipped salt spray. The wind was roaring in his ears, but he could clearly hear someone puking over the side. He had no intention of looking back to see who it was. Instead he concentrated on the view of the marker light through his starlight scope.

A hand tugged on Ali's rubber suit, and he turned around to look. The third Zodiac in line was signaling that its engine was dead, probably flooded by a wave. The fourth boat, which should have moved up to tow it, had already passed by, oblivious to the signaling. Ali pounded on the inflated rubber skin of the Zodiac in frustration. Now all three boats would have to circle about to get the disabled one, and that meant moving back across the path of the waves as they turned. The maneuver was very dangerous in such small craft.

He gave his coxswain the signal to turn and added a shouted threat to be careful. In the middle of the turn, the Zodiac hit a wave and began to flip over. The commandos saved themselves by instinctively throwing all their weight to the side that was rising out of the water. Ali's prayers were answered when the other boats made their turns successfully. As the lead boat cut across the path of the disabled Zodiac, they threw out a line and took it under tow. The other two followed close behind.

Fifteen minutes later they all managed to cross the surf line safely. The two boats that were able to maneuver swung even with the lead boat so they could all land on line.

When the bows hit the sand, the commandos exploded from the boats. All the anxiety of landing in an enemy country was gone in the relief of finally reaching dry land. They cut loose the straps holding the torpedo-shaped containers of arms and ammunition and lifted them free. A few paused to offer the coxswains obscene gestures before collapsing onto the sand. The boats pulled away and headed back to the ship.

A solitary figure trudged down from the dunes and moved carefully toward the men on the beach, obviously aware that many weapons were trained on him.

"Red," Hafiz called softly in Farsi.

"Thunder," Ali replied. "Is the beach clear?"

"All clear, and welcome," said Hafiz. He walked forward to embrace Ali but was held off by an outstretched hand.

"I want to get out of here immediately," Ali said. "Where are your vehicles?"

Hafiz was flustered. He had been expecting words of gratitude and congratulation. "One truck is on the other side of these dunes," he stuttered. "Three others are a distance away; I will have to call them by radio."

"Very well," Ali said curtly, striding toward the dunes and waving for the commandos to fall in behind him.

Now sweating in their rubber suits, the commandos carried the containers over and down the dunes toward the truck. It was a full-sized Ford four-wheel-drive pickup, with a plastic shell covering the bed. On a CB radio Hafiz told the other three trucks to come up.

Ali quickly took stock of the situation. "Put the containers in the back of the truck until the vehicles come," he ordered the commandos, who had been standing immobile with their loads, waiting for guidance. "Where is the sergeant major?" Ali called out.

"Here," came a voice in the darkness.

"Get these people out of the road and into the dunes. Get the suits off and and some security out. And make sure we have everyone." There were muffled orders and the commandos trudged back up the dunes.

Hafiz was walking over to tell Ali the other pickups were coming when a loud "Yai!" rang out from the dunes.

Ali dived behind a mound of sand when he saw the blue lights of a police car come into view. Hafiz stood frozen next to the truck, his mouth open in disbelief.

Ali sprang to his feet, grabbed Hafiz and pulled him down. They were caught in the headlights. Unslinging his Kalashnikov, Ali leaned across the mound and fired a burst into the police car. His first magazine was loaded with all green tracers, and they made it easy to guide the path of the bullets into the car. Once he opened fire, the rest of the commandos joined in, and the top of the dunes lit up with the muzzle flashes. The lines of green light from the tracers gave the illusion of stretching out and slowly floating toward the police car.

Driving up from Surf City, the Onslow County sheriff's deputy had decided that the Topsail convenience store was the best place to pick up a pack of Marlboros. When he saw the pickup, he decided to pull over. Fishermen and kids were always parking on the narrow shoulder, even though there were no-parking signs everywhere and a parking area a quarter mile down the road. He was just picking up the radio handset to call in the license when the first rounds came through the dashboard. The handset was blown to splinters, along with three of the fingers on his right hand. The deputy reflexively stepped on the brake. He stared unbelievingly at his hand. Then the windshield exploded, and he threw himself out the door. The cruiser seemed to be coming apart.

The deputy was left-handed, he was angry, and he wasn't feeling any pain yet. With the glare of the headlights in their eyes, the Iranians didn't see him come out the door. He jerked his Smith & Wesson automatic from its holster, thumbed off the safety, laid it across the win-

dow frame, and fired three quick rounds in the direction
of the pickup—the only clear target he could see. He
didn't fire any more, because the commandos saw the
muzzle flash and concentrated their fire on it. Forty
large, high-velocity slugs punched effortlessly through
the door and killed him.

Two of the deputy's pistol rounds sailed over the truck
and down the road. One went through the open rear
hatch, blew a hole in one of the fiberglass containers,
and struck the detonator of a 60mm mortar bomb.

The mortar bomb exploded, and what resulted is
known as a sympathetic detonation. The bomb exploded
the other grenades, rockets, bombs, and ammunition in
the container; which detonated the other two containers; which detonated the gas tank of the pickup truck.

Ali was just lifting his head to check on the police car
when the first muffled explosion made him pull it down.
Half a second later the pickup exploded in an enormous
deafening blast. Rockets trailed through the air; bombs
and ammunition detonated in the fireball.

Fortunately for Ali and Hafiz, the sand mound they
took cover behind was between them and the truck. The
initial explosion buried them in sand, saving them from
the fireball. Behind the dunes, the commandos were
shielded from the blast. They burrowed in the sand to
protect themselves from the shower of red-hot metal
that was falling all around.

Running out of air, Ali pushed himself out from under
the sand. Feeling Hafiz next to him, he grabbed the spy
by the collar and yanked him out. Heavily stunned, Hafiz
had just brushed the sand from his eyes when the engine
block of the truck fell back to earth and landed with a
thump ten feet away. After instinctively recoiling, it took
Hafiz a moment to recognize what the object was.

Ali got to his feet, felt unsteady, and promptly sat
back down. Musa and Karim charged down the dunes,
expecting to find him dead.

"Are you wounded, Colonel?" Karim shouted. Musa began checking Ali's body for injuries and broken bones.

"I am all right," Ali said shakily.

"He has no wounds," Musa confirmed, his voice showing his disbelief. "Praise be to God," he added quietly.

"What will we do now?" Karim shouted.

By force of will, Ali rose from the sand. He was about to speak when Musa shouted, "Headlights! Get down!" They threw themselves to the ground; Ali remained standing.

Hafiz looked up. "No, no," he shouted. "Don't shoot, those are the other trucks!"

"Hold your fire!" Musa screamed up at the dunes.

"Understood," a voice shouted down.

Karim ran out into the road to flag down the trucks. Seeing the destruction, they had stopped a hundred meters away. When they noticed Karim waving, they slowly drove toward him, dodging the chunks of metal that littered the road.

"God is great!" Ali exclaimed, as the trucks pulled up. He walked over to where the first truck had been. In the glare of the other trucks' headlights, he saw that the engine block and two tires were all that remained. The ground was littered with pieces of weapons, cartridges, and unexploded grenades. He felt nauseated and sat back down. After taking a moment to collect himself, he called Musa, Karim, and Hafiz over to where he sat.

"We have to get out of here—quickly," Ali said. He motioned toward the shot-up cruiser. "Check that car." Musa shouted the order, and two commandos trotted over cautiously. One glance at the shattered body in the road told them there was no need to finish the job. The tracers had ignited the upholstery, and the interior of the car was starting to smolder.

"Now listen carefully," Ali continued. "Have all the men run down to the beach, away from where we landed. Leave two Kalashnikovs near the water. Then have them walk through the water to where we came ashore, and come up the same path we took to the dunes." For a moment they did not move, staring at him with perplexed expressions.

"Just do it!" Ali shouted. "And get the men into the trucks. Make sure they bring their rubber suits. Go, go!" Musa and Karim ran off. Ali pointed to Hafiz. "Be sure the trucks are ready." The spy nodded and staggered off.

Ali lay down in the sand and vomited. Then he sat up and tried to shake off the effects of being blown up. Why did it have to happen again? The commandos came running back from the water. After they had loaded themselves in the trucks, Musa and Karim helped Ali up and into a pickup. "We are in your hands now," Ali said to Mehdi, who was driving. The spy nodded grimly, swung the truck past the shot-up cruiser, and stepped on the gas. The other two trucks followed close behind.

As the three vehicles moved north on Route 6, two police cruisers sped by with lights flashing and sirens screaming, heading south toward Topsail Island.

PART THREE

A thing is not necessarily true because a man dies for it.

OSCAR WILDE

CHAPTER 13

THE ROAD AT Topsail Island was carpeted with rifle and machine gun cartridges. As Richard Welsh made his way across the sand shoulder, they crunched underfoot; there was no way to avoid all the debris. His identification had gotten him past the North Carolina Highway Patrol roadblock, but the crush of law enforcement vehicles made it impossible to continue. He parked his car a quarter mile down the road and walked the rest of the way.

Since there was only the single road on the island, one lane had to be left open for the inhabitants. The rest was blocked off with yellow crime-scene tape barriers.

As he walked past the shattered sheriff's cruiser, Welsh whistled softly at the number of bullet holes. The remnants of the explosion were even more impressive. Only the engine block sitting forlornly off to one side gave the clue that the blackened spot on the sand had been a vehicle. It reminded him of the aftereffects of a demolition class at Quantico. Marveling at the devastation, Welsh followed a line of policemen over the top of the dunes. Watching them struggle in the sand, he was glad he'd decided to wear jeans, sneakers, and a parka to keep out the wind.

The amount of metal on the beach was amazing. FBI specialists were marking the locations of the biggest pieces on maps and placing them in plastic bags. Others had taped off lines of footprints and were making plaster casts. There were explosive-ordnance disposal flags all around, marking unexploded grenades and mortar bombs. Welsh bent down and picked up a rifle cartridge at his feet. It provoked a look of disapproval from one of the technicians, but Welsh ignored him—there were thousands scattered about. He recognized the stubby cartridge as the Soviet 7.62×39mm.

Standing conspicuously apart from the uniformed police and the FBI agents in their prominently marked windbreakers was a short, stocky man with dark red hair, dressed in a well-tailored dark blue suit with a red tie. The man had a definite air of authority and a face that seemed to expect the worst of everyone. He appeared annoyed at the toll the beach was taking on his wardrobe.

Welsh walked quietly up behind him. When he was close enough, he said in a loud voice, "Hey, don't you know beach sand'll knock the shine right off those Italian loafers?"

The man was obviously unused to insubordination. He whirled about quickly, an angry look on his face. It changed to a grimace when he saw Welsh.

"I heard you were coming down," said Special Agent James MacNeil. He didn't bother to disguise the lack of enthusiasm in his voice.

Welsh sighed. He'd been afraid it would be like this. MacNeil was an FBI counterterrorism specialist based in Washington. Nearly every branch of the government had some sort of anti-terrorist role, but the FBI had the biggest domestic slice of the pie. Welsh dealt with them in the course of normal business, making sure liaison was smooth between the FBI and Special Operations Command. Obviously MacNeil believed he had come down to butt in and was worried about versions of events other than the bureau's getting back to Washington. Welsh thought he ought to clear the air.

"My boss ordered me down to see what happened," he said, trying out a disarming smile. "I'm just here to get briefed." There was no response, so Welsh decided to abandon subtlety. "I didn't come to drop dimes on anyone."

MacNeil's face took on an expression of either mild amusement or relief, though he did not seem entirely convinced. "You're here pretty quick," he said. "How did you get down?"

"My car," said Welsh. "That'll give you an idea of my priority. Two minutes after I got in the office, they told me to get my ass down here. Couldn't get a commercial flight, so I drove like a bat."

MacNeil allowed himself a faint smile. "We took a helicopter, almost beat the Charlotte office." There was a pause. "Anybody with you?" he asked pointedly.

Welsh shook his head, as if he couldn't quite believe it himself. "I know you'd like me to get the hell out of here, but I just need a quick briefing and I'll stay out of everyone's way." It wasn't quite true, but he didn't need MacNeil on his ass.

"I'll give you the grand tour," said MacNeil. "I appreciate the sentiment, but your boss sits on the Crisis Committee with my director. And that makes you the five-hundred-pound gorilla—you get to do whatever you want."

"Thanks," said Welsh, genuinely surprised. Amazed to find himself with some clout, he decided not to tell MacNeil he was only there because the secretary was pissed at him.

"Sorry I didn't seem happy to see you," MacNeil said as they walked down the beach. "But everyone's coming out of the woodwork on this, and I've been dealing with them all morning. North Carolina Bureau of Investigation, sheriff, the U.S. Marines, the Naval Investigative Service. There's even a couple of geeks from the State Department around here somewhere."

"Did you say NIS?" asked Welsh. The Naval Investigative Service was responsible for handling major crimes involving naval personnel, including marines.

"Yeah, but they're gone," said MacNeil. "They tried,

but since this took place outside the base and there's no evidence of military involvement, they have no jurisdiction."

"Thank God," said Welsh. The NIS was renowned for seriously screwing up every major investigation it had been involved in: the Walker spy case, the espionage scandal among the marine guards in the Moscow Embassy, and the turret explosion aboard the battleship *Iowa*.

They stopped at a blocked-off column of footprints. "Whoever it was landed here last night," said MacNeil, pointing to the shoreline. It was low tide, and there was a smooth gap between the ocean and the beginning of the footprints. "Probably rubber boats, since nothing marked up the seabed."

"How many do you think got out?" asked Welsh, writing in his notebook.

"About thirty, but it's hard to tell, they must have been wearing something over their shoes—and the North Carolina cops ran around here like idiots this morning. Our nighttime arrivals were met by what looks like one guy; his shoe prints are pretty clear. The mess on the road is probably his vehicle, a pickup of some kind. Then they moved up over the dunes."

"And they got interrupted," said Welsh.

"Sheriff's deputy. He must have surprised them. No radio call, but he got three rounds off. You saw what they did to his car. We don't think he got any of them, but something hit the pickup and it went up like a bomb. A citizen down the road called it in, but the scene was abandoned when help finally got here."

"And the truck was full of what they brought ashore."

MacNeil took out his notebook. "Basically small arms; RPGs, mortars, grenades. Can't give you numbers and types right now, they're still putting the pieces together."

Welsh dug the cartridge out of his pocket and held it up. "AKs, right?"

MacNeil nodded. "Lots of rounds, and empty cases up on the dunes. That's what they used on the deputy. We recovered two intact AKMs from the water."

"What make?" asked Welsh.

"They tell me North Korean, folding stock. That's all we've got right now."

"Well, they sure weren't timid about it. Just dropped off thirty guys and all their hardware on a U.S. beach, easy as you please. Very professional."

MacNeil did not dispute the point.

Welsh closed his notebook and slipped it back into his parka. "Looks like we got lucky again."

"If you want to look at it that way."

"How else would you?" asked Welsh. "It's like the Japanese Red Army operator who got caught by a trooper on the Jersey Turnpike while he was heading for New York with a couple of pipe bombs. If the deputy hadn't shown up, all this firepower would be on its way somewhere. Any ideas on that?"

"That's the thing," said MacNeil. "The footprints come back off the dunes and head into the water, which is where we found the AKMs."

"You think they hauled ass back to their boats when their truck blew up? Maybe dropped some of their gear in the general panic?"

"Everyone would like that," said MacNeil. "But we really can't afford to depend on it, can we?"

"No," said Welsh, "we can't."

"Right now there's no indication of who did it or what their intentions were, or are. Unless you've seen something?"

Welsh shrugged. "I'm not trying to be coy, but we don't get a lot of raw intel where I live. But just wait, people are going to be screaming about their pet bogeymen, whether it's the cocaine cartels, Central American leftists, Palestinian or European contract terrorists, Puerto Rican nationalists. . . ."

"Okay," said MacNeil, "I get it."

"I'm not screwing with you," said Welsh. "Personally, I think Iran is at least behind it, not that anyone I know gives a shit. And I don't think it's a coincidence they picked this spot to land. We have to start thinking about what they were here for."

"You don't need thirty guys to smuggle in a load of arms," MacNeil said in agreement.

"And you can do a lot of things with that kind of force," said Welsh. "The big question is whether all their gear went up in the truck. If it did, then I can't see professionals hanging around, especially so soon after they inserted. And these guys look like pros."

"I hope we can answer that once we put together the data from the scene," said MacNeil. "If we can't find their ship, I think our best chance is to try for whoever was here to meet them. If they were planning something in the vicinity, there's probably a safe house. We'll start checking the last few months' real estate transactions."

Welsh shook his head. "You're forgetting where we are. Do you have any idea how often real estate turns over near a military base? Or how many transactions there are every month? It's big business around here; there's probably a few hundred registered agents."

"That's right, I forgot you were a marine."

"I used to live six miles down the beach."

"It looks like an interesting place," MacNeil said with a smirk. "Little out of the way, though."

"No kidding," said Welsh. "A little out of the way from everything. Never thought I'd be back, either. Well, I suppose I'd better hit the base and find a secure phone. The office is going to want to know what happened."

"We're working out of the Base Headquarters, using their communications center. If anyone bothers you, use my name."

Welsh was about to say that he couldn't do that, they might lose control of their bowels, but was held back by a rare flash of self-preservation. It's not your duty in life to mock the pretentious, you dumbshit, he told himself. He just said "Thanks a lot."

"Where are you parked?" MacNeil asked.

"A ways down the road. I couldn't get any closer."

"Need a ride?"

"No thanks," said Welsh. "I like walking."

He started for the dunes. MacNeil caught Welsh's arm in a grip that, although firm, was mostly for effect. But Welsh whipped about quickly, and the look that came across his face made MacNeil drop the hand. MacNeil thought Welsh was going to attack him. He automatically took a step back.

"Just one thing," MacNeil said, without his previous confidence. The quick change in Welsh had shaken him.

"What?" Welsh demanded. He was aware that he'd narrowly averted a disaster. That asshole MacNeil, throwing his weight around. In Welsh's circles you didn't put your hands on people unless you wanted your ass kicked.

"The bureau is running this investigation," said MacNeil. "I expect you to just observe and, if you do come across something, to keep us informed."

Welsh was back under control. "You don't have to worry about that. We're all going to have enough problems without playing stupid fucking games with each other."

When Welsh showed his ID at Base Headquarters, they practically wagged their tails. He never ceased to be amazed at the effect the Pentagon had—on people who had never been there, of course.

The secretary was in a meeting with his boss, the secretary of defense, and the deputy secretary wasn't around, so Welsh gave his information to Carol Bondurant.

"It sounds as if we got lucky," she said after he finished.

"I said the same thing," replied Welsh. "To tell you

the truth, this is so big I'm getting a little nervous about being the man down here. I'm not anywhere near senior enough, so why don't you talk the boss into sending someone else?"

"He'll say no."

"Then I'm not being paranoid in thinking he sent me down here in the hope I'd give him an excuse to burn me."

"Of course not, Rich. If you do a good job, he takes the credit; if something goes wrong, you're the handy scapegoat."

"You don't have to sugarcoat it like that, Carol, I can take it. Now, is there any more sunshine you'd like to bring into my life today?"

"No," she said, and Welsh could hear her laughter over the phone. "Just be careful . . . and don't antagonize anyone."

"I'm trying," said Welsh. "I swear to God I am."

CHAPTER 14

AFTER THE DISASTER on the beach, the Iranians made the drive to the farmhouse in shocked silence. Ali gave quiet orders to Karim and Musa, then locked himself in a small room that had once been used for sewing.

One of the commandos who had trained as a medic tried to examine him but was firmly ordered away. "I think he has a concussion," the medic told Musa. "He must stay awake."

The sergeant major made a noise in his throat. "Have no worries about that," he said.

The pickup trucks were hidden in the barn. The commandos were allowed to sleep after the sergeant major threatened to kill anyone who left the house without his personal permission. The spies, except Hafiz, led them to mattresses set up on the floors of the unused rooms.

Karim and Musa spent the night going over the status of the commandos' weapons and ammunition. What they found was not encouraging. All the RPG-7s and rockets, the machine guns and ammunition, the mortars and bombs, and the packaged grenades and extra rifle ammunition had been lost in the explosion of the truck. Only the demolition equipment survived, and the commandos' individual weapons. Most of the commandos had expended at least one magazine on the sheriff's car, and none had more than 120 rounds left.

"What will he do?" Karim asked, after the sergeant major returned from giving Ali the information.

"To be honest," said Musa, "this time I do not know."

His AKM was broken down into pieces on the floor, and he methodically cleaned it as they talked.

"But what do you think?" Karim persisted.

"At the moment he is shocked, more from the plan going wrong than the explosion. That will not last. I know him; he will look to carry on with the mission. It is too bad, though. If not for that police vehicle, the landing would have come off perfectly."

"We still have everything we need to deal with the marines," Karim said.

"That is minor," said Musa. "The White House is what we came for."

"We can do it. We have our rifles and twenty-five good men. The American president is just one man."

"You forget that our mission is to kill him in the White House. This unit is organized for a plan that was months in preparation and rehearsal. A new plan, made up here, without all our weapons, is another thing entirely."

"Our mission is to do it. Our lives do not matter."

"Ah, yes. That is why it will be interesting to see what the commander does."

"I was never so happy as when I saw him alive after the blast," said Karim. "It would have taken me too long to decide what to do."

"I thought he was dead," the sergeant major said quietly.

"You have been together for a long time," said Karim, the question in his voice. "He never talks of it."

"There is not much to speak of," Musa said, running a cleaning brush through the short barrel. "We were soldiers before the revolution, in a mechanized infantry regiment stationed in Teheran. I was a corporal, a professional."

"I did not know this," said Karim.

Musa understood the caution in Karim's voice. "If you are the last of eight sons," he said, "and never went to school, there is only the army. It was no worse than the farm, and they did teach me to read and write."

"And you have not stopped since," Karim said, smiling.

"Making up for too much time lost," said Musa. "The commander was a private, a conscript. He wanted to do his national service as a teacher in the Literacy Corps, but his father thought the army would make a man of him."

"Was the colonel in your section, is that how you met?"

"No. One day I saw him in a storeroom, praying. We talked, and soon we and a few others began to meet in a park to read the Koran. We became very good friends. One of the others always had tapes of the Imam's speeches."

"You met in the park so you would not be seen?" Karim asked.

"Yes. The officers were upper-class pigs, always off attending to their business interests in the city." Musa's hands moved faster as he scrubbed carbon from the piston head. "The sergeants ran the unit, and there were informers everywhere. Well, it was 1978, and the demonstrations had begun all over the country. In early September, while our company was guarding the French Embassy, another unit in Jalah Square opened fire on a crowd. Hundreds died. When two days later Carter called the shah and assured him of his support, things were bound to become worse.

"A week later we were assigned to block an intersection. We knew what could happen, and the thought of it was terrible. You see, we had no tear gas. The generals could make more graft buying F-14s, so there was no gas. Only bullets. The passersby on the street would stop and beg us not to hurt the people. They bought flowers and put them in our webbing or through the front sights of our G-3 rifles. All of us were ashamed—it was like standing naked out on the street. Just before noon a

demonstration came toward us, thousands of people.
They were calling through megaphones for us to put our
weapons down. Some in the front ripped off their shirts
and dared us to shoot them. The noise was incredible,
and they kept coming closer and closer. The senior lieutenant, our company commander, ordered us to shoot.
He was standing on a personnel carrier shouting at us
with his own megaphone."

"What happened?" Karim asked softly.

"No one moved. The lieutenant was screaming, the
crowd was screaming—they were so close you could feel
the heat coming off their bodies. Then, without a word,
Ali cocked his rifle, swung about, and shot the senior
lieutenant off the personnel carrier."

"Really?" Karim exclaimed. "That is incredible."

"The senior sergeant was about to shoot the commander for doing that," Musa continued. "So I
bayoneted him through the back." He pointed the AKM
bolt group toward his web gear, which was hanging from
the nearby chair. "I still have the bayonet."

"What did you do after that?"

"We shot all the officers and sergeants. The crowd
went wild and embraced us. That was our discharge.
Soon the shah fled and the Imam returned from France.
When the Iraqis invaded, we joined the commandos,
and he became my commander, which was only proper.
We have been together ever since."

"I have served with him for two years," said Karim.
"And I never heard this."

"And you will tell no one else," the sergeant major
growled. "Especially not the colonel."

"Of course."

"The colonel is a good man," said Musa. "The best I
have ever known. But experience and necessity have
made him hard. So I do not know what he will do. He
never makes crazy plans, but he never gives up. So will
we make the bomb and then escape? Or will he lead us
on, regardless of the cost? Or something else? He is very

resourceful. And there is another complication. The Americans may not believe our ploy on the beach. It was brilliant under the circumstances; I do not know how the colonel thought of it so quickly in the confusion. But the Americans may be hunting us even now." He slid the bolt group back into his weapon, and snapped the receiver cover down.

"You talk as if this were a soccer match," said Karim. "And you were in the stands."

"It has been a very long time since I became excited about such things," Musa said calmly. "God's will be done. Whatever the colonel orders we will carry out. It will be interesting. He is a very intelligent man. And never dull."

In the sewing room Ali removed a hard plastic briefcase from his carry-on bag. He carefully manipulated the lock and disarmed the self-destruction charge of plastic explosive.

Inside were the plans, maps, photographs, and intelligence briefing books. It was a great security risk, but he had felt the chance of a long delay would make it necessary for the men to be rebriefed on the plan. Ali stared at the sheet listing the arms and ammunition. There was ice in his stomach, and he felt like vomiting again. Stupid, how could you be so stupid? He angrily slammed the papers down on the worktable. Only a fool would put all the weapons in one place, even for a second. What would he do? What would he tell the men?

Ali went over the documents page by page, though by this time he had almost memorized them. The briefing book for Camp Lejeune was nearly an inch thick. He was reading it, praying for inspiration, when he fell asleep at the desk.

Hafiz sat alone in the family room, pressing his fingers into his temples to try and relieve the throbbing pain in his head. His ears still rang from the blast, and the four aspirins were doing no good at all. He needed a drink, but didn't dare in present company. He didn't even dare leave the house for fear that short hairy sergeant would shoot him.

A nightmare. No, an unmitigated disaster. They would probably claim it was his fault, try and shift the blame. That wasn't his job anyway; he wasn't a commando.

The mission was blown. There was only one thing left to do. The commandos would have to use their escape plans and get out of the country as soon as possible. He and his men would have to stay behind to clean up the mess. Then he would send a signal to Amir, requesting to remain and continue with their original work. Oh, please let him agree. That would be the only decent thing to come of this.

Tomorrow they could start the escape preparations. The three fools he'd been saddled with for so long would not be any trouble. No sense in taking chances, though; he would talk to them first. The original plan had been reckless anyway, only sheer luck that they were not dead or behind bars.

The aspirins were finally starting to work. Hafiz got up from the chair and left the family room, passing by the kitchen. Two commandos sat in front of a television tuned to the CNN news network. The police scanner next to the TV occasionally broke in. Both were monitored twenty-four hours a day.

It had been decided that all communication with Iran would be severed once they landed. Direct lines of communication were vulnerable to betrayal or compromise and could be used to track them if anything went wrong. In an emergency they could send messages by mail to a cut-out agent in New Jersey, who would pass them on to the Iranian United Nations Mission. Ali had approved the system—no one in Teheran would be bothering him with stupid orders. In any case, they could get more accurate and timely information from the American media than Iranian intelligence.

Hafiz passed them without speaking and went to bed.

• • •

Ali did not emerge from his room the next morning. The sergeant major brought him food but had no reply to the questions the commandos deluged him with. "He is working," was all Musa would say. The commandos passed the time talking amongst themselves, trying to guess what would happen.

Hafiz spent the morning with Mehdi, Ghulam, and Mahmoud, working on a plan to erase every trace of their presence in Jacksonville and then move back to Virginia.

Hungry for news from home, the spies had spent the night talking to any commando they could persuade to stay awake. "They have not been given any orders," Mehdi said, "but they are certain they will at least carry out the bombing they have planned."

"Their cover is blown," said Hafiz. "What can they do now? As soon as I talk with their commander, we will straighten this out."

"Why is it," Mahmoud asked angrily, "that their lowest soldier knows every detail of this plan, all the things we have not been told yet?" Mehdi and Ghulam nodded in agreement.

"How dare you talk to me that way," Hafiz said. "I am still the one in charge here, and I decide when you will be briefed." No one replied. Hafiz realized he needed to strike a conciliatory note. "What happened last night was a terrible shame. We all wanted to see the operation come off. After all, we worked very hard to make it a success. But now it is blown, there is nothing we can do about it. I am sure the FBI is investigating even as we speak. We are in great danger, and if we are to get out of this we must stick together. They are excellent soldiers," he said, lowering his voice. "But they know nothing about this type of situation. We are the experts, and we have to show them the way. It is our responsibility to get them out of the country safely so they may fight again.

Perhaps in the future the operation can be remounted."
Hafiz scanned their faces. They were coming around.

"I suppose you are right," Ghulam said glumly.

Mahmoud nodded. "It was our job to get them here
safely," he said. "And we failed. So we certainly have the
obligation to get them out." Hafiz refused to rise to the
barb. Mehdi stared at him and said nothing.

The spies had just begun to sound out the commandos
to determine their escape plans when the sergeant major
appeared and abruptly told them to mind their own
damned business. No one was escaping yet. And in the
future, he informed them, they would come to him before they bothered his men. Chastened, the spies went
back and reported this to Hafiz.

Hafiz next tried to get past Karim to talk to Ali.

"The commander is not to be disturbed," Karim said,
standing in front of the door with his arms across his
chest, as if guarding a bank vault.

"You do not understand," Hafiz said. "I am the head
agent here, and I must talk to him about your escape
plans."

"The commander is planning how we will continue
our mission," Karim said flatly, giving Hafiz a look of
scorn.

"Look here," Hafiz said, in his most reasonable voice.
"After what happened last night, the American police
services will be up in arms. You must make your escape
now. Believe me," he said in a patronizing tone—the
mature, experienced agent lecturing the hot-blooded
young boy. "I know my job as well as you know yours.
You simply do not understand."

"I understand," Karim said. "I understand that if you
had done your job, we would not be in this situation."

Here it is, Hafiz told himself. You knew they would
blame you. "I cannot tell the police cars where to go," he
said quickly. He had vowed not to get into an argument with them but couldn't help it; it was a matter of
justice.

"You should have picked a spot the police do not go," Karim responded, as Hafiz knew he would.

"I do not want to argue with you," Hafiz said, realizing they were both shouting. He gazed about, and saw they had attracted a group of curious onlookers. "Now I must speak with your commander. Every minute you remain here endangers you even more."

The door to the sewing room opened, and Ali walked out. "What is all this noise?" he asked.

Hafiz managed to speak before Karim. "I must talk with you at once," he said. "It is extremely urgent."

Ali looked Hafiz up and down, as if examining him anew in the light of day. "I will speak to my men first." He turned to Karim. "Have the sergeant major assemble everyone."

"At once," said Karim.

"If we could just talk for a moment before you do that?" Hafiz asked.

Ali seemed to be looking past him. "Assemble your men also," he said.

The commandos and agents packed into the living room, which was the largest room in the farmhouse. They all watched carefully as Ali entered, their soldier's antennae trying to pick up some indication of what was to come. Ali swaggered into the room with the confidence of a lion tamer entering the cage. Except for the streaks of dirt on his face and the sand on his clothes, he had thrown off the effects of the previous night. He did not have to call for silence.

"Did everyone get some sleep last night?" he asked in a loud voice. There were nods around the room. "Good. I am glad someone did." He got a quick burst of the pent-up laughter of men who had lately found little to laugh about.

"The first thing I want to do," Ali said, "is thank these intelligence officers for their work last night. It was a bad situation, but it would have been much worse if they had not kept their heads. After all, we did make it here

safely." He gave a slight bow to the spies. Mehdi, Ghulam, and Mahmoud beamed with relief. They had been
prepared for bitter accusations. Hafiz sat stone-faced,
watching his efforts unraveling.

"Well, now," Ali continued, "I do not have to tell you
our present situation. We were given two separate missions: the bombing of the marines and the attack on the
White House. We still have all we need to accomplish
the first, but we have lost complete surprise. As for the
second, the plan is now useless because our weapons are
gone.

"Last night I tried to find some clue to our predica-
ment. I confess that I fell asleep without the answer."
He had the commandos' complete attention; every eye
was on him as he circled the room. "Then, early this
morning, I woke up and looked at the pages before me.
And the answer was right before my eyes!" he shouted.
Then his voice dropped. "Because I asked myself,
should you give up and go home? Never!" he shouted.
The commandos jumped. Ali's voice reverberated
through the room. "After being singled out for this task,
should we slink home with our tails between our legs?
Never! With the finest commandos in the world, our
rifles still in our hands, and our force still intact? Never!
Not as long as we have only one cartridge left." He had
them now. The men were practically bouncing in their
seats.

"But the question remained," he said, his voice dropping again. "How will you do it? How will you replace
that beautiful plan everyone knew perfectly? Then it
came to me. We sit next to the marines' training base.
We have good intelligence on all their activities. We
need machine guns, grenades, and rockets. Why not take
theirs?" Mouths dropped open all over the room.

"I know what you are thinking," he said quickly. "Is
he mad? Does he not know how many marines are
there? Yes, he knows. But these marines are at their

peacetime base, so safe. Their weapons are filled with blanks." The faces were skeptical.

Ali handed Musa a map and photographs and motioned for them to be tacked to the wall. "Move in closer," Ali said to the men, "and I will tell you all about the base, and exactly how we will do this."

When Ali finished, the reaction was electric. He could see it; they knew it could be done. Now the real test. He asked for questions. A commando stood up and asked about the mission timetable.

"It will depend," Ali said. "Careful preparation is required. All the conditions have to be right. First we must wait for the reaction to last night. Depending on what the Americans do, we could go to Phase 2 very quickly. Or we may have to hide until their security precautions are relaxed. But I will keep you informed." The commando sat down. There were no other questions. We are going to do it, Ali thought in exultation. He struggled to hold his emotions in. Only the sergeant major saw Ali's fists clenched at his side as he began to walk from the room.

Hafiz sat stunned. He could not believe it. They were going ahead after all. Without thinking, he leaped from the chair. "Wait!" he called out. Ali stopped in the doorway.

Hafiz walked up to him quickly. "You cannot be serious about this," he said in a low voice.

"Is that what you wanted to talk about?" Ali asked.

"Yes. You must realize your mission is blown. You have to activate your escape plans at once."

"There is nothing more to discuss," Ali said coldly. "The decision has been made." He began to walk away.

"Wait right there!" Hafiz shouted. He couldn't believe it, he was surrounded by madmen. His head was aching again.

Ali turned, a cruel smile on his face. None of the commandos had moved.

"This is madness," Hafiz shouted. "Can you not see that?" He seemed to be appealing to the room.

"I told you the decision was made," Ali said, trying to make this babbling idiot realize he should shut up. He did not want a scene now that he had the men convinced. And he did not want a split with the spies; he still needed them.

"I am in charge of this part of the operation," Hafiz said desperately.

Ali shook his head. "You are mistaken," he said, slowly and clearly. His normal tone of voice made the effect even more cutting. "The second I set foot on the beach, I commanded every man in this operation. My decisions are final."

The sergeant major sat off to one side, disgusted. As if we did not have enough problems, he thought. This spy had to be a fool to challenge a man's authority in front of his subordinates. He showed the confidence of someone who had never lost a fight; looking him over, Musa decided it was because he had never been in one. Obviously the spy thought his position gave him leverage. He was about to be proved wrong, and Musa hoped Ali would not be too drastic.

"My orders are specific," Hafiz shouted, his voice shrill. Ali said nothing, trying to hold his anger in check.

"I will send a signal to Teheran," Hafiz continued. "They will decide."

At this Ali's temper snapped. "You will send nothing," he shouted. With a sweep of his boot, he kicked Hafiz's legs out. The spy fell heavily to the floor. Ali's right hand flashed to the small of his back, and when Hafiz looked up he was staring into the barrel of a pistol. The bulbous muzzle of the silenced Russian Makarov, aimed directly between his eyes, seemed to Hafiz the most enormous thing he had ever seen in his life. Ali cocked the hammer back with his thumb. As it fell into position with two loud metallic clicks, everyone in the room froze. Hafiz closed his eyes. He could not bear to look into that huge black hole any longer. Karim and most of the commandos seemed to be waiting expectantly. The sergeant major shook his head.

"Open your eyes," Ali commanded. Hafiz did as he was told. "Listen to me very carefully," Ali said. He had everyone's attention. "You make me want to vomit. You and your expensive clothes and your American manner. While you live the rich life over here, safe and warm, we have been bleeding on the battlefield. And when you are finally given something vital to do, you want to run away at the first sign of danger, so you can go back to your rich life."

The other spies sat mortified under the gaze of the commandos. "It is not true," Mehdi shouted. "For him, perhaps, but not us. We are with you." Mahmoud and Ghulam shouted agreement.

Ali turned his attention back to Hafiz. "So you see, at least your people have some backbone. Now I will give you a chance to redeem yourself. You have the choice. You can do the job you are supposed to do and come back to Iran with us, alive. Or I can put a bullet in your brain, right now."

Hafiz looked into Ali's eyes and believed him. "I will help you," he croaked. Ali dropped the hammer with his thumb, and Hafiz almost passed out at the sound. Ali holstered the pistol and walked away, leaving Hafiz sprawled on the floor.

"What do you think?" Ali asked, when he had Musa and Karim alone in the sewing room.

"How did you manage to come up with it?" Karim asked.

"The intelligence briefing book on the marine base," Ali said. "In the early planning stages, I considered an attack on the ammunition storage or on marines training in remote areas of the base. There were reports on ammunition handling and issuing procedures and marine operational methods." He turned to the sergeant major. "Well?"

Musa gave him a familiar look, a raising of the eyebrows.

"Yes," Ali said. "I want to know what you really think."

"You should have killed him," Musa said. "He could be very dangerous."

"Not that," Ali said. "My plan."

Musa shrugged. "It is incredibly dangerous," he said, staring at Ali. The colonel was impassive. "And you know why. First, we will have to split our force. Then we will need exact intelligence, so we will have to send in advance reconnaissance teams. They may be discovered." Musa stopped abruptly, obviously feeling he had made his point.

"Why do we not attack the White House with what we have?" Karim asked. "One of the spies told me that Kalashnikov ammunition is easy to obtain here in America, in any quantity you wish."

"I thought of that," Ali said. "I am not convinced we can do the job on the White House with just rifles. If we have to die to accomplish the mission, then we will die. But we will not die for failure."

"Why not kill the president when he is outside?" Musa suggested. "It will be understood that we could not do everything without all our arms."

"No," Ali said firmly. "We were given a specific mission, and that is what we are going to do."

"But I am sure . . ." Karim began. A glance from Musa cut him off.

"If you are against it," Ali said, showing his first sign of doubt, "then I will reconsider."

Musa and Karim looked at each other.

"Do you truly think we can pull this off?" Musa asked.

Ali did not seem to take offense at the question. "I am positive," he said.

"Then I am for it," Musa said.

"And I also," Karim chimed in a moment later.

"Now are *you* sure?" Ali asked them.

They both nodded.

"Then we cannot fail," Ali said, his voice breaking with emotion.

CHAPTER 15

"IT WAS THE world's most boring briefing," Rich Welsh told Carol Bondurant. "And I say that from long and bitter experience."

"You old salt, you," Carol said, with friendly sarcasm.

Welsh had driven back to Washington for a day of meetings. The secretary wasn't available yet, so Welsh was cooling his heels with Carol in the office.

"I can't wait to hear what they told you," she said. "Now give me all the latest on the investigation."

"I'd tell you," Welsh whispered, "but then I'd have to kill you."

She kicked him hard on the ankle.

"No, not the high heels," Welsh groaned, rubbing his leg. "I'll talk, I'll talk." He leaned back in the chair and put his feet up on the desk. "The FBI is checking the local real estate offices for a safe house, which to me is wishful thinking. There is one good lead, though. The lab boys found a burned ID plate in the pieces of the pickup truck and brought up the numbers. That'll give us the dealership and, hopefully, the purchaser."

"Probably a fake license," said Carol.

Welsh shrugged. "Maybe something will turn up."

"The Coast Guard found what looks to be the mother ship, two hundred miles off the coast. The *Treccano Volturno.*"

"We heard," said Welsh. "On fire; sinking; and no distress call, lifeboats, or survivors in the water. Did they track down her route yet?"

"Kuala Lumpur through the Panama Canal, overdue three days in Wilmington. But nothing else so far. Did the bureau forensics people get anything from the pieces of the weapons? That's where I thought we'd get lucky."

"Oh, they reconstructed them all right," said Welsh. "But they're clean as the driven snow. Most were Soviet design, and the Russians are breaking their asses to give us the records so we won't blame them. Three PKM machine guns, originally shipped to Sudan. Three RPG-7Ds, originally sent to Afghanistan. A Chinese mortar and ammunition, and you know we won't get anything out of them. North Korean AKMs. The grenades were ours, though, M67 frags and white smoke."

"There must be something there."

"You'll love this. The lot numbers are from a foreign military sales shipment to the then-Lebanese army in 1982."

"God," said Carol.

"What goes around, comes around," said Welsh.

"The question, though," said Carol, "is why they were coming ashore in the first place."

"That's what I was trying to tell those dodoes" said Welsh, leaning forward in his chair. "This was no smuggling job, not with just three RPGs, three machine guns, and one mortar. This was a platoon-sized unit with supporting arms. Enough firepower to chew up any hardened target we've got in this country, not to mention all the soft ones."

"And they didn't agree?"

"I got the impression that everyone is hoping fervently that the bad guys got back in their boats and went home after their ride got blown up."

"But they obviously weren't planning to move thirty men with weapons in one pickup truck," Carol protested.

Welsh smiled with obvious pride. "Exactly, Holmes. I should have had you with me to whip some sense into these bureaucrats."

"Rich, what did you do?"

"There was a whole table of them," said Welsh. "CIA, Defense Intelligence Agency, National Security Agency, marines, State Department. MacNeil just sat there like he was carved out of stone. The CIA was too busy bitching about FBI leaks to the press—you know, the ones accusing the Company of being caught flatfooted by all this. And everyone was perfectly willing to wait as long as it took for the investigation to run its course. We're just liaisons, they said. Washington makes all the decisions."

"What did you do?" Carol repeated.

"Nobody was going to stake out any position and take the risk of being wrong. I just got a little vocal, so they'd have to report what I said, if only to cover their asses in case I turned out to be right. I said I thought they were Iranians or Iranian surrogates, that it was a platoon-sized mission, and that we'd better get up on our goddamned toes. If you can't light a fire from the top," Welsh said triumphantly, "light one from the bottom. I put it all in my report," he tapped a binder on the desk, "and it's a beauty."

His phone buzzed.

"I hope the secretary feels that way," said Carol.

"He will," Welsh replied. "If only because it'll make him look good. And this time I'll buy dinner."

The secretary sat him in front of the desk again. Welsh was used to it by now. He made himself comfortable, opened his report to the first page, and looked up expectantly.

The secretary glowered at him for a moment. Welsh fought off the temptation to yawn. After Officer Candidate School that shit just didn't work on you anymore. He decided to take a chance and begin. "Sir, I think you'll be very interested in what I have here."

The secretary held up a well-manicured hand to stop him. "Richard," he said, "all week I have been taking calls from important people in a number of agencies. And all these calls were complaints about you. About you being abrasive, about you being discourteous, about you being uncooperative." He said all this very calmly, as if Welsh was not important enough to become angry over.

Welsh blinked twice, bowled over by the unexpected turn in the conversation. Then he began to get angry. "You didn't get any complaints from the FBI," he said, half question and half declaration.

"They were the only ones who didn't complain," said the secretary.

Welsh opened his mouth to speak, and the secretary once again held up a hand to silence him. "Now I'm telling you this formally, Richard. I want you to go back to North Carolina. I want you to keep me completely informed about the progress of the investigation. I want you to maintain good relations with everyone down there. And I want you to keep your opinions to yourself."

Welsh was on the verge of an explosion. "What about my report?" he said tightly.

"Submit it through channels," the secretary said pleasantly. "Thank you, Richard, that will be all."

Welsh shot up out of his chair so fast that the secretary automatically rolled his own chair back a foot. Welsh turned quickly to go, then turned back and flipped his report onto the secretary's desk. Then he got the hell out of the office before he did anything else.

This time he went directly to Carol's desk. She listened quietly, careful not to interrupt, as he recounted what had happened. "Discourteous," he said at the end. "Discourteous. Well, isn't that just fucking sweet."

"What are you going to do?"

"Drive on," said Welsh. "If the shit comes rolling downhill on you, just say 'Fuck it' and drive on."

CHAPTER 16

FROM THE EXPRESSION on his face, the owner of the Charlotte, North Carolina, Ford dealership would rather have had leprosy than four FBI agents sitting across the desk from him. Not just one or two, but *four* of them. He surrendered his sales records without argument and let off a little of the stress by berating his secretary for being too slow.

"I knew there was something funny about that fellow," Sam Warders confided to Special Agent MacNeil. Even though you understood that the New South had broken with its old stereotypes, you still occasionally ran into a businessman like Warders—a beefy, moon-faced, shrewd old boy who dressed like a tobacco farmer suddenly gone prosperous.

"Do you usually handle customers personally?" MacNeil asked, coldly officious. "Or was this a special case?"

"No, no," Warders said quickly, eager to correct such a horrible misunderstanding. "It was just that I was here, and it was an unusual sale. . . . He's a drug dealer, isn't he?"

"You still haven't answered my question," MacNeil pointed out.

"He paid cash in full for the truck," Warders said glumly, abandoning all efforts to be ingratiating. "I was in the office that day, and Bob, my sales manager, came in to ask me about it." He shook his head. "We don't get much of that around here, and I know you boys put out all that information about cash transactions. . . ."

The four agents sat there quietly, staring at him. Other than experienced criminals, very few people can stand up to that sort of blank, impersonal, cold-hearted authority. Warders's equilibrium deserted him. Desperate to fill up all that empty air, he began talking himself into knots.

"But how're you going to question someone's cash money?" he demanded of the agents. "I mean, you can call them on a check, but what can you do about cash?"

"So you do a lot of cash transactions?" MacNeil asked, leaving him no room at all.

"No, no, no," Warders said. MacNeil thought the man would have hit himself had he been alone. "That's why this was so unusual," Warders repeated, with emphasis.

"We need every possible bit of information on this man," MacNeil said. "And we expect your complete cooperation."

"Certainly, certainly," said Warders, relieved that the pendulum had somehow swung him back on the same side as the law. "As you can see, sir, we even photocopied his driver's license." He pushed the paper over the desk.

"Yes, I see," said MacNeil, looking at the multi-tinted smudge where the machine had failed to copy Hafiz's photo.

"Check the Registry of Motor Vehicles?" asked the agent sitting next to him.

"Even money the license is fake," said MacNeil.

"No, sir," Warders said firmly. "You see, we check all documents very carefully." MacNeil glared at him, and Warders pouted and sank lower into his chair.

"It's a shame we don't have his face," said MacNeil. He turned back to Warders. "We'll have an artist come in and talk to you and your employees."

Warders squirmed in his chair, clearly uncomfortable about something. "Well, sir, um. . . ."

MacNeil decided to provide a little motivation. "Have

you been audited recently?" he asked, as if it was just a matter of personal curiosity.

Warders flinched. Clearly, his day was on the way to being ruined. "We videotaped him," he said.

"You what?" MacNeil said, calmly, as if he couldn't quite believe what his brain had just taken in.

"We've had a couple of lawsuits," Warders explained, sweat beading across his upper lip. "People saying they didn't agree to things they agreed to. So we have this video system—for security you understand—and we taped this fellow while we were dealing. My lawyer said it ain't no crime," he moaned plaintively. "Is it?"

MacNeil let him dance for a few seconds. "Not if you've still got the tape."

Sam Warders took a videocassette from a locked cabinet behind him and slid it over the desk to MacNeil.

CHAPTER 17

ALI WAS PUTTING the final touches on his operation order when the sergeant major knocked on the door of his room.

"The spies have appeared with the truck," Musa said.

"Any problems?"

"If there were, they did not say."

"I am surprised," Ali said. "I did not think they could come up with it so soon."

"We put it in the barn," Musa said. "I told one of the team leaders to begin cleaning out the back."

At that moment Karim crashed into the room. "The truck has arrived," he announced excitedly. "When can we begin work on it?"

Ali and Musa smiled at each other. "I was just about to discuss that with you," Ali said. "My research is finished, and the time has come to see if our intelligence is correct. If it is not," he said to Karim, "then we will have to obtain more Kalashnikov ammunition and do as you suggested."

The one phone in the farmhouse was on a long cord, and Ali had it brought into the sewing room. "Time to make a call to the marines," he said.

Musa and Karim both sat down. "I do not need any help," Ali said. "You may begin putting the truck together." Disappointed, they rose and walked out the door. "Close it behind you," Ali called out. "And under no circumstances am I to be disturbed." Musa nodded from the doorway. "Try not to blow yourselves up," Ali said gruffly.

"I will do my best," Musa said, smiling at him.

Ali looked at the phone and took a deep breath. He hoped he had not lost his American accent. The dialog he wanted to use was on the pad in front of him, alongside the list of telephone numbers obtained from Base Information. Ali took a deep breath, and dialed a number.

The phone was picked up on the second ring. "Marine Corps Base Camp Lejeune, Public Affairs Office, Corporal Melvin speaking. May I help you, sir?" came the monotone reply. Ali was momentarily startled—the introduction had lasted so long he thought it was a recording.

"Ah, yes." Thrown off his stride, Ali stumbled a bit. "This is Bob Perkins from *Pennsylvania Times* magazine." He remembered the magazine from his last time in America. Ali thought Pennsylvania was far enough away to make it unlikely the marines would check. "I was wondering if I could speak to someone who could answer a few questions?"

"If you'd hold for a moment, sir, I'll connect you with one of our Public Affairs officers," the corporal said.

"Thank you very much."

The line clicked open again in less than thirty seconds. "This is First Lieutenant Humphrey. How can I help you?"

To make it sound official, Ali identified himself again. "Ah, yes, I was wondering if you could give me some comment on the recent incident that occurred on the beach near you, where the police officer was killed."

"Well, sir, that did not occur on this base. Therefore, the Marine Corps has no jurisdiction over it. So you'll have to get in touch with the FBI for any information."

"Yes, but it was so close to you. Have you taken any kind of precautions?"

"Well, sir, as a general precaution the base has gone to a yellow alert, which is a security condition."

"And what does that involve?" Ali asked.

"Oh, increased intelligence gathering, heightened security at the gates, that sort of thing. It's nothing drastic," the lieutenant hastened to add. "Just one step up from our normal procedures."

"So you're not really worried."

"No, sir."

"Thank you, Lieutenant." Ali gave it just the right amount of pause. "Say, now that I have you on the phone, what's the possibility of us sending a reporter and a photographer out there to do a feature?"

"On what?" the lieutenant asked, with friendly suspicion in his voice.

"My editor is a former marine," Ali explained. "And he wants to do a story on the new infantry weapons you people have now. You know, take pictures of them being fired and talk to some marines. A short photo story with captions."

"I think we could arrange that," Lieutenant Humphrey said. "You know, we have a brand-new combat town and some firing ranges that simulate urban fighting. The marines use live ammunition and throw live grenades. It's very exciting stuff—it would make great pictures."

"That's exactly the kind of thing we're interested in," said Ali, not having to manufacture the elation in his voice. "Just the foot soldier's weapons, you know, no tanks or anything."

Lieutenant Humphrey, used to dealing with the press, did not correct him on the use of that despised term, "soldier."

"An infantry company firing on the range," he said. "Rifles, machine guns, AT-4s, that sort of thing?"

"What's an AT-4?" Ali asked. He knew very well, but he didn't want to give anything away.

"Oh, I'm sorry. It's an antitank rocket launcher."

"That's exactly what we would want to see," Ali said. "And those other things you mentioned. Now we wouldn't want any kind of a special show, just an average . . . company, did you say? I'm not familiar with these military terms."

"Yes, sir, just an average company firing."

"When could you let me know about that?"

"Well, sir, I'd have to call Range Control and see when a company will be doing that kind of firing."

"I don't understand," Ali broke in.

"When a unit wants to fire on the ranges," the lieutenant explained patiently, "it has to send a request to Base Range Control—they assign the ranges. I'll call and see when a company is scheduled, and we'll try to match it up with your itinerary. But as I was saying, I'll have to clear the whole thing first with Base and then with Division. Then I'll be able to get back to you."

"It will take some time, then?"

"Yes, sir, things move pretty slow in the military. It'll be at least three weeks before I can call you and set something up."

"I understand," said Ali. "Well, before I make you go to all that trouble, let me make sure I can get approval here. The whole thing was only a rough idea my editor had."

"I see," said the lieutenant who was becoming a bit impatient. He was obviously a man used to being jerked around by the press.

"Why don't I make sure up here," Ali continued, "and then I can get back to you."

"All right, would you like to give me your num—"

"Thanks for everything," Ali interrupted. "Goodbye." He broke the connection.

Ali thought it over. He couldn't wait that long for the information, and his cover story wasn't likely to hold up through the number of calls it would take to arrange a visit. As he liked to say: Make up a good plan and then be flexible. He glanced at the notes he had made and

checked his Camp Lejeune special map, a topographic
map that detailed the entire base, including the various
firing ranges. God only knew how Amir had gotten it.
Range Control, yes, that was obviously the next thing to
try. He would have to be very careful.

Ali waited until the lunch hour to make the next call,
reasoning that military units were the same the world
over. Camp Lejeune Information provided the phone
number once again. This time the phone rang for a bit
before it was picked up. And this time Ali was ready for
the introduction.

"Range Control, Lance Corporal Banotz speaking.
May I help you, sir?"

"Yes, Lance Corporal. This is Lieutenant Humphrey
from Public Affairs."

"Yes, Sir?"

"I have some people from the press who want to see
infantry weapons being fired, and I want to take them to
a range where all the weapons can be used."

"Yes, Sir, that would be either Golf-3 or Kilo-305."

"I also want them to see those urban combat ranges, I
can't remember what their names are. . . ."

"You mean the K ranges, Sir. They're right next to
Kilo-305."

Ali tore over the map, trying to find them. "I can't
seem to find them on my map."

"They're on the other side of the river, Sir," the lance
corporal said, trying to be helpful. Public Affairs, Jesus.

"I found them," Ali said. He had. "Now, could you
tell me when an infantry company will be firing on those
ranges? With M16s, machine guns, AT-4s, and preferably mortars." Don't be greedy, he told himself.

"Jeez, I don't know, Sir. Everybody's gone to lunch.
I'm just the phone watch."

"I realize that, but I'm working on very short notice.
Isn't there a list somewhere? I'd really appreciate your
looking."

Banotz had been about to flip the lieutenant off; can't

help you, Sir, I'm just a lance corporal. But this guy sounded like a human being. "If you'd hang on for a minute, Sir, this week's firing schedule is on the board in the other room. I'll pick up in there."

"I'd really appreciate it," Ali repeated, with utter sincerity.

A few seconds later Banotz picked up the phone again. "Sir? This week we've got a unit firing the K ranges and K-305, but they're only shooting mortars and machine guns, nothing else."

"What about next week?" Ali asked.

"Sorry, Sir, only this week is on the board."

"Isn't there a list somewhere?" Ali asked in desperation.

"I dunno, Sir. Wait a minute, here's the binder with the approved range requests. This may take a bit."

"I'm awfully sorry to bother you like this, but it's very important. You know how these things come in at the last minute."

"That's okay, Sir." There was the sound of rustling pages. "These are listed by unit, not range."

Ali was silently praying on the other end of the phone.

"Got one, Sir! The week after next there's a rifle company firing M16s, SAWs, M60s, AT-4s, and 60mm mortars on K-305. And they're firing the K ranges the same week, M16s and grenades. I'll give you the unit and the dates and times when you're ready."

"Fantastic," Ali breathed. His pen was poised over the paper. Lance Corporal Banotz read out the information. "I want to thank you very, very much, Lance Corporal," Ali said.

"No sweat, Sir. Have a good day."

"You too," Ali said, hanging up. He looked at the information as if he could not believe it, then slammed his fist onto the table in exultation. "Yes!" he shouted. "Yes!"

• • •

They had rehearsed the construction of a truck bomb many times in Iran. The commandos broke into teams, each assigned a specific task. Musa and Karim would supervise the overall operation.

Rough wooden tables had been constructed from scrap wood in the barn, and all the materials had been brought out of storage and neatly arranged. The commandos lounged about, talking and joking, waiting for the order to begin.

"Where did they get it?" Karim asked, as he and the sergeant major walked around the truck.

"It was stolen from a depot," Musa replied. "We will put new license plates on it later."

"Yummycakes?" Karim asked, pointing at the brightly painted logo on the side.

"A snack food," Musa explained. "Sold in packages. This type of truck is used to supply shops. I understand they are very common."

They moved around to the back. The commandos had removed the storage racks, and the inside was bare.

"What is the capacity of the truck?" Musa asked one of the team leaders, who was sitting on the bumper. The man jumped to his feet.

"It's manual says thirty-five hundred pounds, Sergeant Major. And it says it is called a step-van."

"I say it looks like a truck."

"Yes, Sergeant Major."

Musa glanced at Karim, whose face was twisted in concentration as he tried to do the conversion. "A little less than sixteen hundred kilos," Musa told him. Karim was crushed.

"We will have quite a bit of explosive left over," the team leader said.

"I am sure we can find a use for any excess," Musa said.

One team would handle the actual manufacture of the explosive. Karim and Musa stationed themselves near the tables to keep a close eye on the process. The commandos donned coveralls, long plastic aprons, and rubber gloves. The quiet made the sergeant major smile; the prospect of handling high explosives had shut off all the joking. The commandos opened the drums and poured the clear chemical into large garbage cans. The empty drums were set aside to be used as containers for the finished explosive. The bags of ammonium nitrate fertilizer were cut open, and the granular particles scooped out with measuring cups.

The explosive had to be mixed in relatively small batches, so effort was concentrated around the large glass mixing bowls. The chemical was carefully poured from the garbage cans into the bowls. Fertilizer was slowly added, and the mixture stirred with a glass rod until the granules had completely dissolved. More fertilizer was added until it no longer dissolved into solution, even after prolonged stirring, and small particles of ammonium nitrate remained in the bottom of the bowl. The resulting clear liquid was more powerful than any military explosive, including C-4 plastic.

Teams of commandos, straining under the weight of the heavy bowls, carried the finished explosive over to the empty drums. They were very careful. The stuff was supposed to be stable, but you never knew. They gingerly poured the liquid back into the drums through a large funnel.

"Easier than baking bread," Karim commented to Musa. The sergeant major grunted.

While the explosive was prepared, other teams were readying the truck and the firing systems.

Three separate firing systems had been brought from Iran, each capable of detonating all the explosive. To power the systems, the commandos mounted three 12-volt lantern batteries on a frame behind the driver's seat.

The first system consisted of a pressure switch mounted on the front bumper. The switch was a plastic box the size of a pack of cigarettes. The box trailed two

wires. The heart of the box was a microchip. When the
bumper received an impact of more than twenty pounds,
the chip would be crushed; two seconds later the circuit
would close, firing a blasting cap. The second system was
a hand-sized device with a protruding spring-loaded
lever. When the lever was pressed down, the system was
armed; when it was released, the circuit would close.
The third system was a simple digital clock timer. Once
the systems were installed and the electric wiring run
back to the driver's cab, the commandos were ready to
place the explosive.

Six of the drums, filled and resealed, were gently
rolled up two wooden planks and into the back of the
truck. The men placed the drums upright against the
outside walls, three drums on each side, and strapped
them to the frame. The commandos set the cylinders of
acetylene gas in circles around each drum, padded them
with rags so they would not smash together, and secured
them with more straps.

The drums would be detonated by separate charges of
C-4 plastic explosive. The men had brought the C-4 from
Iran in their shoulder bags, along with detonating cord
and blasting caps.

Musa and Karim watched while the commandos prepared the charges. The olive-green plastic wrapping was
removed from the one and one-quarter-pound bars of
C-4. This C-4 was American, and the bars were labeled
"CHARGE, DEMOLITION, M112." The explosive was
white, similar to but slightly stiffer than children's mod-
eling clay. Each bar was broken in half, releasing a
distinctive smell of marzipan. The commandos cut four-
foot lengths of detonating cord, quarter-inch waterproof
cord filled with high explosive. Each piece of cord was
doubled, and an overhand knot tied at the loop, leaving
both ends hanging free. The knot was pressed into the
center of a half bar of C-4, and the other half bar was
placed over it. The two halves were sealed together with

electrical tape. The knot was buried in the center, and the two ends of detonating cord hung free. Two blocks of C-4 were taped to the side of each drum, between the acetylene tanks.

A separate twenty-foot–long piece of detonating cord was made into a loop by tying both ends together. Then the two trailing ends of det cord that protruded from each block of plastic explosive were tied onto the longer loop. The ring was taped against the walls of the van to protect it.

All that remained was to connect the explosive to the firing systems. Musa and Karim stepped in to take over this final step. Once the last connection was made, the truck would be ready to explode. If there was a mistake, the blast would vaporize the barn and farmhouse.

The electric blasting caps were smooth silver cylinders two inches long and slightly thicker than a pencil, filled with very sensitive explosive. From the base of each trailed two thin twelve-foot-long electrical wires. Karim selected three caps from a padded plastic box. He gently taped them onto the central ring of detonating cord, passing the wires to the sergeant major in the driver's cab.

"Are the positive and negative wires shunted together?" Musa called nervously.

"Of course," Karim said.

"Well, I hope you know that the static electricity in your hair can explode them if you do not have the circuit closed," Musa said.

"I know," said Karim. "You should be calm, it is not good for your health. See how relaxed I am?"

"You are too relaxed, as far as I am concerned," Musa grumbled. "It is not good to be too casual with explosives."

The sergeant major hunched over the carefully separated bunches of wires and prepared to complete the circuits. The look on his face indicated he was not en-

joying himself. Electric blasting caps were very touchy—
stray currents or even radio signals could sometimes set
them off. With visible perspiration, though the barn was
quite cool, Musa spliced wires from the blasting caps to
the three firing systems. Since the truck would not be
sent immediately, Musa did not connect the batteries.
Instead he quickly twisted the free wires together, clos-
ing off the circuits from any stray sparks. It took half an
hour to finish all the systems, and nothing blew up in his
face. Relieved, Musa began breathing normally.

Activating any switch would close the circuit and fire a
blasting cap. This would ignite the explosive filling of the
detonating cord. The explosion would travel through the
center ring cord and down the individual cords to each
C-4 charge, the detonating cord knot in the center of
each bar of C-4 transmitting enough force to detonate
the charge. Since detonating cord explodes at a rate of
twenty thousand feet per second, the six drums would go
off virtually simultaneously.

Musa looked up to see Karim grinning in the doorway.

"Good work, eh?" said Karim.

"Very good," said Musa. "But there is a bit more to
do." He hung cloths across the rear windows and the
passage from the driver's compartment, so no one could
see in. He removed the batteries from under the seat
and locked both the side doors. Karim padlocked the
rear doors. The sergeant major called the team leaders
over. "Clean up the inside of the barn, which you should
have started while we were working," Musa told them.
"When you are done, come get me and I will check it.
Clear?" They nodded glumly, having thought they were
finished. "Then get started," said Musa.

He and Karim walked out of the barn into the cold
fresh air. They had begun work on the truck after breakfast, and it was now dark.

"The cold here is so damp," Karim said, zipping up

his jacket. The barn had been relatively warm from all the people and activity.

"I have not found anything to like about this place yet," said Musa.

CHAPTER 18

ALI AND KARIM parked their motorcycles in the over-grown yard behind the farmhouse. "Very nice," Karim said, pulling off his helmet and wiping mud from the cardboard temporary license plate. Mehdi had returned from an out-of-town dealership an hour before, and Ali and Karim had taken the bikes on a test drive.

Musa and Mehdi came out of the farmhouse carrying two small daypacks. "Everything you need is in here," the sergeant major said. "And the radios are fully charged."

"Before we leave, we will give you a radio check," Ali said, "and see if this new receiver really works." An antenna extended from the farmhouse roof; the commandos had installed the apparatus the previous night. "If we run into trouble, we will call and tell you. If we are taken, send the truck on its way at once and carry out Phase 3 the best you can." Musa nodded.

"You should have no trouble," Mehdi said. "On Sundays the base is almost deserted." He snorted in derision. "The Americans are easy to surprise. For two days at the end of every week, they cease to be an army."

"We are both students of history," said the sergeant major, smiling and gesturing toward Ali.

"I am sorry your driving licenses are not good for motorcycles," Mehdi said, still serious. "No one back home thought you would need them, I imagine."

"Have no worries about the licenses," Ali said. He tapped the Russian silenced pistol in his belt. "No one will get the chance to ask for it. By the way, you did a good job buying these on such short notice."

Mehdi waved off the compliment. "In this country," he said, "if you have money, you can have anything."

Karim rummaged through his pack. The walkie-talkie was in the front pocket. He put on the headphones with the attached voice-activated microphone, carefully fitting his helmet over it. "I will give a radio check," he said through the visor. He spoke into the radio and received a response from the commando monitoring the larger unit in the house.

Ali did the same. "We are ready," he said, fastening his chin strap. He kicked the motorcycle into life.

The sergeant major walked up to him, his face almost touching the edge of the helmet. Ali flipped up the visor. "Be careful," Musa said. No one else heard him over the noise of the bike. Ali clapped him on the shoulder and signaled to Karim. They sped down the driveway and onto the highway.

Camp Lejeune Marine Corps Base extended out to the Intercoastal Waterway and the Atlantic Ocean and was split into two separate parts by the New River inlet. All the base facilities and a large part of the training areas and firing ranges were on the east side of the inlet. On the west side were the rifle range and, isolated in the northwest corner, the New River Air Station and the Infantry School at Camp Geiger. The rest was heavily wooded training area and ranges. No direct on-base access connected the two sides. To cross from east to west, one had to leave the base through a Military Police checkpoint in the south and cross the Sneads Ferry Bridge onto Route 6, or leave by other checkpoints on Route 24 and circle around on the highway.

Ali knew that his targets would have to be on the more secluded western side. It was God's will the Public Affairs lieutenant had mentioned that the hand-grenade ranges were on that side of the base. His map was taped to the motorcycle gas tank. As they circled the highway around the base, Ali checked off the various possibilities.

The Air Station and Camp Geiger entrances were impossible. The Military Police checkpoints were well guarded and within sight of the highway. Taking a left turnoff in the village of Verona, they followed an asphalt road through the woods toward the entrance to the westside training areas. There were signs ordering drivers to stop, and a small MP shack. Before the MP could get out of the shack, the Iranians swerved about and sped back down the road.

"We will not be able to sneak in this way," Ali said to Karim over the radio. "But with the post in the woods on that lonely road, it would not be hard to kill the guard and drive right in."

"They must have a telephone and check in regularly," Karim replied.

"Probably," Ali said. "We would lose surprise. But the entrance is there as a last resort. We will keep going down the highway and check the other entrances on the map."

They continued south on Route 17. It was a long way; the base was quite large. The were a few homes along the highway, but outside the town of Jacksonville it was mostly undeveloped. Ali's map showed dirt road entrances leading into the training area. When they checked, they found the trails blocked by mounds of earth and barbed wire, remnants of the spasm of security precautions taken after the Lebanon bombing in 1983—precautions that had long since been relaxed.

"We can get the motorcycles through the trees," Karim said. "Nothing larger, though."

"We will come back in if we have to," Ali decided.

They took a left onto Route 6, heading south toward the ocean. Almost missing the well-marked entrance to a firing range, Ali braked hard and almost lost the bike on the turn. The gate was out of sight of the road. It swung open easily.

Ready to turn and flee at any moment, they cautiously drove onto the range and found it deserted.

"This is it," Ali declared. "We are on the base."

"But this is a Sunday," Karim pointed out. "We have to be sure the range will be empty when we arrive."

Ali shrugged. "I will just make another call to the Range Control."

It was a lovely crisp day riding through the old-growth pine forest. They became lost several times in the maze of unmarked tank trails and unimproved roads. Eventually they found the firing ranges and examined them thoroughly. After settling on the routes, they took markers from their packs. The commandos had covered small pieces of plywood with luminous paint from a hobby store. Ali and Karim nailed them to trees along the tank trails and road intersections so they would be able to find their way while driving at night. The plaques would not be noticed among the engineer's tape and ribbon marine units had left along the trail.

They left the training area the same way they had entered. Ali decided to drive farther down Route 6 to see what was there. They discovered two more dirt roads leading into the training area, and Ali marked them as backups. The mission completed, they turned and headed back.

After briefing the commandos on his plan, Ali spent the next week conducting nighttime rehearsals in the woods. The thick stand of pines behind the farmhouse provided them with both excellent concealment and an approximation of the Camp Lejeune training areas.

The following weekend, on Sunday night, Ali assembled the men who would make the reconnaissance and checked the gear they laid out on the living room floor. Mehdi had been sent to one of the several military-surplus stores in town to buy sets of American wood-land-pattern camouflage uniforms and caps. The recon teams would wear these for camouflage and to resemble marines if seen from a distance. Ali stressed that they must remain hidden in observation positions during daylight and move at night only. And they were not to use their weapons unless the situation was hopeless.

One man in each of the two recon teams was armed with a silenced Uzi. The rest carried AKMs, chest harnesses, and two grenades each. Newly purchased green civilian backpacks were stuffed with rations, rain gear, sleeping bags, and radios. Ali and Karim had found that the UHF signals were strong enough to be picked up at the farmhouse from as far away as the training areas.

Ali went over their briefing again until it was dark enough to move. They loaded into one of the pickups. Mehdi drove while Ali navigated and rode shotgun.

They entered the training area through the same empty range, following the luminous plaques. Ali was relieved to see that his marking system worked. A two-man team was dropped off near the K-305 range, to keep it under observation. The other four men were dropped off in the section of training area the lance corporal at Range Control said the marine company would be using. They would trail the marine unit, observe its habits, and locate its bivouac. When the last man disappeared into the brush, they turned around and tested the route out.

On Monday the spies drove away from the farm and returned that evening with two more standard-sized four-wheel-drive pickup trucks with plastic shells. Besides the five pickups, there was the panel truck Mahmoud had transported the chemicals and equipment in. It had been stripped of its Hi-Speed Trucking markings. In front of the house sat the Toyota Celica and Honda Civic Mehdi and Ghulam had purchased new to drive down from Virginia in. By now the barn was full, and the sergeant major was annoyed. "There is no place for me to lead calesthenics," he complained to Ali.

Ali could not help smiling. The men would be devastated to hear that. "Do not worry," he said. "We will leave soon."

"This week?" Musa asked.

Ali nodded. "Mehdi says there is talk that the FBI is asking questions all over the town. I want to be ready to move at a minute's notice."

"We have nearly everything packed up," Musa said. "What shall we do with the leftover explosive?"

"Two drums will go with us," said Ali. "So make room for them."

"There will be two drums left and almost another garbage can full. Adding the fertilizer made too much explosive to fit back into the original drums."

"Take all the glass food containers with tight-fitting lids," Ali ordered. "Fill them with explosive from the garbage can. We will find a use for it."

"And the drums?" Musa asked. "Shall I dump them?"

"No," Ali said. "I have an idea."

On Monday night he called the four *Baseej* into his room. They were Mustafa, Houshang, Hassan, and Selim. "Have you been treated well?" Ali asked. "Any problems?" They told him there were none, thank you, Sir.

"As you know," Ali said, "we are ready to move. You have all done well, but as you know only one will be required for this mission. Before I choose, I give each of you the opportunity to withdraw. You have my personal guarantee that nothing will be said of it, and you will be included in the third phase of the operation."

The four glanced at each other. Ali had intentionally brought them in together. He really did not want any to decline; it would only cause problems. He thought if there was a real coward among them, quitting in front of the group would not faze him. None of them said anything.

"Very well," Ali said. "Then Hassan will be my choice for the mission."

The others looked crestfallen. Hassan was a slightly

built boy who looked to be the youngest. Ali thought him the hardest worker and the most dedicated. The boy beamed as if he had won a prize at a festival. "Thank you, Sir!"

"No need to thank me," Ali said formally. "You others have my assurance that each of you will be given a chance to distinguish yourselves." At this they cheered up.

"That is all I have to say," Ali told them. "Unless there is anything you wish to talk to me about?"

There was not. They left the sewing room with each giving Hassan his congratulations.

Now Ali could only wait for the reconnaissance teams to radio in their periodic reports. Late Monday afternoon the four-man team saw marines drive into the training area on trucks. After a risky daylight movement that Ali authorized, the team reported that they had found the company and were tracking it. Based on the new intelligence, Ali made some last-minute changes to his plan.

Monday and Tuesday passed for the team overlooking the range, but they had nothing to report. Ali did not know what to do. They were packed and ready to go, and the recon teams had only one day's provisions left. Ali vowed to remain calm until Wednesday evening. It would have to be that night—the marines were scheduled to use the ranges the next two days.

Late Wednesday afternoon the team watching the range reported in. After writing down the message and giving the teams their orders, Ali walked into the living room, where the commandos had gathered. They were dressed in the one-piece green coveralls the spies had bought in Virginia. Underneath, the commandos wore civilian clothes in case of emergency. Their false documents and money were wrapped in plastic and secured in inner pockets. Their faces were blackened. Walkie-talkie holsters had been attached to the chest harnesses.

Most were cleaning Kalashnikovs for the hundredth time. They all looked up expectantly.

"It is a go," he said calmly. "Tonight."

After they carried Ali around the room the second time, he demanded they stop screaming and put him down at once.

CHAPTER 19

At 8:30 THAT evening, Special Agent Ken Maher slid into his FBI sedan and slammed the door shut. He turned on the dashboard light and put a mark next to one of the names and addresses on his computer printout. The large number still remaining caused him to sigh mournfully. Having the identical conversation with fifteen to thirty people every day was becoming disorienting. It wasn't good enough to interview these real estate agents at work during the day. MacNeil wanted it done fast, so Maher and the others had to visit some at home. The only way to get MacNeil off your back was to give him what he wanted. Everyone was pushing hard to pin this guy down, since MacNeil had promised that, if they didn't come up with anything in Jacksonville, they'd start checking real estate agents in all the outlying towns. Maher looked at his watch. Only Wednesday night and he was already exhausted. One more interview, and that was definitely it.

The address was in one of those new generic developments where the houses are identical and the streets laid out so that no matter which way you turn, you always end up in the same place. Maher had to stop at nearly every intersection to consult his map before he found the house. He took a minute to gather up his materials and put himself in the proper frame of mind. It helped to be extra nice when you bugged people in their homes after dinner.

The porch light snapped on, and a marine answered

the door. He wasn't in uniform, but the haircut made his occupation quite evident. Before Maher could open his mouth, he said gruffly, "If you're selling anything, I'm not interested."

Maher aired his ID out in front of the marine's face. "I'm Special Agent Maher, FBI."

The marine peered at the ID, and his face suddenly flushed. "Oh, shit. I'm sorry, what can I do for you, sir?"

Maher smiled to put him at ease. "I need to speak to Laura Jackson."

"That's my wife. What's it all about?"

"I just need to ask her a few questions. May I come in?"

"Sure," the marine said, worried but moving automatically now that he was dealing with a higher authority. "Come on in. I'm Jeff Jackson." He shook hands and ushered Maher into the living room and onto the couch. "Can I get you some coffee?"

"That would be great, thanks."

Mr. Jackson returned with coffee and an attractive blond woman in her middle twenties. Maher stood up.

"Hello," she said brightly. "Am I in any trouble?"

"Not at all," said Maher, accepting the coffee and smiling back at her. "A man we're looking for might have bought a house around here recently, and we'd appreciate it if you'd look at some pictures."

"Of course," she said. "But why don't you just check the records at all the agencies?"

"He may have used a name we're not familiar with," Maher explained.

"I'm sorry, you must think I'm pretty foolish."

"Not at all," Maher said gallantly. He handed her a stack of ten photographs. They were large prints, eight by tens. All had been transferred from videotape, so interviewees couldn't focus on anything unusual about the quality of the photographs; they could concentrate on just the faces.

She went through the photos, looking carefully at

each one. Maher leaned back and sipped his coffee. Why couldn't they all be as easy as this? She stopped abruptly at the next-to-the-last photo. "I sold this man a house," Laura Jackson said.

Maher nearly dropped the coffee in his lap. "Are you positive?"

"Yes, I even remember his name. Mr. Bradford. I sold him an old farm about a month ago. I remember, because there was no mortgage. He paid the full amount with a certified check. He seemed to be a very nice man. Has he done something awful?"

"May I use your phone?" Maher asked quickly.

Richard Welsh flipped through the channels of the television in his room at the Jacksonville, North Carolina, Holiday Inn, searching for something to occupy himself. He had just returned from the hotel lounge, having confirmed that things hadn't changed much. It was still largely populated by marines' wives whose husbands were on deployment and who had somehow lost their wedding rings. But to be fair, Welsh had done two deployments, and he knew infidelity cut both ways. He left after one beer. He drew the line at both married women and betraying marines.

TV was hopeless. Welsh pulled a book from his traveling stash and threw himself on the bed. He'd taken a lot of shit in the corps for his literary tastes, but there even readers of military history were few and far between— the commandant might have wanted a corps of thinkers, but what he wanted didn't carry much weight with the people who had to make things happen every day. The good ones were spread so thin and worked so hard they barely had time for their families, let alone books, and everyone else was too busy chasing their own ass in circles. Welsh settled down with a paperback Joseph Conrad, definitely one of those things in life worth taking shit for.

He was just beginning to reread *Nostromo* when the

phone rang. He thought briefly about bagging the call, then picked up.

"We've got the safe house," MacNeil announced on the other end. "Get out to the parking lot, there's a car waiting for you."

"Why don't I drive myself instead of tying up one of your cars?" Welsh suggested.

"I want to keep the vehicles down to a minimum. Hurry up and get moving. Oh, and plan on being outside overnight." MacNeil clicked off.

With the speed of a man who had learned to dress in fifteen seconds flat in Officer Candidate School, Welsh threw on lightweight polypro long underwear and blue jeans, and a sweater. A Goretex parka in a woodland camouflage pattern would go over it—one of the very few decent items of clothing ever issued by the U.S. military. He stuffed the Goretex trousers into the daypack he always brought with him, along with binoculars, thermos, notebook, camera, Mini Mag-Lite flashlight, and *Nostromo*. Over his long underwear top he added a Second Chance armored vest with ballistic inserts. The body armor had never been worn but was always packed for an occasion such as this. Welsh considered it simple prudence, but it was definitely not something he'd want MacNeil to know about.

Welsh made a last trip to the bathroom, grabbed his gear, and locked the door behind him.

CHAPTER 20

LANCE CORPORAL JIM CRAIG was cold, tired, and pissed off. It wasn't enough that he was stuck guarding a load of ammo at night in the middle of the boonies—he had to be doing it with Corporal Davies. And Corporal Davies was a shitbag, pure and simple. Craig didn't doubt for a minute that Davies had fucked something up and was out there for punishment, same as him. Having to be dragged out of bed past reveille three days in a row, on top of failing an inspection, were the causes of Craig's exile to the K-305 range, where he was freezing his balls off.

It really wasn't fair, Craig thought. They told us it was just a uniform inspection. How was I supposed to know the captain was going to open up my wall locker?

When the company commander had popped the handle to open LCpl. Craig's wall locker, a week's worth of unwashed laundry and accumulated possessions had exploded from it at impressive velocity, to the keen embarrassment of Craig's platoon commander, platoon sergeant, squad leader, and fire team leader. Understandably, the ass chewings worked their way down the chain of command until they came to rest on Craig—to use the marine terminology, the shit rolled downhill—and Craig found himself living in the valley. Along with other and sundry tasks and punishments, some quite creative, he was banished to the field to guard ammunition in the spring frost. It was almost midnight, and it was fucking cold—a weather phenomenon well known to infantrymen.

What the fuck, thought Craig, pushing his boots nearer the fire. Just the same old shit. He was stacking more wood on the flames when Corporal Davies crawled out from the shelter half and rummaged around for his canteen cup. Typical, Craig thought bitterly. The motherfucker spends all day in his fucking sleeping bag and only comes out now that I've built a fire. The pile of wood began to catch, and the heat forced him to back away.

Davies placed the canteen cup of water at the edge of Craig's inferno, glancing up as Craig walked around a pile of wooden boxes stacked together thirty feet from the crude campsite. "What's going on, Craig?"

"Nothing."

"That's, 'nothing, Corporal Davies,' Lance Corporal."

"Nothing, *Corporal* Davies," Craig parroted.

"If you want, Craig, instead of sleeping tonight, you can dig all the fighting positions the company is gonna need."

"That's okay, Corporal Davies." The chickenshit son of a bitch made corporal on sea duty, some fucking sub tender, and out in the bush he didn't know his ass from a two-hole shitter. Craig had been on two deployments and was still a lance corporal. The injustice was almost too much to take.

"Hey, Corporal Davies, why don't they just draw the ammo from the dump tomorrow, if that's when we're going to shoot? That way we wouldn't have to sit out here."

"Because the lieutenant told me the ammo dump doesn't open 'til 0730, and it would take until noon to get all this stuff loaded, checked out, and moved across the river. The captain wants to start shooting at 0700, so that's why we're here."

"Okay," said Craig as he walked back around the ammo pile. The dumbshit wouldn't know whether it was right or wrong, just that the lieutenant told him. One thing was right though, it was a shitload of ammo. There was 5.56mm ball and tracer for M16s, a lot of 5.56mm linked in belts for the Squad Automatic Weapons, linked 7.62mm for the machine guns, 60mm mortar shells, AT-4 antitank rockets, and 40mm high-explosive dual-purpose rounds for the M203 grenade launchers. There was a can of smoke grenades and hand-launched pop-up flares. And on top of the pile were six cases of frag grenades, thirty grenades to a case. Craig momentarily brightened at the thought of them. With that many grenades they were probably going to shoot on the close combat ranges. The ranges were shit-hot: You threw live grenades in rooms and followed up with live rifle fire; there was a simulated city street with pop-up targets; and a live-fire obstacle course. Craig imagined they'd shoot everything else here on K-305. Then his funk returned; they'd probably stick him on radio watch.

Ammo for training was a much lower priority in the budget than expensive weapons. The ammo pile Craig was babysitting contained much more ammunition than a rifle company would normally shoot at one time. But the company had been on regimental guard duty and hadn't gone out to the field for a while. The new fiscal quarter was approaching, and the company commander was going to use this ammo up before the next quarter's allocation wiped it off the books. Craig arranged some ammo crates into a seat and decided to relax. There was still an hour before Davies took over the duty and Craig could grab some sleep.

Craig must have been dozing—he was startled by a loud snap in the brush that separated K-305 from the next range. He stood up and listened carefully. Hearing nothing else, he sat back down and lit a cigarette, shivering from the cold. He was acting like a damn PFC. He walked over to the nearest tree to take a piss.

Craig slung the M16 across his back, but it kept banging on the tree branches. He finally rested it against a nearby tree—didn't want to get piss on it. After fighting with the buttons of his fly, he leaned back and grunted with pleasure as the warm flow hit the cold tree trunk and steam began to rise.

Karim's team had spent thirty minutes making its way through the short treeline. It wasn't easy; the ground was covered with sticks of dry pine that popped like firecrackers if trod on. One of the commandos had just stepped on one. The sergeant major, who had been leading, stopped the column to have a few whispered words with the offender. Halted in the tangle of trees and undergrowth that separated the ranges, they were close enough to see the campfire burning but far enough away to communicate without being heard. Karim took the opportunity to call Ali on the walkie-talkie. "Team 1 to Command, we are in position. Over."

Ali's voice came through: "I read you. Stand by." He was with the five pickup trucks, parked half a mile away on a tank trail. "Security 1, report."

"All clear," reported the first two-man security team, watching the north side of the road that led to K-305.

Ali pressed the talk button. "Very good. S2, report."

"All clear," came the answer from the two-man team watching the road south of K-305.

"Understood," Ali replied. "Team 1, clear to go. Over."

"Acknowledged," whispered Karim. "We are proceeding."

Karim pushed the microphone back under his chin. Musa had been listening over his own headset and gave Karim thumbs-up. The sergeant major quietly led the two commandos to positions just inside the treeline, where they could cover the movement. Then he and Karim quickly checked their weapons, made sure their gear was tight, and began crawling slowly through the tall dead grass toward the fire.

• • •

Preoccupied with his task, Craig didn't notice a figure move behind a tree to his right. Then, as the stream trailed off, he noticed movement in his peripheral vision. The shape moved up on him incredibly fast. Craig forgot to yell a challenge while diving for his M16 and tearing at the magazine pouch, trying to get a loaded magazine out and into his weapon. The shape turned into a man who kicked him in the solar plexus. Craig tried to yell but couldn't get any air out. All he managed was a rattling wheeze. The sergeant major grabbed at Craig's hair, but it was too short for him to get a good grip. He compensated by getting a hold on the forehead and pulling Craig's head back. Musa punched his bayonet into the side of Craig's throat, slashing forward and out. There was a cascade of blood and terrible gurgling noises as Craig's windpipe and carotid artery were cut. He could not shout, and would be dead in less than a minute. Musa dropped on the marine's back to stop the final desperate thrashing. He listened carefully to discover whether the struggle had attracted the other marine's attention.

Corporal Davies had been gazing into the fire. He heard a noise and needed a moment to remember exactly where he was. He stood up but couldn't see Craig —the tarpaulin-covered ammo pile blocked his view. "Goddamn Craig, fucking around again," he grumbled. He walked around the fire and raised his voice. "Hey, Craig! Where the fuck are you?" There was no answer, and a wave of anger surged through him. The little shit was behind a tree sleeping. Craig was like the rest of them, trying him out because he was new. Well, he knew how to be an NCO, and Craig was going to find that out.

Corporal Davies was perfectly silhouetted as he walked in front of the fire to get his rifle and go tear Craig a new asshole. Karim had swung around to Musa's left and was lying quietly in a depression near the observation bleachers. He aimed at the marine's knees; held his breath; and gently squeezed the trigger of the suppressed Uzi, quickly releasing it and squeezing four more times. He got off five five-round bursts in less than seven seconds. Of the twenty-five 9mm rounds, ten hit Corporal Davies from the right thigh to the left chest. The rest flew unnoticed downrange. With the suppressor the firing noise was only slightly louder than an air rifle. The only other sounds were the rapid clicking of the Uzi's action, the thump of the bullets' impact, and the popping of burning wood as the marine fell into the fire. There was no muzzle flash.

After making sure Craig was dead, Musa had rolled behind the tree. He waited for a moment to be sure Corporal Davies didn't move, and then got up and trotted over to the fire. As he approached he snapped his fingers at Karim, so as not to be mistaken for a target. Karim had inserted a new magazine and was covering the area near the fire. He snapped back. Musa moved cautiously to the fire and examined Corporal Davies. Davies was alive, but only barely, and his camouflage jacket was smoldering in the coals. Musa pulled the marine out of the fire; Davies, at the edge of consciousness, smiled gratefully. Unstrapping the webbing that held it tight against his body, Musa brought out his Uzi and fired two rounds, single shot, into the corporal's skull. The sergeant major slung his weapon and felt the fading pulse. When it stopped, he took out a blue-filtered flashlight and blinked twice at the treeline. The two commandos trotted onto the range and moved to cover the road.

Karim walked up and unlimbered the walkie-talkie. "Command, this is Team 1. Springtime. Over." It was the code word that signaled success.

Ali's jubilant voice came over. "Understood. Security teams, any movement?"

"S1. Negative."

"S2. Negative."

"Understood," Ali radioed. "Team 1, we are coming in."

"Acknowledged," replied Karim. He got Musa's attention and motioned toward the two commandos. "Our people are coming in." Musa nodded, and walked over to relay the news.

Five minutes later the trucks pulled onto the range, headlights off. The drivers parked them behind the observation bleachers, out of sight from the road. Ali jumped from the cab of the first truck and greeted Musa and Karim. "Excellent work," he said, surveying the scene. "Just excellent." He turned to Karim. "I want equal amounts of each type of ammunition spread between the last two trucks. Put two cans of rifle ammunition in my vehicle. Oh, and wrap the bodies in the sheet that covered the ammunition and put them under these seats." He gestured toward the bleachers.

"At once," replied Karim.

Ali took Musa by the arm and led him over to the truck. "Were there any problems?" he asked quietly.

"No, none."

Ali nodded and spoke into the microphone of his walkie-talkie. "Team 2, this is Command. Over." There was no response. With a look of concern on his face, Ali tried again. Still nothing. On the third attempt he received a whispered reply.

"This is Team 2. Over."

Ali breathed a sigh of relief. "Status report. Over."

"In position in ten minutes," came the whispered reply.

"Understood," Ali replied. "Keep me informed." He called the recon team watching the marine bivouac. They reported that, as far as they could tell, all the marines were present and there was very little movement in the camp.

"We will just have to wait," Musa said. "There is no sense in rushing their movement." Ali nodded nervously; he hated being exposed out on the range. He walked off a few steps and urinated on the sand, paced for a moment, then sat on the hood. Musa rested on the sand, leaning against a tire.

A few minutes later Karim came over with Hafiz to report that the trucks were loaded. "Very good," Ali said. He motioned toward the two corpses. "Did you get their weapons and ammunition?"

"Yes," said Karim.

"Are you clear on the rendezvous?" Ali asked him, ignoring Hafiz, who walked over to the bodies.

"Of course," said Karim, not sensing his commander's anxiety. There was the sound of retching. Hafiz had obviously pulled back the tarpaulin.

"Then leave now," Ali said. He pointed to Hafiz. "And take this with you. I do not think he can stand the sight of blood." Then, haltingly, "God go with you."

"And you also," said Karim.

A few minutes later the walkie-talkie static broke four times. "They are ready," Ali said.

"They have sense," said Musa, climbing into the driver's seat of the pickup, "not to speak when they are so close."

"Are you ready?" asked Ali, trying to hide the fact that his hand was shaking. Musa nodded and started the truck. Ali called the assault and security teams and told them the trucks were moving.

They stopped at the road to pick up Security Teams 1 and 2, which had been watching the road on either side of the firing range. The four commandos climbed into the truck bed, leaving the rear hatch open in case they needed to get out in a hurry.

The three trucks sped down the dirt access road until they came upon an asphalt road. The drivers switched on their headlights and turned right, toward the second objective of the evening.

CHAPTER 21

First Lieutenant Paul Ramsey leaned back against a dead log and wrapped a poncho around his legs, trying to stay warm while he waited for his platoon commanders to show up.

Echo Company was bivouacked for the night in two-man shelter halves, arranged in four neat rows in the middle of a large clearing. Ramsey thought it was Mickey Mouse bullshit, but the company commander wanted it that way—end of discussion. Off to one side of the clearing was the company command post, its center-piece the captain's CP tent, big enough to hold four cots with ease. Ramsey wanted to throw up every time he looked at it. That goddamned tent! Captain Pleister, the last company commander, had been a real hard charger —travel light and move fast, tactical all the time. Everyone carried only ponchos and quilted nylon poncho liners for protection against the elements. And the company's CP tent had gathered dust in the supply warehouse.

The present commanding officer—CO—of Echo Company, Captain Doylan, had recently arrived from Quantico, Virginia, and Amphibious Warfare School. It had been six long years since he'd served in an infantry battalion. As the company executive officer, the second in command, Ramsey had tried to convince Doylan not to take the tent. The captain told him that, after ten years in the grunts, he wasn't going to sleep on the ground if he didn't have to. So the troops slept on the

ground and the captain and the company gunnery sergeant slept on cots. The gunny was a good man, but he
wasn't going to fight the new CO. It made Ramsey
seethe. What bullshit.

In the early days of Doylan's command, Ramsey
thought the captain was just establishing his authority.
After all, everyone had different ways of doing things.
But now Ramsey had come to the conclusion that not
only was the captain a lousy leader, he was also an in-
competent pussy. The first time Doylan led the company
on a forced march, it had taken him four hours to go
only eight miles, a humiliating pace. Afterward, Doylan
was so wiped out that he had retreated to his tent for a
nap while the platoon commanders conducted the training. Now the company rode trucks to the field whenever
it could be arranged. The lieutenants were appalled. Not
only did marine officers consider weakness the worst
human disease of all, but it had been branded into them
from the first day of their training that officers led from
the front and set the example. And here was the company commander, the standard bearer, bringing up the
fucking rear.

The first two days of training had been uneventful.
Today, Wednesday, was a little different. Early in the
afternoon the captain had taken the humvee utility vehicle to the rear for a couple of hours and observed the
training when he'd returned. It hadn't escaped the marines' attention that he'd showered and changed clothes.
One of the first things Ramsey had learned as a boot
lieutenant was that nothing of that nature *ever* escaped a
marine's attention. Now the CO and the gunny were
asleep in the tent—Captain Doylan didn't like to do
much night training—and Ramsey decided it was time to
have a little talk with the platoon commanders. They'd
been grumbling lately, and it was time to get them
squared away.

The platoon commanders approached him in a group.

An ominous sign, it meant they had already been talking.

"XO, we've talked this over, and we want to request mast," announced 2d Lt. Bob Hartman, the Weapons Platoon commander. He had obviously been appointed the group's spokesman.

Ramsey was incredulous. They had to be bullshitting him. "First of all," he said quickly, "keep your fucking voices down. Now, who are you idiots planning on requesting mast to? The battalion commander? The regimental commander? Maybe the division commander? Or are you going to cut out all the deadwood and go right to the commandant?" He was smiling; they weren't.

"We're not kidding," 2d Lt. Al Hanna, the 3d Platoon commander, said angrily.

"Sit down," said Ramsey, trying to sound reasonable. They didn't move. "Sit the fuck down," he said. They sat.

"Look," Ramsey explained, "you're second lieutenants. You can't go to the battalion commander and fucking demand that your CO be relieved just because he's a brokedick."

"Then what do we do?" asked 2d Lt. Ray Ames, the 2d Platoon commander. "The company is going to shit faster by the minute. We used to be the best in the battalion; now everyone just laughs at us."

"You do your fucking job," said Ramsey. "You take care of your platoon. That's how you keep the company going. You go to the colonel and say you want the captain fired because he's a pencilneck, you'll be lucky if he just throws your mutinous little asses out of his office. You're going to be putting your own dicks on the chopping block." He glared at them; they were staring at the ground. "Who told you fuckers you could pick your boss anyway? If the colonel wants Doylan relieved, he'll do it. Look," he said, in a softer tone, "Captain Pleister spoiled you guys. You don't find many like him. He was a real stud warrior. You've got to face it—there are only a few of them around."

"But Jesus," moaned Hanna. "This guy is such a dildo. Look at this fucking bivouac. It looks like a fucking Boy Scout jamboree out here. He even made the gunny use string so the rows of shelter halves would be even."

"Look," said Ramsey, "after your first tour as a lieutenant, you spend four to six years out of the game. When these captains come back to a battalion, they're rusty as hell and all freaked out—after six years behind a desk they've got to impress the colonel quick so they can get promoted to major and not get thrown out of the corps on their asses. Give Doylan a little time. Maybe he'll straighten out."

"It still sucks," Hanna said bitterly.

"Semper Fi," said Ramsey. "The one good thing is that, if we're lucky, we only have to put up with him for a year."

"That can be a long fucking time," said Ames.

"We're stuck with him," said Ramsey. "Now listen, if you guys really want to fuck up this unit, then keep walking around pissing and moaning. Then we'll really be in trouble. Besides, we run the company anyway—we'll keep things on the right track. Okay?"

"Okay, XO," Hartman said. The others nodded in agreement.

"You coming to our party this weekend?" Hanna asked.

Ramsey was relieved that he'd been able to head them off. They were still green—full of the way things were supposed to be, instead of the way they really were. Shit, second lieutenants were supposed to wear their hearts on their sleeves. They kept the corps honest. And first lieutenants were supposed to keep them from stepping on their dicks. "I don't know," he said. "Are you having it at that whorehouse you live in on the beach?"

"Why do you ask?" Hanna said with a grin, knowing what was coming.

"Because the last time I was over there you scared the living piss out of me before I even got in the fucking door."

"Oh, that," said Hanna. "C'mon."

"Yeah, c'mon. I'm a little funny. It's not every day I get greeted on the porch by a naked guy pointing a Ruger Mini-14 between my eyes."

"I was just out of the shower," Hanna shrugged. "We'd been having a little trouble with the neighbors, and I thought you were an intruder."

"Besides, XO," Ames grinned wickedly, "there was no harm done. You chilled right out after you had a few beers . . . and cleaned the shit out of your skivvies!" The others exploded into hysterical laughter, giving high fives and rolling on the ground.

"You guys wear my ass out," said Ramsey. He couldn't keep himself from smiling. "When I was a second lieutenant I was crazy, but you fuckers make me feel like the chaperone at the high school dance. I feel like your goddamned uncle."

"You *are* our uncle," said Ames, deadpan.

"Fuck you," Ramsey retorted.

Just then Ramsey noticed three sets of headlights coming toward them from the nearby tank trail. The vehicles pulled into the entrance of the bivouac area, but the company's humvee utility vehicle in the middle of the trail kept them from going any farther. Ramsey shaded his eyes from the headlights. "Who could that be at this time of night?"

"They look like CUCVs," said Hanna. CUCVs, pronounced "cuck vees," were civilian pickup trucks used by the military.

"But CUCVs don't have shells," Ames observed.

"They're probably lost, let's go see who it is," said Ramsey. They rose and walked toward the trucks.

• • •

In the pickup, Ali turned to the sergeant major. "We must draw in anyone walking about. I want them close enough to make sure of."

"Yes, Colonel," Musa sighed, in the way of senior enlisted men when officers instruct them in the obvious.

"Here," Ali said, oblivious to his tone, "this is the turn. Make a left, and we should see their vehicles immediately on the right." Musa braked and cut the wheel, skidding a little as they made the transition from asphalt road to the loose sand of the tank trail.

Ali looked behind to make sure the other two trucks were with them. "There, pull in behind their vehicle." He cocked the Uzi, made sure the magazine was seated properly, and gave the suppressor a twist. He extended the folding stock and slid the weapon across the seat, gently placing it in Musa's lap. "The safety is on," he said.

"There is a group off to the left," Musa said.

"Do not come out until their attention is focused on me," said Ali, checking his pistol. His AKM was lying on the floor next to his feet. "Use the open door to mask your movements, and keep the weapon behind your thigh."

"Yes, Colonel."

Ali brought the walkie-talkie microphone up to his mouth. "Team 2, do you read me? Over." The static broke twice, the assault team signaling yes. "Are you ready? Over." The static broke twice. "Understood. Stand by."

Two men got out of the lead truck, the first from the passenger's side and the other from the driver's. The first was dressed in marine camouflage utilities. The second stood out of sight behind the open door. Still shading his eyes from the headlights, Ramsey couldn't see the marine's rank, so he decided to be polite and let the man know his. "I'm Lieutenant Ramsey. What can we do for you?"

As if in response, Ali snapped his fingers. Musa rested the silenced Uzi on the doorframe and fired short bursts into each of the officers. He was so quick, and they so stunned, that they dropped where they were standing. Musa quickly changed magazines and ran toward the CP tent. Ali shouted "Go, Go, Go!" into the walkie-talkie microphone. To make sure the message had gotten through to everyone, he put a whistle to his mouth and blew two long blasts.

The assault team of eleven Iranian commandos burst from the edge of the clearing and ran to the rows of shelter halves. Two commandos stood astride each row, with three slightly behind to cover them and prevent anyone from escaping—one man in the middle and one on each flank.

It is a Marine Corps tradition that an unarmed night-time security watch be mounted in garrison and bivouac. Because of the danger of fire in crowded barracks, this duty has always been known as a firewatch. The Echo Company firewatch had halted his tour of the bivouac to chat with three marines sitting in front of a small fire built between the rows of shelters. As they saw the lieutenants shot and the attackers emerge from the trees, the four Americans jumped to their feet and ran toward the edge of the clearing and the trees bordering the road. All they could do was run; most marine units did not carry live ammunition for protection while training at Camp Lejeune.

The Iranians had placed a two-man stop group in the trees at the far edge of the clearing, just off to one side. The group was out of the attackers' line of fire but positioned to cut down anyone trying to escape the clearing and reach the road. The two commandos sighted carefully and fired their Kalashnikovs into the running marines. The cover men of the assault team also opened up. The lines of tracer bullets from the two groups reached out, wavering slightly as the shooters came on target, and quickly converged on the group of marines. The runners dropped reaching for the treeline, still fifteen feet away. There were other marine units in the area, but the sound of gunfire at night is common at Camp Lejeune. Several ricochets flew into the air, but no one noticed that the tracer bullets were Soviet green instead of American red. Ali stood in the trail, watching the action and monitoring the walkie-talkie, keeping an eye on the CP tent in case Musa needed any help—which he doubted.

The shelter halves started to shake as marines woke up and struggled to get out and see what was going on. The AKM gunners walked down the rows, firing short automatic bursts into each shelter half. When a commando needed to change magazines, he signaled his backup man to keep up the fire. It was over quickly. At the end of one row, a marine tried to get out of his shelter half and escape, but a backup man shot him before he could stand up and start running. When the attackers finished, they changed magazines and listened for any movement. When they heard rustling in a shelter half, one would walk over and fire a short burst into it.

By this time the four Iranians riding in the back of the lead pickup made their way to the marine humvee to move it off the trail. The driver and company corpsman had been sleeping inside. The Iranians found them playing dead and pulled them out of the humvee to be shot, to avoid damaging the vehicle. After a moment of study, a commando managed to start the engine and drive the humvee into the clearing. The other three walked back to the pickups to guide them in, since Ali had insisted the headlights remain off.

The Iranians in the third pickup were guarding the entrance to the bivouac site. The three security men relieved them at the entrance so the truck driver could move the vehicle into the clearing to join the others.

From the CP tent the sergeant major walked over to the pickups, straining under a load of PRC-77 backpack radios. He wore a marine camouflage hat on his head, a souvenir. Smiling, he dumped the radios on a tailgate and went back for more booty. The drivers covered the area with their weapons while the assault team formed into pairs and moved down the rows again. One held a flashlight and AKM while the other slit open the side of a shelter half and removed the occupants' weapons. The dead marines' webbing was dropped into plastic garbage bags.

Musa stripped the CP tent of everything useful, picking up all the radio batteries he could find. He left the blank ammunition but took the pop-up flares and smoke grenades.

Ali stationed himself near the pickups, examining the weapons as they were loaded and making sure they were evenly distributed among the vehicles. He called one of the team leaders over. "Make sure they get all the cleaning equipment and spare barrels for the machine guns," he said. "And especially the accessories for the mortars. Leave nothing behind." The team leader dashed off to tell the others.

When all the weapons and gear were loaded, Musa walked over to Ali. "Shall we drop the Kalashnikovs?" he asked. "There is very little ammunition left."

"No. We will leave them nothing but their dead."

Now each of the Iranians had an M16A2 rifle, and they loaded magazines from the two ammo cans of 5.56mm ball ammunition saved from the attack on the range.

The commandos stripped off the green coveralls, exposing sweat-soaked civilian clothes. They threw their bloody gloves into a plastic garbage bag. They climbed into the trucks as Ali counted heads, making sure everyone was present. The bulk of the weapons left little room for passengers in the beds of the pickups; the commandos were wedged in uncomfortably. They sat on the discarded coveralls to cushion the hard metal, wrapping themselves in blankets to keep warm. Ali was the last to board. He stripped off his camouflage uniform and

made a final flashlight check of the ground in case anything important had been dropped. Then he climbed
into the front seat of the lead pickup, accepting the congratulations of Mehdi, who was driving. Musa took the
front seat in the last truck.

With the headlights still off, they drove down the tank
trail, stopping to pick up the two-man security team.
From the tank trail they turned onto the main asphalt
road. Only then did they switch on the headlights. Ali
looked at his watch. It was ten minutes past 2:00 in the
morning. Including the strike on the range, the action
had taken just under two hours.

The pickups did not head toward the only gate and its
MP guard; the Iranians drove deeper into the training
area. Carefully following his map, Ali ordered Mehdi to
turn onto a sandy tank trail. After pausing to shift into
four-wheel drive, they moved steadily. When they hit
intersections with other trails, they followed the luminous plaques nailed to the trees. The trails were loose
sand, and the trucks heavily loaded. When they bounced
over humps, Ali could hear the rattling of weapons and
muted cursing from the back. Several times the drivers
narrowly avoided getting stuck in the sand, provoking
more obscene comments from the passengers.

Finally the trucks emerged onto the impact area of
the unoccupied firing range. Mehdi was momentarily
startled when the headlights played over the targets on
the range; it looked like real soldiers were waiting for
them. After a slight hesitation they raced up the range
access road, past the firing berms and control tower. Ali
directed Mehdi to a right turn onto the asphalt road that
would lead them off the range. Mehdi, still spooked
from the targets, was going too fast and nearly collided
with a bewildered herd of white-tailed deer frozen by the
headlights. He slammed on the brakes, and the truck
almost spun off the road. Ali braced himself against the
dashboard and closed his eyes, waiting for the other

trucks to smash into them. The heavy brakes of the pick-ups stopped them just in time.

Ali turned to Mehdi, whose knuckles were white on the steering wheel. He began speaking quietly and deliberately, his voice reaching its upper register toward the end. "We have not gone through all this, just to have it end because of *stupid driving. Do you understand?*" Mehdi nodded quickly.

"Then continue," Ali said, this time in a normal tone of voice. "And keep your wits about you."

The gate was fifty meters down the road. Ali got out to open it. Two hundred meters past the gate the trucks left Camp Lejeune and pulled out onto North Carolina Route 6.

CHAPTER 22

IT WAS SLOWLY beginning to get light. Rich Welsh stood beside an old pine, watching the world take shape. The temperature was in the thirties, but he was warm in his parka. Welsh had spent most of the night in an FBI van reading Conrad, but he felt claustrophobic and decided he'd be much more comfortable out in the open air. He reached inside his pack and poured a cup of coffee from the thermos. Now that it was dawn, he thought he ought to walk over to the communications van and see what the FBI had decided to do.

There were four vans and three cars in a small clearing out of sight and hearing from the farmhouse. After the FBI did some sneaking and peeking in the woods, they brought the vehicles up the plow road that led to the back of the house. The long driveway in front was useless for their purposes, since it offered a clear view to the main road. But there were teams a quarter mile up and down that road to cut off any escape. There was also a hidden roadblock on the plow road to bag anyone driving up that way before they could make it to the house. Virtually every agent in the FBI's North Carolina field office was somewhere in the vicinity, along with the dozen MacNeil had brought down from Washington.

MacNeil was just outside the communications van, talking with a group of agents, including one in a black jumpsuit. Welsh recognized him as the special agent in charge of the FBI Hostage Rescue Team. The team members had arrived in Jacksonville at 3:00 that morning by helicopter from the FBI Academy at Quantico, Virginia. MacNeil had been keeping them on alert. The Hostage Rescue Team (HRT) was responsible for counterterrorist operations in the United States, with Special Operations Command oriented toward missions overseas.

In the late seventies, hostage rescue was all the rage, and the bureau got into the game to protect its domestic law enforcement turf from the military units that were then forming. To its credit, it went to the very best for help—the British Special Air Service Regiment. In the early eighties the HRT had been counted among the best-trained forces of its type in the world, but the FBI brass couldn't understand why they should keep fifty agents waiting around for something that might never happen when they could be out crushing crime. So it was decided to assign HRT personnel other duties and only bring the team together periodically. The bureau eventually realized that this course was disastrous and went back to a full-time force. But, like every other counterterrorist unit, the HRT still had problems with personnel turbulence and maintaining proficiency during long stretches of inactivity.

Welsh had been trying for over a week to get permission for a team from SOCOM's J3, the operations and planning section, to come down and observe. The normal drill was to send observers only when a U.S. hostage incident had already occurred, so there was a bitch about travel authorizations and whether observation was really necessary. Welsh had argued that if an incident went down, there probably wouldn't be enough time to send the J3 team. He prevailed, but the people hadn't arrived yet.

Welsh walked up to the group. The wind was with him, and the aroma of coffee preceded him. The FBI men began sniffing the air like bird dogs.

"Is that coffee?" one asked.

Welsh passed the large thermos cup around. "Aaaah," another agent sighed, taking in a large draft.

Welsh grinned. "This is the same guy who was pissing and moaning when I made him stop to get my thermos filled."

"We're tough and hard," the HRT commander said, winking at Welsh. "We don't need luxuries like hot coffee."

"Speak for yourself," said MacNeil, taking his turn at the cup.

"What's happening?" asked Welsh.

MacNeil gave everyone a subtle nod to go ahead. Welsh smiled. The fucker didn't need vocal cords.

"We've got the farmhouse all scoped out," said the HRT commander.

Welsh took back the coffee cup. "What's inside?"

"We couldn't get close; it's open ground all around the house. Thermal scan didn't tell us much. All the lights are on, and the imager picked up a lot of heat from appliances. There may be bodies in there, but we can't be sure."

"What about sound?" asked Welsh.

"We used a parabolic mike," said the HRT commander. "And we bounced a beam off the windows."

Welsh nodded. A laser beam directed at glass picked up vibrations caused by sound inside a room. With the right conditions, you could hear everything.

"At least two TVs and a radio are on, upstairs and down," continued the HRT commander. "And loud. They're drowning everything else out."

"So we don't know if anyone's in there," said Welsh.

"There's two cars out front," said MacNeil. "We just couldn't get close enough to use the more sophisticated equipment. I doubt they went off and left *everything* on."

"So what are you going to do?" Welsh asked him.

"We're going in as soon as we get just a little more light," said MacNeil.

"What's the hurry?" said Welsh.

"I've got the Sheriff's Department and the rest of North Carolina on my back," said MacNeil. "I could deal with that, but either they made too much noise or they leaked, because I hear we've got press on the way."

"And any of the boys we're looking for who happened to be out of the house is going to run into the whole circus later on this morning," said Welsh.

"Exactly," MacNeil said angrily. "It'll be a mess, and I'm not going to wait around to have that happen."

"When exactly are you going to move?" Welsh asked.

"Half an hour," said the HRT commander. "We're all briefed, rehearsed, and ready to go."

"You don't think there are any hostages, do you?"

MacNeil shook his head. "But we'll give them a chance to surrender first. We'll find out then."

"I'm not a big fan of giving them fair warning," said Welsh. The FBI had a mindset toward effecting an arrest and shooting only as a last resort. That was fine for bank robbers, but terrorists were something entirely different. The military units had no such scruples; they were trained to locate, close with, and destroy the enemy.

The HRT commander shrugged. "If there are hostages, we'll pull back, begin negotiations, and wear them down before we move. If not, we'll use gas and go in hard, a simple clearing operation. That's why we're ready now. You don't have to cut things as fine if there aren't hostages."

"Too bad the boys from SOCOM aren't here yet," said Welsh. "They'd enjoy this."

At 6:15, MacNeil, Welsh, and the senior agents were crouched behind a low stone wall that marked the edge of the woods. They had a clear view of the farmhouse. Mindful of the bureau's image, MacNeil had allowed a network camera crew to tape the operation. They had agreed to pool their pictures. The crew's requests to transmit live and to accompany the Hostage Rescue Team on the assault had been denied. The camera crew was hidden nearby, with an agent watching to make sure they didn't get into any trouble.

Twenty feet down the wall were several HRT sniper teams. They worked in pairs—a sniper and a spotter. The teams had removed the lower stones from the wall, so they could fire from the prone and under cover. They wore walkie-talkie headsets with voice-activated microphones, to keep their hands free. The radios had encrypted channels, so no one else could listen in. They were using the Marine Corps M40A1 sniper rifle, a customized heavy barrel Remington bolt action, chambered for the 7.62 × 51mm NATO cartridge. Welsh wasn't surprised. The Marine Corps scout-sniper instructor school, the very best in the business, was just down the road from the FBI Academy at Quantico.

At 6:18, MacNeil picked up a microphone lying beside him. When he pressed the button and began talking, his voice went through a line of amplifiers back in the woods. With all those watts behind him, Welsh thought MacNeil sounded like God. Welsh hoped the creeps in the farmhouse were impressed, because he certainly was. MacNeil made the standard come-out-with-your-hands-up speech, but there was no response from the farmhouse. Another agent with a remote unit made a telephone call to the house. Again, no response.

"Okay," said MacNeil, making the decision. "Cut the power, cut the phone, and tell HRT they're clear to go." His minions passed the orders by walkie-talkie.

Welsh could see the snipers tense up and get ready. There were coughing noises from the treeline. Dark objects arced in the air and crashed through the farmhouse windows. White smoke quickly billowed up. Welsh smiled. CS tear gas, and from personal experience in the marines he knew it was a bitch. When those little crystals hit, you started pumping mucus from every orifice—eyes, nose, mouth. It even felt like it was coming out your ears. The only drawback was that the burning grenade had a tendency to set things on fire.

Under cover of the gas, twelve HRT men made a dash for the back of the barn, which shielded them from the house. A smaller team broke off to clear the barn, but the rest waited, crouched against the walls.

The basic HRT assault unit was four men, taken from the Special Air Service. Equipment and tactics were also influenced by the SAS. They dressed in one-piece black jumpsuits and black balaclavas, and their primary weapon was the West German Heckler & Koch MP5 9mm submachine-gun. A few also carried folding-stock 12-gauge shotguns. A variety of 9mm automatic pistols were worn as backup weapons in tie-down hip holsters. Body armor sheathed their torsos, heavy enough to stop an AK-47 round. Over the armor was worn a vest carrying submachine gun magazines, stun grenades and pyrotechnics, and a radio. All the men were wearing gas masks. Larynx microphones led to the radios, allowing communication even with the masks on.

There was the sound of a helicopter. Welsh looked up in time to see a Bell Jet Ranger pop up over the trees. Two HRT men were leaning against the doors on each side, with their feet on the skids. The Ranger darted over to the farmhouse roof, and the men jumped off. Welsh nodded with approval. It was easier to fight from the top of a building down than from the bottom up.

The roof had two tiers, as if part had been built on as an extension. The HRT jumped onto the lower part, which gave them easy access to a second-floor window. Backed up against the side of the house and well covered by other HRT members, one man punched out the glass with a small sledgehammer. His partner threw in a stun grenade, and it exploded instantly. Both dived through the window behind the grenade, and the rest followed, one after the other. Then another Jet Ranger flew over to the roof and disgorged four more HRT. They went in through the same window.

Simultaneously, the twelve men waiting behind the barn dashed toward a corner of the house. They stayed low to the foundation, weapons trained on the windows above. Covered by the others, two agents fixed an explosive frame charge to the back door, being careful to stay out of any line of fire. There was a pause, a signal was given, and the door disappeared in a sharp explosion. Before the smoke cleared they threw in stun grenades and charged through the opening.

MacNeil had a walkie-talkie tuned to the HRT net, and he put the volume up so everyone could listen. There was no idle chatter. All the rooms had been given a designation, and the HRT teams reported in as each one was cleared. So far they hadn't encountered anyone. The special agent in charge warned them to stay alert.

Welsh couldn't fault them so far. The tactics were classic. Surprise everyone by coming in from above, get their attention fixed to the upper floors, and then give them another problem by coming in downstairs from another direction. He'd been taking pictures with his little 35mm camera, but after everyone was inside he put it away and watched through binoculars, even though the white CS smoke made it nearly impossible to see. There hadn't been any shooting, so he decided to take a calculated risk. He stood up and used a pine tree for cover, leaning his head and upper body around it to look through the binoculars. MacNeil yelled to get down, but Welsh ignored him.

Inside the farmhouse, an HRT team had just blown the hinges off a locked door with a twelve-gauge shotgun. They now faced an alcove leading to the downstairs hallway. A stun grenade went in, and two HRT followed —one on each side of the doorway. The alcove was clear. The hallway was empty; there was a closed door at the far end. Following carefully rehearsed routine, the team started down the hallway to deal with the next door.

Halfway down the hall, at calf height, was a standard two-plug electrical socket. However, close examination would have revealed that there was no receptacle, just the faceplate. Mounted inside the wall in the receptacle box was a burglar alarm, available at any well-stocked electronics store. Through the top hole in the faceplate, a photo-relay sensor projected a beam of infrared light across the width of the hall. On the opposite side the beam hit a reflector, also recessed into the wall. The reflector bounced the beam back to a receiver, positioned where the bottom plug should have been.

The Hostage Rescue Team had undergone extensive training in the detection of booby traps. They had cut all electrical power to the farmhouse, and they took great care upon entering each room. But they were looking mainly for trip wires.

The first man broke the infrared beam as he moved down the hall. As a burglar alarm, this would have turned on the house lights or a siren. Instead, the sensor closed the circuit on a wire loop leading to a 12-volt lantern battery, two electric blasting caps, and two fifty-five-gallon drums of liquid explosive, which were in the basement.

As Welsh watched through his binoculars, the farmhouse blew apart. Something hit him very hard all over his body.

He must have been out only a few seconds, because when he opened his eyes debris was still falling from the sky. He looked up and saw branches, and found himself beneath a tree in a bed of pine needles. Welsh tried to get up, but things were still too fuzzy. There was dust everywhere, and he heard sirens. It was very nice to be able to hear something. MacNeil came running over, looking very shaky.

"I'm okay," Welsh told him calmly.

But MacNeil looked down at him and exclaimed in horror, "Oh my God!"

Welsh was puzzled by this and thought he ought to look himself over. He quickly discovered the cause of MacNeil's distress: A chunk of wood two inches thick and five inches long was protruding from his parka just below the rib cage. Welsh thought about it for a second, then extended his arm.

"For God's sake, don't move!" MacNeil shouted.

Before he could get closer, Welsh reached down and yanked out the wood. MacNeil moved in to try and staunch the expected flow of blood, but there was none. Welsh handed the sharp chunk of wood to MacNeil, who stared dumbly at it.

"Remind me to write the Second Chance people a really nice letter," said Welsh.

Realization slowly made its way across MacNeil's face. "You bastard," he breathed. Then he shouted. "You son of a bitch, you nearly gave me a heart attack!"

"Stop yelling and help me up," said Welsh.

The dust was finally settling. The farmhouse and barn were gone. Only the foundations remained. Fire trucks and ambulances were moving in; people were running about.

"Those bastards," said Welsh, from the bottom of his heart. "Those dirty motherfuckers."

Everything stopped as the ground rumbled, faintly but distinctly. Welsh's first thought was that some more explosive had gone off in the foundation of the house.

"What the hell was that?" MacNeil shouted.

Welsh saw it first, a thick pillar of black smoke rising far to the west. "Oh, Jesus Christ," he moaned. "That's Camp Lejeune."

CHAPTER 23

AT 5:45 ON Thursday morning, Hassan and Mahmoud stood beside the Yummycakes truck in the parking lot of one of Jacksonville's twenty-four-hour supermarkets, taking in the pleasures of the new day. The barometer was dropping; it made the air feel thick and heavy.

"The night seemed to go on forever," the boy said.

Mahmoud nodded. "I do not know why the commander refused to let us to stay in the house after they left last night. I tried to convince him, but orders are orders." He noticed a strange look on the *Baseeji*'s face. "Do you feel all right?" the spy asked.

"I am fine," the boy said quickly. He looked embarrassed. "I had a dream last night that they caught me, and the mission failed."

Mahmoud wasn't quite sure what to say. He didn't want to upset the boy, so he took refuge in banality. "Try not to worry. Just remain calm and remember your training, and you cannot fail. You are doing a great thing, and we are all very proud of you."

Hassan smiled shyly. "Really?" he asked.

"Really," said the spy. He paused. "It is time to go now," he said gently.

"I am ready."

"You will never be forgotten," Mahmoud said, embracing the boy. "God willing, we will meet again in Paradise."

"So it is written," Hassan said. He started the truck.

Mahmoud waved as the truck pulled out. The boy

waved back. Mahmoud's panel truck, where they had spent the night, was on the other side of the parking lot. The other three *Baseej* were sleeping inside. Ali had left them with Mahmoud for security and in the event Hassan developed a last-minute change of heart that would necessitate his being shot. Now the four of them would drive directly to Virginia.

The truck moved through Jacksonville, picking up green traffic lights all the way. Hassan kept an eye on his watch; he did not want to be too early. He turned left onto North Carolina Route 24 and headed for the main entrance to Camp Lejeune. The road was a long strip of gas stations, bars, and auto dealerships. The traffic grew heavy. Hassan took the well-marked exit and passed the sign that announced "The World's Most Complete Amphibious Training Base." Ahead was a military police post and signs requesting drivers to slow down and dim their headlights.

The boy panicked when he saw movement in the guard shack. It was not supposed to be like this. Merciful God, he was too early. Other drivers tapped their horns as Hassan began to slide his truck out of its lane. Hassan was about to step on the gas and run the checkpoint when he noticed that the MP in the guard shack was reading a newspaper. The boy quickly cut his speed to five miles an hour and followed the traffic onto the base.

Normally, any vehicle coming onto Camp Lejeune had to pass by an MP standing in the middle of the access road. If a vehicle did not display a Department of Defense sticker, it was ordered to turn off and stop at another guard shack, where the driver was required to show license and registration and explain his or her business on base. But Camp Lejeune had a population of over fifty thousand, and a large number of marines lived off the base. Because of the massive flood of traffic streaming in during rush hour, the sticker check was suspended for a short time every morning, to accommodate the commuters.

Hassan increased his speed down Main Service Road. The light was green, and he held the truck at fifty miles per hour. He fought the temptation to push down on the gas pedal. Discipline, he told himself, discipline. You have waited so long, and it is so very close. Concentrate and be patient, you are almost there. The route was familiar. He had practiced in Iran on an exact copy built in a lonely area near Shiraz and had twice driven down this road on the back of Ali's motorcycle. But now that he was alone the boy was terrified of making a mistake. He passed over a bridge and checked the landmark off in his mind. The signs told him to slow down, and he did. He passed the Burger King on his left and the Hostess House on his right. He slowed the truck to twenty-five miles per hour as he passed the Post Exchange. Hassan cut the wheel and swung around the traffic circle, careful to stay in the lane that continued down Main Service Road. Tears came to his eyes; he was almost there. The boy tripped a toggle switch attached to the dashboard, which he thought activated the time-clock mechanism.

Actually, the switch was not connected to anything—but the boy did not know that. Mahmoud had activated the device before the truck left the parking lot, and the clock had been running ever since. It was simple insurance against a last-minute failure of nerve. If Hassan surrendered or abandoned the truck, the bomb would prevent its being examined.

At the end of the road, the truck came up on the 2d Marine Division headquarters. For a moment Hassan was tempted, but he had been briefed that there was no one in the building this early. He took a right turn onto Julian Smith Drive. The speed limit was twenty-five miles per hour, and he was careful not to exceed it. He passed a regimental headquarters, another landmark. Then came the headquarters of a different regiment. He turned right as he passed it. Six hundred meters down the road, a parking lot appeared on the left. Hassan pulled into the parking lot and swerved between two parked cars. He slowed down so the bumper would not impact on the curb, and he bounced the truck over the concrete walk and onto the grass. Two staff sergeants arriving for work stared in amazement.

The boy heard the bellow of typical staff NCO outrage: "What the fuck do you think you're doing, asshole?"

Hassan whipped the truck hard to the left, straightened the wheels, and stepped on the gas pedal. He picked the hand switch up off his lap, depressed the lever, and held it tight. The ground was damp, and the rear wheels kicked up a fountain of turf and mud as the truck accelerated. The wheels wobbled on the slick grass, and with one hand on the wheel Hassan fought to even it out. He picked out his target, the Bachelor Enlisted Quarters in the center of a group of barracks, and his aiming point, the exact center of the BEQ.

The new Bachelor Enlisted Quarters at Camp Lejeune were large, three-story, flat-roofed concrete buildings. A departure from the old-style communal squad bay, they had more than ninety rooms, with a central lounge on each floor and one room per building for a duty NCO. The rooms, each with its own bathroom, were designed to be occupied by three marines. A battalion normally used two of these buildings and half of another, grouped together in a regimental area.

The poor traction on the soft ground made it hard for Hassan to hold the overloaded truck on the aiming point. From the first-floor passageway, a bareheaded marine wearing a cartridge belt stepped out of the duty NCO office and began waving wildly at him. Hassan found this enormously funny and began to laugh, the tension washing away now that he knew he was going to make it. The duty NCO stopped waving, turned, and ran down the first-floor passageway.

The front tires blew out when the truck hit the concrete edge of the first-floor walkway—the vehicle's progress was not slowed. It crashed through the thin brick outer wall and entered the duty NCO office. The impact with the outer wall activated the pressure switch on the front bumper; Hassan had dropped the hand switch when his body crashed through the windshield. But the van was completely inside the building when the charge detonated.

The velocity of the explosive blast completely sheared the nearest support columns, and the center of the building fell in upon itself. The columns farther away buckled and fell inward. The acetylene gas enhanced the already terrible force of the explosion and created an enormous fireball that followed the initial shock wave. The noise drowned out any screams. When the dust cloud settled, the center of the BEQ appeared as a collection of huge chunks of concrete carelessly heaped together, like building blocks a child might meticulously construct and then knock down. Only the two far walls of the structure remained slightly intact. A mound of debris lay between, covered by the roof, which rested in pieces on the top of the pile.

The force of the blast blew in the flimsy fronts of the two nearest BEQs. The explosion was contained within the semicircle of buildings, but marines in the regimental area two blocks away were knocked off their feet by the explosion. Debris fell to the ground in an eight-hundred-yard radius, and the cars in the large parking lot were perforated by chunks of concrete and steel reinforcing rods. The fragments of glass, concrete, and metal caused heavy casualties among commuting marines just arriving at work.

In the 2d Marine Division headquarters, GSgt. Ron Blakely, the command duty staff NCO, had been brushing his teeth when the blast knocked him from his feet. His first thought was that there had been an explosion in the ammo dump. He looked out the window and saw the cloud of smoke over the infantry areas. The phone rang, and he ran into the office. Major John Delburton, the command duty officer, pushed the enlisted phone watch aside and took the call himself.

When he hung up, his face was ashen. "A BEQ was just bombed."

"Did they say how, Sir?"

"They said there was nothing left of the building."

"Mother of Jesus, now it's happening over here."

The major had been gazing out the window. For a moment he seemed lost, then quickly snapped back. He grabbed a yellow legal pad off the desk and began writing. He was the assistant communications officer for the division and had personally revised most of the emergency SOPs. "Gunny, this is a list of people you've got to call. I'm going to have to get on the phone with the general and let him know what happened. Then I'll have to call Fleet Marine Force Atlantic and Washington. You get ahold of base headquarters and the MPs. Tell them to seal off the base and keep a road clear to the hospital for ambulances. Tell the provost marshal's office that I'm activating the Alpha Increment Air-Alert Company for base defense. Call New River Air Station, Camp Geiger, and Camp Johnson and tell them to do the same. Tell New River to be prepared to send its fire fighters and crash crews over here and to get some helos ready to transport casualties. Then get the hospital and tell them to be prepared for mass casualties. Call Bragg, Cherry Point, and Bethesda and tell them the same thing. Call the command duty officer at Force Service Support Group, and tell him to stand by with earth-moving equipment from Landing Support and Engineer Support battalions. Don't let him send it; I don't want a clusterfuck in the disaster area. Just have him get the drivers in the vehicles and stand by. Do the same thing for 2d Combat Engineers." He ripped the paper off the pad and handed it over. "Okay, Gunny?"

"Jesus Christ," breathed the gunny.

"Let's get moving," the major said sharply.

"Aye, aye, Sir," said the gunny, swinging around to the phone.

"And you," the major snapped at the phone watch, a mild-looking private first class who shot out of his chair to attention.

"Yes, Sir?" he squeaked.

"Sweep this building for field-grade officers," the major ordered. "If you find any, send them up here—we have to get the command center set up."

"Aye, Aye, Sir!" yelled the phone watch as he dashed from the room.

"Of course this had to happen when I was on duty," mumbled the major as he walked to his office to break the news to the commanding general.

The situation on the base was chaotic. Not everyone had arrived at work yet, and those who had were little help. Because everyone wanted to take charge and insisted on an explanation, it took too much time to get moving. Marines poured into the blast area from all corners of the base, wanting to help. But they impeded the flow of ambulances and heavy equipment. The usual morning traffic jams were made even worse, stranding the people who were most needed. The Division Command Center had trouble getting through to the various units because the phone lines were jammed with dependent families calling to find out what happened and make sure their loved ones were all right.

The 2d Marine Division has, at all times, an infantry battalion organized and on alert to move anywhere in the world by air in a matter of hours. That battalion has a rifle company prepared to move out as its lead element at even shorter notice. When it assembled, the company was sent to the bomb site as crowd control and security. For as in Beirut, the leaders at the scene felt that another attack might be launched as soon as large crowds gathered. The air-alert company also kept the area clear, allowing the engineers' cranes and earthmovers to move in and start clearing rubble in the search for survivors.

Luckily, four battalion surgeons had been on the base before it was sealed off. They rushed to the bomb site and allowed doctors who had been trying to stabilize casualties at the scene to move back to the hospital. There were at least 150 navy corpsmen there also—they grabbed their Unit 1 medical bags and rushed over from all directions. Even the duty dentist of Dental Company came over with his equipment and enlisted technicians.

Elsewhere on the base, dump trucks raced about carrying sandbags to gates and important buildings. Each gate and main headquarters soon had sandbag bunkers, concrete blocks, and rolls of concertina wire blocking the entrances. The military police at the various gates traded their dress uniforms and Beretta pistols for camouflage utilities, helmets, flak jackets, M16s, M60 machine guns, and AT-4 antitank rockets. When the TOW heavy antitank missile section attached to the air-alert battalion arrived for muster, live missiles were issued and each squad of TOW humvees was sent to a gate. The other two rifle companies of the air-alert battalion stood by on trucks as a mobile reaction force should any part of the base be attacked.

All over Camp Lejeune shocked, scared, and very angry young men waited, hoping someone would try something now that they were ready.

PART FOUR

But helpless Pieces of the Game He plays
Upon this Chequer-board of Nights and Days;
    Hither and thither moves, and checks, and slays
And one by one back in the Closet lays.

The Rubaiyat of Omar Khayyam

CHAPTER 24

At 0730 that Thursday morning the commandos were driving up Route 29 north of Greensboro, North Carolina, approaching the Virginia border.

After leaving Camp Lejeune the three pickup trucks had followed Route 17 south down the coast to the city of Wilmington, North Carolina. When making his escape plan, Ali had resisted the temptation to immediately head north, even though it meant risking more time in the state.

In Wilmington they stopped at three commercial parking lots in widely separated locations: at the New Hanover Commuter Airport, near the access to Wrightsville Beach, and in downtown Wilmington. To his fury, Ali lost his way no less than three times. At each lot they traded a pickup truck with North Carolina plates for a van registered in Virginia. During the drive down, the commandos had wrapped the weapons in green tarpaulins to make the transfer as unobtrusive as possible.

The convoy of pickup trucks soon became a convoy of three sporty passenger vans: a Toyota, an Aerostar, and a Grand Voyager. Ali hadn't wanted to risk bringing the captured ammunition to the attack on the bivouac, so Karim and Hafiz had driven directly to Wilmington from the range. In a parking lot near the USS *North Carolina* Battleship Memorial, they transferred the ammo to two Econoline vans, one blue and one red. The rest of the unit linked up with them there.

Ali knew the trucks would be discovered in the parking lots sooner or later; that was his main reason for driving south to Wilmington. It was a busy port, accommodating ships from all over the world. A natural avenue of escape. God willing, the Americans would think they had abandoned their vehicles and fled the country by sea. Or perhaps used the airport to connect with an international flight out of Charlotte or Atlanta.

They made it out of Wilmington onto Route 40 just before the start of the morning rush hour. The long, winding route through the North Carolina flatland took them through Raleigh and then Durham. The vans finally turned north onto Route 29 at Greensboro.

Inside the vans some commandos were still on an adrenaline high from the night's action; others fell asleep as soon as the vans began moving. Ali was wide awake in the front seat of the lead van, driving Mehdi to distraction by continually switching through radio channels for news.

At 0740 the radio announced an explosion at Camp Lejeune Marine Corps Base in Jacksonville. Ali slammed his fist into the dashboard in exultation, nearly causing Mehdi to swerve off the road. His war cry woke the commandos in back, and soon they crowded behind the front seats to listen to the news. The laughter and chatter grew so loud that Ali had to shout for silence.

The North Carolina media, shocked and somewhat giddy at finding themselves in the midst of a national news story, were promising continuous coverage. But the only information available was that the base had been sealed off and large numbers of casualties were arriving at area hospitals. This provoked cheers from the back of the van. Sources suspected the explosion to be an act of terrorism. The commandos began booing. "It was an act of war," one shouted. This started a long argument about whether they were engaged in war or vengeance. Ali had to turn up the volume to drown them out.

As they left North Carolina after what seemed an

eternity, Ali allowed himself a brief celebration, accepting a sandwich and soft drink from one of the commandos in back. Chewing the sandwich, he reflected that Karim had to be given due credit for the provisions. They had been discussing the escape plans, plotting an indirect route north to Virginia, when Karim abruptly inquired what they would eat on the trip. Ali and Musa had looked at each other and, to the amazement of Hafiz and his agents, had burst into laughter. For all the detailed contingency planning, none of them had given it any thought. Of course it had to be Karim with his appetite. As they talked it over, it was clear they had a serious problem. Even the most dim-witted gas station attendant or fast-food clerk would not forget five vanloads of foreigners passing through just after a marine barracks had been blown up. So a number of extra gas cans had been purchased and filled. Coolers packed with drinks and sandwiches were added to the list of items to be brought along. Once they left Wilmington the only stops had been in secluded areas. Gasoline was added to the tanks, and empty soda cans filled with urine were thrown out the windows.

In Virginia they followed Route 29 northward, skirting the edge of the Blue Ridge Mountains. At Culpeper they turned east and followed the Rapidan River into Fredericksburg. It was night when the five vans arrived at the house Mehdi had purchased months earlier. Mahmoud and the three remaining *Baseej* were waiting with food laid out in case the commandos were hungry.

The sergeant major laughed uproariously as the commandos hobbled about the lawn, trying to get their legs working after sitting so long. Even those who had napped in the vans were exhausted from the stress of the previous days, and they longed for sleep. But Ali would not allow them to eat or sleep until the vans were hidden in the garage and barn, and all the weapons, ammunition, and stores were unloaded and secured in the house. The sergeant major posted a guard schedule, which included monitoring the police-band radio at all times. Only then were the commandos allowed to collapse on the mattresses scattered throughout the house. They were safe for the moment, and that was the extent of their concern.

CHAPTER 25

THE FBI JET RANGER circled over mainside Camp Lejeune at a thousand feet, out of the way of the medevac helicopters darting in below. Rich Welsh felt like a ghoul. Such a godlike perch almost made you forget that those tiny things being pulled from the rubble were men. Almost. But the distance made it easier in a way. You didn't have to hear or smell what was going on, or watch too closely.

Welsh hated helicopters. After a dozen close calls as a marine and half a dozen friends killed in crashes, he'd vowed never to set foot in one again. But this time it was necessary—all the roads in the vicinity were jammed.

The report of the terrorist bombing at the Camp Lejeune Bachelor Enlisted Quarters had come in a few minutes after they'd felt the actual explosion. MacNeil tried to get a forensics team to the BEQ explosion scene by helicopter, but his efforts did little good. There was too much confusion, and the marines were in no mood to deal with the FBI when men might still be alive in the rubble. MacNeil told them to just stand by. He'd already called Washington for bomb experts after the explosion at the farm.

Welsh felt sorry for MacNeil. Even if what happened wasn't his fault, the guy in charge always took the spike. MacNeil had spent a long time in the communications van after the explosion, explaining things to Washington. And there was plenty to explain. Only three of the twenty Hostage Rescue Team members who went into the house survived the blast, and they were all in critical condition. And there were two dead and seventeen wounded among the men surrounding the farmhouse. But the most humiliating part was that the bombers had escaped the farmhouse and gotten through to the base. The first reports from Camp Lejeune made the damage sound very bad.

Then, a few hours later, while they were still putting things together at the farmhouse, a report came in of a massacre in the Camp Lejeune training areas. MacNeil ordered the rest of his forensics people at New River Air Station to drive to the scene, and decided to take the remaining helicopter and check it out personally. Welsh thought it was also to get away from the phone to Washington. He'd been surprised when MacNeil offered to take him along, but it made sense when he thought about it. It was always nice to have a neutral party to talk to.

MacNeil's voice came through the headset. "We can't set down here. I want to go to the other site and take a look. Do you know any place close where we can land?"

Welsh leaned into the space between the two front seats and pointed to a spot on the map the pilot held up. "The ammo dump here is abandoned. We could land inside or anywhere around, and just walk across the road."

The pilot nodded, spoke a few words to New River Control, and swung the Ranger into a sharp turn across the river. Welsh held on to the sides of his seat. He knew it wouldn't do any good, but he couldn't help it.

They landed in a field of tall grass next to the old ammunition storage area. The pilot stayed with the helicopter, and Welsh, relieved to be on the ground again, guided MacNeil through the brush to the asphalt road.

Military police had the area cordoned off. The FBI forensics team was already hard at work. Frank Sears, the team leader, met MacNeil and Welsh at the entrance to the tank trail.

"What does it look like?" MacNeil asked.

"The same people," Sears said flatly. "Same 7.62 × 39mm M43 cases, all spent. Other than tire marks and footprints, that's all they left behind. They used pickup trucks. We may be able to get fibers off the bushes, but that's it."

"How bad?" asked MacNeil.

"Total. Over sixty so far. A few tried to run, but they didn't make it."

"Who found them?" Welsh broke in.

"The company first sergeant," said Sears. "He drove over here right after the bombing."

"What did they do to them?" Welsh demanded.

Sears hesitated. MacNeil nodded for him to go ahead. "They all were shot," Sears said. "Most in their tents, they never had a chance. Every weapon was taken. But the bodies weren't mutilated," he added, as if that made all the difference in the world.

Without saying anything, Welsh left them and walked toward the clearing.

The bodies of the five lieutenants were still lying in the trail. Someone had covered them with two camouflage ponchos. Welsh noticed that whoever had done it had tucked the ponchos very neatly around their legs. He thought of a first sergeant taking care of his lieutenants. He checked the CP tent and then circled the clearing until he could see how it had been done. There was a group of marines standing off to one side, talking quietly among themselves. Welsh could make out a bird colonel and a lieutenant colonel, probably the regimental and battalion commanders. He didn't go over. He had nothing to say to them, and it was probably for the best, since in his present mood he felt like spitting on any marine officer over the rank of lieutenant.

FBI technicians and photographers were working among the shelter halves. Welsh walked down the rows. The trampled dead grass was bathed in thick sheets of dried blood. There was no way to avoid it, so Welsh tried to put it out of his mind and keep walking. Most of the bodies had been pulled out of the slashed-open shelter halves. Dead men gazed blankly up at him. Welsh heard the voices of marines in his head. They became too loud, and he walked quickly into the treeline, almost running. Far enough not to be seen, Welsh sank to his knees and took several great, deep, rattling breaths.

MacNeil was looking around the clearing when Welsh appeared from the treeline. "Are you okay?" he asked, very concerned, when he saw Welsh's stricken face.

"Yeah," Welsh said heavily, staring at the little green tents. "I just never thought I'd have to see another dead marine." He looked over at MacNeil, embarrassed by what he had said. "Sears said they took all the weapons, right?"

"Right," said MacNeil.

"So they've got M16s, Squad Automatic Weapons, M60 machine guns, and 60mm mortars."

MacNeil looked back blankly, and then it clicked. "Everything they lost on the beach," he breathed.

"I think," Welsh said quietly, "you had better send someone to check all the firing ranges on this side of the river. Right now, because there's probably a few more dead marines and a load of missing ammunition."

MacNeil was puzzled, so Welsh explained how things were done on the ranges. "Oh, my God," MacNeil exclaimed. He ran to find the officer in charge of the military police.

An hour later the MPs found the two bodies under the bleachers at range K-305, and MacNeil had to make another series of calls to Washington.

Welsh was getting a feeling he had sometimes—that he ought to stay away from people for a little while. Or people ought to stay away from him. He knew MacNeil was going to be tied up for some time, so he went for a walk in the woods. It was just as well. There weren't any ambulances left, so the marines brought in a working party to load all the body bags on two 6 × 6 trucks. Both trucks were filled quickly, but there were still bodies left over, so the marines had to take all the bags out and restack them.

When Welsh came back an hour and a half later, he found MacNeil sitting alone in one of the technicians' cars, his notebook open on his lap.

"C'mon," said Welsh, sticking his head through the window. "Let's confiscate this car and get the hell out of here. I know the back roads; we'll miss the traffic."

"I suppose there's nothing else to do here," MacNeil sighed.

Welsh took a circuitous route back to Jacksonville. After they passed a few familiar landmarks, MacNeil sat up and took notice. "Where are we going?" he demanded.

"To get a drink," Welsh informed him.

"You've got to be kidding," MacNeil said. Welsh could see he was angry. "Turn this thing around right now."

"Look," said Welsh. "It's over. Nothing either of us could do right now is going to make things any different. So let's go get a couple of drinks and try to tune it down. Believe me, it's a lot better than staring at the walls of your hotel room all night." He glanced over at MacNeil, who didn't say anything.

"We're all standing in the shit," Welsh added. "The only difference is the depth, and that's no fucking difference at all." He snuck another quick look, and MacNeil was smiling faintly.

"All right," MacNeil said. "Let's go."

Welsh made a few more turns, and MacNeil asked, "We're not going to the Officers' Club?"

"Shit, no," said Welsh. "Outside of Friday night happy hour, the only people who drink at the club are alcoholic colonels who crawl across the lawn to their housing after last call. I know someplace more congenial."

They went to one of Welsh's former favorite bars, a

neighborhood spot nestled in a little mall off all the main drags. It was nearly deserted. They took a booth.

MacNeil ordered scotch and water. Welsh had a beer. He made sure to hide a few bills for cab fare; he felt the drinking was bound to become serious.

MacNeil started off talking shop. Welsh figured it would take more than a few drinks to change the subject.

"But how in the hell did they know everything?" MacNeil asked him. "The bastards knew *everything!*"

Welsh shrugged. That didn't seem important. "I don't know, maybe they had really great intelligence. It's not like we're hard to spy on, or that the U.S. military has any great appreciation for security. Maybe they grabbed some marine off the street and tortured it out of the poor fucker."

"You're pretty cold, you know that?"

"Whatever you say," Welsh replied.

They drank in silence for a while, then MacNeil started again. "But why the weapons?" he said. "It breaks every rule in the book. They should hit once and then run like hell for home."

"They're planning something big," said Welsh. "So big they wouldn't give it up even after they lost everything on the beach. I'll tell you the truth, these people scare the living shit out of me. This is not your usual brand of fanatic freak. Christ, they're professional. The landing, the booby trap in the house, the raid on the bivouac—all right out of the textbook. The *advanced* textbook," he added.

"Whatever it is, they're fully armed now," MacNeil said glumly.

"And they could be anywhere. Oh, and I wanted to tell you," Welsh added, "before I get shitfaced. I'm going to call the office tomorrow and suggest that the secretary of defense petition the attorney general to suspend *Posse Comitatus.*"

"That's the law that prohibits the military from assuming police powers inside the U.S., other than at government installations, right?" said MacNeil.

Welsh nodded. "We have to do that before we can activate Special Operations Command for missions in this country."

"Well, there's not much of the HRT left. I'll give the director a call tomorrow, if he still wants to talk to me."

Welsh ordered another round. "This shit is *not* your fault," he said forcefully.

"You didn't want me to send HRT into the farmhouse so fast," MacNeil said.

"That's personal judgment," Welsh replied. "If they'd gone in later, the fucking bomb would still have been there and they still would have hit it."

MacNeil was becoming looser as he got drunk, and Welsh more talkative. "What did you mean out there in the woods?" MacNeil demanded. "When you said you thought you'd never have to see another dead marine."

"I was in Lebanon," Welsh said.

"Oh."

"Not for the bombing. We were just coming off as the air-alert battalion. When the BLT headquarters was destroyed, they needed a battalion headquarters and a rifle company right away. There's a story, I don't know how true, that they first called the CO of the battalion that was relieving us and he said they weren't ready. If it's true, you've got to admire the guy's honesty, because things would really be screwed if they weren't prepared. But in the corps you've always got to be ready, even if you aren't. So the guy supposedly was fired, and we got flown over instead. That's just what we heard. It's one of those stories that, even if it isn't true, it fits with everyone's personal experience, so they believe it."

MacNeil downed some more scotch and shook his head.

"When we got to Beirut, they were still pulling bodies out of the rubble," said Welsh. "Fucking Lebanon. Jesus, setting up shop in that country might have sounded like a peachy idea in the beginning, but then we took sides in the family feud and everything went sour. And we couldn't leave, because that would have sent the wrong message. Working in Washington and seeing all these assholes close up, man, I can see how it happened. And the press, those fuckers. I was a kid during Watergate, and I thought they were the guardians of democracy. But they're just a bunch of lazy ass-kissers, or so fucking stupid even military Public Affairs officers can con them—and that's pretty fucking stupid." He took a drink to cool off. "Anyway, I got my ass out in one piece; did me good, stripped away all those small-town illusions."

"Is that what gave you this fixation on Iran?" MacNeil checked Welsh's face quickly, afraid he was going to get mad.

Welsh only shrugged. "You know they were the ones behind Beirut—them and our new Syrian pals. Afterward I tried to learn everything about the Iranians that I could. We think they're crazy, but that's just simplistic shit. They have a completely different set of values, a different outlook on the world. Islam is all about revealed truth, religion providing the final word on every aspect of life. That kind of system creates people with no doubts, and that's the most dangerous thing in the world. And they hate us. Don't underestimate hate, my man; it'll keep you going through anything. These people live on it."

"We're going to get them," said MacNeil.

"Even if we do, it's not the end of it. Right now, at this very minute, we're at war. And our massive, expensive military machine is completely useless. There are no ships to sink, no planes to shoot down, no armies to fight. That truck was their Stealth bomber. Terrorism is the warfare of the future, and our military doesn't have a clue."

"Do you think it's really that bad?" asked MacNeil.

"We're not capable of changing our mindset toward

European-style conflict. Iraq saw to that. Terrorism is just another form of guerrilla warfare, and conventional, heavy-firepower armies don't do well against guerrillas. The lesson we came away with from Iraq is that we're pretty hot shit. But it was like the NFL All-Pro team playing in the Super Bowl against Harvard. Every other country in the world is going to take a *different* lesson—that the only way to fight us is in the shadows. After all, one truck bomb in Beirut killed more marines than the entire fucking war against Saddam Hussein."

"But now we have to learn from our mistakes."

"Bismarck said only a fool learns from experience," Welsh replied. "He learned from the experience of others." MacNeil seemed taken aback at the reference. "Anyway," Welsh continued, "we won't learn. We never have, and we never will. The military operates on a zero-defects system. So does our government. You see, when you claim to be perfect, then only perfection is acceptable—mistakes are not allowed. And if mistakes are not allowed, then we can never, ever, admit that they occurred. So the institution can't uncover and correct its own defects. And to keep from making mistakes we do the minimum, take no risks, look good on paper, and pass it off as perfection."

"Anybody ever tell you that you're a cynic?"

"I'm not a cynic," Welsh said firmly. "I tell the truth as I see it, and that seems to piss people off wherever I go. I'd call myself a skeptic—I have to run everything through my bullshit detector. I found out the hard way that when someone in authority invokes national security, patriotism, or loyalty to the team, what it usually means is that something got screwed up and they're looking to sweep a load of shit under the rug. I'm definitely a realist." He broke into a loopy smile. "But anyone who looks at reality long and hard enough is bound to become a little cynical. What I really hate is complacency. That's what killed those marines."

"I've been at some bad scenes," said MacNeil. "But that was the worst I ever saw."

Welsh drained his beer and started on another. "I loved enlisted marines. Lot of officers didn't. Of course, I never let my marines know how I felt. It's like your kids —you love them even when they're a pain in the ass. I thought they were the greatest guys in America. But a lot of times they get treated like just another piece of gear. I could deal with basic stupidity, but that kind of unfeeling negligence always pissed me off."

"Is that why you left the marines?"

"There were a lot of reasons. If you work for IBM and your boss fucks up, it doesn't mean much. But if you're an infantryman and your boss fucks up, you're dead— nothing you can do. And in the lower levels, where it's most important, everyone gets his shot as a commander, whether he's Captain America or Bobo the Simple-minded. Napoleon said there were no bad regiments, only bad colonels. And believe me, the little bastard knew what he was talking about." Welsh looked over. MacNeil was stiff and almost comically attentive.

"I'll tell you why I got out," said Welsh. "And there's even a no-shit war story. One day they dropped some mortars on us. I say 'they' because it could've been any one of about six groups of assholes. Only one of my guys was hit, in the leg; he was a real good marine. The leg was bad enough to get him back to the States, but not bad enough to lose it or anything. Well, when we got back I called his home address in Arkansas to see how he was. I get his dad on the phone, and he was real cool —ex-marine himself. But then his mom comes on, and she's still pissed. I couldn't blame her. A mother wants to know why her kid was hurt, not a lot of political shit. You know, for her there might be some good reasons, but they're never acceptable. So she asks me, flat out, to tell her exactly *why* her boy was in Lebanon, and *why* he got hurt. And I just sat there, looking at the phone and feeling like the world's biggest asshole. I couldn't give her any bullshit speech, so I just hung up. 'Cause there wasn't any good reason. That's when I decided to get out."

"I'm going to have to make some of those calls," Mac-Neil said.

"One thing Lebanon did for me, though," said Welsh. "Most people in this country get so comfortable and insulated they forget the world is a very dangerous place. Not me. Not ever."

CHAPTER 26

THE IRANIANS SAT around the television set like children watching Saturday-morning cartoons. With elbows firmly planted on the rug, chins cupped in hands, and mouths slightly open in concentration, they watched taped images of the farm in Jacksonville. Ali sat in an armchair in front of the set. The Hostage Rescue Team had been more than he hoped for.

The sight of Special Agent MacNeil calling on those inside to surrender provoked snorts of disgust from the Iranians in front of the TV.

Then the farmhouse blew apart and the tape stopped. The commandos cheered and pounded on the rug as if they had witnessed a brilliant soccer play. The spies were shocked by the magnitude of the explosion.

Karim reached over the arm of the chair and took Ali's hand. "What a wonderful idea," he said.

"More than that," Musa said. "It will be some time before they are ready to go into action again. And any evidence we may have left is now gone."

A picture of Hafiz's face suddenly filled the screen. Hafiz stared at the TV in shock. The commandos hooted and threw cushions at him.

Ali motioned for Karim and Musa to follow him into the kitchen. "So they have Ghalib's picture," he said.

"The idiot probably left a trail," Karim said angrily.

"If he were captured, it would take the Americans at least five minutes to make him talk," said Musa.

"He will not leave the house," Ali ordered. He filled a

glass of water at the sink. "Yes," he said idly, "we will have to do something about this."

There were happy shouts from the living room. The sergeant major turned to quiet them down, but Ali stopped him. "Let the men enjoy themselves for now," he said. "But we must guard against overconfidence." He took a long drink. "Because compared to what we still have to do, this was nothing. Nothing at all."

Every morning after that, Ali took up position on the living room couch, surrounded by all the fruits of the American press. That first week the coverage took on a tone of incomprehensible outrage. Ali imagined it reflected the American mood. With the bombing, the slaughter of the marine company, and the elimination of half the Hostage Rescue Team, Americans were having an unpleasant week. He was quite pleased; they had had their own way for far too long. An editorial mentioned that it was the first combat on American soil since the Civil War. Ali only laughed. They were always so eager to bomb anyone who annoyed them; let them try and keep their appetite for it when they were bombed in return.

The first item of business now that they were settled was to attend to the new weaponry. The American weapons, though solving most of Ali's problems, created a set of new ones. The commandos would have to quickly become expert in the operation of an unfamiliar family of small arms.

Mehdi toured military-surplus stores in the area and purchased the technical manuals for the M16 rifle, the M249 Squad Automatic Weapon, and the M60 machine gun.

Ali knew the commandos would have to fire the rifles and machine guns before the attack, if only to zero the sights. And bitter experience had taught him that men were doomed if they needed to consciously think about using their weapons in the stress of combat. So they needed to find a place to shoot. Karim suggested traveling to a secluded stretch of forest. Ali thought it too risky. They might be stopped by police or discovered by some hiker. He was determined to stay hidden until the attack on the White House. While he thought about it, the commandos began preparing the weapons.

Karim and Musa decided that the repeated disassembly and assembly involved in cleaning the weapons was the best way for the men to become familiar with their operation. The arms were unpacked and spread throughout the rooms, and the commandos set to their labors. Each new discovery would provoke a round of conversation as they argued over a weapon's merits. Ali would watch with a bemused smile. What engines of creation could provoke such fascination among human beings as engines of destruction?

Few were happy with the M16A2 rifle. The sights were much better than the Kalashnikov, but there was no provision for fully automatic fire—only three-round bursts. And the M16 magazines were terrible. They were so flimsy it was impossible to load the intended thirty rounds—the spring would only operate with twenty-eight. They also had some M203s—M16s with a 40mm grenade launcher mounted under the barrel. The launcher was a single-shot, pump-operated weapon that fired a grenade out to three hundred meters.

Compared to the more substantial West German and Soviet weapons the Iranians were used to, the American M60E3 machine guns seemed flimsy, though they appreciated the extra penetrating power of the big 7.62mm NATO round.

But the weapon they all loved without reservation was the M249 Squad Automatic Weapon, or SAW. It was a light machine gun that fired the 5.56mm round of the M16. It could use M16 magazines or a 200-round belt carried in a green plastic box that clipped conveniently to the underside of the weapon. The SAW was light, had superb firepower, and was extremely reliable. They had captured fifteen of the weapons, and Ali planned to use as many as he had ammunition for.

The commandos taped small flashlights to the stocks of their weapons, for both emergency lighting and as an improvised close-quarters low-visibility gunsight.

The AT-4 antitank rocket was a one-shot disposable launcher, thirteen pounds and a meter long, that fired an 84mm rocket. The rocket had a three-hundred-meter range, and the warhead could penetrate 450 millimeters of armor. Fortunately the firing instructions were simple, and printed, with diagrams, on the side of the launcher tube. They had sixteen rockets, more than enough; they could afford to miss with a few.

The grenades and pyrotechnics were the same type they had trained with in Iran. They had nearly two hundred fragmentation grenades. The M224 60mm mortars were identical to similar weapons the world over, except for a much longer range.

That first week the commandos also put together the rest of the ordnance they would need for the attack, in case they were discovered and had to move quickly. They made firebombs first. These were sophisticated versions of the Molotov cocktail. They had a filling of napalm, or gasoline brought to a gel-like consistency. The burning gel would stick to whatever it touched. The clever ignition system would not have to be lit with a match—it would explode upon hitting anything hard. Except for the gasoline, the ingredients were available in any supermarket.

To deal with any armored doors or obstacles the shotguns could not handle, the commandos made small breaching charges from leftover plastic explosive packed into soap dishes. A grenade fuze was screwed into the top. To attach the charges, Mehdi purchased rolls of tape with adhesive on both sides.

Ali settled on the date of the attack during their fifth week in Virginia, while reading the morning papers. He called Karim over.

"What is it?" Karim asked, leaning over the couch.

Ali pointed to the article. "The president is to sign important legislation next week."

Karim read it over Ali's shoulder. "Do you think it is the proper moment?" he asked.

"Perfect," Ali replied. "We will be able to depend on the president being at a specific location at a specific time, which is all we need. And with luck there will be other important officials present. It would be an achievement if we could kill some of them, also."

"But that means a daylight attack," Karim said, biting his lower lip as he studied the article.

Ali shrugged. "Less easy perhaps, but the streets will be crowded so the confusion will be greater. It evens the chance of escape after the job is done. And we have plenty of smoke grenades. After all," he said, "we must take the opportunities we are given."

Karim bobbed his head in agreement. "The paper does say that the signing will take place in the Oval Office instead of the Rose Garden, for reasons of security."

"Even better. They are worried about snipers. So instead of the rats staying in the open, where they can run in every direction, they put themselves in a box for us."

"It says they have extra security. What will they use?"

"Extra police and Secret Service." Ali smiled. "But I think we will be able to surprise them."

"Really?" said Karim. "After all that has happened?"

"Exactly. When you are weak, you worry about everything and prepare for the worst. Any other country would have a battalion of troops guarding the White House. But the Americans do not think that way."

Suddenly, shouting erupted from the kitchen, where the morning cooking detail was at work. Ali and Karim were both pulling themselves up from the couch when the sound tapered off. They sat back down.

"Well," Karim said, "in that case. . . ."

He was interrupted by a shrill scream from the

kitchen. They both sprang off the couch, but Ali made it through the door first. A commando was lying on the tile floor, bleeding from a puncture wound in his side. Another stood over him waving a bloody kitchen knife. He had his back to the door, but whirled about after hearing Ali enter.

"Drop the knife!" Ali shouted.

The commando's eyes raced wildly about the room, as if looking for a friendly face or a way out of his present situation. He made a quick slashing motion with the knife. It may have been a bluff to keep Ali away long enough to gain time to think, but Ali chose not to interpret the movement that way. He swept a container off the counter and hurled it at the knife wielder's head. The man ducked and Ali moved in. He grabbed at the knife with his left hand. The blade sliced into his forearm, but he had a grip on the commando's wrist—and the knife was immobilized. Their chests were almost touching. Ali brought his right hand up from his waist in a sweeping movement, and with all his strength jammed his thumb in the man's eyeball. The thumb went in over the knuckle; the sensation was disgusting. Ali remembered it described in an unarmed-combat course as a most effective technique—if you could bear to do it. The man let out a piercing scream and automatically threw his hands up to the eye, the knife clattering to the floor. A snap kick to the side of the knee brought him to the floor. Ali swept the blade away with his foot and sagged back against the counters. He picked up a washcloth and wiped the viscous ocular fluid from his hand as quickly as he could, before pressing the cloth onto the slice in his forearm. Karim rushed in and applied a battle dressing to the wound. The commando writhed on the floor, his screams filling the kitchen. Then there was an oily metallic snap, and the screaming stopped abruptly. The sergeant major stood over the body on the floor, smoke trailing up from the barrel of the Russian silenced pistol in his hand.

The dead man was buried in the yard that night. The medic tended the slash wounds on Ali's arm and the other commando's side with stitches and antibiotics.

"Did you find out what caused it?" Ali asked Musa after the evening meal.

"There was an argument over who would clean the vegetables."

Ali grimaced. "Idiots!" He thought for a moment. "He was with the second support team. I will replace him with one from the mortar team. That leaves only two men to operate the mortar, but there is nothing else we can do."

"Is that all you have to say?" Musa asked in disbelief.

"What else is there?" Ali countered. "The incident is over. I only hope we do not have a repeat of it."

"That is not what I mean; I expected this would happen."

"What are you talking about?" Ali demanded impatiently.

"Their nerves are raw. They are men of action, and they have had to sit in this house for weeks, like caged animals, listening to the police radio and watching out the window, waiting for the Americans to charge down the drive at any moment. There is too much time to think."

"I can do nothing about all that," Ali said angrily. "They should be able to take it, not turn into wild beasts."

"I do not know anymore," Musa said. "I have never seen you like this. You did not need to stop the fight that way—no one was really hurt. And one of our own is dead, a good soldier. Combat discipline is one thing, but this is something else. You used to care about such things."

"And you have always been soft about these things," Ali taunted. "Perhaps you have lost your stomach for what we must do?"

Musa stared at him as if he was looking at a stranger.

"Maybe I am too sentimental. But maybe you have fought too long, and all the emotion has been burned out of you."

Ali rose from the chair and walked out of the room.

For the next few days, the colonel and his sergeant major studiously ignored each other. The commandos knew something was wrong, and talked about it amongst themselves. After the incident in the kitchen, there were no further disagreements.

Ali had been taking short naps in the afternoons, partly to fight the boredom but also in an effort to avoid a recurring dream he had been having at night. Possessing the infantryman's ability to sleep lightly with the senses still alert, he snapped awake at the first sound of a commotion in the house. When the noise was followed by a distinctly feminine scream, he snatched the M16 from the pillow next to him and charged out the bedroom door, nearly colliding with the commando who was rushing in to wake him.

The mob of commandos in the hallway near the front door parted to reveal two American women, one in her late twenties and the other middle-aged. Both were impeccably dressed and prosperous looking, and Karim was slapping heavy tape over their mouths to prevent any further screaming. One of the commandos pulled out a curtain sash to tie their hands.

"What is this?" Ali shouted. He looked at the women in despair. "How did they get in here?"

The commandos did not meet his gaze. "Someone left the front door unlocked," Karim said eventually, seeing that Ali's patience was wearing thin. "They must have knocked and walked in. They saw the arms in the front room," he added.

"Merciful God," Ali breathed. "Are you sure there were only these two?"

"We saw only the two," Karim said. The others nodded.

"I do not think they will be alone," Ali said. He closed his eyes, trying to think. "Sergeant Major?"

"Yes, Colonel," Musa said from the background.

"Pack everything," Ali said. "We leave tonight."

"Where will we go?" the sergeant major asked.

Ali was taken aback. He actually had not thought of that. "I know," he said, after a moment. "You have homes, do you not?" he asked the spies.

"Yes, of course," Mehdi replied.

"We will go to the home of whoever lives closest to Washington," Ali said.

"That would be Hafiz," Mehdi said, with a slight smile.

"No. If they have his picture, they may be waiting."

"Then mine," said Mehdi.

"We leave at once," Ali said.

"What will we do with them?" Karim asked, gesturing toward the two women. They were utterly terrified, moaning behind their gags. Seeing the weapons and hearing a foreign language spoken, they had no doubt what was happening.

From the edge of his vision, Ali could see the sergeant major watching him intently. "Take them down to the cellar and shoot them," Ali said.

"Commander . . ." said one of the assault team leaders.

"What is it?" Ali snapped.

"They are women," the team leader said.

"Yes?" Ali said.

"They are holy people, religious people," the team leader said persistently. He held up the Bibles and religious pamphlets the women carried in their purses. "The attack is in two days. Could we not leave them bound and locked in the cellar?" The other commandos looked at him with expressions of respect and trepidation. No one else wanted to argue with Ali.

"Are you serious?" Ali asked.

"Yes, Commander," the team leader replied hesitantly.

"Are they Muslim?" Ali asked.

"No."

"Then allow them to pray—and then shoot them," Ali said, looking directly at Musa.

"As you order, Commander," the team leader replied.

As the commandos rushed to load the vans, the sergeant major sat in an easy chair and looked at the family pictures he found in the women's purses. Ali walked by, and two heavily muffled shots could be felt through the floorboards.

"Have you ever loved anyone?" Musa asked him.

Ali stopped abruptly and fixed the sergeant major in a cold stare that lasted for some time. "No," he said finally. "You see, all the emotion has been burned out of me."

CHAPTER 27

BASED ON THE number of police cars, Rich Welsh guessed they didn't get much of this kind of thing in Fredericksburg. Every cop in town had to rush in for a look. But why did they always have to leave their stupid lights on? It was making him see blue spots in front of his eyes.

He had a hassle with the cops at the front door of the house until one of MacNeil's men came out and cleared him.

"You checked the place out, right?" Welsh asked him, before they got through the front hall.

"You won't believe this," the agent replied. "The local cops were looking for two women who disappeared in the area yesterday afternoon. They talked to all the neighbors this morning, and somebody remembered seeing a bunch of cars leaving here last night. So the cops get a warrant, tramp all over the house, and then give us a call. That's how we know there's no booby traps."

"Jesus," said Welsh.

"But we had a team go over the whole place, in case the cops just got lucky and missed something." He directed Welsh to the basement stairs. "There's a lot of prints, but otherwise the place is clean," he said. "Except for down here."

"And I have to be surprised?"

The agent shrugged. "MacNeil wants to fill you in himself. . . . Hey, how come he likes you all of a sudden? You two didn't exactly hit it off before."

"I guess we just grew on each other."

As Welsh went down the stairs into the basement, he could see something was different, but he couldn't figure it out in the dim light. When he got to the bottom, he was dumbfounded. The basement had been turned into a firing range. The walls and ceiling were sheathed in cork soundproofing material. Piled up against one concrete wall were trash cans filled with dirt, two high and three deep. The cans were perforated with bullet holes. Welsh took out his pocketknife and stuck it in the cork wall. It didn't hit wood, so the cork was over four inches thick.

"Look at this," MacNeil said from behind him. Welsh turned, and MacNeil was pointing to a large stainless-steel object set in the ceiling. "Restaurant fan," said MacNeil. "To get all the gunpowder smoke out. Ran the vent up to the second floor and out a window."

There was more. MacNeil led him over to the far corner. There were more trash cans and a pile of silhouette paper targets. The cans were filled with small, shiny objects. Welsh plunged his hand into one. "They even policed up their empty brass," MacNeil said. "All 5.56mm and 7.62mm NATO." He pointed to two chalk outlines on the floor. The outlines approximated human forms. Two small, dark stains marked where the heads should have been. "Two ladies out spreading the Gospel. They must have stumbled across something, because they were taken down here, each shot twice in the head with a 9mm, and then these creeps bolted to a new hole."

"And you're telling me that the neighbors didn't hear or see anything until they *left?*" Welsh shouted.

"Now, after the fact, a few people might have heard something that sounded like hammering. But that's it. They might have noticed a van drive out a few times, but nobody saw a license plate or anyone who lived here. You notice we're at the end of the drive, set away from all the rest of the houses."

Welsh just shook his head. "Yeah, what could be in poorer taste than introducing yourself to the neighbors. Well, the assholes have their weapons all zeroed, and plenty of practice. Unless they're waiting for a specific date, they should be about ready to go."

"I didn't think of that," MacNeil said quickly. "But wait a minute, all the spring holidays are over. There's no major ones for a couple of months."

"What about Islamic holidays?" Welsh suggested. "Or terrorist anniversaries?"

"We'll check it out," said MacNeil, writing in his notebook. "They pulled out of here in a big hurry; maybe they screwed up this time. Or left something we can use."

"Maybe we can get lucky before they move again," said Welsh. "God knows we rate it after all this."

"I'll call you when we get everything back from the lab."

"You know their being here means two things," said Welsh.

"What?"

"Well, now that they're in range of D.C., our bosses will hopefully put everyone and everything on a high level of alert. . . ."

"And?" said MacNeil.

"And it means now I have to go back to the office."

MacNeil chuckled and shook his head. "Good luck this time. If you'd like, I'll write you a testimonial."

"Thanks," Welsh replied. "But I doubt it would change anyone's mind about me."

CHAPTER 28

THE DEPUTY ASSISTANT secretary of defense for special operations, the number two man in the office, was a one-star admiral, a SEAL. Welsh was directed into his office the moment he arrived.

"Does this mean I'm not on the secretary's A list anymore?" was the first thing Welsh asked. He knew he could joke with the admiral.

"Rich, sit down," said Rear Adm. (Lower Half) John Booker. "I'm going to counsel your sorry ass."

"Is this personal or official, Sir?"

"Personal, goddammit. Let me tell you something, Son, you're on damn thin ice around here. You make one false move, you're gone—and more than a few people can't wait for that to happen. I'm not one of them—I think it would be a great loss for this office. Now, this is the bottom line: If you want to quit, quit right now and get it over with. But if you want to stay, then for the time being you're going to have to keep a low profile and do *exactly* what you're told. It's your choice."

Welsh was chastened. "I appreciate you talking to me like this, Sir. I want to at least stay and see this thing through, so I'll be a good boy."

"Nobody expects *that* much from you," the admiral said with a smile. "Okay, let me fill you in on what we're going to do around here. Team 6 and a detachment of helos from the 160th are moving out to Andrews. And just in case this thing in Fredericksburg is just deception, Delta and another helo detachment are going out to Los

Angeles. They'll respond to anything that goes down west of the Mississippi."

"That's the best news I've heard all month, Sir," said Welsh. "But with all due respect, you're a lousy poker player. The look on your face says I should be ready to take it like a man . . . again."

"Okay," said the admiral, "I'll be straight with you. You're going out to Andrews as a liaison to the SOCOM command group."

"You mean to make sure the boys are getting their chow all right," Welsh said, with more than a little bitterness. "Sit and drink coffee until my bladder rots. High-priority shit like that. I know where these orders came from."

"I expect you to do your duty," said the admiral.

"I have always done my duty," Welsh said firmly. "And I've always accomplished the mission, whatever it was. I'll go."

"You know," Welsh said later in the evening, spearing a forkful of swordfish, "if I keep having these setbacks, I'll never have to pay for another meal."

"It's wonderful you haven't let it ruin your appetite," Carol Bondurant replied.

"Nope, as a matter of fact I'll probably have to run an extra five miles a day to keep from buying new clothes."

"At least I'm picking the restaurants now."

"Carol, I'm just that kind of modern, free-thinking guy."

"How's the sauce for the fish?"

"Beautiful. Garlic and butter, and just the way I like it —not too fussy. How's the pasta?"

"Just fine. Rich, at the risk of bringing up a tender subject, have you gone out to Andrews yet?"

"Tomorrow," said Welsh. "The advance party flies in tomorrow."

"Are you going to do what the admiral told you?"

"I don't see why not," said Welsh. "But you know me; I'll try to keep my hand in."

"That's what worries me," said Carol, twirling pasta on her fork with great concentration.

"Don't. I may be crazy, but I'm not stupid. There's a big difference."

"I'll take your word for it." She put down her fork. "You know, I've been trying to put the chronology of this whole thing together back at the office, and it's got me completely stumped."

"What do you mean?"

"Well, if the bombing of Camp Lejeune was the main effort, why did they bring all those weapons?"

"It obviously wasn't," said Welsh, with his mouth full.

"Then if there's a bigger attack, so big that they had to risk replacing the weapons, why bomb Camp Lejeune and lose the element of surprise?"

"As a distraction for killing the rifle company to get their weapons?" Welsh suggested. "Hoping that it would be a longer time before we found the dead marines."

"It took a lot of planning, demolitions gear, and training to do that bombing," Carol pointed out.

"You're right," said Welsh. "That's what I get for thinking more about my chow than what you're saying."

"Camp Lejeune is the wild card. I just can't understand it."

"You're supposed to get into your opponent's head," said Welsh. "I can see the logic of what they've done, because they hate marines with a passion. But I can't get the rationale behind the sequence of events. You're right. If something bigger is yet to come, why alert us?" He shook his head. "They're operating on a different frequency than we are, as usual."

"I'm sure that the next attack is going to happen here in the D.C. area, though," said Carol.

"I think you're right, as usual," said Welsh.

"I'm also coming around to your way of thinking about them being either Iranian or Iranian-hired. I can't see what else they could be." She paused. "What if this is some kind of long-term series of suicide attacks? You know, they have a list of targets and just keep hitting us until they're all killed."

"Your guess is as good as mine," said Welsh. "I'm afraid we're just going to have to wait and see."

"I hate that," Carol said vehemently.

"I know," Welsh said affectionately. "The rational mind. But this isn't rational or logical—it's much more elemental than that." He laughed. "Just like our office isn't rational or logical."

"Don't worry," Carol said. "The boss'll get his one day."

Welsh shook his head. "At the risk of being called a cynic again, he won't. Guys like him always do just fine. They may leave disaster in their wake, but they cover their asses, blame someone else, and glide on to the next thing. If you're well connected and know how to play the game, you'll always be taken care of."

"Well that just stinks."

"You know what the problem is?" said Welsh, with a gleam in his eye. "The assholes are starting to outnumber us. We really ought to give some serious thought to reproducing, to restore the proper balance."

"Is that a proposal?"

"Just a topic for discussion."

"There's only one thing I've got to ask," Carol said dryly. "Will I still have to pay for dinner?"

CHAPTER 29

SERGEANT MAJOR MUSA Sa'ed peered cautiously through the kitchen door of Mehdi's house in Falls Church, Virginia. Ali was sitting at the breakfast table. He was alone, drinking tea and going over his plans for the thousandth time. Except for issuing a few perfunctory orders, he had hardly spoken to anyone since leaving Fredericksburg.

Taking a deep breath, Musa walked into the kitchen and poured himself a cup of tea from Mehdi's samovar. He held back for a moment, as if unsure how to proceed, then set the cup down and walked over to the kitchen table. He stood at rigid attention.

"Colonel?"

"Yes, Sergeant Major?" Ali replied, eyes fixed on his papers.

"I wish to apologize for what I said."

Ali looked up from his plans and examined Musa's face. "I regret that it happened. The tension has made us forget all we have been through together. Please, sit down."

Musa pulled up a chair and made a space between the diagrams for his teacup. There was an uncomfortable silence, Ali ruffling papers and Musa sipping tea.

"I must talk to you for a moment, now that we have privacy," Musa said.

"Oh?" Ali replied uneasily.

"Something is bothering you." It was a statement.

"Everything is bothering me," Ali said. "We are only attacking the White House tomorrow."

"No," Musa said. He took hold of Ali's arm. "Something is wearing away at you. It has been ever since we came to America. Perhaps you should tell me."

"Will it do any good to bring this up again?" Ali asked in exasperation.

"I think we should talk about it, whatever it is."

"You are being presumptuous."

"How can I be, after all we have been through together? It is not just what happened in the last place. You have not been able to sleep since we arrived here. Whatever it is, I know it must be cleared away. I ask you to do this, as your friend, for your own sake. I know you went to school here," Musa continued, "even though you will not speak of it. Does it have something to do with the Americans?"

Ali looked at him for a long while, as if weighing a decision. He put down his pen and settled back in the chair.

"Very well, old friend. Since you are so determined, I will tell you the story of my education in America. The great dream of my life was to attend university. It was always unattainable, as you know. Then I was chosen to be in the first group of the revolution to go abroad, picked because we deserved it, not for our families' influence. We were given applications to those American universities who had contracts with our National University. They were eager to establish good ties with the revolution, so the windfall of money they received from the shah would continue. I was accepted by the University of Pennsylvania.

"My education began the day I arrived. From the airport to the university, people would listen to my accent and ask where I had come from. None knew where Iran was."

"And the university?"

"The university was like an island in the area of the

city called West Philadelphia. It was full of white faces and unlimited promise. Leaving it, you entered another world of black, brown, and yellow faces, and little hope."

"A familiar story," said Musa.

"Yes. My English was not perfect, but it improved over time. The classes were not difficult, but the other students were beyond belief. It was through them I learned of the American character. They were as ignorant in their own way as the common people I met in the streets, but without the excuse. They would read a book, and that would determine their philosophy until a different idea became fashionable and took its place. You see, they were convinced they knew the absolute truth about everything. They made a great show of their liberalism, and when they took their degrees they would join the government and corporations that use the rest of the world for their own purposes. . . . It was at that time the spies in the embassy were taken."

"I can imagine their feelings about that," said Musa. "We would watch on television."

"Outrage, of course. They simply could not understand why we had done it. They imagined all American diplomats do is issue visas, instead of spying and overthrowing governments. Even when our women pasted the shredded papers together and proved their crimes, they called us barbarians. All they could see was that they had been wronged. When the hostage crisis— as they called it—began, they showed their true colors. On the street they would shout obscenities and call us ragheads."

"Ragheads!" Musa exclaimed. "They said this?"

"Why not?" said Ali. "You remember the shah used that word for those of us who kept the true Faith."

"Disgusting," said Musa.

"It is how they see us," said Ali. "But to them we have always been too much trouble to try and understand."

Musa felt that Ali was close to revealing something. He asked gently, "What did they do to you?"

Ali took a deep breath. He placed his forearms on the table as if to steady himself. "It was fall. Every night the television would have some fantastic story, and they would show the embassy and our people giving their support. At the end they would say how many days the spies had been held. This was to keep the masses aroused.

"I had been studying in the library and afterward went to a cafe. Then I walked to my dormitory. Along the street were student houses that were called fraternities, private clubs filled with the most fascist elements—all white, of course. They drank alcohol constantly, and in public they would insult any woman they did not find attractive and proposition those they did. Like pigs they would abuse whoever crossed their path: women, blacks, Orientals—anyone different. They would wear shirts calling us obscenities, insulting the Imam, and demanding that we be bombed."

"I would have guessed it," said Musa. "Did the authorities encourage this?"

"Their general behavior was tolerated," Ali explained. "There would be protests from women and blacks they had abused. But their behavior toward us was ignored. We were not in fashion with the so-called liberals at that time."

"Go on," said Musa.

"As I said, I was walking back to my dormitory. I passed one of these fraternities where a party was taking place. My attention was attracted when the music became louder; the front door had been opened. The people of the house were ejecting someone from their party. I should have left, but my curiosity was too great."

"What of the neighbors?" Musa asked.

"Animals like themselves. These people were beating a man on the front steps. They dragged him down the steps and threw him onto the lawn. Then they went back into the house to continue their drinking.

"I thought of running away, but the man on the lawn

was moaning. I walked over and began to examine his wounds. I could not go to the house for help, and if I called to anyone on the street they would think I was trying to rob them and run away. Then I heard voices, and bright light hit my eyes. There were many police vehicles, and policemen running toward me. A voice shouted, 'Get him!' Before I could speak, I was hit with a club, and they swarmed on me.

"You must understand that the American police had many rules that governed their conduct," Ali said bitterly. "Those in their hands had rights that protected their safety. But the police of Philadelphia did not know of these rules—they had a fearsome reputation for violence and corruption."

"Go on," said Musa.

"Soon they stopped hitting me with their clubs and put handcuffs on my wrists. I cannot bear to be confined, and I screamed and thrashed with my legs. I think I kicked one. That infuriated them. They took hold of the handcuffs and dragged me across the lawn. They dragged me across the concrete sidewalk and threw me into the back of a van. They beat me until I lost consciousness." He stared at the table, as if trying to decide whether or not to continue.

"One of them was a woman," he said.

"A woman!" exclaimed Musa.

"Yes, they have women police. The last thing I remember was her beating me with a club, and her look of enjoyment."

"An abomination!" Musa said.

"When I woke up I found myself in a hospital, but there were bars on the door. My face was so swollen I could barely see, and my jaw was wired—it was broken. My ribs were broken, and one wrist. The next day a judge came to the hospital, and I was charged with attacking the police."

"They accused *you* of attacking *them?*"

"Yes. The lawyer defending me said it was to keep me

from charging them with brutality. That is the word he used, 'brutality.' A brother from our embassy came with a man from the Department of State. This was before our diplomats were expelled. I was given a choice. I could leave the country at once. Or I could make a complaint against the police, in which case the police would say I had gone berserk and they defended themselves. I would go to prison, and then be expelled from the country."

"Wonderful choices," said Musa.

"Yes, it did not take me long to decide. The embassy arranged a flight, and I was home in a week, in my bandages."

"So this is why you hate them," Musa said flatly.

"I vowed one day I would have my vengeance. But that is a personal thing. The whole world hates them, why not I? They deserve to be hated. When I discovered how they thought, it all became clear to me. They believe the world must live by their orders. Their arrogance is equal to their power."

"The rich are always like that," Musa said knowingly.

"Yes, they have everything they could desire. Everything, but it is never enough. For years their companies would take our oil for a pittance, and we could buy their goods that we could not afford and did not need. Their plan for us was permanent poverty, poverty that would pay for their luxury. When we took our wealth back and made them pay fairly for once, they screamed in outrage."

"Like a spoiled child, who pushes another away from a bowl of sweets even though he has had enough," said Musa, indulging him, wanting Ali to be rid of it.

"You understand," said Ali, "to be among them is intolerable. They live in freedom, with no enemies on their borders. But they support animals like the shah and his torturers all over the world because they will do as they are bid. So, for the sake of their security, their prosperity, their freedom, others must live under tyranny and in poverty."

"I always wondered when I read of them," Musa said, "after they fought so well for their own freedom, why they should begrudge it to others."

"Why should they care?" said Ali. "They already *have* their freedom." His voice rasped; his mouth was dry. "They were shocked we should call them spies, the same CIA that once overthrew our government, trained our torturers, and plotted against the revolution. Then they were hurt we did not embrace them when they held out their arms. To them we were returning to the Middle Ages when in fact we had gained not only our freedom, but our souls. Now we frighten them because we are the few they cannot control."

"They attack us, and they attack the Faith," the sergeant major said, almost sadly.

"That is because they have none," Ali said, his voice winding down. "When all Islam rose up against the blasphemous book, they were amazed to find people who took God seriously, whose religion was a matter of life and death to them."

Several commandos, attracted by the conversation, stood in the doorway, watching silently.

Musa gripped Ali's shoulders with both hands. "Now I know why you feel as you do." He noticed the men in the doorway. "Go back to your work!" he snapped. Grudgingly, they returned to cleaning weapons.

Ali gently removed the hands from his shoulders. "I am sorry, old comrade. I have never told the entire story. Before the war I dreamt of it often. Then I had other things to occupy my nightmares. Now the dream has come back every night since we landed." His face took on a strange look. "Perhaps tomorrow night it will go away."

"Because tomorrow you will be revenged."

"Or dead. I always knew I would be back. Now the

chance has come . . . another chance in America. But we may all pay for my vengeance."

The sergeant major drank down his now-cold tea, trying to absorb what this rigidly self-contained man had revealed. He had seen many under stress break apart without warning, and he prayed that Ali's actions were not a sign of this. But we are all human, Musa thought. We all have our limits and our many motives. "We come for our country's vengeance," he said.

"But before, under the pressure of events, it was easy just to act. Now I have had time to think. I made you all take a great risk at the marine camp."

"And we won," Musa interrupted.

"We take a much greater risk this time."

"Is it the mission? Is that what you worry about?"

"I worry what will happen to Iran if we succeed, what the Americans will do. I worry about the men."

"Then do you think we are doing the right thing?" Musa asked quietly.

Ali waved his hand impatiently; some of his fire was coming back. "You misunderstand. I am sure it is the only way we can defend ourselves. All this talk about war waged by rules is a Western invention, to soothe their troubled consciences. These 'humanists' were the first to use poison gas, nuclear weapons, and drop bombs on cities of unarmed civilians. The only rule in war is to win. You owe your enemies nothing—certainly not mercy. It is like prisoners," he said pointedly. "You take prisoners because it makes the enemy more willing to give up without much fight. But if prisoners are a burden, you kill them. Who or what they are makes no difference. That is war."

"I know it is true," Musa said. "It was just that, at the time, I did not want it to be. But the way you said it, the way you did it, you made it so hard."

"I never try to put a pretty face on reality," Ali said. "My only worry is what we may do to ourselves."

Musa sensed that Ali was not so much stating a philosophy as trying to convince himself. He realized his friend was asking for his approval, to share at least some of the responsibility. No wonder, he thought, with the strain of the past weeks, knowing the consequences of a mistake. "I do not worry for us, Ali. You are not one of these empty-headed children who has learned to hate life, heard too much talk of martyrdom and Paradise, and rushes toward death with a plastic key in his hand. . . . I believe in you."

Ali rubbed his eyes again. He felt sickened by his show of vulnerability. Then the door in the man slammed shut —Ali was gone, and the colonel had returned. "Have no fear, my good, good friend. I am tired, and I talk like a fool. We have nothing to be ashamed of. And tomorrow we will accomplish our mission. All debts will be paid."

Musa smiled sadly. "I have always trusted in your skill. And I have always prayed. God has always protected us. What happens tomorrow is in His hands."

CHAPTER 30

RICH WELSH STOOD in the rear of a Military Airlift Command terminal at Andrews Air Force Base in Maryland, sipping a Pepsi and taking in all the activity around him.

Andrews has the largest capacity of any military airfield near Washington, D.C. In addition to handling the transportation needs of the president, incoming foreign dignitaries, and the upper levels of the political establishment, the base accommodates a full range of strictly military missions. When the air force was ordered to give up a space near the flight line to Special Operations Command, it meant someone would have to be kicked out. The howls of outrage could be heard all the way to the Pentagon.

Welsh accompanied the SOCOM advance party that had checked out the first facilities offered by the air force. The facilities were inadequate, but that was expected. As in the Middle Eastern bazaars, in such situations the bargaining was an accepted part of doing business. After a call to Washington, a Military Airlift Command terminal and a transient barracks were put at SOCOM's disposal. There were no further problems. It was Welsh's experience that the air force handled the transport and accommodation of large numbers of men and equipment better than any other service—and with immeasurably less chickenshit.

On the tarmac outside was a line of helicopters belonging to the 160th Aviation Regiment, the U.S. Army's special operations helicopter unit based at Fort Campbell, Kentucky. Formed in the early 1980s, in less than a decade the 160th had ballooned from a composite unit to a regiment of three battalions operating 163 helicopters. Though a quantum leap in capability, this fast growth exacerbated a serious shortage of fully trained pilots able to handle the extremely demanding night and low-level flying the regiment conducted. It was a classic Special Forces problem. Any rapid expansion created intense competition with other units for the limited number of first-class personnel, and overall quality nearly always dropped off. In the 160th the pilots were all volunteers, selected and trained by the regiment.

The three different helicopter types flown by the 160th were all represented. Most numerous were the medium-range assault transports, the MH-60Ks. This was the army's Blackhawk utility helicopter with uprated engines and in-flight refueling probe, terrain-following radar, forward-looking infrared for night flying, comprehensive navigation systems, and extra fuel tanks.

Next were two versions of the McDonnell Douglas/ Hughes H-6-530, best known in civilian clothing as the helicopter on the television series *Magnum PI*. The helicopter was small, fast, nimble, very quiet, and able to land in incredibly small spaces. The MH-6, as the army called it, was the short-range assault transport. Platform seats were mounted outside the cabin above the skids, for rapid dismounting. The AH-6 was the gunship variant, armed with rocket pods and 7.62mm Gatling guns. The army's regular gunships, the AH-1 Cobra and AH-64 Apache, were too slow to get into action after being transported inside cargo aircraft. The AH/MH-6s and the Blackhawks had special bladefolding and stowage systems that made them flyable within ten minutes of being unloaded.

The long-range transport was the MH-47E, the Vietnam-era twin-rotor Chinook with the same avionics and special equipment as the Blackhawk. It was almost equivalent in capability to the air force's well-tried

MH-53 Pave Low special operations helicopters, but the Chinook had been developed at great expense because the air force no longer wished to be in the special operations helicopter business, and the army did not wish to add a new aircraft type.

After the aborted Iran hostage rescue, the American military had finally learned a few lessons about having sufficient helicopters to both accomplish the mission and allow for the inevitable technical malfunctions. The same necessity applied to other forms of transport. Delta had once been delayed in responding to an overseas mission when the single transport aircraft assigned to it went down with mechanical troubles. As a result there were more than enough helicopters on the strip to meet any conceivable mission requirement. Some were already prepared for transport in the two C-5B and two C-141 cargo planes also standing by, along with a pair of KC-130s to refuel the helicopters in flight.

If a terrorist incident went down within helicopter range of Andrews, SEAL Team 6 would fly in directly. If something happened farther away, the unit would fly in the C-5Bs and C-141s to the nearest capable airfield.

The members of SEAL Team 6 sat together on one side of the terminal. Although other services might disagree, the SEALs were widely regarded as America's military elite. The special operations craze had pumped them up from four to seven teams in only a few years, and the SEALs had to fight hard to keep their high standards from being diluted. No one could touch them in the water, but many thought they lost some of their edge on land when the underwater demolition teams were merged into SEAL and swimmer delivery vehicle teams in 1983. And since SEAL officers had begun to make admiral, some were even mapping out career paths in good regular navy fashion.

For all that, they were still the cream of the elite forces. And Team 6 was the SEAL elite: highly experienced and specially chosen men, all first class petty officers or above. The platoon leaders were lieutenant commanders, and the officer in charge was a captain, the equivalent of a full colonel in the other services.

Small groups were reading, playing cards, or sleeping. Others pored over maps or checked equipment. They were dressed in their usual combat uniform, the U.S. sage green flight suit made of fireproof Nomex. Most were wearing their sidearms. Team 6 used stainless-steel Smith & Wesson revolvers, for better functioning after immersion in saltwater and the ability to use exotic ammunition that would not feed reliably in an automatic. The pistols were worn on belt rigs with holsters that strapped down on the thigh, and pouches for speed-loaders on the opposite side. For quiet work they also had available 9mm automatics with snap-on sound suppressors. They had originally used Berettas, but the slide of one blew off during firing and took out a SEAL's front teeth. With typical SEAL humor, Team 6 maintained that "You're not a SEAL until you've eaten Italian steel." After that, most SEALs switched to pistols by SIG or Heckler & Koch. These had replaced the Vietnam-era Smith & Wesson "Hush Puppy."

The rest of their personal equipment was neatly stacked on the plastic chairs of the terminal. Heavy body armor. Parachutist goggles for eye protection. Gas-mask bags worn on the hip. Load-bearing vests with submachine-gun magazines across the front, Motorola radio in back, and stun grenades and pyrotechnics in pouches on the sides. Team 6 also wore lightweight plastic helmets, like kayaking helmets, with built-in earphones and microphone, and a strobe light taped to the back.

Their primary weapon was the ubiquitous Heckler & Koch MP5 submachine gun, but a model designed specifically for the SEALs with custom handgrips, sights, and safety. It was used without any stock and normally had a powerful light mounted under the barrel. The MP5s were stored in mount-out boxes, as were the rest of the SEALs' family of weapons. Other mission equipment was stored on pallets outside the terminal, ready to be loaded into either the planes or the MH-47s.

There was no common physique among the SEALs; they were alike only in their spectacular physical condition. But they all had the utterly confident look of men who as part of their daily work do things normal people would only regard with abject terror. All a product of the Darwinian selection of the Basic Underwater Demolition/SEAL course. Survival of only the fittest and the craziest.

The pilots and flight crew of the 160th gathered in another part of the terminal. They also wore green flight suits and had an attitude similar to that of the SEALs, which was to be expected of the most shit-hot pilots in the army.

Wandering in and out were members of the 160th's ground crews, dressed in regular army camouflage field uniforms, BDUs. Most were young soldiers chosen solely for their technical expertise. They had given SOCOM fits during several exercises with their typically American inability to keep their mouths shut about what they were doing.

Like the rest of the SOCOM support staff, Welsh wore a flight suit with no markings. He finished his soda and tossed the can.

"What's up?" said a voice behind him.

Welsh looked over his shoulder. It was the CO of Team 6. Captain Al Hasford was tall and lean, with a carefully maintained moustache and the glittery eyes of an all-pro linebacker.

"Just checking out the scene," Welsh replied.

"You look worried," said Hasford.

"I am."

"Well, you're the guy who should know. What else do we need to do to be ready?"

Welsh felt comfortable around Hasford. The man was a real leader, and secure enough to listen to any point of view. As far as Welsh was concerned, that was what got the job done. "Smash all that shit," he said, gesturing toward the office down the hall where the SOCOM communications detachment had set up what looked to be two of every type of radio in existence.

Hasford laughed. "No, really."

"I mean it," said Welsh. "If comm with Washington goes out at the right time, we might just make it."

"I signed for it all," Hasford said with mock horror. "My kids would have to forget about going to college."

Welsh smiled in spite of himself.

"Seriously, though," said Hasford. "Did we forget anything?"

"We're as ready as we can be," Welsh replied. "But I was thinking about Punta Paitilla."

"Now I see," said Hasford. In Panama a SEAL platoon from Team 8 had been given the job of destroying General Noriega's private jet at Punta Paitilla airfield near Panama City, to prevent its being used in an escape. But, at the last minute, staff officers at U.S. Southern Command had ordered the SEALs to only disable the plane, so the next government wouldn't have to buy a new one. Instead of firing a rocket into the jet from a distance, the SEALs had been ambushed while approaching it. Four died, and the plane was shot up anyway.

"What if some staff puke fucks us up this time?" asked Welsh.

"You don't worry about something that's out of your hands. All you can do is make sure *your* shit is together."

"It chills my balls when I think about the consequences of a screwup."

"We're locked and cocked," Hasford said confidently. Then he whispered, "I'm not even worried about Clark." The CO of the army's Joint Special Operations Command at Fort Bragg, Major General Clark, was in operational command at Andrews.

"Yeah, the army's done all right in the special ops

business," said Welsh. "Shit themselves a whole bunch of new generals. They got a four star as SOCOM commander in Tampa, a three star for army special ops at Bragg, a two star for Special Forces, and one for all the joint commands."

"Amazing anything gets done at all, ain't it?" Hasford said with a grin. "But Clark'll be fine."

"Seems to know his shit," Welsh admitted. "But he sure gets Van Brocklin uptight, though." Lieutenant Colonel Van Brocklin commanded the detachment of the 160th.

"Nervous as a whore in the front pew of church," said Hasford. "Brock's worried about his fitness report, wants to be a general too. Look, chill out. You've been working your ass off getting everything we need. Getting that secure fax line for blueprints of federal buildings was a great job."

"It wasn't easy," said Welsh with typical military humor. "I nearly had to suck every dick in Washington."

"That," Hasford said emphatically, "is exactly what liaison officers are for." They both burst into laughter.

"I know," said Welsh, shaking his head. "I've been a real downer lately. And I've got no right to be, since you guys are a hell of a lot more fun than the FBI. But I am fucking sick and tired of watching firsthand while these bastards do a job on us."

"Where do you think they'll hit next?"

"D.C.," said Welsh. "My money is all on D.C."

CHAPTER 31

THE TRAFFIC AROUND the White House was light at 4:00 in the morning. Hafiz and Karim made excellent time as they methodically toured the streets in their sporty little Toyota van. Resting on the bench seat behind Karim was a collection of jars and bottles. The containers were filled with liquid explosive brought up from North Carolina, each one primed with an electric blasting cap wired to a nine-volt battery and a simple watch timer. Whenever they passed a trash receptacle near street poles carrying traffic lights or electrical transformers, Karim would wrap a bomb in newspaper, jump out the passenger door, and bury the device deep in the trash can. They had no illusions that the bombs would disrupt operations at the White House—the building had its own self-contained power supply. The explosives were intended to cause confusion and snarl traffic around the executive mansion at the appropriate time.

After seeding their packages at all the crucial intersections leading to the White House, they turned down Constitution Avenue and crossed the Theodore Roosevelt Bridge into Arlington, Virginia.

Except for Karim's occasional orders, it had been quiet most of the ride, though the atmosphere was not unfriendly. Hafiz was in a magnanimous mood; Ali had told him the day before that he would not be participating in the attack.

"I just want you to know," Hafiz said, as they were crossing the bridge, "that I wish you every success."

Karim did not reply.

"I realize there have been hard feelings between us," Hafiz persisted. "But I want to tell you I am sincere; I really do wish you the best."

"That is good of you," said Karim. "Pull in here," he added quickly, pointing to an exit at the end of the bridge.

Hafiz was glad there was no traffic; the van was moving fast and he barely made the turnoff. They circled around the brightly lit Iwo Jima Memorial on the edge of Arlington National Cemetery. Hafiz followed Karim's finger to a narrow road that separated the memorial from the cemetery. "Turn around," Karim ordered. "Pull in behind that tree and stop.

"Turn off the headlights," Karim said in exasperation. "We are trying not to attract attention."

"Sorry," Hafiz said apologetically, turning the switch. "What are we doing here?"

"We have one more package to drop off," Karim said, producing a brown paper bag from under his seat. He sat back for a moment, as if thinking. "Say, would you mind doing this for me? I feel a bit tired from all the running around."

"Of course," said Hafiz.

"There's a good fellow," said Karim, handing him the bag. "It's all ready to go. Just put it next to that bush, on the other side of the wall."

Hafiz got out on the driver's side. He walked in front of the van and gave a little wave to Karim in the passenger seat. Karim cheerfully waved back. A low brick wall bordered the cemetery. Hafiz carefully laid the package on top of it before climbing over. It took some time—he showed no evidence of muscular coordination. Watching from the van, Karim could only shake his head in disgust. Once he was safely on the other side, Hafiz retrieved the bag and headed for the bush. What he saw made him pause for a moment. The moon was setting, and its last reflections illuminated the endless symmetrical mounds of white stone. The light made it seem that the tombstones were leaning forward, straining to reach the nearby hill that dominated Washington. After an uneasy shiver, Hafiz hurried to the bush.

Karim had opened his passenger door before the van had come to a stop. During the conversation with Hafiz, he had held it slightly ajar with one hand. The interior lights had been disconnected to avoid attracting attention. Once Hafiz was over the fence, Karim slid silently out of the van. He sprang over the brick wall without making a sound.

Hafiz was gently laying the bag on the grass when he heard the quiet snap of fingers behind him. He whirled, and, incredibly, Karim was standing before him pointing a pistol at his face. Karim was far too experienced to say anything melodramatic, or give Hafiz time to cry out. By all rights he should have shot the spy in the back of the head while the man was leaning over. But he indulged himself by letting Hafiz see what was going to happen.

The Russian silenced pistol had a slide lock to keep the mechanism from cycling after a round was fired, so there was not even a metallic snap—just a slight hiss. Karim unlocked the slide and ejected the spent 9mm Makarov case into the pocket of his jacket. He methodically emptied Hafiz's pockets and removed the watch and rings, putting everything in the paper bag. There was no bomb there, only trash. Karim rolled the corpse under the bush and made a last check of the ground. After peering cautiously over the wall to look for any passing cars, he leaped over and got into the van, throwing the paper bag into the back.

Whistling, Karim guided the van around the cemetery and onto Route 66. He thought he hadn't felt so good for a long, long time.

When he arrived back at the house, Karim found Ali staring out a picture window facing the backyard. A working party of commandos was burying the plastic-wrapped bodies of Mehdi, Ghulam, and Mahmoud beneath a flower border.

"I want you to know that this was done according to the orders I was given," Ali said, still staring out the window.

"I understand," said Karim. "The secret of our country's involvement cannot be known. We all understand."

"Did you have any problems?"

"None at all," said Karim. "But you were right, I did need him to drive. The route was very complicated."

"I am only sorry I had to leave that job to you."

"Think nothing of it."

"Where did you leave the body?" Ali asked. Karim told him. "Fitting," Ali said, with a slightly bemused look. "Very fitting. You should get some sleep."

"I will. Just an hour or two."

Karim ordered the guards to wake him in two hours.

The bill-signing ceremony was scheduled to begin at 10:15 in the morning, in the Oval Office.

At 8:00 Ali was lying on Mehdi's couch, checking the morning papers for any changes to the president's schedule and trying to get the taste of breakfast out of his mouth. Once again he had ignored the signals from his stomach, which was always the one part of his body to desert him under stress. He stretched out with his arms tucked behind his head, staring at the ceiling. His repose was interrupted by Karim, who announced that the commandos were assembled in the recreation room for the final inspection.

The men were lined up in their team organization. During the training in Iran, they had been broken down into four assault teams, three support teams, and a mortar team.

Three of the commandos in the four-man assault teams were armed with the M249 SAWs, the fourth with a SPAS-12 shotgun and an AT-4 rocket launcher.

Each of the three-man support teams had one commando armed with an M60 machine gun, one with an M16/M203 grenade launcher and an AT-4, and a third with an M16 and three AT-4s.

The two-man 60mm mortar team would use one mortar and M16s. The team would operate from its own van.

The commandos were dressed in blue jeans, sneakers, and a variety of civilian shirts and jackets. Automatic pistols were secured in holsters beneath their clothing, along with fake IDs and money so the men could make an escape in everyday clothes, with the pistols for protection. To identify each other in the confusion of the attack, they wore red bandanas on their heads.

Over their clothing they wore Marine Corps cartridge belts with suspender harnesses. On the rear of each belt, resting over the small of the back, two firebombs were snapped into a pair of canteen pouches. The rest of the space was taken up by pouches for M16 magazines or Squad Automatic Weapon two-hundred-round belt containers.

Since Ali felt that the Americans would use tear gas, the commandos had done all their training wearing gas masks. They used a French model with a wide bubble faceplate; high-capacity filter; and a valve that allowed the breathing of outside air, if desired.

The men carried radios in holsters secured to their cartridge belts. Each man wore an earphone in a plastic mounting that slipped over the ear and held it in place. Small push-to-talk hand microphones were plugged into the walkie-talkies and hung at collarbone height on the suspender harnesses.

The Iranians knew that only the foolish or inexperienced haphazardly hang hand grenades all over themselves; the grenades tend to drop off during rapid movement, with the embarrassing prospect of accidental explosion. The assault teams stored their grenades in green canvas shoulder bags; the support teams, in extra canteen pouches. The nonexplosive cylindrical smoke grenades were hooked onto the suspender straps of the equipment belts.

Those men armed with M203 grenade launchers carried the 40mm grenades, which resembled huge bulbous bullets, in the plastic and cloth bandoliers the ammunition came packed in.

The M60 machine gunners arranged the straps of the cloth and cardboard assault packs so that each pack, holding a hundred-round belt, hung at their waists. They did not drape bare belts of ammunition over their shoulders because dirty or bent ammunition causes weapons to jam—especially ones as finicky as the M60.

When the inspection was over, Ali took the sergeant major off to one side. "Bring everyone up to the first floor," he said. "There is not enough room here."

"Will you give them a talk before we leave?"

"No, the time is long past for that. They are more than ready, and they have no need of any speeches I could give."

"Then why do you wish them all together, if I may ask?"

"To hold prayers," Ali said. "We will pray for victory in battle and the destruction of our enemies."

CHAPTER 32

At 9:40 in the morning, two Econoline vans filled with Iranian commandos were parked on H Street near the northern side of Lafayette Park, directly across Pennsylvania Avenue from the White House.

Ali had been passing the time gazing at the White House through the trees. It was almost a letdown seeing it for the first time, since every small detail of its plan had already been committed to memory. A seven-foot iron fence surrounded the mansion grounds. To Ali's left was the East Wing; in the center the famous visage of the North Portico, with its four massive supporting columns. The portico was fronted by a fountain that was ringed by flowers just beginning to bloom. The main driveway was a semicircle; the two open ends began at vehicle gates spread far apart on Pennsylvania Avenue and joined in front of the North Portico. Branching off from the right side of the main driveway was a smaller drive leading directly to the West Wing entrance. And the West Wing was their target. Projecting off from the main White House, it held the offices of the executive staff and the Oval Office of the president of the United States. To the right of the West Wing, separated by a fence and a parking lot, was the old Executive Office Building, home to executive branch staffers not important enough to rate an office in the West Wing.

Ali did not see architecture. He saw fields of fire, cover and concealment, and obstacles. The wait had compacted his stomach into a tight knot, and he had to urinate though he had done so barely a half hour before. The bench seats of the van had been removed to facilitate a quick exit. The commandos looked otherworldly in their gas masks. Ali and the driver would not don theirs until the last minute.

Agent Dan Latimer strolled back and forth across the Oval Office carpet while a camera crew assembled its equipment. As was usual for televised events from the Oval Office, most of the furniture had been moved out into the hall to make room for the cameras. Today even more space was needed because the president, seated at his desk, would be flanked by key members of Congress and his cabinet while he signed legislation. As usual only one network camera crew would provide the pool broadcast of the event.

Latimer was assistant leader of the 7:00 to 3:00 shift of the White House Secret Service detail. As the number two man, he normally found himself directly responsible for the president's safety. It was the last month of his White House tour, and Latimer couldn't wait to get back to the relatively stable schedule of a field office and get reacquainted with his wife and kids.

The president was in the small private study just off the Oval Office, getting his makeup done. Another agent was with him. Along with the TV crew, various aides were flitting about, making sure the TelePrompTer was loaded and spreading out the legislation and note cards on the desk. Others were putting down tape so the various VIPs surrounding the president would know where to stand; it wouldn't do for anyone to get crowded out of the picture. The White House chief of staff was moving about the room supervising everything—the man was all raw nerves before a television appearance. Latimer kept a careful eye on everything but still remained cool and impassive. He liked to think of the Secret Service as the eye of the hurricane when White House hysteria really cranked up.

The armored glass door leading to the Rose Garden was closed. A few TV crews were set up in the garden, but most waited near the driveway on the other side of the West Wing to record the impressions of the congressional participants.

Corporal Brian Hawkins, in full-dress blue uniform, stood at rigid parade rest outside the West Wing entrance. The Navy and Marine Corps Medal for gallantry hung over his left breast pocket and, beside it, the Purple Heart. He had received both, along with a meritorious promotion to corporal, for his actions on the USS *Makin Island.* Hawkins considered the hardware more a curse than a blessing. The general who pinned them on had come to the sudden conclusion that such an outstanding marine should be assigned to the ceremonial unit at Marine Barracks 8th and I, in Washington. In the revelry over his inspiration, the general neglected to ask Hawkins's opinion. So Hawkins—who had previously considered it a major effort to shave daily, iron a set of utilities, and buff his boots—now found himself in the most rigidly spit-and-polish outfit in the corps. He hated it.

Now Hawkins was sweating in his blues, the heaviest article of clothing known to man, and mentally cursing the lance corporal whose flu had put him on the door. He sighed wistfully, remembering how uncomplicated life had been as just another snuffie. Now, in addition to those whose only concern in life seemed to be the length of what little hair he was allowed to retain, the corps was divided into two kinds of marines: those who had heard about *Makin Island* and expected daily proof that he really deserved the medal and those experts who thought he hadn't done anything special.

At least the White House detail was better than burying people at Arlington or drilling eight hours a day back at the barracks, but it was still a pain in the ass. It pissed Hawkins off that his sole occupation was to open a door and salute people who paid less attention to his physical presence than they did the color of the carpet. At least it was only a couple of hours at a time.

At 9:45, the Grand Voyager van carrying the mortar team pulled into a parking space on the road circling the Ellipse, the small park facing the south lawn of the White House. Actually, there was no open parking space. The driver of the van created one by discreetly bumping a small Honda out of the way. The mortar team was on the southern end of Ellipse Road, close to Constitution Avenue, with the front of the van aimed at the White House.

The modifications to the vehicle had been made in Fredericksburg. A large section of the roof was cut away and covered by a removable piece of plastic. One of the 60mm mortar baseplates was welded to the floor of the van, along with metal cups to hold the two legs of the mortar bipod. To roughly aim the mortar, the front of the van was pointed toward the target. The gunner would then sight through the windshield and dial in any fine adjustments. Accuracy was less important than concealment and using minimal manpower.

Comfortably parked in the sun, the two Iranian mortarmen deflated the tires to make a stable firing platform. They would make their escape on foot. They adjusted the azimuth, placing the vertical line of the sight on the West Wing. Then they dialed in the range, converting to elevation in mils with the help of the firing-table card thoughtfully included in each can of mortar ammo. Since the range was so short, they removed all but one of the explosive increment disks from the fins of the shells. The fuzes were set for groundburst, also called HE Quick. They would not remove the plastic cover from the top of the van until ready to fire.

At 9:55, Ali gave the order, and Selim, one of the three remaining *Baseej,* was let out of the van and began walking slowly across Lafayette Park toward the White House. Selim wore a baggy trenchcoat over a business suit and carried a briefcase. He had what appeared to be stereo headphones over his ears.

Ali spoke into his radio. "Van 3, are you ready?"

Van 3 was the Toyota, driven by the second *Baseeji,* Houshang. He was parked on 17th Street, across from the Ellipse and southwest of the White House. "Ready," Houshang answered.

"Understood," Ali replied. "Van 4, are you ready?"

Van 4 was the Aerostar, driven by Mustafa, the third *Baseeji.* He was parked on 15th Street, near Ellipse Road, southeast of the White House. "Ready," said Mustafa.

"Understood," said Ali. He had checked with the mortar van moments before. "All units, stand by."

The minute hand of Ali's watch moved agonizingly slowly toward 10:00. He could see Selim between the trees. The *Baseeji* had crossed the street at the light and was walking past the Executive Office Building toward the White House. The second hand swept to the final minute. "Start the engine and pull out," Ali commanded the driver. They crept toward the traffic light at the Pennsylvania Avenue intersection. The second Econoline van followed behind.

When they stopped at the red light, Ali shouted into the microphone: "Van 3, go! Van 4, go!" There was rattling in the back of the van as the commandos shifted anxiously and checked their weapons. Their quickened breathing could be heard in metallic rasps through the gas-mask voice transmitters. Ali and the driver put on their masks, secured earphones, and tied on bandanas.

When the command came over his radio, Houshang pulled out of the parking space and aimed the Toyota van down 17th Street. He took a right onto E Street, which separated the White House from the Ellipse. A quick left and he was on West Executive Avenue-State

Place, driving toward the two vehicle-access gates located on that street. One was for the executive parking lot reserved for high-ranking staff and visiting members of Congress. Twenty feet to its right was the Southwest Gate of the White House, leading to the sunken drive that cuts across the South Lawn and circles the South Portico.

To gain access to the two gates, a vehicle had to pass through a security chute where credentials could be examined and the vehicle searched. A square concrete island sat at the end of the chute, requiring a sharp turn at very slow speed to approach either gate. Vehicles exited around the opposite side, through a narrow gap in the concrete barriers that bordered the sidewalks all around the White House.

The gates were thick reinforced steel, designed to withstand the impact of a vehicle the size of a tractor trailer, to keep a truck bomb from crashing through and driving on to the White House. Six members of the Secret Service Uniformed Division were stationed outside the gates, and more manned the three guardposts inside.

Traveling at about twenty miles per hour, Houshang guided the Toyota van past the entrance chute, as if he were merely continuing on State Place. Steering with one hand, he picked up a fragmentation grenade wrapped with detonating cord. The cord led back to the passenger compartment, where a fifty-five-gallon drum of liquid explosive, 460 pounds in all, was resting on the floor, secured against one of the bench seats. He pulled the pin from the grenade and held it tightly.

Approaching the exit, Houshang slowed down and dropped the grenade to the floor, letting the spoon fly free. He swung the van left, then cut the wheel sharply to the right. Even with the extra weight, the vehicle handled well. It slid through the exit space in the concrete barrier. Jagged stars appeared in the windshield; they were shooting at him. Houshang tried to make it around the concrete island, but the side of the van scraped it, slowing him down. No matter, he thought, close enough. Then the grenade went off.

There was a huge blast and fireball. It took more than a minute for the dust to settle and reveal what had occurred.

The van had completely disintegrated, leaving a twenty-foot-wide crater in its place. The island was destroyed, and the two nearest guardhouses blown apart.

The gates were designed to withstand impact, but not the equivalent of a five-hundred-pound bomb. The blast bent the thick steel frame of the executive gate around the central locking mechanism as if pushed down by a heavy wind. The Southwest Gate hung sideways, only half attached to the pillars. Large chunks of concrete were scattered about. Trees were knocked over, and both drives were blocked. There were heavy casualties among the gate guards and pedestrians, and most of the cars parked on the street were wrecked or on fire.

After receiving Ali's signal, Mustafa, parked near the opposite side of the White House, began driving north on 15th Street. Inside his Aerostar van was a bomb identical to Houshang's. Mustafa turned left on E Street and made a quick right onto East Executive Place. He headed toward the Southeast Gate of the White House, a lesser-used vehicle gate directly across the South Lawn from the gates Houshang had been assigned. The guardhouse was inside the fence, and access only slightly restricted by a concrete barrier.

Mustafa was approaching the gate, a grenade tightly grasped in his fist, when Houshang's bomb went off. The shock wave buffeted the van, and Mustafa automatically stepped on the brake. Recovering, he dropped the grenade and stepped on the gas, swinging around the concrete barrier and coming to a stop with the front end of the van resting against the center of the gate. A uniformed Secret Service guard began firing at him from behind one side of the guardhouse. Mustafa sat upright in the driver's seat, eyes straight ahead and fingers tightly gripping the steering wheel, as if to support himself against an inevitable impact.

The blast crumpled the gate and the guardhouse like aluminum foil. The closest trees were blown down. Although White House tours had been canceled, there was considerable pedestrian traffic, and casualties were heavy. The Southeast Gate was completely destroyed.

The guards and plainclothes Secret Service agents who had been running to reinforce the Southwest Gate were knocked off their feet by this second explosion. Now they had to split up and cover both gates.

Ali's deception plan had succeeded brilliantly. Not only did the two *Baseej* block all vehicle access to the grounds and kill a number of guards, but the explosions focused the attention of everyone in the vicinity on the two gates and the area south of the White House.

The alarms came in automatically over special lines to the communications center of the Washington D.C. Metropolitan Police. A sergeant first class from SOCOM's communications section, who had been standing by on duty, made an excited call to Andrews over his secure voice line. The phones were working, so he didn't have to use the backup portable satellite communications set.

The metro police dispatched every available radio car to the White House. Then they set about informing the numerous law enforcement agencies of the nation's capital: the National Park Service Police, the Capitol Police, the FBI, and the small security units that protected installations such as the Pentagon. Secret Service headquarters had already received the alarm over their own lines.

At 10:00 the trash-can bombs Karim had planted began exploding. The bombs maimed nearby pedestrians, knocked over traffic lights and electric lines, and smashed passing cars. Not a great deal of damage was done, but the streets leading to the White House were effectively blocked. Only police on Constitution Avenue or on foot patrol could get through.

The first explosion was the signal for the mortar team. The gunner threw off the plastic roof covering and began dropping bombs down the tube in a slow but steady rhythm. The observer watched with binoculars for the first impact on the South Lawn near the Oval Office.

At 10:00, the president was sitting at his desk in the Oval Office, preparing to give the television crew a sound check. The members of Congress and the cabinet were scattered about the room, casually chatting until the time came to get before the cameras. Present were the speaker of the house, the house whip, the senate majority and minority leaders, and the vice president. Most of the line of presidential succession.

When the first vehicle bomb detonated, the floor rocked and everyone standing fell over. The president reflexively grabbed the top of his desk to steady himself. After a moment of disorientation, Agent Latimer quickly bounced back on his feet and made a wild running leap over the desk, knocking the president off his chair and onto the floor. Ignoring the president's protestations, Latimer jammed him under the desk. Alarms began to sound. Some of the VIPs were just getting to their feet when the second bomb went off, throwing them back onto the floor.

A Secret Service agent crawled over to the door leading to the Rose Garden and made sure it was locked. The news crews in the garden had been scattered by the explosions. Most ran in the direction of the blasts. Some were calmly filming. Others had run in search of cover.

Two Secret Service agents burst in from the outer hall, Uzi submachine guns in their hands.

"What is it?" Latimer shouted from behind the desk.

"Explosions on the two side gates," shouted one of

the agents. "Radio's so jammed with people screaming I can't find out anything. It's a mess out in the hallway, everyone's running around and knocking into the furniture."

The first mortar bomb hit the roof, and small pieces of plaster fell from the ceiling. The two agents reflexively dropped to a crouch. "Jesus Christ!" one of them exclaimed, much louder than he intended. "That sounds like a mortar."

"We're getting shelled," the other said in disbelief.

"Okay," said Latimer. Ten years of waiting and here it was. "We're not going anywhere until I find out what's happened. I'm not walking into any ambush. Pull the curtains," he ordered the agent near the door, who hurriedly moved to comply. He pointed to the two with the submachine guns. "Both of you secure the outer office. When you're set up, get me a couple more people in here."

The VIPs began to get very vocal, raising the noise level. "Listen up!" Latimer bellowed. Not accustomed to being spoken to in that fashion, they fell silent. "Everyone move against the walls," Latimer ordered. "Right now. Sit down on the floor, and be quiet until we find out what's going on. Sir," he said to the president, still under the desk, "I want you to stay here."

"Okay, Dan," said the president, quite calmly, though his voice from beneath the desk was slightly muffled. "But can I at least come out from under this thing? It just doesn't look right."

"Sure, sir," Latimer said, relieved that he wasn't going to have any trouble with the boss.

At the West Wing entrance, Corporal Hawkins automatically hit the deck at the first explosion. Looking up, he saw the news people still milling about near the driveway. "Get down!" he yelled at them. They weren't listening. He thought to himself: Jesus Christ, Hawkins, you went and stepped in it again.

• • •

The United States Special Operations Command detachment at Andrews Air Force Base handled the alarm with admirable calm. Every day they had run two full-scale drills that included loading the helicopters and circling the base. The commanders quickly decided on the number and mix of helicopters they would use, and the flight crews dashed off to get them warmed up. The SEALs strapped on their personal weapons and gear and got into their helicopter teams. The support personnel began moving the SEALs' palletted equipment out to the big MH-47 transport helicopters that would follow them in.

There was only one problem. Major General Clark, the detachment commander, was not present. He had flown one of the MH-6s to the Pentagon for a 9:30 meeting.

Welsh stood beside Lieutenant Colonel Van Brocklin, the helicopter commander, watching Captain Hasford trying to get in touch with the general on the secure phone to the Pentagon. Precious minutes ticked off. When the general came on the line, Hasford quickly described the situation. After a few seconds he fell silent, obviously interrupted. He began to protest, and was cut off again. The SEAL's face took on an expression of absolute fury. "Yes, Sir!" he shouted into the phone. He slammed down the handset and turned to Welsh and Van Brocklin. Veins were standing out on his neck. "We're not to move until the general gets here," he told them. "He's flying back right now."

Welsh's stomach dropped. The stupid bastard wasn't going to let anyone else lead the fucking charge. He'd rather have it all go down the toilet than pass up his chance at glory. The other officers in the room were practically crying with frustration. Welsh began pacing back and forth, furiously trying to think of something. "Do you know what the country is going to do to us if the president dies because we didn't move?" he asked them.

They didn't have to say anything. They just gave him the look that said—we got a direct order, asshole, what do you think we *can* do?

Welsh stopped pacing. He remembered a major in OCS saying that someday people's lives would hang on a decision they made, and that they'd better not choke. Welsh dashed over to one of the desks and grabbed a legal pad. He put down the date and time and wrote

As the personal representative of the Secretary of Defense, I authorize SEAL Team 6 and Det. 160th Av. Regt. to conduct nonexercise operations on this date. No rules of engagement. I assume complete responsibility for this order.

Richard S. Welsh.

Welsh tore off the sheet and handed it to Captain Hasford. The captain read it, passed it over to Lieutenant Colonel Van Brocklin, and looked Welsh in the eye.

Welsh knew it took a wild sweep of the imagination to picture him in the chain of command. And the captain knew it, too. Lieutenant Colonel Van Brocklin looked dubious, but Hasford was the senior man—it was his call. Welsh was counting on the SEAL mentality; he knew he wouldn't have a chance with an army officer.

Captain Hasford thought about it for a few seconds, then folded the paper carefully and put it in a pocket of his flight suit. He smiled at Welsh. "Let's go," he said.

North of the White House, on Pennsylvania Avenue, the *Baseeji* Selim walked toward the pedestrian entrance directly opposite the West Wing. He was twenty yards from the gate when the first bomb went off. Recovering his balance, he sprinted toward it. Ten yards away, he placed his briefcase between two shafts of the wrought-iron fence and pulled the fuze igniter dangling near the handle. He leaped back and ducked into the pedestrian entrance.

Access through the gate could be gained only by entering an electric door on one side of the guardhouse that abutted the gate, presenting identification to a guard protected behind bulletproof glass, and then waiting for the guard to electrically open a second door onto the White House grounds.

Immediately after the explosion both doors were sealed. As the guard watched through a bulletproof window and alarms sounded, Selim ran up, pulled the pin from the hand grenade in his pocket, and plastered himself against the door. Four seconds later the plastic bags of liquid explosive strapped to his body, twenty pounds in all, detonated. The explosion blew in the side of the guardhouse, killing the guard inside. Seconds later the bomb in the briefcase went off, opening a four-foot gap in the fence.

The two Econoline vans screeched across the Pennsylvania Avenue-Jackson Place intersection. Both the rear and side doors were thrown open. The vans weaved through the cars on Pennsylvania Avenue, most of which had come to a stop after the explosions. A plainclothes Secret Service agent on foot patrol in front of the Executive Office Building fired from behind the sidewalk barrier as they sped by him. Both vans squealed to a stop opposite the gap in the fence. The Iranian commandos poured from every available door as soon as the wheels stopped moving, leaping over the concrete barrier onto the wide sidewalk and screaming that God was great. The first ones over directed automatic fire down the length of the sidewalk. The Secret Service agent never had a chance. Neither did any of the people nearby.

The drivers of the vans, the last men out, threw grenades behind them into the vans as they ran toward the fence. The vans exploded, and the burning hulks blocked the street.

The sergeant major and the three support teams were first through the fence. They spread out in a wide fan along both sides of the gap and beside the ruined guardhouse. A machine gunner dropped, shot through the chest. Another man took up his weapon. The two gunners on either side of the path began shooting parallel to the fence, then sweeping their fire inward toward the White House, at knee height. The third machine gunner concentrated on the West Wing.

Corporal Hawkins barely made it through the West Wing entrance before the first machine-gun rounds hit. He locked the door and dropped down as the slugs impacted above him. He chanced a look out the window beside the door. The TV crews had been shot down where they stood. The few survivors crawled away as the attackers concentrated on more important targets. Hawkins thought it was about time to get the hell out of there. He began crawling down the hall.

The Iranian AT-4 gunners ran awkwardly across the grass, with the rocket-launcher tubes slung in clusters under their armpits. Laying their rifles and extra rockets down, they kneeled, exposing the sights. Each nestled a launcher easily onto his shoulder, cocking the mechanism, sighting carefully and holding his breath, and then smoothly squeezing the firing button. The rockets blew from the tubes at high velocity, flame and backblast shooting out the rear. The firer had no sensation of recoil, nothing but the noise and the sight of the rocket to tell him he had actually fired. The men threw the empty tubes away and took up new launchers.

The first pair of rockets streaked off to the right, aimed at the guardhouse straddling the walkway between the West Wing and Executive Office Building. Because of a fold in the ground, the gunners could only see the post from the windows up. One rocket missed; the second hit a window dead center. Designed for use against infantry fighting vehicles, the armor-piercing shaped charge of the AT-4 incorporated a high-pressure rise and flash, creating a blinding and incendiary effect to deal with protected troops and stored ammunition. The guardhouse windows blew out with a crash and a quick blaze of white light. Another rocket did the same damage to the guardhouse serving the vehicle gate on Pennsylvania Avenue, off to the far left. Other rockets were aimed at the windows of the West Wing, or wherever heavy return fire was coming from. Some smashed against the building walls, or went high or low, but enough hit their targets. Few inside survived when a rocket hit their window. The blasts pockmarked the formerly unblemished white facade.

The third leg of the support teams, the grenadiers, fired 40mm grenades as fast as they could work the single-shot launchers. They aimed at the depressions in the lawn, behind the hedges and ruined guardhouses, and the raised curbs where the guards who had survived the initial machine-gun fire were taking cover and firing back.

The sixteen commandos of the assault teams followed the support men through the fence, throwing out smoke grenades and staying away from the backblast areas behind the rocket gunners. The commandos spread out on the grass in a line, facing the West Wing entrance, firing their own rockets and automatic weapons, waiting for the smoke to billow up. It took only seconds. The wind was blowing toward the White House, and the different clouds of white, green, and yellow mixed into a thick surreal mass and floated over the grounds.

The fast chattering of the Squad Automatic Weapons blended with the more deliberate hammering of the M60 machine guns, the crash of the rockets, and the smaller explosions of the 40mm grenades, which seemed almost delicate by comparison. The heavy volume of automatic fire the Iranians were putting out was suppressing the defenders' return fire.

As the smoke covered the grounds, the support teams shifted to prearranged sectors of fire. To the right of the West Wing entrance and the driveway leading up to it was a tall tree. The commandos of one support team sighted in on the tree before the smoke came up, the machine gunner driving his bipod into the grass so the barrel could not swing to the left. Now, even with the area covered by smoke, they could restrict their fire to the right of that tree. Another team did the same with a tree to the left of the West Wing entrance. This formed a clear channel, a bullet-free tunnel, encompassing the small driveway and the entrance to the West Wing. Where seconds before they had been under open skies, the Iranians were now encased in a dense, multicolored fog.

Ali was on the far left of the assault team line. When the smoke had covered the entire area, he shouted through his microphone, "Assault teams, go!" He tapped the man on his right and crawled toward the driveway. The rest followed in single file, keeping low.

The driveway was slightly lower than the lawn, and the lawn sloped downward from the central fountain. So moving low along the drive gave the commandos good cover. More important, the driveway was their path; the smoke was so thick they could not even see the White House. And no one in the White House could see them. They were being fired upon, but it was aimed blindly through the smoke. They could hear the support teams' machine-gun bullets snap past on both sides but were safe so long as they stayed in the driveway.

The smoke was acrid and choking. Ali flipped the valve on his gas mask and began breathing filtered air. The smoke grenades lasted for over a minute, and when they began to dissipate more were thrown out.

The driveway dipped downward and the entrance loomed out of the haze. Ali stopped, and the commandos spread out beside him. "Grenades!" Ali shouted. Those in front lofted fragmentation grenades toward the portico, to clear away anyone hiding behind the hedge. When the grenades exploded, Karim's assault team charged toward the entrance while Ali and the others fired into the adjacent windows.

Karim chose to enter through an office window to the left of the door; he didn't relish coming in where he was expected. The armored glass had been pierced by a rocket but was still intact. Karim attached a charge of plastic explosive to the lower part of the window. He pulled the fuze igniter and jumped out of the way.

Seconds later the window and part of the wall exploded in a shower of splinters. Karim tossed a grenade through the hole. When it exploded he knocked away the loose glass with the butt of his SAW and jumped into the room. The fluorescent and emergency lights had been blown out. Karim jumped to his left and sprayed the room with automatic fire, the red tracers bright flashes in the darkness. The commando following him jumped right and sprayed his sector. Only then did Karim remember the flashlight taped to the front stock of his weapon. Embarrassed, he switched it on. A bleeding man was hiding in a corner of the room, behind a file cabinet. The short burst from Karim's SAW blew him open from the navel to the collarbone.

Someone fired at them from the doorway of the adjacent office, and Karim's partner went down, shot in the throat. Karim dropped behind a desk and stitched a long burst across the doorway and the nearest walls, at the same time yelling over the radio for the rest of his men to come in and help. The two-hundred-round belt of the SAW made it easy to keep up a continuous fire, and the high-velocity 5.56mm rounds punched right through the wall. The two other members of his team came through the window and fired at the doorway. Karim whipped a grenade through the open door, and his teammates moved up to fire into the office. Karim made another radio call, and Ali and the rest of the men in the driveway got up and ran for the entry.

Once Ali was inside, he took stock. Three of the assault element, including Karim's man, had been killed in the move. Without the smoke it would have been many more. He made a call on the radio, "Support, up!" The support teams threw the last of the smoke and sprinted toward the West Wing.

The remaining smoke was not enough to cover them completely. As it blew away, a Secret Service counter-sniper team that had rushed to the White House roof was finally able to make out targets. The sergeant major was waving his arms at the other commandos, urging them to run faster. They picked him out as the leader. The sniper fired just before Musa disappeared behind the cover of a tree. The jacketed hollow point bullet tore away the lower part of his face, leaving a gruesome red mask. He dropped to the asphalt without a sound. Ali saw it happen from the window. Before he could speak four commandos from the support element ran back into the driveway to get their sergeant major. Ali screamed for them to stop. The Secret Service sniper killed all four in succession, and Sgt. Maj. Musa Sa'ed drowned in his own blood.

Ali turned away from the window. Karim was still waiting beside the door. "Go!" Ali screamed at him. "Go! Kill them all!"

Karim threw another grenade into the adjoining office, and Ali led his team in. The room was abandoned. Two Secret Service agents lay dead on the floor, killed either by the grenades or Karim's men firing through the walls. One more room down and they would be in position to assault the Oval Office entrance across the hallway. They were already able to cut off anyone trying to escape out the West Wing exit. Ali assigned two men to cover the hallway. It was filled with white smoke; the Americans were throwing tear gas.

The other two assault teams passed them to clear all the offices to the left and cut off any escape back into the main White House. Even if Ali did not find the president in the Oval Office, they would have the West Wing isolated and could hold out long enough to search every room for him.

The four-man assault teams leapfrogged through the rooms with quick, well-practiced efficiency, using shotguns to blow hinges off doors, throwing in grenades, and spraying automatic fire. The trail teams checked for hidden survivors, killing any they found, and upon leaving the rooms threw in firebombs as the coup de grace.

The surviving members of the support teams moved in to cover them. The machine gunners kept up a steady fire down the length of the hall, through the tear-gas smoke, to keep the Secret Service from moving up.

When the Iranians took casualties, the wounded were stripped of ammunition and grenades and left to fend for themselves. Every man carried a morphine injector with an overdose, knowing there would be no way to remove casualties from the White House.

The SEALs of Team 6 stood in groups before the turning helicopters on the Andrews tarmac. Captain Hasford had opted to use the Blackhawks for transport, along with four AH-6 gunships for support. When the helicopters were ready, the crew chiefs signaled the waiting SEALs and each group began boarding.

Hasford would travel with his radiomen in a special command Blackhawk outfitted with extra communications equipment and flown by Lieutenant Colonel Van Brocklin. The executive officer of Team 6 rode in another identically equipped Blackhawk flown by Van Brocklin's deputy.

Hasford was plugging his headset into the radio console when Richard Welsh climbed through the helicopter door.

"Get the fuck out of here!" the SEAL shouted over the screaming of the turbines.

"No way," Welsh shouted back. "If you think I'm going to hang around and greet the general when he arrives, you're fucking crazy."

As Welsh had calculated, the captain had no time to argue and little inclination to boot him out forcibly. He threw up his hands in resignation, and the Blackhawk lifted off, followed in turn by the others.

There was less opposition than Ali had expected. The diversionary explosions caused the Secret Service to spread themselves too thin throughout the White House and the gates. The remaining agents had to be split between the family quarters and the West Wing.

Corporal Hawkins dived out of the office where he'd been hiding, just ahead of an Iranian assault team's grenade. He ran across the hall to the alcove facing the Oval Office, and only his dress blues kept him from being shot by the five Secret Service agents behind a heavy barricade of furniture.

The first thing Hawkins did when he got over the barricade was strip off his blouse. He felt twenty pounds lighter. An agent slapped a gas mask and the carbine version of the M16 into his hands. "Know how to use these?" the man snapped.

"Are you fucking kidding?" Hawkins replied. That brought faint smiles to the others' faces. While Hawkins was putting on the mask, a grenade exploded against the barricade, and everyone ducked. The furniture absorbed the fragmentation. The agents opened fire and threw concussion grenades and tear gas, all they had, out into the hall.

The thick smoke made vision almost impossible and caused the fighting to take place at very short range. Hawkins and the Secret Service cut down the first three commandos who tried to reach them. The Iranians threw more grenades across the hall, but the furniture rendered them ineffective.

• • •

From a nearby doorway Ali moved two grenadiers into position, but even 40mm high-explosive dual-purpose grenades could not dislodge the men behind the barricade.

The volume of grenades slowed as one of the launchers jammed. The heat from repeated firing had caused the plastic shell of the M203 to swell—the action was frozen shut. The glue securing the handguard on the other grenadier's launcher melted, and the handguard fell off. The commando had to wrap a bandana around his hand to operate the hot mechanism.

Ali knew he was running out of time. He called for an M60 machine gun. The big 7.62mm bullets would do the job.

Then Ali was knocked against the doorframe when someone pushed by him. It was Karim. Ali knew what was going to happen as soon as he saw the look on Karim's face. Karim sprinted down the hall with a firebomb in each hand, screaming, *"Allahu akbar!"* He threw one bomb at the barricade, and it burst into flame.

Hawkins had just slapped in a fresh magazine when the fire blew up in front of him. Through the flames he could see a terrorist come screaming down the hall. Though his face felt like it was being broiled, Hawkins centered his front sight post on the man's chest and squeezed off three rounds, single shot, just as he'd been taught.

Karim staggered, then dropped. He fell on the other firebomb and it exploded, showering him with burning napalm. Karim writhed on the floor, screaming and beating madly at the flames. Ali leaned out of the doorway and fired a burst into his friend's body.

"I got him," Hawkins yelled, "I got the son of a bitch!"

One of the agents had been badly burned. "Take him in the office," the leader ordered Hawkins.

"You got it," said Hawkins. He picked up the burned agent in a fireman's carry. The Oval Office door opened to admit him.

In a cold fury, Ali slung the SAW behind his back, took up a grenade in each hand, and charged the barricade. He let the spoons fly free, underhanded both grenades over the flaming furniture, and rolled away to one side. There were two sharp explosions, and no more firing from the barricade.

Ali stopped to put a new belt in his SAW and shouted to the commandos to use their rifles to push the burning furniture out of the way. The flames were too intense; they couldn't get close enough. The attack was stalled. Ali snapped the feed cover over a fresh belt and ran back into an office. He emerged with heavy window drapes wrapped around his head and shoulders. Taking a running start, he crashed into the burning barricade, knocking it over. His momentum carried him over the top, and he quickly shed the drapes. Some of the napalm stuck to his clothing, and he rolled to put it out. It took him through an open doorway. Three commandos followed, leaping over the flames.

They found themselves in the office of the president's secretaries. The Oval Office door was directly in front of them. The torn bodies of four Secret Service agents lay nearby. One was still alive. The commandos finished him off.

"Where are the others?" Ali shouted. One of the commandos shook his head. "Move up to the barricade," Ali called over his radio. There was no answer. He repeated the message. After a quick check he found that the radio had broken in the fall. He told the other commandos to try. The heat from the gas and the fire was brutal. Alarms were still sounding but, amazingly, the sprinklers were not working.

One of the men managed to get through. "Ten are covering the hall," he reported. "But there are no more left."

"What of the other two assault teams?" Ali shouted.

"That is everyone," the commando said flatly, making a chopping motion with one hand.

Ali glanced at his watch: 10:16. Only sixteen minutes. He stayed low to the floor—the smoke was making it hard to get air through the gas mask filter. The sweat had poured down his face and pooled in the bottom of the mask. It felt like being underwater, but he didn't dare break the seal.

The commando with the working radio cupped his hand over his earphone. "They say the fire is becoming too great in the hall," he informed Ali.

"Have two men stay to cover our rear," Ali commanded. "The rest move into the main White House and escape through the East Wing. Burn everything they can. God go with them."

The commando relayed the order.

When the marine brought in the wounded man, Agent Latimer knew he'd made the worst mistake of his life. Mortar bombs were dropping regularly in the Rose Garden. The shrapnel barely scratched the armored windows of the Oval Office, but there would be no escape in that direction. And now the other side of the hallway was closed off. They were in a box. He thought he'd played it right, but it turned out all wrong. Whoever was running this not only had firepower, they knew what the hell they were doing.

There was no alternative but to hold out and wait for help to arrive. Latimer had three agents with him in the office, and he kept calling for help on his radio. They had Uzis, M16s, gas masks, and plenty of ammo. All the doors leading to the Oval Office were locked and barricaded. They could hold on. Latimer worried about a rocket coming through one of the windows. The presi-

dent was holding up well, and the VIPs were so fright-
ened they weren't making much noise.

Hawkins set the burned agent against the wall. The
man must have been in terrible pain, but he was hardly
making a sound. Hawkins turned around, and the most
powerful men in the government were staring directly at
him. He looked down at his grimy T-shirt and blackened
trousers, grinned self-consciously and blurted out,
"How's everybody doing?" He received no answer. Then
the grenades exploded in the outer office. Everyone
flinched. With an enlisted man's unerring gift, Hawkins
picked Latimer out as the man in charge. "I don't want
to start a panic or nothing," he said. "But I think we're
in a shit sandwich."

As the helicopter formation crossed the Anacostia
River, Rich Welsh sat jammed into the cabin of the lead
Blackhawk with his knees up around his ears. He was
miserable, and it wasn't just the helicopter ride. It was
what he'd done. He pictured himself sitting in front of a
congressional investigating committee, maybe even
something like the Warren Commission, telling them
that he wiped his ass with the Constitution because he
thought it was a really neat idea. That he might have
been right made no difference. Welsh knew that, in a
democracy, the ends *are* the means.

The helicopters came in low over the Tidal Basin. For
the last few miles Captain Hasford had been talking to a
very excited White House Secret Service detail on the
radio. He ordered the rest of the helicopters to hover
over the Tidal Basin while he went in for a look with two
of the gunships.

As they came in low over the Mall, Welsh could see
what were obviously mortar rounds impacting in the
Rose Garden. The two AH-6 gunships broke off to try
and find the tube. Noticing some faint smoke over the
Ellipse, one of the AH-6s moved in lower. A figure with

a rifle popped up from a hole in the top of a van and opened fire. The gunship took two M16 rounds through the windshield, and the pilot quickly whipped the little helicopter over the trees. While he checked his systems for damage, the other gunship pilot asked Captain Hasford for permission to fire. He got it, and an admonition to be careful of civilians.

The AH-6 popped up over the Commerce Department Building. Its 7.62 mm Gatling gun gave off a high-pitched whine, firing so fast the tracers flew into the van in what seemed a solid stream. Glass blew out, metal flew off, and the van went up in a series of sharp explosions.

"Yeeaaah!" the gunship pilot whooped over the radio. "Got some secondaries off their ammo."

The Blackhawk flew over the White House, and Hasford knew he'd have to make an immediate assault. It was always a last resort in hostage rescues, but there was no time to set up a containment perimeter and develop a detailed plan.

As they flew back over the Mall, Welsh listened in admiration as Hasford made up his operation order and radioed it to the platoon commanders in the other helicopters. It took only a few minutes, and Team 6's finely honed standard operating procedures made all the difference.

They linked up with the other helicopters over the Tidal Basin and swept back over the Mall at high speed, with the gunships buzzing out in front.

Most of the SEALs were let off onto the White House roof, joining up with the Secret Service agents who would guide them through the building. The president's family was also there. They were taken off in the first helicopter and flown immediately to Andrews. The SEALs left snipers on the roof to cover the grounds, and began the assault downward.

The rest of the Blackhawks, led by the command helicopter, popped up over the South Lawn in a violent assault landing, almost brushing the trees. Welsh held on tight as the Blackhawk stood on its side. It was disconcerting to look directly at the ground from the side door. Welsh felt weightless—unpleasantly so. If his seat belt had broken, he would have floated right out.

They touched down on the South Lawn. A group of SEAL snipers ran for the small hill off to the right. The rest of the SEALs made a beeline through the trees for the Oval Office. As he went out the door with his radiomen, Captain Hasford grabbed Welsh by the flight suit and yelled, "You stay the fuck here!" Welsh opened his mouth, and the captain motioned to the helicopter door gunner, who looked at Welsh and smiled. Welsh sat back in the cabin. As soon as all the SEALs were out, the helicopters took off again.

Staying close to the walls, Ali and his three commandos began attaching soap-dish charges to the armored door of the Oval Office. "Put them near the hinges," Ali said, as quietly as he could through the gas mask. Waving the others back, he pulled the pins. The commandos hunched over, palms pressed against their ears. Ali prepared to throw a grenade as soon as the door blew.

The Secret Service agent positioned at the door thought she heard something outside. She was trying to see through the blocked peephole when the door blew apart.

Latimer had been watching the helicopters land on the lawn. In the shock of the blast, he automatically rolled over on top of the president. When he saw the open doorway, Latimer pushed the president behind the desk and leaned over the top, taking aim with his Uzi.

Something small sailed through the doorway. It looked like a dark baseball and was moving very fast. The object hit a sideboard and bounced into the air. Sensing rather than knowing what it was, Latimer dropped the Uzi and sprang across the room. He made a great one-handed catch and was cocking his arm to throw the grenade back when it exploded.

Latimer's body absorbed most of the shrapnel. More grenades came flying into the room. They hit the walls and floor and bounced wildly. The explosions were incredibly loud, and the Oval Office filled with swirling dust.

After the door blew, Hawkins rolled on top of the burned Secret Service man. He was trying to pull a chair over them both when a grenade went off nearby. The blast hit him like a baseball bat, and he couldn't move or think.

The SEALs in the Rose Garden couldn't get through the armored door to the Oval Office. They began attaching a charge to blow it open, and a few pounded on the windows, shouting for someone to unlock the door.

Hawkins's head cleared a little, and he saw the SEALs at the window. The sight of his left arm made him sick— he couldn't feel it, but it didn't seem like there was much holding it together. Hawkins knew the grenades were mainly for shock, and that someone would be coming in soon to finish the job. Even though he was afraid his arm would fall off, Hawkins began crawling across the carpet to open the door.

The president was unhurt behind the desk, but his vision was fuzzy and he couldn't hear a thing. There was an awful stench of spilled bowels and high explosives, and blood was splattered everywhere. Knowing what was about to happen, the president picked up Latimer's Uzi from the floor and managed to take it off safe. He braced the weapon on his desk and aimed it at the doorway.

Ali told his men that they would all go in after the last grenade. Just after it went off, Ali thought he heard something behind them. When he turned around quickly to look, the commandos mistook it for the signal and rushed screaming through the doorway.

Hawkins grabbed the molding of the door with his good arm to pull himself up. His nerves weren't numb anymore, and the pain was searing. He strained to keep conscious.

The SEAL platoon commander positioned his men on either side of the door. He could see Hawkins, but the charge was in place and he knew he'd have to blow it—whether anyone was in the way or not.

As the platoon commander was about to fire the charge, Hawkins tripped the lock and fell out of the way.

Six SEALs burst through the door, almost together, just as the Iranians charged in firing from the opposite side. The SEALs abandoned all fire discipline and emptied their MP5s. It was a gunfight through a haze of explosive smoke at a distance of fifteen feet, and the best and fastest would win.

Two SEALs took hits on their body armor and were thrown back through the door. But the three Iranian commandos were nearly dismembered by the concentrated submachine-gun fire. It was all over in four seconds, but the SEALs changed magazines and kept firing through the doorway.

Ali watched in disbelief as his men surged past him. He was about to follow when a hail of bullets came through the doorway. The intensity of the fire drove him back out of the office. He couldn't believe it, they had beaten him again. Then a surge of anger forced the thought down.

Not yet. Backing away through the secretaries' office, Ali took the last fire bottle from his pouch. He pulled the safety strip from the cover and lobbed it through the open doorway into the Oval Office.

• • •

The SEALs immediately wrapped the president in body armor and a ballistic helmet. The corpsmen were starting to attend to the wounded when the firebomb came through the doorway and exploded at the feet of a SEAL. They dragged the burning man out into the garden and extinguished the fire with dirt dug up with their helmets. The president was the next out, surrounded by four SEALs who set him beside a pillar and pressed so close that he could barely be seen. Other SEALs braved the flames to drag the rest of the wounded and dead out. The two SEALs who had been hit on their body armor were only stunned.

A SEAL corpsman put a tourniquet around Hawkins's arm, gave him a shot of morphine, and started an IV. "Don't worry, pal," he said, "you're going to be just fine."

The morphine had started to work, and Hawkins smiled weakly. "The fuck you say," he told the SEAL. "Looks like another medal. . . . They'll probably send me to fucking Alaska this time."

"What was all that?" a nearby SEAL asked the corpsman.

"Nothing," said the doc. "He's just a little shocky."

Captain Hasford, concerned about his men but relieved beyond words to have the president safe, radioed Lieutenant Colonel Van Brocklin to bring in his helicopter so they could evacuate him immediately.

Diving back into the West Wing hallway with the window drape around his shoulders, Ali knew he would have to move quickly or be trapped by the flames. The men supposed to be waiting for him were gone. He was furious. The hallway into the main White House was blocked by fire. Praying that the rooms farther down the West Wing had not been burned, Ali crawled down the hall. He knew it was only a short way to the end. The hall was full of smoke, and he had to hold his breath. The heat made it feel as if his gas mask was melting. Just when he thought he could hold his breath no longer, Ali reached the exit. Now the smoke was thinner, and he could breathe close to the ground.

Ali looked out the window and couldn't see anyone nearby. Deciding that speed was better than caution, he burst out the door and dashed to the left, along the side of the building toward the South Lawn. Nearly running into several White House police, Ali dropped low and crawled into the border of trees and shrubs that screened the Rose Garden from the surrounding buildings.

Crouching behind a clump of bushes, Ali removed his bandana and tore off the tape holding the walkie-talkie earphone in place. He took off his equipment harness and threw it into the bushes. The one hand grenade left in the carrying bag went into the pocket of his windbreaker. Finally, he stripped off the gas mask, reveling in fresh air that did not taste of rubber. The air was cold against skin used to the heat of the mask.

It felt strange to be completely alone for the first time in months. Ali took stock. He had a full belt left in the Squad Automatic Weapon, and the silenced Makarov pistol was in the holster at the small of his back. He could hear Americans talking off to his left, but he needed a clear field of fire. Ali decided to follow the thick foliage around the edge of the formerly pristine South Lawn, now pocked with mortar craters and the debris of explosions.

CHAPTER 33

THE HELICOPTERS WERE circling over West Potomac Park when Captain Hasford's call came in. Lieutenant Colonel Van Brocklin passed the orders to his deputy and the other flight leaders. The command helicopter, accompanied by a backup Blackhawk and two gunships, broke off from the formation and headed for the White House. Rich Welsh cinched his seat belt tighter in preparation for another assault landing. The two doorgunners readied their weapons.

The ten surviving Iranian commandos moved through the ground floor of the main White House, throwing their last few firebombs. They set fire to the Red Room, the Green Room, and the Blue Room. When they tried to enter the East Room, they were ambushed by a team of Secret Service agents. Any escape in that direction was cut off.

The commandos dragged their wounded back through the burning Green Room and tried to flee out the South Portico, but the first two were shot dead by overeager SEAL snipers firing from the small hill on the South Lawn.

A group of SEALs with Secret Service guides came down the Grand Staircase from the second floor and trapped the commandos in the State Dining Room.

The Iranians ignored repeated calls to surrender. After their ammunition ran out, they chose to charge the

Americans with their last grenades. None survived, but two SEALs and a Secret Service agent died with them.

Lieutenant Colonel Ali Khurbasi crept cautiously through the trees of the South Lawn, skirting the driveway that crossed the lawn and curved in front of the South Portico. He picked a spot where the van bomb had blown two trees across the drive and checked to be sure the way was clear. With his SAW at the ready, Ali crawled across the driveway as fast as he could, concealed by the tree trunks. Once on the other side, he followed the treeline bordering the outer fence, then cut back in toward the lawn.

Ali moved slowly on his stomach until he reached a spot where the trees opened up onto the South Lawn. He slid under a large, thick, flowering bush. He couldn't imagine them taking the president out one of the destroyed gates. No, they would call a helicopter, and as soon as they left the safety of the Rose Garden he would have a clear shot. Ali carefully broke off some low branches and laid them over himself to cover his jeans and blue windbreaker. He extended the SAW's bipod legs and made sure the barrel didn't protrude from the foliage to give him away. He checked once again that the weapon was loaded properly. Then he took the grenade from his pocket and placed it beside him, removing the safety clip and straightening the pin for easy removal. He would not fail this time, he promised himself. There was much blood to be repaid.

Van Brocklin brought the Blackhawk in along the same route he had used before. Welsh didn't like it one bit. It would only make it easier for anyone sighting in on them. Welsh was listening to the radio traffic over his headset when the unit crackled and went out. He reinserted the plug and banged it a couple of times for good measure, but no luck. He took off the headset and put it aside, since he didn't want to accidently screw something up.

As they came in over the trees, Welsh leaned his head out the open door to get a better look. He wasn't afraid of heights, just helicopters. As the rotor downblast blew away the branches, Welsh thought he saw a flash of blue in the treeline between the helicopter and the White House. He looked away and then back, and thought he saw it again. Dark blue is not a color that occurs often in nature.

Ali cursed as the wind from the helicopters blew away the covering branches, but he didn't dare move.

Welsh popped the catch on his seat belt and scrambled across the cabin to the left doorgunner. "I think I saw somebody in the trees," he shouted.

The gunner followed Welsh's outstretched arm. "I don't see anything," he shouted back, as Welsh knew he would.

"We can't take the chance," Welsh yelled, slowly so the man could make out the words over the engine noise. "Tell them to keep the president under cover."

"What?"

Exasperated, Welsh lurched forward and grabbed Van Brocklin by the shoulder. The colonel jumped, then pulled up the bottom of his helmet so he could hear.

"There's someone in the treeline," Welsh screamed in the colonel's ear. "Don't let them come out on the lawn."

The colonel's eyes widened, and over the intercom he asked the doorgunners if they could see anything.

Through the windscreen Welsh could see the SEALs bringing the president through the thinly spaced trees that screened the driveway. No one was moving fast enough, and there was no way he was going to sit there and watch the president be gunned down before his eyes. Welsh reached behind the copilot's seat and

grabbed the man's personal weapon, an MP5 with a re-
tractable stock. He brushed past a surprised doorgunner
and jumped out the opposite side door. He kept the
Blackhawk between him and the White House. The
treeline was only thirty feet away, and Welsh sprinted for
it.

Once he was in the trees, Welsh extended the MP5's
stock. He made sure the magazine was loaded, and reinserted it into the weapon. There were two thirty-round
magazines held together side-by-side with a metal clip.
He pulled back the cocking handle and let it fly forward,
then did it a second time. A bright 9mm cartridge
popped out the ejection port, and Welsh knew the
weapon was charged. It suddenly dawned on him that
there was an excellent chance of being chopped into
hamburger if the doorgunner's vision improved and the
kid saw him moving around. Or the SEALs might start
clearing the woods and grease him by accident. And he
hadn't taken a radio. Nothing like a little fear to focus
the mind. Just don't fuck up, Welsh, he told himself. *Do
not* fuck up.

Recalling the techniques of silent movement, he began making his way through the shrubbery. The green
flight suit was good camouflage, and the snug fit kept it
from snagging on the brush and making noise. The Adi-
das GSG-9 boots he was wearing were also very quiet.

Once he got through the bordering shrubs it was very
open between the trees. The groundskeepers were obviously efficient, and that pissed Welsh off. He went
deeper into the treeline so he could come up behind
whoever it was.

Ali saw the Americans in the green uniforms heading
toward the lawn. There were four out in front, and the
president was completely surrounded by another four. It
didn't matter. With the SAW he could knock them
down, bulletproof vests or not, then charge them and
finish the job before the rest could react. The helicopters

wouldn't fire if there was a chance the president was still alive. Ali pressed the stock into his shoulder and leaned into the bipod until the weapon was locked tightly against his body. The safety was off, and he sighted in on the walking figures.

Welsh cautiously moved from tree to tree with his weapon ready, keeping his eyes toward the border of the South Lawn. He saw a patch of blue and dropped quietly to the ground. He crawled up to the nearest tree and peeked over some large exposed roots at the base of the trunk. There was a man under some bushes about fifteen yards away. The navy blue windbreaker made Welsh hesitate for a moment, but no Secret Service agent or plainclothes cop would be lying out in the brush. This guy was waiting in ambush with what looked like a Squad Automatic Weapon. Welsh knew what the SAW could do, and there was no way he was going to tell this stud to drop it and put his hands up. Welsh had no idea where the MP5's sights would hit, so he decided to fire full auto and walk the bursts along the ground. The adrenaline was pumping and his hands were shaking. It was nothing at all like qualification day on the rifle range. He leaned his head and shoulder against the tree trunk, rested the MP5 on the roots, and looked out over the sights. It's time for a little payback, you bastard, he thought.

Ali heard the MP5's safety click and instantly whirled around. The barrel of the SAW hung up in the bush, and the ground erupted next to him. He yanked the weapon free and fired a burst in the direction of the sound. Then he felt a sharp blow to his side, then more, and lost his grip on the weapon. His first thought was that he had been hit with a club.

The rounds cracked just over Welsh's head and leaves fluttered down around him. He kept firing short bursts and could see them hitting. The terrorist rolled over on his stomach, and the submachine-gun magazine ran out. Welsh ducked behind the tree, changed magazines, and knocked the charging handle forward. Thirty rounds left.

Welsh felt a terrible urge to rush forward, but he stayed behind the tree. He got up on one knee to see better, keeping the MP5 ready. The terrorist was still moving a little. His arms were under his body. "Get your hands out in front of you!" Welsh yelled. "Get 'em out, or I'll shoot your ass again."

There was a cracking of branches off to his left, and Welsh raised his weapon. Two uniformed Secret Service guards, a man and a woman, burst through the trees, pistols ready. "Don't shoot!" Welsh shouted, staying behind the tree just in case. "I'm with Special Operations Command, the terrorist is over there." When they saw Welsh's flight suit they lowered their weapons. Welsh noticed that the branches above his head had been chewed up by the SAW burst. He was shaken by how close it all had been, even though he'd had the advantage. Where the fuck are the SEALs? he thought.

Ali tried to raise his head to see who had hit him, but it was too heavy to move. The earth smelled wonderful, and as he lay there he felt for the first time released from all obligations, content to simply rest under the trees.

Then, out of the corner of his eye, he saw a woman advancing with a gun in her hands. The reverie was broken. The woman. The woman in uniform. She was coming for him again. She would beat him and laugh at his weakness.

Ali was frantic. He sobbed into the earth—the SAW was out of reach, and he could not get to the pistol. Once again he was helpless. It was so hard to think, to move. There was something under his chest. He felt with his hand, and cried with relief. The grenade felt marvelous, smooth and cold: an engine of deliverance. He hooked his finger through the pin. He could feel it coming out, but there was not enough time. She would take it away and laugh at him.

Welsh watched as the male Secret Service guard kept the terrorist covered. But when the woman moved in with the handcuffs, Welsh shouted for her to stay back. She just waved him off. Welsh was remembering all the tricks from prisoner-searching classes in the marines. "Don't go near him," he bellowed. "For Christ's sake, don't touch him!"

Ali heard yelling, but paid no attention. The exertion brought the coppery taste of blood to his mouth. Then the pin was out, and he knew he was safe. "There is no God but Allah," he whispered into the ground, "and Mohammad is the Prophet of Allah." With the last of his strength, Ali rolled over on his back.

Welsh couldn't fire; the Secret Service guards were in his way. He dived behind the tree.

Both of the guards fired into Ali's body. The woman took a few steps toward him. Something twitched on the ground, and she went closer to look. It was green, and she was furious with herself when she realized what it was. But all she could say was, "Oh, shit." Then the grenade exploded.

Captain Hasford came through the trees with several of his SEALs as Welsh was trying to stuff pieces of the woman's uniform into the largest wounds to stop the bleeding. Her partner was dead. Though he'd been farther away, he'd taken a fragment right through the heart.

Welsh was shaking her, pleading, promising. "You've got to stay awake," he told her. "If you stay awake you're going to be all right."

"I'm trying," she said dreamily. "But it's so hard." The

SEALs applied battle dressings to her wounds, but she died before a corpsman could arrive. Welsh closed her eyes.

Captain Hasford was standing over Ali's body. Welsh got up and walked over to him, wiping the blood from his hands onto his flight suit. "Did the president get out all right?" Welsh asked. "I didn't hear the helicopter."

"Yes, he did," said Hasford. "Van Brocklin was screaming at us not to bring him up, but some idiot on the radio net had his finger down on his transmit button. The helo couldn't get through to us, and we couldn't talk to them."

Welsh shook his head. He was suddenly exhausted.

"You did just fine," the captain told him.

"He was one hard-core motherfucker," said Welsh, looking down at Ali's body. There was a hole in the abdomen the size of a basketball. Pinkish white viscera were spread over the ground and nearby bushes.

As they stood there, another uniformed Secret Service guard came through the bushes from the South Lawn. He took one look at the body and threw up. Welsh and Hasford politely looked away. Welsh saw the black smoke pouring from the windows of the White House and all he could think of was that he'd never been inside.

The guard had wiped his mouth, but he was still staring at Ali's corpse. He wanted to know what had happened, so Hasford told him.

"How can anyone do that with his life?" the guard asked.

Welsh, tired of explaining things to people who would never understand, simply said, "Beats the shit out of me."

EPILOGUE

SINCE AT THE time there was no way of knowing the scope or objective of the terrorist attacks, the President of the United States was immediately flown to the emergency national command center known as Mount Weather, a huge underground complex dug deeply into the solid rock hills near Berryville, Virginia.

Fifteen members of Congress and the Cabinet had been killed in the attack, and many others seriously wounded. Few of the White House staff who had been in the West Wing that morning survived. Seven Secret Service agents and three SEALs of Team 6 also died. The West Wing was nearly gutted before the fire department could make its way into the compound, and the lower floor of the main White House was severely damaged.

None of the terrorists survived to be interrogated. In the end, everyone in authority came over to Welsh's view that the terrorists had been Iranian. Unfortunately, dead Middle-Easterners and untraceable weapons and documents provided absolutely no proof that would justify any military reprisal against Iran.

For its part, the Iranian government heatedly denied any involvement in the attack, calling the U.S. accusations yet another attempt to provoke war. A month later Iran closed a deal with China for the purchase of a complete nuclear reactor capable of producing weapons-grade fuel.

After the smoke cleared, the President expressed his undying gratitude to Welsh, SEAL Team 6, and the helicopter crews of the 160th Special Operations Aviation Regiment.

Corporal Brian Hawkins recovered fully from his wounds and was awarded the Navy Cross, the nation's second-highest decoration for valor, along with yet another Purple Heart. He was meritoriously promoted to the rank of sergeant and assigned, again without his consultation, to the Marine Corps recruit training depot at Paris Island, South Carolina, for duty as a drill instructor.

Welsh's boss, the Assistant Secretary of Defense for Special Operations/Low Intensity conflict, basked in the general acclaim that resulted from the successful rescue. Given time, Welsh had no doubt that he'd find a way to take credit for the whole thing.

Although publicly complimentary, the Army leadership and Secretary of Defense were privately furious with Welsh. The story of his usurpation of command had found its way into the press, forcing them to send Major General Clark into immediate retirement. They were not men who accepted embarrassment with good grace, and the inevitable editorial cartoons of Army generals in togas fiddling while the White House burned did little to improve their mood.

Rich Welsh knew that they would eventually find a way to ambush him through the bureaucracy. Completely fed up anyway, he left his position.

Then, on the verge of entering law school, Welsh was offered another job. But that is another story.